EDEN

A Novel

W. A. SCHWARTZ

Black Rose Writing | Texas

ISBN: 978-1-68513-181-4
PUBLISHED BY BLACK ROSE WRITING
www.blackrosewriting.com

Printed in the United States of America
Suggested Retail Price (SRP) $24.95

Eden is printed in Georgia Pro

*As a planet-friendly publisher, Black Rose Writing does its best to eliminate unnecessary waste to reduce paper usage and energy costs, while never compromising the reading experience. As a result, the final word count vs. page count may not meet common expectations.

For Olivia, Bella and Nick.

EDEN

"Secrets, silent, stony sit in the dark palaces of both our hearts: secrets weary of their tyranny: tyrants willing to be dethroned."
—James Joyce, *Ulysses*

PROLOGUE

Gwen|Eden

January 6, 1982

There is a fear I live with all the time. It's like a shawl around my shoulders that I can't remove. Today has been a hard day. Gray skies and a chill in the air that bites like razors. Clothes refuse to dry on the line, and a particular angry whistle passes continuously through the house.

He was in town with his family, and I saw him across First Street, heading to lunch maybe or shopping. My mind raced in all the directions he might have been going. The pain was excruciating, but still, it made me happy to see him looking good. He was smiling, reaching down to lift his smallest child to his shoulders. The last time we spoke, it devastated him. I think in my life there will never again be such a love. I am now resigned to it. When I think of the damage our love has caused and the responsibility we bear for others' lives, I feel ill all over again, and yet, I am again fortified against my weakness for him.

I've not been right since I got home this afternoon. These pages are where I will say the truth. I can't trust myself to speak it aloud or maybe it's that I can't trust others. An icy terror sits within me. A feeling, or more than that, a certainty that something terrible is about to happen, or has already occurred. Some form of destruction, an unraveling. I see shadows following me; I find objects in my house no longer where I left them—sometimes things are moved and lost for good. Yesterday, I went to get the mail, down to the box, a five-minute walk, and found the box empty. When I came back, the mail was stacked neatly on the kitchen table. John says I must have forgotten I'd gone to fetch it. I'm sure I would remember if I was the one who'd put it there. I tell my doctors someone is watching me, but they only want to give me more medication, so I stop telling them. This is not a sickness. This is real. Why will no one listen?

    -Gwen

PART ONE: DEAD GIRL

Saturday, June 3
Present Day

CHAPTER ONE

Eden, Louisiana

The day they found the dead girl, the sky was the color of marble, and the air stank of rubber and mud. Spring had escaped Bonfante Parish early that year, and it was much too hot for early June. Ray Lee Beaumont was thirteen years old, skinny as a jackrabbit and brimming with the sweaty, excited newness of burgeoning adolescence. He stood, with the self-conscious, impatient, cool, peculiar to young adolescent boys, under the shade of a live oak, half-moons of damp staining his T-shirt underarms and smoking a stolen cigarette. Legs apart, shifting weight from one foot to the other, head down and cocked, peering out from under a lock of shaggy black hair. One hand to his lips, he held the Lucky Strike between his first two fingers, the way he remembered his daddy had done when the man still lived with them. A thin curl of smoke wafted into the still, hot air and hung there for a while before breaking up into nothing. Sporadically, he held the cigarette away from his body and tapped at it, letting the ash fall to the ground next to his feet.

All at once, he flicked the butt aside, took two steps forward until he was standing just outside the shade of the tree, and he shouted. "Basco, what in the hell is taking you so long?"

Gene Basco, twelve, just four months younger than Ray Lee but six inches shorter and lacking the peach fuzz that darkened Ray Lee's upper lip, materialized from the woods, pulling up his pants.

"I don't know Ray Lee. I don't feel too good. I got the diarrheas."

"Oh, shoot, Basco. You ain't got the diarrheas. You're just scared I'm gonna shoot you full of holes before you get one round off," Ray Lee said, laughing.

"I ain't scared," insisted Gene. He approached, and Ray Lee studied his face. Pale, big-eyed. "I'm telling you; I don't feel too good."

"Yeah. Well, don't be thinking we're going back now that we're all the way out here, and I got my brother's gun and all. No way. Like my daddy says, time to man up."

Ray Lee gave the younger boy a hard stare, so he'd know there wasn't a choice. Not now. Ray, who'd been practically shooting out of his shoes with excitement since waking up this brilliant Saturday morning to find Mack's paintball gun, and all his gear, sitting by the back door, had no intention of turning back. Mack never left his gear or anything he cared about, out where Ray Lee might get into it. He must have come in drunk or too tired to think straight, or both. Ever since Mack made sixteen and started driving and got a girlfriend, he thought he was all that. Ray Lee had secretly snatched up the gun and the half-full box of yellow paintballs and made his way out of the house. He'd ridden his bike straight over to Gene's since Gene was the only other kid he knew owned a paintball gun which, Ray Lee was pretty sure, the little softie shit never even used.

"And look," added Ray Lee, picking up the weapon from where he'd laid it on the ground. "I gotta get this gun back before Mack wakes up, or he'll kill me. So, get your stuff and come on. I already loaded yours for you."

They started out back behind a wood structure that looked like, once upon a time, it might have been an outhouse. Everything out here looked like it came from another century. As far as Ray Lee knew, nobody had lived out at the Crazy Yates Place since the old man died, and that was almost before Ray Lee was born.

"Ray Lee," came Gene's whine. "Are you sure we ought to be doin' this? I mean, what if we get caught? My mama says the Sheriff will arrest you for shooting outside in, like, the wild. I don't know."

Ray Lee turned around, peering at his friend. "See, I told you, you was scared."

"I ain't!" Gene took another step.

"Well then, quit jabbering." They trudged across the field about a hundred yards before Ray Lee stopped just on the edge of the forest. "Ok. Here's good." He looked at Gene, softening. "Hey, look, I won't aim at your face, ok? Or your neck. And I'll give you first shot. Ok?" The twelve-year-old nodded, looking reluctant. Ray Lee felt a little bad for him. Getting splatted with a paintball hurt like a bitch, and Gene knew how good a shot Ray Lee was, too.

They crept into the forest in opposite directions, counting off before they turned and began. Immediately, Gene started firing indiscriminately, all his balls hitting tree trunks or rocks, leaving neon yellow and green paint splatter everywhere. He'll be out of ammo in five minutes, thought Ray Lee. Idiot.

Ray Lee avoided the shots, snuck deeper into the woods, and circled behind a live oak's thick, gnarled trunk. When the toe of his runner clipped a fat root and sent him sprawling, face first, into the earth, the gun spilled from his grip and went skittering off into the darkness. Once he'd caught his breath, he pushed himself onto his hands and knees, peering around for the weapon. A tiny kernel of panic seeded itself in his belly.

Mack would murder him if he lost that gun.

He screamed back at Gene to quit firing and come help him and continued to scrabble around in the half-dark. Finally, there it was. Brown plastic sticking half out of the muck. Reaching for it, Ray Lee wrapped his palm around the hilt and at once knew the thing in his grasp was not the plastic gun. Fear shot through him like ice water, and he yelped, drawing his hand back so rapidly that droplets of mud splashed his face, stinging his eyes. He scrambled away from whatever it was and leaned against a rock, panting and peering into the darkness.

After a moment, he pulled a penlight from his jeans pocket and, using it to navigate, took a few steps forward. It seemed suddenly darker inside the cypress wood. His foot sank into the mud so thick it overflowed the top of his shoe, oozing through his sock, like fingers. Inside the jungle of plants, he was briefly disoriented. He swung his head this way and that, panic rising, and suddenly, he saw it. Sticking out of the wet earth, it was small and appeared dipped in layers of sludge and rot. Picking up a branch, Ray Lee used it to poke at the thing, trying to separate it from his gun. No way did he want to touch it. Pushing some filth away, and leaning in for a closer look, he jammed the branch underneath it. As he did so, a brownish bowl-shaped object appeared from the earth. He stared, horrified, as a clump of long hair fell away in a thin, stringy sheath. He made a garbled gagging sound, dropped the stick, turned, and pushed his way out of the trees, slicing the skin of his forearm on the spiny petioles of a giant palmetto as he stumbled past. Emerging from the forest edge, he paused, bent at the waist, and vomited into the dirt.

CHAPTER TWO

Evelyn | San Francisco

Monday, June 5
Present Day

It was happening again, the sleepwalking. When Evelyn was a child, she'd called it *dreaming,* but that wasn't correct. Dreaming was that thing people did while staying in their beds. Dreaming had a sort of pleasurable connotation. The word *nightmare* wasn't right either. Evelyn's ex-husband, Stuart, had called it her "Linda Blair Thing" and thought it hilarious. Of course, Stuart was a prick, and he'd witnessed only two episodes, both of which had involved copious amounts of alcohol followed by nakedness combined with something having to do with mud and nocturnal enuresis, so Evelyn wasn't even sure it had been the same thing. But these more recent events were too familiar, occurring too often.

Evelyn picked up the tweezers and leaned into the beveled glass over her sink. She'd think about the sleepwalking thing later. Right now she had other problems. She pushed closer to the mirror, the marble vanity edge digging painfully into the soft flesh of her abdomen. She pursed her lips, tilted her head, and expertly plucked at an errant eyebrow hair. Behind her, Libby appeared in the glass reflection. Right away, Evelyn knew this was going to be one of those ugly interactions, the ones they'd been having more often than not lately. The teenager was fidgeting from foot to foot, arms folded across her chest, ready for battle. Her mass of black clothing virtually shrouded the pale skin of her face. Her fierce dark eyes were laser focused as she spoke.

"You said it, and if you take it back now, I'll hate you," she spat, pressing her lipstick-blackened lips together so that the baby fleshiness of her mouth became a hard line. Evelyn leaned away from the mirror, set the tweezers down on the marble counter, and turned around. Then she folded her arms and stood to wait for what would come next. "I can't stand it here anymore," Libby continued, her eyes wet, "You do this all the time; you say things, and then say you didn't." That, Evelyn thought, was unfair. Sure, sometimes she did that, but not *all* the time. Did she? "I'm going anyway," Libby continued. "You should say ok and let me do what I want."

"Uh-huh," Evelyn said, weariness rolling over her. She resisted an overwhelming urge to lie down right there on the cool tiles of the bathroom floor. "Look, Lib, there's just no way I would have approved it. So, no. You can't go. Sorry." She hoped she sounded, what? Parental? Certain? Like an adult?

"I am," said Libby. "I am going. You said I could. Last night, you came into my room, totally fucking blotto, and you said I could."

Evelyn considered which part of that sentence she should address. The curse word, the accusation she'd been intoxicated (which was true, of course), the claim she approved of her sixteen-year-old daughter attending an overnight party for graduating high school seniors? Hmm, parenting supplied so many opportunities to screw up. There seemed no good choice. She gave up, deciding instead to change the subject.

"You know, Libby, I think that thing is getting infected. It's pretty awful looking." Evelyn uncrossed her arms and reached a hand, forefinger outstretched, toward Libby's right eyebrow, which sported a small silver ring surrounded by a quarter-sized bruise the color of a ripe plum.

Libby ducked out of the way. "You are not even listening to me!" Evelyn jerked back against the sink, banging her hip bone on the porcelain.

"Fuck, ouch," Evelyn said, rubbing at her hip, fighting the urge to say what she should not. She wasn't good at this. At least not first thing in the morning.

"Whatever, I don't care," Libby hissed, rolling her eyes. She ferreted in her purse and pulled out her phone.

A more direct approach, Evelyn said. "Look, Libby, I listened. I said you couldn't go. You're barely sixteen; it's a ridiculous request. I don't have time to argue about it. I don't know what you guys would do all night in a hotel." She fumbled around in her cosmetics drawer for something, although she was not entirely sure what.

Libby's reflection in the mirror stopped texting. Evelyn turned around to look at her. "Mom, again, you are not listening to me. I told you what we would be doing. We will be *doing nothing*. We won't be out all night; we are staying at the hotel."

Evelyn sighed, the breath coming from a deep, tired place all bone-dry and withered and lost, a place where remorse and guilt and something incomprehensible lay. Her mouth tasted like stale chardonnay. She tried to remember how much she'd had to drink. It had started with the voice mail message in the early afternoon. *I'm calling from Eden. Please call me back as soon as possible.* She'd already been reaching for the wine bottle as she listened to it, but, in fairness, she'd seen the area code when the call came in, and she'd known. *It's important, Mrs. Adamsson. Please call me back.* Mrs. Adamsson? She hadn't been Mrs. Anybody in over five years. The name hit hard. Then there was the other name: *Eden.* It conjured images she'd thought had evaporated from her brain or been drowned out by life and booze. *Her father at the kitchen table. His long narrow face, eyes sliding over her like she didn't exist, knobby fingers gripped around the neck of a beer bottle, dusty sunlight on pine floors under bare feet, and Carolyn, there was always Carolyn.*

She reached out to touch Libby's shoulder with the tip of one finger. Her daughter jerked backward, arms up as if preparing to defend herself from attack. Evelyn snapped her hand back. Rivers of eyeliner ran down Libby's cheeks, and slashes marked the inside of her left arm from wrist to elbow. Some delicate white lines like embroidery cloth, and some new ones, freshly scabbed. A tidal wave of love and terrible grief washed over Evelyn's heart, and she tasted vomit in her mouth. Libby followed her mother's gaze and quickly dropped her arms, allowing the fabric layers to cover her skin below the wrists again. They both looked away.

Evelyn checked her watch. "I'm late. I have to go to my office and finish that Clark thing." Only a part-lie. She had to go to her office, just not at any particular time. "Let's talk about this tonight. When I get back?"

Libby rolled her eyes. "Right, whatever." A car honked.

"It's your carpool." Evelyn nodded her head toward the window.

"I'm going on Friday. You can't stop me," Libby said over her shoulder as she walked out. Evelyn closed her eyes and sucked in air through her teeth in long, tough strands like twine.

•   •   •   •   •

It was early summer, and the city was pale and chilly. A gray mist hung low, obscuring the neighborhoods and erasing street signs. The Honda was freezing, colder than the street outside, and Evelyn fiddled with the heater knobs. She headed toward Market Street, where pedestrians lurched off sidewalks without warning like carnival surprises. The sky, occluded by the architecture, left the streets feeling airless and claustrophobic. She poked her fingers into her right temple, growing angry with hangover pain.

Fighting with Libby didn't help. A drink would help. She shooed the thought like a picnic pest.

One hand on the wheel, one eye on the road, she reached into her bag on the passenger seat and fished around for the Tylenol. Not there. She pictured herself placing the medicine on the bathroom counter after the fight with Libby. She tried to remember if she'd taken any of the pills. Likely not, given the pain in her temple.

She thought about the trellis of scars on her daughter's lovely arm, her eyes simultaneously radiating guilt and accusation. Evelyn had considered just letting Libby have what she wanted. She'd do anything to be left alone with her pain. Her thoughts. *Eden. Eden. Eden.* Instead, she'd tried to hold her ground. Be some version of a good parent. The resulting fight had not been worth it. Anger rose in her chest when she thought about Libby, intentionally choosing that moment for a confrontation. *What did you expect? She's angry. You drink. You lie. You sleepwalk (or whatever). She's pissed off, and you have no right to be surprised.* Probably it was only partly about going to the party on Friday. It was also about Libby's resentment of Richard. Libby detested him. She thought he was a player, whatever that meant. Libby had confronted her in the bathroom precisely because she knew Evelyn would feel awful. Hungover, sleep-deprived.

So, she'd made a promise. Another one she wouldn't keep. Shit. She told herself she'd genuinely forgotten about her evening commitments when she promised Libby they'd "talk about it" tonight. But it wasn't true. A familiar pang of guilt hit, squeezing her gut into a tight ball. She shook her head as if she could dislodge the thought. What choice did she have but to make promises? Libby pushed her into corners all the time. She was practically a single mom. She was doing the best she could. *Are you? Doing your best?* What did it mean that thinking about Libby sometimes made Evelyn feel as if she had no power over her life? It was as if she were observing from somewhere high above the ground, like a witness.

She'd practically had to shove Richard out the door. He'd been so nasty. What had he said to her? Something awful. Something Libby had heard, no doubt. There was a space in Evelyn's head where memories were missing; it happened like that. Was it getting worse? Maybe. Probably. It was like the tape recorder had run out of batteries and just lay dormant in her brain for a few hours until someone dug out the double A's and replaced them. Then the recording started up again as if nothing unusual had happened. Often, she filled in the blanks: "I was home at ten," or "Sure, the movie was great," or "My car? I left it at the office. Too tired to drive home." Not lies as much as best guesses.

The last thing she remembered was her anger at Richard for being such an asshole when she asked him to leave. Looking around the kitchen this morning, it appeared she'd finished the second bottle of wine after he'd left. She'd gotten into the good vodka as well, but had no idea how much she'd consumed. It was after two in the morning when her brain resumed full operations. She knew this because she'd stood in the kitchen, in the dark, leaning into the digital clock on the oven, trying her best to interpret the numbers on the LCD. A two, a one, and a five, in that order. 2:15 am. Fuck. Last she remembered, she'd swallowed a couple of sleeping pills and gone to bed. She wished she could recall what she'd said to Richard exactly, what he'd said to her. On second thought, not remembering was better. He'd left, but not without hurling her house key across the front hall and slamming the front door. For some reason, she had that one isolated memory.

The whole day had collapsed after that goddamn phone call. A man's voice calling from Eden: *Please call me back... Important.* He'd left a number. Evelyn stared at the phone, telling herself it was nothing. Just as her finger hovered over the button to delete the message, she'd changed her mind, and left it in voicemail. Infecting her phone. Her life.

She'd woken up this morning with a head heavy from a hangover and the weight of the phone message she'd never returned. And the memories. Her brain buzzing with the memories.

Carolyn's small fingers dancing across Evelyn's scalp like butterflies. Trying to make French braids out of Evelyn's unruly hair; the flip of Mama's pretty cotton skirt in the breeze as she hung laundry on the old line between the house and shed; Carolyn that last day, the man from social services carrying her across the yard, his broad back, her flailing arms and legs, the soles of her shoes sticky with mud. Moving away, into the distance, into the glare of the morning, until they both got so bright, they disappeared.

CHAPTER THREE

Nick | Eden

Detective Nick MacCallum arrived at the Eden station early Monday morning. As he walked across the dimly lit parking lot, he could hear the cacophony of growls and whispers as a summer storm gathered in the distance. Its breeze, still weak but gaining, unfurled over his skin like lace shot through with electricity. Lightning split the sky and, just as he pushed open the door, a massive thunderbolt cracked across the atmosphere behind him, and the rain began.

At his desk, Nick checked his watch. Not even seven. Lambert came in by eight, and Nick preferred to be away by then. Martin Lambert wasn't so bad, he did his job efficiently, was smart enough, and hard-working. Although not as good as his swagger and crewcut implied, he was a decent detective. People liked him, some people. But underneath, Nick thought, such an asshole. Rigid, hostile, and quick to find fault, they'd never gotten on. Nick was convinced Lambert hated him for being a relative outsider; for showing up two years earlier, transplanted from Jackson, and getting promoted to a position slightly higher in rank over Lambert the year before. Lambert's bleached tooth smile of congratulations had been too broad, his handshake too firm. "Way to go, man," he'd said. "Straight to the top," he'd added, pale eyes so bright they looked feline.

All of it felt poisoned by threat.

Sipping his coffee, Nick paged through the file on his desk. Photographs, newspaper articles, various internet printouts, case reports, and other documents, including an initial tox screen. Reading the words there, he needed all his professional mental muscles not to yell or push the whole folder to the floor. When he'd finished, he picked up one photograph, which had been slipped into a sterile-looking fitted plastic sleeve and labeled in neat block letters.

"Jesus fuck," he said out loud to the empty office and dropped the photograph onto the pile. It slid sideways, coming to rest at an angle that made the corpse in the picture look obscene. He turned it over, stood and pushed a fist into the small of his back. He grabbed from the rack a ceramic mug decorated with tiny pictures of the Eiffel Tower and je t'aime printed in feminine font around the base and poured himself a cup of chicory coffee. Then he stood at the window a minute, watching steam rolling off the black pavement. The day had gone hot already. The rain had stopped, and a gang of middle school-aged boys were rolling homemade skateboards back and forth across the Piggly Wiggly parking lot. School had been out for two days, and they'd already lost their shirts, exposing their pale, malnourished, genetically suspect upper bodies to the light. Soon a store manager would come outside and chase them off, but, for now, Nick thought, what the hell? It was summer.

He stepped back to his desk and, again, began studying the pictures in the file. This girl, he thought, this dead girl, did she skate when school was out? Did she even go to school? Plenty of kids around here didn't. He could feel the muscles in his face tense, his teeth clench. The doctor said his blood pressure was too high for a forty-three-year-old guy. He'd replied he felt a hundred-forty-three. She hadn't laughed. *This job,* he thought, *this goddamn job.*

He took a breath, pushed the photos around again, and lifted one between two fingers, holding it up to the light from the window behind him. Squinted. The crime scene, close up, emerging from the dirt, an object that, except for one detail, looked to be completely benign, maybe a root or the blackened branch of a lightning struck tree. Nick drew the photograph closer, studying the image. It might have been a root or branch, except it wasn't. It wasn't even a dead animal. The thing sticking straight up, small fingers reaching skyward, was a human hand.

Anger surged through Nick and he slammed the picture down. How in the hell was he supposed to deal with a dead girl resurfacing after thirty years? Chief Deputy Broussard was already going crazy, gearing up for a fight with the medical examiner, and Sheriff Savoy was doing the political dance and staying out of it. That put pressure on Nick to sort it out ASAP. That's what the Sheriff said: *Nick, I'm relying on you to sort this out ASAP.* This job, he thought again, this goddamn job.

CHAPTER FOUR

Evelyn | San Francisco

Traffic slowed near the Embarcadero Center and stopped altogether. Evelyn dragged her purse from the passenger seat to her lap, fumbled around inside, and produced a cell phone, ignoring the flashing notification: *Missed Calls (4)*. She jabbed the speaker key and hit the number for Stuart. It rang once.

"Stu here."

Evelyn had learned over the twenty-plus years she'd known Stuart that it was best to get to the point. It gave him less opportunity for malicious sarcasm. This had been especially true since their separation seven years earlier.

"Look, Stuart," she said. "Libby has this insane demand about the dance on Friday. I promised her we'd talk about it tonight, but I've got this thing I have to do. I need you to step up and deal with it. Sit her down, have a real talk with her."

"Oh, come on, Evelyn, you fucked up again, right? You lied to her, and now you want me to fix it for you? You promise her and bail out all the time. I won't do it. It's your week; I've got plans tonight." She knew he was frustrated, but he still sounded like a boy clutching a prize. For Stuart, this would count as a win.

"Jesus Christ, Stuart, come on. I have no choice here." She squeezed back tears and slapped her face with the back of her hand. The traffic started moving. She stepped on the accelerator.

"You have a choice. I have plans," Stuart said.

Plans, she thought. Plans meant a date for sure. Regardless of whether he had one, Stuart never failed to imply that he did. "Look," Evelyn said, trying to sound practical and detached. "I need you to do this. I have a job, remember? Just pick her up from school, okay? Don't talk to her about the dance if you don't want to, but I need you to get her from school." She squeezed her eyes tight. She had to say it, even though it killed her. Stuart had no responsibilities; his parents' money paid for his life. His pretend position in his father's company made him a pretend adult and somehow gave him the right to treat her like she was imposing on him when she needed flexibility. Stuart had earned nothing in his life. Not really. And he'd never been afraid of losing anything either. Stuart floated through life with the underserved, impenetrable confidence afforded only to the born wealthy. Evelyn sucked in her breath and let the word out like it was poison: "Please."

She could hear his mouth stretch across into a bitter smile as he said, "Fine, I'll pick her up. But I'm not giving her your excuses. I'm not covering for you. You can talk to her about the dance yourself. When do you want her back?"

"I'll get her from you tomorrow morning. Tell her..." she hesitated. "Tell her I'm sorry I forgot about this dinner meeting tonight, okay?"

"Right. Fine. Whatever." His words were hard and clipped like fingernails. He wouldn't say she forgot. He'd be faithful to his promise and not cover for her.

"Ok," she said.

"And listen, no more drink and dial, ok? I had to block you last night."

"Huh?" Her heart thudded in her chest, and she was acutely sicker.

"Seven calls Evelyn. I mean, for Chrissakes, seven fucking voicemails. Get it together."

Evelyn could feel the heat on her face. He'd saved this tidbit for the right moment in the conversation. She said nothing, hung up, and gripped the steering wheel hard with one hand, still clutching the phone in the other. Traffic had slowed again. She glanced down at the phone. Jesus, had she mentioned the call from Eden? Her fingers trembling, she hit the RECENTS button, pulling up her phone history. 1:10 am to 2:10 am. She'd dialed him twelve times. Five calls must have been after he blocked her. Motherfucker.

Must have been the zolpidem. The sleep medicine was potent, a lot stronger, taken in double doses. Maybe that's what the label meant: DO NOT TAKE WITH ALCOHOL. Part of her was glad she did not know what she'd said. Perhaps, she thought, unreasonably, he'd deleted the messages without listening. Five years since the divorce and interactions with Stuart still left her feeling stupid and small.

CHAPTER FIVE

Libby | San Francisco

Carpool sucked. Libby sat in the backseat, smashed against the door of the white Mercedes SUV Sheri Kennedy's mother was driving this year. Last year, it had been some other environmentally inefficient monstrosity in a color called Winter, which looked to Libby suspiciously like white. Sheri said her mother dumped it when she could no longer stand the color.

Libby shifted her weight again to escape Sheri's high-pitched prattle. She stared at the floor around her feet.

"So, I was like, no way are you coming with us, you know? I mean, how rude, right? It's like so rude to just assume you're invited," Sheri said. Her words dipped and danced around the car like gnats.

"I know, right? She's totally like that. It's so annoying," Lindsay Pizarro replied. She was sitting on the other side of Sheri, dutifully agreeing with anything Sheri said.

"Yeah, so I'm like, look, I'm sorry you don't have any of your own friends, but that does not mean you can just follow mine around," Sheri said.

"You said that?" Lindsay asked, sounding appropriately impressed.

"No, I didn't say that. I wanted to, though," Sheri replied and lifted her phone, which was set on reverse camera mode, more closely to her face. She examined her forehead, wrinkled her brow, and sighed heavily, as if deeply concerned by whatever she saw reflected there. *Contemplating the disturbing ethical dilemma of teenage social exclusion,* Libby thought. *Or her zit.*

She might have been contemplating her nonexistent zit. "Anyway, I just said I wasn't going, and it was no big deal. She dropped it, thank god. How annoying, right? She's such a bitch, anyway."

"Wait," Libby interrupted. "So, you lied? Sheri, what about your Instagram pics and all those Snapchats you sent out? She's gonna know, and she's gonna be really pissed." *Hurt,* Libby thought. *Darla Cooper, the subject of Sheri's character assassination, would be really, really hurt.* Darla's family wasn't wealthy enough for Darla to rate as somebody who mattered to Sheri, but still, she was popular enough to cause problems if she thought Sheri was intentionally excluding her, which, of course, Sheri was. *Stupid,* Libby thought, *Sheri was stupid. They're all fucking stupid.*

Sheri glanced at Libby for the first time since she'd gotten into the car, a look of profound disapproval on her teen queen face. "Whatever, I mean, she's totally got to know I didn't want her there, right? If you like her so much, you hang out with her. It's not like you're doing anything else these days, right?"

"That's true Lib. I mean, Sheri's right about that," Lindsay said, once again offering her unconditional love and support whenever Sheri was concerned.

Libby stopped talking and resumed staring at her feet.

•   •   •   •   •

Getting out of the car at school, Libby dug a fist into her belly and winced. Taking a couple of breaths, she willed herself to stand upright before continuing. No one noticed. Even though her mother accused her of intentionally starting their arguments, Libby hated the fights. They made her chronic stomachache worse, and, afterward, she always obsessed about the mean words she'd said. She wished she knew how to make the fights stop. Instead, they were getting worse.

It hadn't always been like this. Libby could remember when things were good, and it wasn't all that long ago. She'd adored her mother. When she was small, they'd spent time together. Those memories appeared in Libby's mind, as if illuminated in brief flashes by a flickering flashlight.

Libby digs all ten fingers into a mountain of play-do and laughs when her mother pulls them out to show her the red goop under her nails. Both of them sit on the floor of Gam's enormous bathroom and play with Gam's costume jewelry and lipsticks. They clutter their wrists with gold bangles and pretend they are gypsies, and her mother says she's the prettiest gypsy girl in the world. Libby sits in her mother's lap on a wide stretch of grass, and they watch the sky as Libby's balloon, now the size of a nickel, floats off into what Libby assumes is outer space.

Every memory was laced with the scent of the ocean or the city or the vanilla soap and lemon wax of Gam's bathroom. But later things changed. Evelyn was always tense, her mouth twisted into an angry frown. *Not now*, she would say, *we need to hurry, stop dawdling.* Libby would look down at her shoes until Evelyn snatched her arm to pull her forward.

Then the fighting began. Or maybe, Libby thinks, she just noticed it. Dinners were alone in the kitchen while her parents' muffled voices pitched and broke through the ceiling in angry bursts. Then the drinking. It used to frighten her; it made their voices sound different, especially late at night. All dark rumbles and unfamiliar inflections mixed sickly sweet with the smell of wine and perfume. How old had she been when she first recognized the sound of lies layered on secrets? When she'd first seen the sickness that lived with them. Now hiding in her house. Under the bed. In the laundry where her mother stashed the bottles, she thought no one knew about.

Libby stopped inviting friends over, but she still had friends, and she did well in school. She loved swimming and horseback riding, the things most adults considered *normal*. Evelyn kept her anger contained for a while, (until later when it overflowed Evelyn's brain and shot out into space like fireworks) and briefly, Libby could pretend her life was normal.

Then her father became more distant, remarkable because he'd never been a person who favored intimacy. Stuart was sociable, charming, and easy-going, at least on the surface, but limited in his ability or willingness to relate on a deeper level. He'd charmed Libby up to a certain point. She'd loved him terribly; thought of him like a fairy prince. Beautiful. He smelled of leather and cinnamon candy. He had the habit, seductive, even for a child, of dancing into her room late at night, *actually dancing*, placing a soft kiss on her forehead and a few sweet words in her ear before evaporating again into the darkness. Libby always pretended to be asleep. It seemed like a rule. The pretending. She was always awake when he left the house afterward. She heard the side door close behind him, the gentle electric hum of the garage door opening, the car motor purring softly. Sometimes she thought the car was pretending too. Sometimes he left presents behind.

The young Libby was unaware of Stuart's limitations. She never questioned his nighttime excursions. It wasn't until the separation that Evelyn's words (borne of her pain) would slice through Libby's heart: "He's no good," her mother said. "He's a liar." And the worst, the most damaging of all, "He's loved no one but himself." That one (which Evelyn often repeated when drunk) caused Libby to question her unflagging loyalty to her father. Those words systematically dismantled Libby's world, leaving her confused, guilty, exhausted, and angry all the time.

Libby thought she might have tolerated the divorce if her smiling and beautiful mother had not morphed into someone she no longer recognized. Now Evelyn, frequently drunk, often angry, and always unhappy, was as unpredictable and alien as a stranger. Libby, too, was different. She'd become one of the school's ugly, unpopular emo kids. The sort she used to laugh about, along with her pretty and popular friends. She doubted she'd even rate the effort of covert exclusion by people like Sheri Kennedy. Libby didn't care. Nobody cared. Even the teachers seemed not to notice. If she was quiet and did most of her work, they said nothing. Everyone believed she was doing fine. She fought with her mother, was ignored by her father, and, day by day, grew increasingly empty and hopeless.

There were days, like today, when Libby's exhaustion with the whole thing pushed her brain to its limits, and she found herself on Google searching up awful things like self-immolation. Reading stories about girls in places as far away as Afghanistan. Desperate girls. Not that she'd do that, of course. Never. It was a horrible way to die. But gradually she understood what might make someone choose it. That was the scary thing. Dousing oneself with gasoline and striking a match was starting to make sense.

CHAPTER SIX

Evelyn | San Francisco

It was still early when Evelyn parked underground at the Embarcadero Center. She took the first elevator from the garage to the lobby. When the doors opened, she had a clear view of the reception desk. Jake Simms, the building's impossibly young and improbably good-looking security guard, sat at a bank of computer screens. The last time she'd seen him, she'd been drunk, and he'd had to call her an Uber to send her home. It'd been after a late-night office party for one of the other companies in the building, and she'd overstayed her welcome. The results were nearly disastrous. It would have been disastrous had Jake not been there to call Uber. She straightened her posture, tugged at her blouse and was considering smashing her palm into the panel button marked "Close" when he looked up and straight at her.

"How are you doing today, Ms. Yates?" he said, smiling. His perfect teeth reminded her of blank dominoes.

The day, so far, had been a total bust. The hangover from hell, an ugly altercation with an entirely off-the-wall teenage daughter, followed by the always unpleasant phone call to asshole ex-husband, and now headed into the office to complete a project which was already two days overdue. All before eight am. "I'm good, thanks," she said, her smile broad, making her cheeks ache. Stepping out of the elevator, she took a few steps forward, stopped, and fumbled in her bag for nothing. "Lose something, Ms. Yates?"

"Huh?" she said and looked up. "No, I, uh... nothing. Sorry." Stepping up to the reception desk, she was careful not to look him in the eye as she bent over the iPad and used the stylus to sign in. Her hand shook. The boy smelled of cheap shampoo, aftershave, and something vaguely young, like bean sprouts. Her mouth tasted like Crest and pencil lead, so she held her breath. Perhaps, she thought, he'd forgotten the whole awful Uber event. That would be helpful.

"Have a nice day, Ms. Yates," he said, his voice emotionless, like a bank teller. What was he? Twenty? Twenty-two? She looked over her shoulder before rounding the corner to the second bank of elevators. He'd gone back to reading his paper. Of course, he had not forgotten. He didn't have dementia, for God's sake. He just didn't care. She was inconsequential in his life. Invisible. She wasn't entirely sure which was better.

•   •   •   •   •

A law firm, a behemoth calling itself Bernstein Corning LLP. Bernstein Corning occupied almost entirely the tenth floor, employed hundreds of lawyers, mostly young, overworked, and perpetually stunned-looking. Evelyn avoided them in case whatever they had might be contagious. Her office was one of the very few non-Bernstein spaces on the floor.

She got off the elevator and hauled her belongings down the long corridor to the last door at the end, bent her knees and did a sort of tipped curtsy to the right, letting everything slide off her shoulder and drop unceremoniously to the floor. Glancing back up the hall, she fished around inside one bag and pulled out a set of keys. Unlocking the door, Evelyn pushed it open, gathered up all her belongings, and stepped inside. She poked her head out into the corridor, rechecked it, and then closed the door and locked it from the inside.

The space was small, but she hadn't rented it for the size. Two narrow windows stretched seven feet upward on the south wall and, depending on the time of year, light the colors of spun gold or honey or amethyst, ribboned through them and careened off the floor onto the walls as if shot through stained glass. The effect was spiritual, like a chapel. She stood inside the office and tilted her face up toward the light.

•　　　•　　　•　　　•　　　•

Three years earlier, the conversation had been brief. They were in his living room in Pacific Heights. He'd invited her over for drinks. He wanted to talk.

"You understand, Evelyn, right?"

"Yeah, LC, I know, but I think you should tell me to my face anyway," she said, watching raindrops fat as green peas slide down the double-hung windows outside his lovely apartment.

"Really? Is there a need? I mean, honestly, it's so very unpleasant. Why don't you just do what needs to be done, Ev? Clean it up, take care of it. You know what I mean?" He paced around the cream-colored room, unable to look at her, fiddling with objects, rearranging things.

"Yeah, right, I know." *Prick,* she thought, watching the rain. *Just say it, spineless prick.*

"You know we all love you, Ev. We just love, love, love your work," Lanterman Causey said, rolling the word *love* around in his mouth as if it were strawberry flavored. "But, well, you know, the unreliability. We can't have that on individual projects."

And there it was. Give the man a prize. *Unreliability,* and by *unreliability,* Causey meant *drinking.* Unreliability at work always meant *drinking,* but people were too embarrassed to say it. At least it always meant *drinking* unless it meant *crazy,* in which case people were certainly too embarrassed to say it.

"Yeah, you're right, LC, I get it. I will. Thanks." *Maybe the rain turns to hail and smashes his beautiful windows to nothing. Nothing. Nothing.* "I appreciate your honesty," she said and looked at him, but he averted his eyes. "Really," she said.

"Well, that's good, okay, you understand, we had no choice. Letting you go is, well, the best thing to do for everyone. Anyway, we'll work out the details later. Andrew will talk to you about whatever projects you have pending and all that. I am so glad you understand. You know Ev," he said, picking up a glass globe which he held aloft, studying its contents intensely–a perfect miniature replica of Frank Lloyd Wright's Falling Water. "Perhaps you can use the time to, uh, you know, take care of yourself, right?" He returned the globe to its spot on a bookshelf and looked at her.

"Right," she said.

"Right," he said.

She'd left Lanterman Causey Design LLC and signed a five-year lease on a place she couldn't afford with a plan to live off of the divorce settlement payments and overflow work from LCD only until she got on her feet. That was three years ago. Things hadn't changed. At least not for the better.

•   •   •   •   •

Evelyn pulled the sample board towards her and ran her fingers over its surface. After a minute, she tipped it up and balanced it edge-wise with one hand. She studied it, tilting her head from side to side. She laid the board back on the table, slid a drawer beneath the counter, pulled out a square of rose blue chintz fabric, and held it in the air above the board. After a few seconds, she tossed the chintz onto the board, puffed up both cheeks, and blew an obnoxious stream of air out of her mouth.

She hated this project. One of Lanterman Causey's contract nightmares, he'd sent Evelyn's way because nobody in the firm wanted to deal with it. None of the actual employees. The wife had zero taste. The husband also had zero taste, but that was irrelevant. Blue. This woman wanted everything, and by that, she meant *everyfuckingthing* to be blue. The husband had no input except that if his wife didn't wind up happy, Causey's business would be out of business, or so he threatened. Not realistic, of course, but Causey enjoyed passing along the threat. He passed it along via text to Evelyn at least thrice hourly. In all fairness, she should have completed the project two days earlier, but for various reasons, spelled u-n-r-e-l-i-a-b-i-l-i-t-y, it wasn't finished, and now she was under considerable pressure to finish within the next few hours.

Evelyn checked her watch. Again. She'd been at the office for two hours, switching out bits of silk and chintz. Hopeless. Her phone buzzed, and she reached for it, caught the edge with one finger, pulled it towards her, and read the text message display.

LC: Done yet? On my way at 11.

She yanked it closer and typed a reply.

Evelyn: Almost

Lying by text was even easier than lying by phone and lying by phone had never been a problem. Interesting since she was a terrible, albeit frequent, liar face to face. Evelyn sometimes wondered if she even had the capacity for telecommunications honesty. It seemed almost unnatural.

She swiped the screen off and closed her eyes and waited for another wave of hangover nausea to pass.

•　　　•　　　•　　　•　　　•

An hour later, the landline shrieked, and she jerked backward and dropped a piece of glass tile to the tabletop, where it shattered and lay in spiky bits. "Shit," she said as the phone rang a second time. She scooped at the wreckage with her palms, and the phone rang a third time. "Okay, okay," she said, abandoning the effort. She stood and reached across the big table for the receiver, her brain scrambling for a lie to tell Causey; an excuse for missing yet another deadline.

The call, however, was not Lanterman Causey. It was Chief Deputy Tom Broussard calling from the Sheriff's Office in Eden, Louisiana. *Please call me back, Mrs. Adamsson. It's important.* She never had. He'd tracked down her office number.

Kids said the man on the phone. *A couple of boys were messing around by your father's place on Road 12. They found her, they found the body.*

Evelyn felt herself float upward toward the ceiling. She watched herself lean forward over the drafting table; the landline cord twisted so tightly around her hand two fingers turned white. *Carolyn turning towards her in bed, their small faces inches apart on the same pillow. It'll be ok, she says. Don't worry, go to sleep.*

As he spoke, the traffic sounds outside on the street seemed to expand and contract, like listening through a vent, continuously opening and closing. She watched her head shaking slowly back and forth as she listened.

"Yates," she interrupted him when he called her by Stuart's last name-Adamsson. "My last name. It's just Yates. But please, just call me Evelyn." She wasn't sure why that seemed important. Maybe it was all she could think of to say. She listened to the man talk a bit longer, trying to make sense of the words. Finally, he asked, "Ms. Yates, Evelyn, can you tell me how long it's been since you've seen your sister?"

Without hesitation, she answered, "I think you've made a mistake, Chief Broussard. I don't have a sister." The response was a reflex, like when someone asked zip code or date of birth, or last four of your social security number. *I don't have a sister*, she said.

"I apologize for this, Ms. Yates, but didn't you live at Road Twelve with your father, John Yates? Until let me see." He was checking something. "Until 1994?"

A beat. "Yes, I did, but -"

"Uh, Ms. Yates, according to our records, there was another girl in the house-"

She cut him off sharply, not wanting to hear the rest. *A girl in the house. A girl in her bedroom. Searching for something.* "Look, I'm trying to say that I had a sister once. But, uh, she died. A long time ago, she died. So, whoever or *whatever* you've found, it's not her. It's not Carolyn." She liked the sound of that word, *whatever;* there was distance in that word, coolness. A concrete wall two miles high. Whatever you found, Evelyn thought. Whatthefuckever, you found.

The sheets fluttering there on the line... his broad back... her flailing arms and legs... until all at once... she was swallowed up by the sun.

She listened for another minute. He told her about the situation. His voice was gentle and patient. He was a nice man, Evelyn could tell, nice in that genuine, he'd give a guy five bucks for a burger just because he asked, kind of way.

Carolyn was *difficult*, Evelyn explained to the nice Chief Deputy. That's what they called it. They had made arrangements.

"What type of arrangements?" he asked.

It'll be better for her, Daddy had said. You'll see. This will be better.

Gradually, Evelyn's brain was coming back to her body. Slow, deep breaths. She wiped beads of sweat off her brow despite the chill in the office. "Mental hospital arrangements. She wasn't... well. My sister had a hard time. She wasn't right. My father had her hospitalized up in New Orleans. A special facility for adolescents. They came, and... took her." *The man... his broad back... his broad back... her flailing arms and leg.*

"Who? Who took her?"

"Social workers, I guess, hospital people." Evelyn hesitated. Swallowed the lump in her throat. "She was there a few years. Until she passed away."

The Chief told her he was sorry to hear that... understood how confusing this must be. He asked the name of the psychiatric facility in New Orleans, and Evelyn said she'd have to look it up for him. He told her thanks and by the way, would she mind coming down to Eden and help clear things up? Would she be willing to do that?

No! Hell no! she screamed inside her head. She would not come to Eden. She'd never go back, and nothing he could say would change her mind.

"Yeah, ok. I'll come."

Setting the phone back in its receiver, hand trembling, she shoved the sample boards across the table, planted her elbows and buried her face and rubbed at her forehead with all ten fingers. Her heart was pounding, and it annoyed her to find her cheeks wet with tears. She felt somehow naked. Exposed. She snatched at a drawer under the desk. Reaching into it, she fumbled around and came up with a flask for emergencies. She unscrewed the silver cap and took a long drink. Focusing on the calming warmth in her chest as the liquid did its magic. After a minute, she set the flask down and exhaled. She'd cope with this. Somehow, she'd figure it out. She always did.

Sisters. She hadn't had a sister, hadn't *been* a sister, in over thirty years. The idea of becoming one now, again, was intolerable; it filled her with a familiar angry ache that glowed orange hot inside her belly. *You left me, Carolyn, alone, with that man. You have no right to come back to me now.* Evelyn took another draw on the flask. This was not the time to think about it. She tossed about in her mind for another memory... a good memory... anything.

Mama is calling them, but they pretend not to hear. They've been out in Back Field since shortly after breakfast, and the sun is now coming through the grass in fat, white ribbons. They lay on their backs, daring each other to look up into the light, and

Evelyn can feel the mud squeezing out between her toes. It's a warm spring day but not so hot because the morning's rain has cooled everything down. Carolyn calls it a big old car wash, and that's what it's like too. Just like sitting inside a big old hot car wash. "You know how mad Mama's going to be if we don't go, Carolyn, we got to go now," she says, moving nothing except her toes, which feel lovely in the mud.

Evelyn and Carolyn have been coming to Back Field ever since Evelyn can remember, which is a long time. It's not a field at all; it's like a wild garden behind the old barn that Daddy uses only as a tool shed now. A hole between the wall slats in the back of the shed, is big enough for one girl at a time to squeeze through. Behind it, fenced on three sides, a quilted expanse of wild grasses and flowers: pink cosmos and yellow coneflowers and larkspur; iris and mulberry, violet, and magenta; white bloodroot and banana colored black-eyed Susan's, which Evelyn calls black-eyed Betties because of a woman they both know at church, named Betty, who often shows up Sunday mornings with a blackened eye. Two pecan trees sit in one corner and never fail to drop nuts in the fall. The squirrels steal a good many, but Evelyn and Carolyn find plenty left. They sneak Mama's nutcracker from the kitchen and eat them raw until their stomachs hurt. Giant sunflowers grow head high in summer, and, if the girls beat the crows, they can pick the seeds and have a feast. There are no sunflowers today since it is only April, but that's all right with Evelyn. She likes April the best, anyway. In the springtime, daisies sprout, interspersed among the other wildflowers, perfect for making chains. They sit for hours weaving princess jewelry, dreaming they are royalty. In the fall, when the flowers die, they make mud pies with the leaves and twigs until it gets too cold. Sometimes, they cannot get all the mud off their hands and shoes before squeezing through the hole in the slats and running back to the house. When this happens, Mama looks at them and says, "Now, what in the world have my two girls been up to?" She doesn't much like the mud and always makes them go outside and use the hose to wash it off, even when it's cold, but she always smiles at them and never pushes for an answer about where they've been. So, the Back Field stays their secret.

"Oh, hush now, Lynnie, we don't have to do no such thing. Can you see that over there?" Carolyn asks and raises an arm and points at the sky, one finger stretched into the distance. Evelyn squints. Sees nothing.

"Nope, I don't see nothing, Carolyn, and I don't want to get in trouble." She doesn't like how she sounds whiny, but she can't help it.

"Shh, I said. Look." Evelyn looks. Finally, she sees it. A plane in the distance coming toward them. It's tiny at first but getting bigger and louder. A buzz as soft as a bumblebee and then louder and choppy, like the engine of their Nana's old Ford.

"Where do you think it's going?" Evelyn asks.

"I don't know," said Carolyn. "Where would you want it to go?" Carolyn does this. She has a wonderful way of turning everything into a game.

Evelyn smiles. "I don't know, Florida maybe. Or Mississippi, where Mama's from."

Carolyn sits up and looks at her. Sitting like that in the deep grass, dewy sweat on her brow, tall larkspur and foxglove around her, and the sun creating a halo behind her mass of blonde hair, she looks like a fairy, a garden fairy. "Nah," she says. "Come on. Somewhere better than that. Somewhere far, really far."

Evelyn doesn't know any distant places. Celeste is as far as she's been, and that's not even a different parish. She picks at a piece of grass, separating the thick blade into two green ribbons. She tries to picture somewhere exotic. "I don't know. I can't think of anywhere far. You mean like the moon?"

"Maybe. Maybe the moon." She has to raise her voice as the plane approaches, and the sound grows louder, "or how about... how about the beach? Yes, the beach. That's where they are going. Definitely."

The ocean scares her a little. She's seen it on TV, in books, vast and anonymous, like outer space. The airplane is directly overhead, and Evelyn frowns and shouts, "What beach?" She needs to know who is going? How are they getting there once they land? What have they packed?

"Oh, I don't know, Lynnie, maybe Hawaii. They are going in the right direction for Hawaii." Carolyn sounds mildly frustrated, but she is smiling. The plane has passed and is retreating into the distance. "Yep, that's it. There's a family in there, and they have all their beach towels packed and bathing suits and nice summer dresses, and that's where they are going. To the beach in Hawaii." They both lay back down and watch the tiny airplane until it disappears.

Evelyn let her gaze drift to the windows. *And you did it, didn't you? You flew away and left me behind.* The day was opening up into something glittery and bright. She spun her chair around until she was full face toward the sunlight and shut her eyes, letting the warmth bathe her skin. No, Evelyn thought, Broussard was wrong; the thing they'd found down there, it wasn't Carolyn. She imagined Carolyn laughing at the thought. *Me? In Eden? That's silly. You know Lynnie. You know what happened,* she would say and smile as the summer sun glistened off two rows of small, perfect teeth.

CHAPTER SEVEN

Gwen | 1982 | Eden

February 20, 1982

He's dead. They're saying his own son shot him down, but I wonder if that's true. A hunting accident. Anyway, his death makes me feel safer. That word again, safer. I think now I have to tell someone. I promised I would let it go, but that was before. Now, he's dead. It'll be ok. I'm sure.

I've made an appointment at the Orleans Clinic. They know me. They've treated me. It'll be ok.

-G

March 1, 1982

I drive myself to the clinic for my appointment. It's raining, and the drive takes a long time.

As soon as the doctor comes in, I explain everything to him. I tell him all about what happened, even though it was so many years ago. Then I tell him the rest of the story up to the girl Wanda who died last year. All about Eden. I can see he's having trouble believing me, but he's trying. At least he's trying.

I tell him that my life is in danger. My children might be in danger, as well. The more I talk, the less I can stop myself. He's very kind. He listens patiently. After a while, he leaves the room, returning with a young nurse. They tell me they believe me, and I cry. I suppose it's a relief. The nurse brings me tea and tissues. She says I need to rest and gives me some pills to calm my nerves. The drugs make me sleepy, but I feel much better. They leave the exam room door open, and I can see them talking in the hallway.

I wait for a long time.

When the doctor returns, John is with him, which surprises me. John says the doctor asked him to come and pick me up. The rain. My distress. Driving wouldn't be safe they tell me and I agree. On the way home, John is mostly silent. I feel tired and relaxed. I don't want to talk. But I ask what the doctor told him. At first, he says nothing, but I ask again, and he says I still have symptoms. That's the word he uses symptoms. John says I'll have to take the medication every day because I'm not well. I know he thinks it's like last time. Like what happened after Carolyn. He doesn't say so, but I can see the fear in his eyes. And the sadness too. He is worried.

I am silent the rest of the way home, but I know I will never take that medication again.

-G.

CHAPTER EIGHT

Nick | Eden

Nick set the phone down and looked at his notes. He was trying to make sense of the data in the file, to reconcile it with what he'd been told by Broussard.

Remains buried 25 to 30 years ago.
Child/Young teenager. Female, age 12-15.
Prelim. Tox screen negative.
Prelim. ID: Carolyn Yates

They'd need further analysis of the soft tissue from the bones to complete toxicology. To rule out drug use. It might be impossible in a corpse this old.

Picking up his pencil, he added to the notepad,

Location found: Road 12, Yates Place.

They'd found a child's body buried on the family property. The house and five-acre grounds sat abandoned since the old man died there in 2007; everyone in town knew it as *The Crazy Yates Place*. Nick had initially believed the nickname came after John Yates died alone in his bathtub-the sad result of heart disease and chronic alcoholism-but later, he'd discovered the property had carried the name since the 1970s, a cruel reference to Gwen Yates's psychiatric difficulties. People could be assholes.

Nick wondered why the house remained unsold, although, he reasoned, with depressed property values, the lousy location -

Eden being virtually synonymous with "lousy location" in terms of real estate- and the old man's death occurring on the premises (a fact that had to be disclosed to potential buyers in Louisiana) maybe selling wasn't an option. Then again, perhaps someone did not want it sold. There was a body buried there.

Sitting back in his chair, he glanced out the window and noticed the rain starting again. Within seconds it was coming down in torrents, beating like tiny fists against the glass, so hard and fast it obscured visibility. He might as well have been in an airplane, flying through one of those storm clouds. Or a submarine. He liked Louisiana rain; the indiscriminate power of it.

From the pile before him, he pulled the last page and held it between his fingers. It was fragile and yellowed with age. It was a stroke of luck that Nick found these records, and a miracle they'd been in shape good enough to read. He lay the paper down on his desk and began to read.

John Yates, (father of the missing child Carolyn Yates) called the station on August 8, asking for help to find his daughter and yet no one had filed a formal report. There was a handwritten notation at the bottom of the page; an officer followed up with Yates the following day, at which time he (Yates) reported his daughter found and safe. It appeared there'd been no follow-up investigation; not even a series of follow-up questions.

The floaters had put together a next of kin report on Carolyn Yates. Pretty simple since, other than Evelyn Yates, the sister in California, she had none. The mother, Gwen, deceased in 1986 of suicide, and the father, John, deceased natural causes in 2007.

According to Evelyn Yates, Carolyn had suffered significant psychiatric problems. The family had her hospitalized in New Orleans not long after the mother's suicide and she'd later died during the summer of 1989. Some type of infection. She'd never left the institution. An internet search revealed only one public psychiatric hospital for adolescents in Southeast Louisiana.

There were several private institutions but none within Orleans Parish, and, besides, how likely was it that the Yates family had the funds for one of those places?

NOAH, or New Orleans Adolescent Hospital, had been in continuous operation for over a hundred years when it closed for good in 1995. Nick figured, like the rest of Louisiana, it suffered from a chronic lack of funding and administrative corruption. Getting records would be difficult. He had a floater headed up today to check it, but he wasn't optimistic. Records back then would have been paper, and the chances of finding anything on one girl who died there thirty years ago seemed slim.

If Carolyn Yates died in an institution in 1989, then who the hell was the body in the ground? He closed the folder on his desk, stood, stretched, trying to work out the kinks in his back. It would be a long day. He grabbed his coffee cup and shuffled toward the kitchen for a refill.

CHAPTER NINE

Libby | San Francisco

School was going pretty much as Libby had expected. It sucked slightly less than carpool and only because she'd found several hiding spots where she could be alone during the day.

That's where she was now, hiding in the girls' toilet, sitting on the pot, lid down, feet up, hidden from view. Journal out. Writing. She'd found that writing helped work the kinks out of her brain when she couldn't paint; at least it smoothed them down a little for a time.

.

The moon turns. Goes.
With it, the soft forgiveness of the dark.
Here again, another one.
Bright and mighty. Ceaseless. fierce scratching behind my
eyes. while Poison knives in my gut blind me
Waiting. Waiting. Waiting.

Libby would show no one what she wrote. She had a vague sense that it was wrong or even unhealthy. She'd made the mistake of exposing her writing once. It had been a poem-something about social stress- she'd entered into a school contest back in middle school. She hadn't won the contest, but the work had alarmed her English teacher, who contacted her parents, who subsequently threatened to make her see a shrink. She'd spent the rest of the school term plastering a smile on her face and chatting up her peers whenever the stupid teacher looked her way. Anything to appear not fucked up.

She closed the little journal and shoved it into her jacket pocket along with the pen, stood, flushed the toilet, and exited the stall. The bathroom was empty, but that wouldn't last. During breaks, girls came and went almost continuously, chatting, screeching, laughing, applying lip-gloss, reapplying lip-gloss. She washed her hands out of reflex and was just reaching for a paper towel as the heavy door swung open, and three girls came in, laughing loudly.

Sheri Kennedy and her two main hangers-on: Lindsay, from carpool, and Megan LaGiardino, whose father owned LaGiardino's Grill, a chain of mediocre steak places that Evelyn called *Giardia's* after the intestinal disease.

Libby knew for sure that Sheri only gave Megan the time of day because of her money. Back when Sheri and Libby had had some sort of relationship, Sheri said the absolute worst things about Megan behind her back. The girl was short, chubby, and boring. But she was rich and a first-class licker of asses.

The three girls came giggling and chattering into the lavatory, half-stuck to one another like soap bubbles. They huddled over Sheri's bejeweled iPhone, which, even without the case, was practically the size of a laptop computer. Libby watched as Sheri's white-tipped fingernails clicked away at the screen. "Oh my God, wait till you guys see this," Sheri was saying. "He was like, ok, I'll send it if you send it, and I was like no effing way am I sending you that shit, right? I mean, I'm totally not like that. And then he's like-" The girl stopped mid-sentence. Looked up. Big blue eyes, mechanically curled eyelashes thick with mascara, Tiffany gold bracelets tinkling as she dropped her hand to her side.

"Hi Sheri," said Libby, keeping her voice flat. No need to acknowledge the other two. They were like accessories.

"Hi Lib," said Sheri, her voice sugary. False.

Libby, unable to think of anything clever to say, opted for silence. She would have bolted, but the three girls were blocking the door. She had no choice but to wait for them to clear the way.

"Hi Libby," said Megan and then added, unnecessarily, "I like your top." Sheri glared at the girl as if she'd just said something obscene. Megan wasn't bad, really. Stupid and a brown-noser but not cruel. Not like Sheri and Lindsay. Of course, it was only a matter of time until she was eaten alive by the other two.

"Thanks, Megan," said Libby. "I gotta go. It's almost bell." She started past Sheri but stopped as the girl held up a manicured hand.

"You know, Libby, it's kind of rude for you to just... I don't know. Like, stop hanging out or whatever." It was true that Libby had been avoiding Sheri and the others for weeks. She'd become increasingly less tolerant of the bullshit. More irritable. Sheri was precisely the sort of girl who would take that personally. In Sheri's world, everything that happened was directly related to Sheri. She was the girl who wore her first initial stamped in solid gold around her neck and signed her own name in giant loopy letters, with a big heart over the "i." Sheri took up too much space.

"Right," said Sheri. Her tone disbelieving. "Well, whatever. But you should realize that when you act like a bitch, people notice." She put a special emphasis on the word "bitch" so that it came out with a peculiar snarl.

Libby flinched, then looked up at Sheri. Arched eyebrows, her mouth pursed. She was pissed. Libby forced herself not to care.

"Right. Whatever. I have to go."

As she exited the bathroom, she wondered if that had been a mistake. As much as she disliked Sheri Kennedy, the girl had social clout and, should Libby ever feel like re-joining the ranks of the popular, she'd need Sheri on her side. Fuck it, she thought. Fuck it all.

CHAPTER TEN

Evelyn | San Francisco

Evelyn used her hip to push open the front door of her apartment, then dropped her bags just inside. She leaned back against the wall in the semi-darkness, kicked off one leather pump, then the other, and let her body slide down the wall until she was sitting crumpled, on the floor. A wave of anxiety rose from her gut and suddenly, she was choking, coughing, her stomach was heaving. She gagged as if she would vomit or sob or scream. Something enormous within her wanted out but wouldn't come. She grabbed at her purse and dumped everything onto the floor. The little plastic pill bottle rolled away, and she had to stop it with her foot. Leaning forward, she snatched it up, popped off the top, and dumped three into her mouth, swallowing them dry. What did the label say? *Take one every six hours for panic.* Or something like that. They were such tiny goddamn things-she needed to ask for a larger dose. She lay on the floor, closed her eyes, and waited for the alprazolam to coat her brain in its soothing balm.

Later, when the spasms settled, she rose from the floor and padded into the kitchen. Pulling a bottle of chardonnay out of the fridge, she grabbed the opener off the counter and picked up a glass sitting next to the sink. Carrying the lot into her bedroom, she set everything down on the table next to her bed. She opened the wine but didn't pour it. Instead, she sank back onto her unmade bed, where she lay on her back, eyes open, staring at the plaster ceiling. The shades remained pulled and curtains half-drawn, leaving the room in semi-darkness. The air smelled of stale perfume and old wine or was it old perfume and stale wine? Silk lingerie lay in crumpled heaps of lilac and pink. Sun pierced a hole in the shade and illuminated the scene with a lonely shot of harsh white light. It felt sad and cheap, like a whorehouse.

Evelyn sat up and poured wine to the top of the glass, leaned over it, lips to the rim, and took a long, noisy slurp. Pulling back, she checked the fluid level, picked it up, and swallowed deeply, nearly draining the glass. She refilled it, the bottleneck banging the glass rim as her hand swayed. She grabbed the phone next to the bed and hit Stuart's number.

"Yeah, Stu here." His voice was bright, shiny like a new penny.

"Stuart, it's me." She rubbed her thumb up and down against the glass in her lap. "I need another favor."

"Fuck me."

"Stuart, come on. It's important. I need to... to leave town." The decision became obvious only as she spoke. The words, unfortunately, sounded slurry.

"What the fuck?"

Here we go, she thought. Stuart knew little about her past. To be fair, neither did Evelyn; much of it seemed shadowy and skittish, her memories elusive, morphing. If she chased them, focused on them, they receded faster, disappearing into the grooves and back around dark corners in her mind. Not secrets exactly, more like lost objects. Temporarily misplaced like a set of keys or a favorite book. Or an old friend. The thing about Stuart was that Evelyn had chosen him precisely *because* he allowed, even encouraged, her to let those memories stay lost.

She'd been crazy about Stuart. Beautiful, rich, exotic, well-spoken. His family had Southern roots, but he'd been raised exclusively on the west coast. He was one of those men who, when they were nice, could be very *nice*. They'd met in college at LSU. He was, she'd believed, her prince. Utterly uninterested in emotional intimacy, Stuart could not care less what made people tick, and he rarely asked questions. Evelyn had only to drop one hint about childhood abuse at the hands of an alcoholic father to guarantee Stuart would avoid all topics related to family for the rest of their years together. His tendency toward narcissistic self-involvement-his favorite topic of conversation being himself-was a bonus. That made it easy to cleave her history, her family, and Eden, her whole past life, and start anew. Not Carolyn, however, she'd never let go of Carolyn. They rarely talked, choosing instead to drink, smoke, dance, and fuck. Perfect. A way out. Stuart was Evelyn's way out.

Other friends, who were *not* Stuart, sometimes asked the tough questions. Some of them pressed. Evelyn avoided disclosure with intentionally vague or remarkably discomfiting statements: *They're all dead*, or *I never got along with my father*, or *my mother died in childbirth*, or *I never had siblings-my parents hated children.* Most people made awkward noises of sympathy and changed the subject.

Libby was trickier. Intelligent, curious, and anxious, not knowing was hard for her. She wanted names, and details, forcing Evelyn to fabricate fresh stories for her as she grew older. She invented an exotic illness for her mother, Gwen, the name of which she could not quite recall. Libby had been only five when Evelyn's father, John Yates died, alone, drunk, and estranged from his only living family. No longer having to skip around the truth about him was a relief. Nothing else about the man's death, however, had been easy.

"They called me...." Evelyn said into the phone. "I don't know what's going on down in Eden, but you have to keep Libby for a while." She wasn't making sense. Her brain felt thick, and her mouth wasn't cooperating.

"Who called you? What are you talking about, Evelyn?"

Her thoughts came slow and sticky, like trying to crank them out of a brain drenched in molasses. Her family hadn't come up in so many years. Evelyn was struggling through the booze and anxiety pills to recall precisely what she had told Stuart. Surely, he knew about Carolyn, but how much, or rather, how little he knew Evelyn couldn't remember. "The police, the Sheriff down there. He called me." Why had she chosen to tell the truth about that? She back peddled. "Look, I can't go into the details. I just need to go down there for a couple of days." She inhaled deeply. It was like breathing sand. *Why was it that everything that had anything to do with Carolyn felt messy? Dangerous.*

"Is it your father's house or something?" He sounded genuinely interested. Not concerned exactly but interested. Probably thinking money would be involved. Stuart's number one passion was money. Maybe number two, after fucking little girls closer to his daughter's age than his own.

"I... I don't know. Not exactly. I'll find out when I get there." She could hear him sigh on the other end. Frustrated with her. Exasperated, as if she were a petulant child. He knew she was lying, which was strange, since Evelyn thought she might be telling the truth. Sometimes she wasn't sure.

"Yeah, yeah. Ok, Ev, whatever. What do I tell Lib?"

"Please don't explain anything to her, Stuart," Evelyn said. "Just tell her there's a schedule change or something." She heard the familiar suck of air. That sound meant something was coming she wouldn't like. A criticism. A judgment. If she'd been standing in front of him, it might have been something as subtle as a flick of an eyebrow, letting her know she'd been a bad girl. They'd been locked in the same set of choreographed movements for so many years, sometimes Evelyn was disoriented when he did not take the next pathological step.

"Libby is not a baby," he said. "She knows you hide things from her. She knows you lie."

And there it was, she thought. The punch. And her response: "Stuart, please, stop. I have enough to deal with right now," she said without enthusiasm. "I don't need the criticism. Isn't this why I divorced you?"

"Evelyn, I left. Remember?" Stuart replied.

Evelyn shut her eyes, and when she opened them again, her insides had gone the size and density of a bouncy rubber ball. He had executed his moves perfectly. Throwing the first punch allowed her a weak defense, followed up with something worse. "Just pick her up, Stuart. Tell her I'll call." She went into the kitchen, pushed a chair up against the cabinets, and climbed up high to the place she kept the very best booze.

•   •   •   •   •

Evelyn opened her eyes and sat up in bed with a violent jerk. She kicked aside the brocade spread and blanket. They slid off the side of the bed, landing on the floor in a heap. Pulling her knees up to her chest, she folded her arms around her legs and closed her eyes. Tried to concentrate on slowing her breathing. She hated being afraid. The weakness of fear made her angry, and nothing scared her like the dreams.

Shhhh, Carolyn whispers in the dark. Go back to sleep. It's ok—the wool of her sweater rough against Evelyn's cheek.

But it wasn't ok, was it, Carolyn? Not fucking ok at all.

Blinking her eyes open, she reached for the glass on the bedside table. She brought it to her mouth and took a long draw. Her fingers trembled as she set the glass back down on the table. Leaning back against the bed pillows, Evelyn ran a hand through her hair. She thought about smoking but doubted she had any cigarettes, not after quitting years ago and then again *for real,* six months ago. She swung her bare legs over the side of the bed, leaned forward, and twisted uncomfortably to avoid standing up. Yanking open the drawer to the bedside table, she rummaged blindly around for a cigarette, feeling way in the back where the dust bunnies and paperclips slept, promising herself if she found just one, she'd smoke it and quit again tomorrow. Her fingers stretched into the void. Nothing. Ok, she thought, as she got out of bed and crouched down to search the drawer more thoroughly. For one cigarette, she'd run a mile tomorrow. Swear to god. Two miles.

Still nothing.

She was slamming the drawer shut when her gaze caught on the little silver clock on the nightstand, glowing at 9:09 PM. Guilt shot through her like physical pain as she remembered her promise to call Libby. How long since she'd been asleep? They would be angry—both of them. She picked up the phone, and hit speed dial for Libby's cell, then at once pressed the end button. Texting would be easier. She thought about texting and thought she would do it in just a minute. Then she set down the phone and picked up her drink.

CHAPTER ELEVEN

Tom Broussard | Eden

Tuesday, June 6
Present Day

Chief Deputy Tom Broussard made the wide turn off I-10 onto Road 41 and checked the pink box on the passenger seat, wincing slightly as he saw it slide precariously close to the edge. He reached out a hand in time to yank it back and pulled up behind three cars parked at the first red light. "Shit," he said to no one, and checked his watch. He wasn't late, but he preferred to be early. He drummed his thick fingers on the steering wheel and waited.

Broussard had taken this inconvenient route home at lunch once a week for years. He would exit the highway early, cross-town, and drive over the poorly maintained cutoff road up to his house, arriving promptly. Vera always met him with lunch prepared and a kiss. He looked forward to their Tuesdays. He sometimes wondered if she knew how much.

There was only one bakery worth a damn within a hundred miles of Eden, and Vera, tiny as she was, had a sweet tooth. He couldn't give her much, but Olson's Tuesday Pies, he could give her. So, he did, every week. Broussard's car grumbled down the cutoff road about halfway between the highway and home. He'd thought briefly about skipping the bakery today, even skipping lunch with Vera altogether. *So busy,* he thought. He'd told her this morning he wouldn't make it today. He'd be outside-of-town all day on business. He smiled when he thought about the surprise on her face when he showed up with pie in hand.

Unfortunately, it would have to be a quick lunch. This case was swallowing him whole. Missing kid, now a dead kid, and that bastard Finney was trying to get around doing his job. He sighed deeply and leaned forward over the wheel, peering into the bright daylight ahead. With one hand, he yanked at the cross-chest seat belt, trying to loosen the pressure on his big stomach. "You're an old fat bastard," he said aloud. *Gotta go on a diet,* he thought. *Tomorrow. After the pressure's off. I'll talk to Vera about putting me on a diet.*

He entered a dark, cool stretch where the road became shadowed by overhanging trees. One hand over the wheel, his mind comfortably drifting.

Suddenly, the interior of the car exploded with white light. Blinded momentarily, Broussard blinked a few times, squinted into the rearview mirror, and, unable to see anything, turned to check his side mirror. Light bounced off the glass, making it no more helpful than staring into the sun. He heard a vehicle gaining speed on him as he slowed down. *The idiots were on top of him.*

His vision cleared. It was one of those ridiculous, dressed-up F-150s with massive headlights perched overhead, wholly illegal and capable of blinding another driver, even in broad daylight. The lights blinked three times, and the vehicle seemed to accelerate up into him. Broussard swerved toward the road's dirt shoulder. "Goddammit!" he said. Two more flashes and the driver revved the car's engine, coming within what seemed like inches of Broussard's rear fender. Broussard pulled over to the shoulder and slowed, allowing the truck to pass. He could see the vehicle's rear plate was missing, and the lights had blinded him, making it impossible to catch the front plate. *He'd call it in when he had a little more info. Idiots. Trying to run a marked Sheriff's vehicle off the road. Drunk teenagers daring each other to behave like assholes.* Broussard could count on one hand the suspects. A patient man by nature, he had no tolerance for these kids. Spoiled, rich, loud, stupid, lazy. Everything he never was.

Checking over his shoulder for oncoming cars, he pulled back into the lane, flipped his blue lights and siren, and sped up down the highway after the truck. As he approached, it immediately slowed, pulled to the right shoulder, and stopped. He pulled up behind the F150 and parked. Broussard reached for his radio to inform Tracy at dispatch about the stop just as a man stepped from the driver's side of the vehicle. "Well, I'll be goddamned," Broussard said, recognizing the man. He slipped the radio receiver back into the dashboard holder and hauled himself out of the vehicle. "Awe, for cryin' out loud, what in the hell, man, what in the hell were you thinking?" He was shaking his head and walking toward the man, relieved but also a little surprised that this particular idiot was the one behind the wheel.

The man held his arms behind him and stepped toward Broussard with a smile on his face. "Hi there, Chief. What's up?" His tone was oddly menacing. Probably high, thought Broussard.

Broussard stopped moving. Kept his eyes fixed on the individual's face while drifting a hand back toward the pistol at his side. Chief kept his voice low and controlled, "Well, like I said, what are you doing way out here? And what did you think you were doing b-" He stopped talking when he saw the gun.

He had time to think about the pink box sitting on the passenger seat of his car, and a split second to wonder how the pie would get to Vera before being ruined in the heat. Then, a great white boulder ripped through his brain, smashing his thoughts into a billion tiny pieces of light.

CHAPTER TWELVE

Evelyn | San Francisco

Evelyn peeled back the cellophane wrapper, opened the tin box, held it there for a moment, then snapped it open, picked out one of the white mints and popped it into her mouth, and clicked the box shut. Leaning back, she closed her eyes, inhaling the familiar cab scents. Pine tree air freshener, and plastic. The streets were empty at this hour, and the unencumbered ride to the airport felt like a cheat. She opened her eyes and gazed out the window. After a minute, she pulled her cell phone from her bag, touching the screen. Not dialing. She slipped it back into her bag. Pulled it out. Put it back.

She sucked the mint; tried not to think.

If you run away every time you don't like something, you'll solve nothing, Evelyn. Stuart loved saying that. He could apply it to almost any situation in which Evelyn was involved. Inevitably he would do something awful, like fuck a twenty-year-old in their living room and, when Evelyn refused to discuss it with him, he'd accuse her of running away from her problems. The one time they'd seen a marriage counselor, the guy told Evelyn she needed to *be more patient, more open to hearing Stuart's side of the story.*

How many times had it gone like that? She'd put up with Stuart's lies, infidelity, his incredible condescension. For what? Love? It felt like love. Now, five years since the divorce, seven since the separation, and thousands of dollars of therapy later, she wasn't sure it didn't still feel like love. Her love for Stuart was like a self-replicating, irrepressible, chronic, and deadly virus.

Yes, she thought, she'd marry him all over again. And that wasn't the worst part. The worst part was an ugly, spiky, raggedy little secret. It was herpes, chlamydia, and HIV all rolled into one. The pimple on your ass, the weed in your garden, and every dark hidden thing from your past, you'd rather die than have anyone ever reveal. The worst part was that *she still lived for her love for Stuart*. She would never let it go. Of all the things for which she hated herself, that secret was worst of all.

No, she thought suddenly. That wasn't true. There was the other thing. There was Eden.

A girl is in her room, searching for something, pulling back the bed linens and opening drawers. Her face in the moonlight from the window is tense. Not angry. Frightened. Shhhh, she says. It's ok, Lynnie. Go back to sleep, she says, and Evelyn does.

Evelyn sucked harder at the mint. Looked out the window. This time, she wasn't running away. What was the opposite of running away? Going home? But this didn't feel like that either.

The cab pulled up to a red light. Outside, a homeless man sat huddled in a doorway, his legs folded around a coffee can with a paper sign taped to it reading: "No Work Help." He was eating something wrapped in greasy-looking paper, focused on picking scraps of food out of the crunched-up wrapping, and, for just a second, Evelyn envied him his freedom. The day was emerging gray and dark, and melancholy descended on her like a scrim.

CHAPTER THIRTEEN

Libby | San Francisco

Libby sat in the passenger seat of her father's car and stared out the window. He was saying something, and she was trying not to hear him. She'd gone as far as shoving earbuds into her ears, but he just kept right on talking. Unlike her mother, Stuart didn't notice the small things. She had a bet with herself that they'd get all the way to her school in Pacific Heights; he'd give her pickup instructions and kiss her goodbye, without ever noticing the iPhone earbuds smashed deep into both of her ears. Unfortunately, he had a deeply resonant voice that refused noise cancellation by even her best headphones, let alone her easily concealed earbuds.

"So, your mother will be gone for a while. She didn't tell me how long, but I expect at least the rest of the week." His stream of words broke through the white noise space she'd tried to create around her head. She felt violated and turned up the volume.

The minute her father, instead of her mother, had shown up at school yesterday, Libby had known it would be another one of *those nights*. Her mother was always doing this. Late dinners, late meetings, coming home drunk, not coming home at all. Whatever it was this time, Libby did not care.

Despite the increased volume, her father's voice pierced the rap music in an off-centered staccato beat. "Friday... see... ok... don't." It went on like that for another ten minutes.

As much as Libby wanted the insufferable drive to school with her father to end, she wanted an early school arrival even less. Unlike Evelyn, her father was always prompt. Libby hated the conspicuousness of early arrival. It meant trying to find something to do with herself until the first bell rang. Walk about, fiddle in her bag, avoid eye contact, and try desperately not to be noticed by any of the three hundred other posh, private school kids milling around in the halls and out front.

They pulled up right in front of the school, where exactly one hundred percent of the waiting students could get a good look at Libby's ridiculous father and his stupid blingy "I wannabe a racecar driver but I'm really just a middle-aged loser with money" car that he actually flew to Europe to pick out. Her father flashed a smile as she got out of the car. Libby was sure it was his too-white smile and his too-blue eyes that made him so appealing to his young girlfriends. Well, that and his wallet, she thought. Despite his weaknesses, including his inability to understand anything about her, she loved him. And, despite her mother's vitriolic rants, she thought he loved her too in his way. She leaned in and kissed him on the cheek. "Bye, Daddy," she said and slammed the car door, starting up the path toward the entrance. A minute later, she checked over her shoulder to be sure he was out of sight, then veered left behind the back of the student services building. No way was she hanging around school for twenty minutes, waiting for the bell. In fact, better to skip it entirely today. She passed into an alley behind a row of shops on Jackson Street. After checking to be sure no one was following her, she jogged down the driveway and turned again at Laurel. She came to a narrow, cream-colored townhouse halfway down the block and mounted the steps. The front door opened before she knocked. "Hi," she said.

The young man stepped back to let her in. "Hi, you." He leaned down and kissed her gently on the lips.

Conner pulled her to him, sliding one arm around Libby's waist; he yanked at her baggy sweatshirt and ran a hand up underneath. "What's up, girl?" His voice was throaty and soft as he cupped her breast under her bra.

"Hi," Libby said, pulling away from him and straightening her top. He moved into her again, hands groping. "Hey," she said. "Wait."

"For what?" he asked, pushing her against the wall in the front hallway.

She didn't really have an answer. Wait until we close the door? Wait until we are not standing in the hallway? Wait until I grow up?

She liked Conner. Really. The boy was hot. He was older. He didn't treat her like she was sixteen. She liked the way his muscles curved smoothly over his chest and shoulders. She didn't mind kissing him. The thing was... the other stuff... not so much. She didn't want it and couldn't figure out how to tell him without hurting his feelings. Or worse, making him angry.

So, she'd let him do a few things to her. He'd gotten her clothes off and touched her. Everywhere. He enjoyed looking at her, which made her highly self-conscious. It felt like a medical exam, the light too bright, the eyes too clinical, but she allowed it to make him happy. She had touched him and then kept touching him; he pressed her hand down so she couldn't move it away until he finished. The whole thing was awkward and oddly wrong, although she could not figure out exactly why. So, she said nothing. Just hoped he'd stop pushing her. But it seemed like the more she allowed, the more he wanted. The more urgent his demands, the more difficult it was for her to resist. Increasingly, she felt like she had no choice. Not if she wanted him to keep paying her attention, which she did.

"Come on, baby," he murmured, lips pressed wetly against her ear. When he pulled back, a breeze from the overhead fan hit her face, and it was cold. He took her by the hand and led her to the sofa where he sat and pulled her between his thighs. She imagined how much he must love her. He'd never said it, but he must. Why else would he want her so badly?

Slowly, he unhooked her jeans and slid them down around her ankles, and then he pulled off her underwear. When she tried to sit down next to him, he said, "No, no, I want to look." He held her by the hips and stared at her. Ran one finger from her navel down her belly to her crotch. She could feel her face going crimson. "Please don't, please." He was not paying attention. Not to her words, anyway. She wondered if he could even hear her. She was like a rag doll, without her own internal structure, dangling there, waiting for him to do whatever he wanted. He pulled her down on top of him. As her thigh grazed his erection through his sweats, she recoiled involuntarily.

"No," she said, finding her voice and shifting her weight sideways onto the sofa beside him. "I... I'm sorry," and she was.

He let out a long breath. Said nothing for several beats and then, "Yeah, ok whatever." He reached forward and grabbed the TV remote and switched the mute button off. The ESPN anchor's enthusiastic and yet somehow slightly braindead, baritone filled the room, and Libby realized Conner had never turned the set off; he'd just muted it for her arrival. He looked annoyed; his lips held in a tight line, his eyes staring straight ahead at the screen.

"Come on, Conner, don't be mad," she said.

"Who says I'm mad? It's fine. Like I said, whatever."

He was mad. She was sure of it. He thought she was a baby. A girl. Not a woman. And who could blame him? He was twenty-one, for fuck's sake. She didn't even want to have sex. How long did she really think she could keep Conner without sex? She couldn't lose him. She'd be all alone then.

They lay together on the big sectional sofa in Conner's TV room. Conner's family had so many things Libby wished she had in either of her houses. Frozen mini-pizzas, sodas in big two-liter bottles, a sofa with plastic holes in the arms to hold your giant tumbler of ice and diet coke. The whole concept of a TV room - a special space devoted solely to watching television- was foreign to her, and she loved lounging on the oversized sectional, legs entwined around Conner's, face on his chest, listening to his breath rise and fall softly as he concentrated on the gigantic screen. Sports. They always watched sports. Conner watched. Libby ignored. Conner was a fan of just about everything that involved a ball, although he seemed drawn to athletic activities involving a fair degree of violence. Football, hockey, and rugby rather than soccer or tennis, for example. But he'd watch any sports as long as he could watch on his big TV.

He'd played in high school-she knew because of the football trophies that still lined a top shelf in his bedroom- but he seemed more of a watcher now. Libby suspected the chronic weed smoking had something to do with his proclivity for the couch, but she didn't mind it. Low on energy herself these days, she found his tendency toward immobility comforting. She looked forward to spending a few hours with him, curled up warm and safe on that sofa. It didn't matter what he watched, just to be with him, to fall asleep, inhaling his scent was enough. Axe body spray and Colgate shot through with the sweet, earthy smell of marijuana. She loved that this room, this couch, and this boy were a respite from everything vicious and sharp about her world.

Their relationship, less than three months old, had suffered from what Conner called "misunderstandings" on multiple occasions. The misunderstandings went like this: Conner dropped off the face of the earth, stopped answering his phone or returning texts. Libby panicked and called or texted with increasing frequency the longer he maintained radio silence. Finally, after a day or three or even more sometimes, he would re-surface with some lame explanation, like he'd had to help his mother with something, or he'd been out of town. Libby wouldn't believe him, but she'd say nothing for fear of driving him underground again. He wouldn't apologize, and she'd feel resentful until he was "nice" for a day or two. She'd feel better, and the entire cycle would start again. They'd ridden this merry-go-round a dozen times. Maybe more.

On this day, they were in the *Conner is being nice phase*, having just come out of three days during which he was utterly unreachable. Libby was anxious about how long it would last. She wanted reassurance from him, reassurance he never gave. She imagined all the ways she could phrase the statement so that he would understand her feelings without getting angry. Without thinking, she was being bitchy. Conner hated bitchy. Coincidentally, so did her father. She said nothing.

She glanced at the TV. Golf. The world's dullest activity, next to maybe geometry. Old guys pushing tiny balls from hole to hole over a zillion acres of over-tended, water-sucking, wildlife-killing lawn. Dull and environmentally irresponsible. The only good thing about golf was the silence. She snuggled her face into the crook of Conner's arm let her eyes softly close, breathing deeply. Maybe it would be ok this time. Hopefully, he'd got out of his system whatever drove him away from her sometimes.

Maybe, this time, he'd stick around.

CHAPTER FOURTEEN

Evelyn | New Orleans

Evelyn stood with the other passengers at baggage claim and watched the empty conveyor belt slip past again. She glanced down at her watch without noting the time. Sweat rolled down her neck and gathered in the small of her back. *Why was it so hot already?* She longed to peel off the sweater she'd stupidly thrown on to avoid carrying it off the plane. She shifted her weight to one leg, then the other and glanced down again. There was a slight pain in her stomach. *This was not a good idea. Leaving Libby with Stuart. Louisiana. Summer. Carolyn. Fuck. Carolyn was never a good idea.*

The belt came around again, carrying no bags, and she thought how useless it looked. Pointless. Going around and around, getting nowhere, doing nothing. She felt sick. More beads of sweat trickled down her back. She gave up and turned away. Looked around for somewhere to sit. She headed towards a row of molded plastic chairs ten paces away.

The entire row was blessedly vacant, and she dropped her carry-on bags in one seat, sat down in another. She pulled out her cell phone, hit the buttons, and checked the call history. Twelve missed calls, every one of them from Lanterman Causey. *Shit.*

She accessed her email and sent him an intentionally vague message. Causey was not bright. He was one of those people who considered himself *right-brain smart,* which just meant he was lucky. The great thing about his lack of intelligence was that Evelyn could confuse him with convoluted email messages long enough to buy some time. *Screw him.* She stood. Shook out her arms and straightened her spine as if guilt were a powdery residue she could displace from her soul with a good rattle. Leaving it behind, she headed back towards the baggage claim belt, which was rendering luggage once again.

•   •   •   •   •

Airline Highway out past the airport remained as Evelyn remembered. A wide ribbon of asphalt, bleached in stretches, patched ink-black in others, laid out like a gash through the flat landscape. On this day, the underside of summer storm clouds gathered, bulbous, thick, and ominous. Their fat bellies sank into the roofs of the low-slung strip malls that lined the highway, appearing to threaten suffocation rather than rain.

Deteriorated signs, paint flaked off, letters missing. FAMILY DOLLAR. DAO D O DENTAL. CHEC CASHING N W. Evelyn wondered how many were operating. How many were abandoned? The flood had been hard all over the southeast and the damage in Orleans Parish was significant. But then, had this ever been any better? Abandoned parking lots sprouting weeds in the cracked concrete; long, low warehouses covered with aluminum siding in anonymous colors. The few attempts made at construction appeared pathetic among the boarded-up windows and evidence of decay.

A young girl, eighteen or nineteen, took quick, short steps along the roadside. She wore heels much too stiff and tall for daylight, the skirt too short, top too tight. As she passed the girl, Evelyn slowed the rental car and checked the rearview. A device in her hands, a phone. Busily clicking at the buttons, she never looked up, but Evelyn could see cheap silver rings on her slim fingers and the blonde hair falling around her face. Knees knobby and elbows too big for her arms, like a colt. She was young. Not eighteen. Not close. Thirteen. *God, thirteen.*

Nothing's changed, Evelyn thought, *not really.* Overwhelmed with fatigue, she was too tired to drive to Eden, too tired to *be* in Eden. Was it too late to turn around? Run home. *Home,* she thought. Where was that? Of course, it was too late. She'd run once, so many years ago. She'd thought she was free of this place. But she'd been wrong.

Carolyn screams as he scoops up her thin body, whirling away before Evelyn can see her face. Arms and legs... the soles of her shoes... away... away... across the yard... past the laundry line... until she's gone... taken... leaving only questions and pain behind.

This time, Evelyn would finish it. Whatever was required, like a gangrenous limb. Hack it off. Wrap it up and bury it deep.

•   •   •   •   •

Just clear of the airport, she pulled off at a nameless motel. The lobby smelled like twenty-five years of Lysol spray and stale cigarettes. Evelyn stood for a moment inside the glass doors and sucked deeply at the air-conditioned coolness. The desk clerk was a short, fat, unsmiling woman with tired eyes and a grease stain on her blouse just above her heart. Efficient as a parking meter, the clerk nodded at Evelyn, ran the credit card, and then swiveled a clipboard towards her to which was tied a length of yarn with a pen attached. All without ever taking her eyes off the television screen. This was an impressive individual, Evelyn thought. She signed the form. The clerk shoved a white card key across the counter. Evelyn headed to her room. The TV continued to prattle on, in a voice part cheerleader, part evangelist, espousing the benefits, *low cost, and easy financing*, of a Diamonique tennis bracelet to the tired-eyed lady with the grease stain on her blouse.

• • • • •

She is alone in the dark. Around her, the bald cypress forest seems to twist and thicken by the second. She is trapped in a deep ditch and can move nothing but her head and her fingers. Yet, she can feel her entire body. Something rough pokes into her sides, and she thinks it is tree roots. A slimy thing crawls over her belly, and she wants to scream, but her mouth won't open. She can only make gurgling sounds. Nothing more. In a weird dance of defiance, the mud poured between her toes. The mud does not like her body being down here among the roots and creatures. The soft buzz of an airplane in the distance serves as her only compass point. Her neck hurts as she cranes it to peer up into the black sky, searching for a visual. She catches a glimpse, but it shoots by so quickly she loses sight of it almost at once, and her heart sinks. She is nothing but a small girl lost in the woods. Buried in the woods. The trees bare their teeth and close in with ever more ferocity. The desperation in her heart grows like cancer, eating her from the inside until finally, there is nothing left, not even tears.

She closes her eyes tight, and when she opens them, Carolyn is there. Her body lying next to Evelyn's in the ditch, just inches away, wrapped in tree roots as if she has been there for a long time. It takes Evelyn a few seconds to understand what is happening as she watches an earthworm crawl out of the open space that was her sister's mouth. The worm makes its slow way up Carolyn's blackened and ruined cheek and then disappears into the empty socket where her eyeball used to be.

Evelyn tries to scream, but there is no sound. Frantic, she turns her head away, plunging her fingers into the surrounding mud, trying to escape. Suddenly, she is terrified at the thought of what else might lurk in the depths of the earth. She struggles fruitlessly to move her paralyzed body, and finally, her fingers, exhausted, come to rest against the cool, welcoming void of nothing.

•   •   •   •   •

Her body was being shoved up, and out of darkness so deep it was like death. Evelyn opened her eyes and lurched forward to sit up in bed, her heart banging against the inside of her chest. Her palms, neck, back, and face sweat-slick, and wetness on the pillow and sheets around her. She sucked air through her teeth. *It's only a dream.* Gradually, she could feel the thud of her heart calm. She leaned over to switch on the light next to the bed, her hand still trembling. Her elbow thumped against the side table. She winced, her eyes filling with tears, and she jabbed blindly for the button on the switch plate. Harsh artificial light flooded the room and Evelyn huddled against the headboard; knees folded against her chest.

According to the digital display on the bedside clock, it was 2:59 AM. The gloomy non-time that lives too long after midnight to be romantic and too far before dawn to be healthy. The hour of drunks, criminals, insomniacs, drug addicts, and shift workers.

At three o'clock in the morning, people get arrested for beating the shit out of their wives and kids, ghosts arrive, and people die, and towns sleep, and little girls curl up inside themselves and pray to Gods they don't believe in to please make their Mamas stop being dead.

CHAPTER FIFTEEN

Evelyn | Eden

Wednesday, June 7
Present Day

Evelyn ran a finger over the steering wheel and watched the wilderness outside grow thicker, meaner looking by the second. Bonfante was a tiny parish by Louisiana standards. Comprising three townships, Celeste, Juliet and Eden, with a total population less than 15,000, it ranked at the bottom in every category for the state: population, per capita income, productivity, education, and, as far as Evelyn was concerned, desirability. Most of those 15,000 residents lived in the parish seat, Celeste, and this created a financial, educational, and cultural imbalance that was devastating to the other two townships. Curiously, folks from Juliet and Eden rarely emigrated to the larger and more prosperous part of the parish. It was just off-limits, like marrying outside your religion.

Bonfante parish had always appeared to Evelyn as if it were doing battle with the surrounding wetlands and losing. Now, much of the road between Celeste and Eden looked as if it had surrendered the entire war. At some points, gnarled tree branches met over the narrow strip of blacktop, creating a ceiling so dense that it entirely blocked the sunlight, leaving behind a startling darkness. Elsewhere, the treetops dipped so low overhead as to impede the passage of a medium-sized truck; or waist-high wild grasses crowded inward from the roadside like impatient spectators, leaving no discernible shoulder.

The road rolled unevenly beneath the car wheels, gravel here and slick, new tar there. The familiar sensations came back to her, and with them came all the rest. It had been waiting. The heat, the sky, the mud and bayou, the roaches and sticky-sweet flowers, the people; folks like the teenager working at the Stop-Go, with his canoe face, sad, nowhere eyes, and acne. She felt all of it snake over her lips and tongue down her throat, down passages, under doorways, around corners inside her where it unfurled like fingers. The great and vicious spirit of this place, with its lifetime of secrets, its magic, and all the special poisons of her youth.

Between Eden and Celeste, thirteen poorly maintained and mostly unpaved roads sprouted off the Parish Road. Running into the cypress groves and marshes like varicose vessels, most came to nothing, dead-ending at an ancient and now-obsolete clearing so deep in the overgrowth of honeysuckle and wild berry vines as to be impassable. One or two remained alive if severely withered and continued to the sites of tragically deteriorated family homes dating back to the Civil War. Develpers had surgically dissected a very few to prepare for new construction. Evelyn suspected that her Road, creatively named Road 12, was one of the former. At one time, Road 12 had led off the Parish Road and looped around a back way into downtown Eden but Evelyn doubted very much that was still true.

Claustrophobic anxiety descended on Evelyn as her car approached Road 12. She'd known, of course, that she'd need to do this drive to get to the house. She'd tried not thinking about it as a method of preparation. Her therapist called that method 'avoidance' and strongly recommended against it. Evelyn, therefore, used it all the time.

PTSD. Posttraumatic Stress Disorder. ICD 10 Number F43.10 according to the receipts Evelyn received from her therapist's office on the occasions she attended appointments. Mostly she didn't go because she thought the whole thing was a load of crap. She had almost no memories associated with childhood, so how could she have been, as the therapist had explained to her, "traumatized." Nevertheless, Evelyn had memorized the criteria written in the doctor's little cheat sheet of a book, the DSM-V (She, Evelyn, had something like all the fucking criteria): A. Exposure to actual or threatened death, serious injury, or sexual violence in one (or more) of the following ways: (1) Direct Experience. (Check) (2) Witnessing, in person, the events. (Yup) (3) Learning that the traumatic event (s) occurred to a close family member. (Uh, yup) (4) Experiencing repeated or extreme exposure to aversive details of the traumatic event (s). That last one explained why Evelyn's therapist had specifically recommended she not travel back to Eden, another medical suggestion she'd wound up ignoring.

She'd read and re-read the other half of the diagnostic criteria as well. The half that explained the symptoms she was supposed to be experiencing:

(1) Recurrent, involuntary, intrusive, distressing memories of the traumatic events. (Nope)

(2) Recurrent distressing dreams related to the traumatic events (Uh, maybe?)

(3) Dissociative reactions (WTF? That one scared the crap out of her, so she preferred not to think about it at all.) There were about a million other symptoms as well: Intense or prolonged psychological distress at exposure to internal or external cues that symbolize or resemble an aspect of the traumatic event; physiological reactions to cues; avoidance of stimuli associated with the traumatic event (s); negative alterations in mood; memory loss (that one also scared her); persistent and exaggerated negative beliefs about oneself; persistent negative emotional state; feelings of detachment or estrangement from others; persistent inability to experience positive emotions; irritability; anger; self-destructive behavior; hypervigilance; exaggerated startle; sleep disturbance. The list went on.

Overall, PTSD looked like it sucked balls, and Evelyn decided she'd just as soon not go to that party. She told her therapist she was opting out; she'd take something a little more standard, maybe a nice neat short-term depression or something feminine, like lightweight anxiety or "nerves," maybe. None of this heavy-duty crap. The therapist refused to budge and kept putting the same diagnostic code on her paperwork. Evelyn fought back by attending only about twenty percent of the appointments, following thirty percent of the behavioral instructions, and taking one hundred and fifty percent of the prescribed medications, always WITH ALCOHOL.

She stared through the glass of the windshield and tried to control her breathing. The painted center line, faded and flaked from years of harsh weather and neglect, turned the two lanes into one, leaving Evelyn with the sense that she was riding down the middle of the road. Her breath became short as she envisioned colliding with another car, coming round a curve and doing the same thing. Not a car, she thought, but a truck, a goddamn eighteen-wheeler, hurtling itself at her, crashing through the treetops, unstoppable, blind, and ready to swallow her whole. She rubbed her right palm on her jeans, noticing the dampness. The drive seemed longer than it had the last time she'd been here. Longer and more treacherous.

There'd been only two houses on Road 12, addressed predictably, 1 and 2. The Yates family occupied 2. Even as a small child, Evelyn was aware of the despair in those addresses. They were lonely, gloomy numbers, and the awkward sign stuck carelessly in the dirt at the roadside looked like an afterthought underscoring the pathetic nature of the place. Besides that, everyone in town called them "Old Miss Coolidge's" and "The Crazy Yates Place," respectively. She suspected even the mailman used those names, and it always surprised Evelyn to see her address written on envelopes or in school directories any other way. She wanted to live on one of the town streets, lined with gingerbread Victorian cottages and hundred-year-old oaks with made-up names like Spiceberry and Cherrywood. Later, when developers arrived and built the new tracts out east of town (in anticipation of a spike in population growth that never came), under a big sign that read Country Estates, Evelyn wanted to live there even more than on Spiceberry Street.

She'd had a friend who lived in the new estates. Carla Purcell, a slight girl with golden curls that made Evelyn think of fairy tales. Carla's house was a clean, flat-roofed, boxy place with wall-to-wall carpet, a green lawn, and a real asphalt carport. The sidewalks were so bare and white you could draw hopscotch games in every chalk color, and if it didn't rain, they'd still be there the next day. Streetlights stood, evenly spaced, parallel, upright, and dignified as soldiers, outside Carla's house. Evelyn liked to think they were guarding the neighborhood.

She wondered briefly where Carla was now. Her family moved away when the girls were still in junior high school. Evelyn had been relieved when Carla left. It took away the burden she'd created with so many lies over the years. For whatever reason, Evelyn had spun stories for Carla. Her real father, she'd said, was a wealthy foreigner, possibly royalty, and he'd had to return to his country to fight in a war. On her mother's side, she was pretty sure they were related to George Washington. Once, she'd told Carla, she'd been to Paris, and when the girl started asking excited questions about the city, Evelyn had to change her story quickly. Well, she said, she'd been so young she couldn't remember it very well. Carla listened to the lies. Attention rapt, twisting one gorgeous yellow lock of hair around her forefinger, gap-mouthed, and swallowing every detail like a gospel. It made Evelyn feel whole. Lies, she discovered, could fill in the gaps where her life held nothing but space.

One night, Evelyn slept over at Carla's. Long after her friend had fallen into a Hershey bar and soda pop induced child-sleep,

Evelyn was still awake, watching out the window. She studied the moonlit sidewalks. Bikes lay sideways in the yards, forgotten. Skates and Frisbees and squirt guns scattered across the grass. The entire neighborhood was sadly empty, and yet, in all the darkness, hope remained; no actual death existed there, only sleep. With the morning light came rebirth. Another chance, everything new again.

• • • • •

She rolled the rental car to a stop and sat for a minute, staring up at the house. The paint was so badly peeled, that the wooden siding appeared almost colorless, wisteria had overgrown the tiny front porch with branches thick around as a man's arm, weeds sprouted nearly waist-high in the front yard, and Evelyn detected a definite sway to the roof, the result of ten years without maintenance. People say houses, places from childhood, seem much smaller when revisited in adulthood. This house seemed huge. Physically, it remained, the two-bedroom cottage-not much more than a shanty, but it seemed to have gained mass. As she sat in the car, reluctant to open the door, she felt the house pulling her inward. The force was overwhelming, like a black hole.

Shhhh, says Carolyn. It's ok. Go back to sleep. It's for the best, says Daddy. Try not to cry for your sister.

Evelyn stepped out, the gravel crunched under her heel. Looking down, she saw it wasn't gravel, but seashells. When had that happened? She hadn't been back since her father died. Had he put down the shells? A stab of something. Guilt. She shrugged it away and stepped forward toward the house.

The front door opened with difficulty. Its hinges rusted. Stepping inside, she pushed it closed behind her, stood still, allowing her eyes to adjust. Dust motes danced across the living room, illuminated by a single shaft of light that peered in under one of the roller shades. The shades were yellowed, and her mother's curtains were gone. The bright ones with huge red roses and poppies. Why had she imagined those would still hang in the house? That was thirty years ago. Were they here in 2007? She couldn't remember. Her father wouldn't have removed them. Their absence made her sad. Her father's old chair-the leather cracked, the cushions sagging- sat in the spot she remembered, although the TV, always switched on in those days, was gone. In its place, on the TV table, was only a thick layer of dust and a flowery dinner plate. Empty. Staring at it, gooseflesh rose on her arms.

"Please, Daddy eat," she says.

"Ain't hungry, Lynnie, Lynnie, but thanks," he says without moving his eyes from the silent screen. Then he picks up the bottle and drains it, and she watches the tendons in his long, thin neck strain as he sucks in the last drop.

In the kitchen, she found the old table they'd used ever since she could remember. Staring down at its Formica surface, she studied the glittery inlay. How old had she been? Ten? Eleven?

"I don't want to talk about it," her father says. "I've told you that. Let it go, Lynnie."

She stares at him, angry. "I won't," she says. "You can't make me stop thinking about it. I'm not a baby. You need to tell me."

"There's nothing to tell," he says, looking more exhausted than ever, the gray circles under his eyes deepening.

"I won't eat." She sets her fork down on the shiny tabletop, studying the surface. Refusing to look at him. "I won't eat until you tell me what you meant. I heard you tell Mrs. Coolidge,

Daddy. You said it weren't no accident, and it weren't no suicide. I heard you." She looks up, wrinkles her brow, trying to make her face appear grown-up.

He stares at her, cocking his head to one side. Not angry. Just sad. He runs a hand over her head, strokes her hair. Leans down and kisses the top of her head. Then he walks out of the room.

Eleven. She'd been eleven. It was the year after. It was hot, so it must have been summer again, the summer of 1987. Mama and Carolyn had been gone a year. She hadn't given up. She'd begged and hounded her father for at least a week, pleading for more information. Despite that, he'd refused to tell her anything more. That's how it was with him. Once John Yates made his mind up, there would be no changing it.

Evelyn eyed the closed door to the room she'd occupied with Carolyn. She couldn't make herself go in there. Instead, she pushed open the door to what had been her parents' room. It was smaller than she remembered, barely big enough for the double bed and one dresser that sat pushed up against the wall. The mattress was bare and looked dusty, but otherwise unblemished. She'd brought her own bedding, sheets, and a travel blanket from home.

She unpacked the few other items she'd brought along, began stuffing them inside the old dresser, then realized it needed a wipe down. Still sturdy despite its age. She yanked open the bottom drawer, a damp rag in one hand. As it jerked free, she found, to her surprise, it wasn't empty. Inside was a large shoebox, which she gently lifted free and set down on the creaky iron bed. She chewed her lip, staring at the closed box for a moment before removing the top. Inside was an assortment of old photographs and a few papers, postcards, and letters. On top of the stack was a photograph, which she lifted carefully and held up to her face. Faded and yellowed, it was still clearly a picture of her mother. Gwen looked fifteen or sixteen, although it was hard to tell. Gwen had been small, barely an inch over five feet, and slight. Her size, her huge, brown eyes, and her perfect skin had always made people think she was younger than she was. Three teenage girls stood before a large sign that read IT'S ALWAYS 5:00 AT O'HARES! Two of the girls wore sundresses with wide skirts that looked almost, if not entirely, identical. Evelyn peered more closely at the figure in the middle. Gwen. She wore a dress that, even in the black-and-white photo, Evelyn could tell was swirling with color. Across the front were large peonies printed into the fabric, and Evelyn imagined they'd been red. Like blood. Or wounds.

Mama, she thought, you never belonged here in Eden. Why did you come? What trick of fate could have led you here, Mama? Evelyn looked hard into the photo as if the answer would lift off the faded picture and present itself, appearing like letters from invisible ink. Evelyn moved the photograph closer to her face. It must be there, she thought, the answer or a clue, at least.

Gwen held her narrow body at an angle and turned slightly away from the camera. Her mouth partially open, and her head tilted back as if responding to something the girl on her right was saying. She might have been laughing. Gwen laughed all the time, Evelyn remembered, until she didn't anymore. She looked as if she'd shifted her gaze over her shoulder and looked toward the camera at just the moment the shutter clicked. Despite her girlish pose and wide-open expression, her eyes sliced into the viewer like scalpels.

The other two girls, both taller than Gwen, looked straight at the camera, frozen in a pose, keenly self-aware. The hems of their dresses appeared blurry as if they'd been in motion.. Evelyn did not recognize them. They glowed with the sort of spectacular hope and curious energy reserved for the very young. Although pretty in the photo, the girls were ordinary, and Evelyn suspected their looks had devolved rapidly over the years after that picture;

all that youthful energy would have become bitterness and knife edged anxiety poking and cutting them into middle age, then old age, and finally death.

Gwen was different. Her eyes harbored something else, something extra, as rare as genius or the beginning of lunacy. Her eyes suggested Gwen might be less fit for the world than her friends. Evelyn wondered if she was seeing something that wasn't really there. She had the advantage of hindsight, and, looking at this photo, it was impossible not to consider Gwen's life, what had happened next and her ultimate fate. Gwen Martin had been like a child dancing maniacally on the edge of a cliff, tragically unaware of the raging sea below.

CHAPTER SIXTEEN

Gwen | 1965

June 1, 1965

Dear Diary,

So, I'm out in the barn with one of Daddy's straight razors when they find me. James is so angry that he runs to get Daddy before I can stop him. He thinks he knows everything since he made seventeen. I try to show him the cuts aren't that bad, but then I realize there are just so many.

Daddy says he doesn't understand why I do it. I tell him it helps. I tell him that sometimes when the pain inside is too big; it feels like the cuts are all I have. Like cutting my skin on the outside makes the pain on the inside smaller. I try to explain, but he won't listen.

They pull my hair and drag me back up to the house. I try to bite Daddy but only get as far as putting my teeth on his shirtsleeve. It tastes like sawdust. I hear Daddy tell James to snatch one of Mama's sheets off the line, and they bring it with me into the house. Up to my room. They wrap me up like a burrito, with only my face showing. Daddy uses his teeth to tear off long strips of duct tape and bind the sheet around my body. His teeth are sharp and yellow like a wolf.

At first, I holler some, but no one comes so I just stop. It's dark and hot, and I worry I might stop breathing. Finally, Mama comes upstairs and uses her kitchen shears to cut away the tape. She dabs my tiny wounds with iodine, and I watch as brown droplets spill over onto my pillowcase and the yellow posy quilt nana made me. She lays out clean clothes and leaves me to get dressed. She says nothing. Mama was never one to say much about the hard things.

I sit on the edge of my bed and stare at the rug.. I count the squares and daisies in the pattern until I stop feeling mad or even scared. I'm just tired. So tired trying to think about what to do. At first, I can't make my brain figure it out. Everything seems stuck. Gluey. But then, it comes to me.

I wait until I hear Mama in the kitchen getting lunch -opening and closing cupboards-then I get dressed. I'm real quiet, so maybe she'll think I am asleep. I creep down the stairs, careful to jump over the fourth step because I know it cracks loudly with weight on it. In the pantry, I take the twenty-six dollars' grocery money Mama keeps in a coffee can on the top shelf. I think she doesn't know I know about it. I stuff my pockets with peanut butter and saltines. Careful not to make any noise with the cracker box as I slide it back onto the shelf. Then I open the front door and walk out. I keep thinking someone will stop me. A hand on my shoulder or mama's voice. It never comes.

Down the front walk, out the little gate Daddy built last summer onto the road. I just stare down at my boots, watching one foot in front of the other in the dirt. The sun is shining hot on the back of my neck, and I think its warmth is pushing me forward. The idea makes me feel better even though I can't stop crying.—G.

CHAPTER SEVENTEEN

Evelyn | Eden

A lump rose in Evelyn's throat. She swallowed it down, and quickly shoved the photo back on the box, replaced the top, and stuffed the whole thing back into the drawer. She couldn't look at the rest of it. Not right now. Shoving the drawer closed, she let out her breath and sat back on the bed. Rattled. The disconcerting feeling, something terrible, had had her in its grasp.

Carolyn- eyes shining in the moonlight. Something in her hands. Frightened. What is it, Carolyn? What are you looking for? Shhhh, she says. It's ok. Go back to sleep.

Evelyn checked the bathroom, turned on the faucets, and realized the water was off. She'd have to call the water company. She'd got the lights turned on before her arrival, forgetting completely about the water. There'd be no shower for now.

Using a makeup remover pad, she wiped her face and armpits, brushed her teeth, changed her clothes, and went back out to the car.

Yellow crime scene tape encircled the trees in the distance. A few hundred yards from the house. She hadn't noticed it when she pulled up. Approaching the tape, she could see where they must have found the body behind the spot where the barn used to be. They'd called it Back Field in those days. She'd loved it then. A uniformed deputy stood guard. Several other official-looking people were milling around. Doing what? In typical Louisiana fashion, she thought, probably not a whole lot.

"Hi," she called out to the deputy. He nodded at her, tipping his hat.

"Hey, Ma'am."

"I'm um, Evelyn. I." She hesitated, unsure how to explain who she was, settling for, "I live here. I'm staying here."

"Yes, ma'am," said the young cop, unsurprised.

"Oh, ok. Did you expect me?" she asked.

"Yes, ma'am," he said. "We cleared the house, checked everything out for you. Is there anything we can do for you?"

She wasn't sure if that was an invitation to leave or a genuine offer of service. "No, no, I'm fine. I mean... is that where-" she stopped, feeling awkward. She had no idea what "cleared the house" or "checked everything out" meant but she didn't really want an explanation.

"I apologize, ma'am, but I'm not allowed to discuss anything with you."

"Ok, well, that's alright. I'll be back."

"Yes, ma'am."

Evelyn stood for a moment, staring at the spot among the cypress trees where the earth had been turned. For just a second, she forced herself to imagine Carolyn's body buried there. Her thin arms, her lovely back, her shoulder blades so sharp they looked like wings, her long, thick hair. No, Evelyn thought, it wasn't possible. Carolyn had been hospitalized at NOAH. They might have found a body there but, whoever it was, it was not Carolyn. It was not her sister.

CHAPTER EIGHTEEN

Libby | San Francisco

The day had gone gray and cool, dousing the sidewalks and townhouses in a depressing, watery mist that turned everything colorless. Her mother called as Libby was leaving Conner's. It had been a risk, cutting school two days in a row to hang out with Conner, and she needed to get back before third-period science class — (Mr. Sanchez took a rigorous role and called your parents from his cellphone if you didn't show up)—so she was walking, albeit slowly, toward the school when her phone rang. She'd been busy fiddling with her phone, compulsively checking her posts on Instagram and Snapchat. How many likes? How many comments? She didn't want to care, but she did. She and Evelyn had argued about it more than once. Evelyn, who couldn't be bothered with social media, didn't even use Facebook, had exclaimed, "But why?" after Libby had suffered a series of particularly humiliating cyber-taunts. "Why does it matter to you, Libby? You don't even like some of those people."

"Because, mom, because. I can't explain it," Libby had answered. Evelyn had responded with a half-snort, half-laugh that made Libby feel small. As if her concerns were trivial. It enraged her. Of course, she couldn't explain it. Nor could she explain why her heart sped up and her palms got sweaty when she was around Conner. Why couldn't her mother put aside the why of everything and just accept that, to Libby, it mattered. Her pain was real. What certain people thought and said had power over her? Not everyone. But girls she knew. Even some girls she didn't know that well. Girls like Sheri and Lindsay. And they were cruel, selfish people. No, she didn't like them, but liking them had nothing to do with caring about what they thought. In fact, at Libby's school anyway, it was the very nastiness of certain girls that gave them so much power.

She thought again about the incident in the bathroom two days earlier. Why hadn't she tried just a little harder to ingratiate herself with those girls? There'd been a time when she would have done it reflexively. As automatic as breathing, she would have smiled and charmed and said something smart and complementary. Something so over Sheri's head, she'd have had no choice but to respond positively. In recent months, however, Libby pulled away from all of it. Bored, irritated by the immature and quixotic behavior of most of her so-called friends. Sheri, with her Tory Burch sandals and array of handbags that cost more than Libby figured most people earned in a month, and her belief in what she called social survival of the fittest. A theory she'd obviously filched from her parents because poor people were, by definition, losers. Or something like that. Sheri and most of her circle were assholes, badly in need of a punch in the nose, but they'd never get it. That was the thing. No such thing as justice. Life's not fair, Evelyn would say. Quit whining.

The whole thing was insane, really, because as soon as Libby started to not care, Evelyn became concerned she was isolating. Not socializing. What happened to all your friends? Her mother would ask, as if she'd never intimated, they were all a bunch of vacant, spoiled, self-absorbed bits of cotton candy. In fact, Libby recalled, Evelyn had once said something very close to that. Her mother didn't remember. Of course, she didn't. Evelyn said her worst things while drunk and always, or almost always, conveniently forgot she'd said them by the next day, sometimes by the next hour.

So, this phone call was nothing new. Evelyn would be intoxicated (something Libby would hear in her mother's voice even from two thousand miles away) and probably little or nothing of the conversation would register in Evelyn's long-term memory. It was like talking to a person with Alzheimer's who asks you the same question a million times. Or like that movie where the girl keeps waking up in the same day over and over again, getting so frustrated with the meaninglessness brought about by endless do-overs that she does outrageous things. Breaking rules, breaking laws. Whatever. Much of Libby's life felt that way. Nothing she did, nothing she said, made any difference. She pictured herself walking right through people without so much as a stir in the air, like a ghost.

When she'd seen the caller ID, she'd considered letting it ring through to voice mail. Then something, a tiny voice, in her mind had suggested Evelyn might be in trouble, needed her, and Libby couldn't do it. Couldn't ignore the call. Sometimes she had feelings like that. She knew things sometimes before they happened.

Libby hit answer and knew at once it had been a mistake.

"Sweetie," gushed Evelyn on the other end. Her voice was thick and sweet and droopy, the way it got when she drank. "I miss you so much. Whatcha doing?"

Libby gritted her teeth, held the phone to her ear, stepping around a giant dog turd someone hadn't bothered to clean off the pavement. Evelyn's attempts at casual concern always made Libby feel crazy, annoyed. She looked up the street at the school, estimated the distance between her body and the building was shrinking too quickly (arriving early could be as bad as arriving late) and slowed her stride. "What do you think, Mom? What do you think I'm doing on a school day, in the middle of the day?" Her words came out in one giant turtle snap, and she felt a brief pang of guilt.

"Oh, don't be like that, Lib. I just wanted to talk to you. That's all." A beat. "Is that ok? Please, baby."

"What? What is it? I'm at school," Libby lied.

"Oh. Right. I'm sorry. I didn't realize the time. Well..." Evelyn took a breath, and Libby thought she heard a shudder in it, the sort that comes after a hard cry.

"It's ok," Libby said before she could stop herself. Why, she wondered, did guilt come so easily to her? She'd done nothing wrong.

"Listen uh... Libby, I need to tell you something, ok?" Evelyn sounded sharper. Not completely clear, but almost. Maybe she wasn't wasted. Libby was annoyed at herself for caring enough to hope that was true. "I haven't been totally honest with you about things." No shit, thought Libby, saying nothing. "I should have told you the real reason I'm here. In Eden, I mean. You're not a baby."

"Right, I'm not." She stopped walking. Turned away from the school. Just in case anyone was out there, watching her.

"Right," said Evelyn. "So, here goes. You need to know this because I might have to stay a little longer than I thought. I want you to understand." Libby listened. Evelyn was not drunk. Drinking, for sure, but not yet shit-faced drunk. Something tickled at Libby's spine, and she was suddenly afraid.

CHAPTER NINETEEN

Gwen | 1965

June 26, 1965

Dear Diary,

It's been almost three weeks since I left. Nobody's following me. Why would they? Daddy always says I'm more trouble than a pantry full of ants. Or something like that. I'm in a new place. Eden. I'll say, in a minute, how come I'm here. The name is funny, like the bible, I guess. Except it's no garden. More swamp than anything. The air is so full of water I don't even need a shower. It's not New Orleans, which is where I thought I might go when I first started out. It's not even Clarksville. Eden's downtown is no bigger than a postage stamp. Just one little street running up and back. I walked the whole thing in a minute, and the Stop-n-Go is smaller than Clarksville, but the clerk-the day clerk anyway is a few tools short of a shed, which makes stealing easy.

Money keeps me moving. What I got from the pantry didn't last long, and there's no work for a girl too young to have papers. The thing is, I'm good at disappearing. I'm small. Fast. The crowd just swallows me up. I'm magic. I just take what I need from stores out of folks' pockets. I won't lie. I don't feel bad about taking it. Sometimes that worries me-like what kind of girl steals and feels nothing bad about it? But I figure hunger makes folks do all sorts of things they'd never do normal. Sometimes, I ask for what I need. Seems like most adults, especially ladies, are quick to help. I look younger than fifteen on account of being small. The trick is never to stick around long enough for anyone to ask questions. So, yeah, I ask sometimes, but I'd rather steal. Don't owe nobody that way. Up in Shreveport, I met a few girls selling themselves. The money was good, but I'll never do it. That's no way to live. Besides, I'm saving myself.

So, it was last week, and I'm hitching a ride from Lafayette, and this man picks me up. Old, like granddad. Says he's headed all the way to the Florida panhandle. Says I can go along if I want. Sunshine and the beach, and I hear the ocean is warm as a bathtub out there. I remember a picture postcard, or, at least, I think I remember it. Florida by the sea and all the houses the color of saltwater taffy. Bubblegum pink and powder blue and soft yellow. So, I tell him, yeah, I'll go all the way to Florida.

Then he starts acting funny. Hand on my leg. Asking me how old I am. When he stops for gas in this place called Eden, I just get out and walk up the road a good piece before he can see what I'm doing. Walking away is getting easier. I'll say that much.

Pretty soon, the afternoon is coming down hard, bringing mosquitos big as hummingbirds and awful heat. Also, I'm getting hungry since I had nothing since a hostess pie I stole from the Easy-Buy in Lafayette. I'm crossing the street toward this diner thinking I can get ice water, if nothing else, when all of a sudden, I feel someone tap my shoulder, and when I turn around, it's a man. A grown-up man, but younger than Daddy. Smiling. Real nice blue eyes. He isn't tall, and he doesn't seem scary. His arms are sticking out of his shirt where the sleeves are rolled up, and he has tattoos covering the muscles, which are thick. Makes me think of beef jerky on account of his skin being tanned so dark or on account of being hungry.

I almost don't go with him because of the tattoos. Partly naked women with long hair that covers the private parts. Also, he smells like cigarettes and fried fish, so I'm taking a minute to consider, but then, he smiles again, and I am so hot and so hungry.

He asks if I just arrived in town, and I tell him, yes, and he says he knows about a house. A place where kids without nothing can get some food and sleep if they need some. I say I could use some food but I ain't never heard of place giving food away like that. He says that a lot of young people come down the highway through Eden, so they have this set up for them. When he offers to give me a ride, I say okay, even though I don't really like the way he smells or his tattoos.

That's where I am now, this house. But it's not really a house at all. Just a bunch of little rooms inside an old church, and each one stuffed up with beds and mismatched dressers. All broken. Missing knobs and such. And there are girls here. All kinds of girls. Different ages. I saw one who looked to be only twelve, her shorts and blouse dirty and too big for her. Like they belonged to an older sister. Or even a grown-up. Most of the girls are lying around reading magazines or sleeping. A few of them smile when I come in. Most just ignore me and go right on. But this one girl, the young one, she's just sitting near the door. Looking out. Like she's expecting somebody.

I get something to eat and a bed-more like a mattress on the floor really and a blanket. It's not bad. I think I'll stay on a little, just until I get myself feeling strong again.

Love G.

July 3, 1965

Dear Diary,

I'm dreaming of Clarksville again. I thought it had stopped. But I dream of Mama, little Katie, the weeping willows and our tabby cat Martha. Not about Daddy; I hope I never do. When I wake up, my cheeks are wet with tears, but I don't remember crying.

Today my new friend Tara-she's fourteen, only small for her age- says she's come all the way from Memphis. That's further than me. She knows lots of things. Like how to fold a dollar bill into the shape of a swan and how to swipe candy from the Stop-n-Go without the clerk spying you in the big fisheye mirror, and how to make lipstick out of cherry pits and beeswax.

Tara says she never had a home-not one she can remember-and she never knew her daddy at all. She says she can't remember when she got here, to Eden, but I think it was a long time ago. When I ask about her Mama, she only gets this look on her face like a person gets when they're thinking about something they'd rather not be thinking about. So, I quit asking, even though I still want to know. Also, I keep wondering how anybody could not have a home. She had to live somewhere, right?

Sometimes, at night, I wake up and see her fidgeting all around. Skittish, like a mouse caught in one of Daddy's sticky traps. Like what she really wants is to get free, only she can't figure out what is holding her down. I feel like that sometimes too.

The fourth is tomorrow. We're going to have cupcakes and sparklers.

Love G

July 5, 1965
Dear Diary,

Tara. This morning when I wake up, she's just disappeared, along with all her stuff. Not that she has much. I try asking Meg, one of the older girls. She's been here a while. But she tells me to hush up, she tells me not to worry, and Tara is fine, just moved along, is all.

I should get used to losing people.

Something isn't right. I know it, the way sometimes I know ahead of time what folks are going to say before they even open their mouths. I'll be leaving soon.

G.

July 6, 1965
Dear Diary,

That man, the one with the tattoos, comes by today. He asks me if I'll help him pick out a birthday gift for his wife. Says her birthday is tomorrow. I tell him I will even though I'd planned on leaving today. I figure I owe him that much for bringing me here.

I decide not to worry about Tara. I'm sure Meg is right. Lots of girls come and go. Right?

I'm all packed up. Tomorrow morning, I'll get back to the highway. Hitchhike down to New Orleans, I think. The tattooed man says he'll drop me right after the shopping.

   -G

CHAPTER TWENTY

Libby | San Francisco

By the time Libby reached the school, class was out, and the housekeeper was already waiting. Fuck. Early fucking release day. How had she not remembered? Not that she cared all that much about getting into trouble with her father, but she did not want to listen to a lecture from her grandmother. Gam could nag so long Libby would go cross-eyed. The phone call from her mother had made her even later. She'd slowed and stopped walking as she'd listened to what her mother wanted to tell her. Then, when they'd hung up, she'd had to sit down on the curb and get her breath back before continuing.

What Evelyn had said made no sense. A sister? Evelyn had never said a thing about a sister. In fact, she'd outright denied having any family beyond a mother she never knew and a father who was, in Evelyn's words, not worth the paper his birth certificate was printed on. It wasn't like Libby hadn't tried. She'd asked questions, so many questions she couldn't even remember Evelyn's answers, or non-answers, to all of them. It was clear to Libby that family was a topic that made her mother unhappy, so she quit asking.

"So, where is she? Now, I mean," Libby asked. "You said she left. Where did she go?"

Evelyn had hesitated, and Libby braced herself for another lie. "She... she had to go to a hospital. A special hospital."

"Why? Why did she have to go?" asked Libby.

"Carolyn had problems, sweetie. Lots of problems. Mood swings, anger, sometimes even violence. She just needed more help than family could give her, so..." Evelyn's voice sounded heavy. "So, my father sent her to a psychiatric hospital. For kids." She paused, then added, "for teenagers." Evelyn was withholding something, like she always did. She picked through the truth like it was a salad bar, hanging onto the bits she liked and tossing back the ones she found distasteful.

"And then what happened? Where is she?"

"She died, Libby. I didn't see her after she left, after they took her. That was in 1986. I was only ten. Then, a few years later, she got really sick, she had an infection in her brain, and she died before I ever had time to see her again."

Libby struggled hard to stay focused. The story was terrible, but it wasn't the first time she'd heard something heart shredding from her mother. It wasn't even the tenth or the fiftieth time. "You shouldn't have lied when I asked you. When I asked about your family."

"I know." Evelyn swallowed, and Libby pictured the little silver flask she carried around in her bag. Now Libby just wanted to hang up. "I know. I'm sorry," Evelyn continued. Libby gave no response, and she added, "Lib? Are you there?"

"Yeah, I'm here." She wanted to hang up but couldn't help herself. One more question. "I don't get it. Why are you down there? If she died, then why do they need you down there?"

"Oh, Lib." Now Evelyn just sounded exhausted. "They found a girl. The body of a girl. They think it's Carolyn, but it's not. They asked me to come down, supply DNA, help clear this up. Anyway, I'll call you, keep you posted when I get more information, ok? But not this minute. I have a meeting this afternoon with some people. I'm on my way now."

Of course, she had a meeting. Wasn't that always the response? I've got a meeting. I've got a project. I've got people to call. I've got to go.

"Whatever. I don't care," said Libby.

"I love you, Lib. I'll call you later."

Libby wanted to say she'd be busy later, but she didn't. She wanted her mother to call her back. Despite herself, she wanted to talk to Evelyn, she wanted to know about Carolyn.

CHAPTER TWENTY-ONE

Evelyn | Eden

Evelyn parked the rental car in the small lot which fronted the Sheriff's station. She wiped the sweat away from the back of her neck and wished again she'd worn the sleeveless T-shirt instead of leaving it stuffed into her suitcase back at the house. The town was dismally hot for this time of year, and the humidity felt more like August than June. Evelyn hated the sticky heat. It turned the ground boggy, and the people bedraggled. She saw no romance in any of it. Only memories. Eden might have grown a different sort of people had it been blessed with a different climate, like plants. Instead, Evelyn thought, Eden had gone right on growing the same sort of folks she remembered: slow-moving, hollow-eyed, and sweat-stained, but something else too. Some other thing was uniting them. It wasn't sadness, she thought, although it should have been sadness, given the state of the town, of their lives, and it wasn't anger exactly or fear. Still, it was something like that, and it was alive within them. A sort of meanness. As a child, she'd thought it was her fault. She still wondered.

According to Chief Broussard, who'd called her in California, it was precisely the excessive heat and humidity, combined with a couple of out-of-bounds adolescents, which had created the conditions ideal for the discovery of a thirty-year-old corpse. Bodies didn't stay buried in Louisiana. Not forever. The ground, restless and shifting, was upending itself, giving back. Most of the dead were never buried at all. The state was strewn with cemeteries crammed with above-ground mausoleums. Macabre-looking structures ranging from modest stone boxes to enormous constructions of marble and granite, elaborately carved with names and epitaphs dating back centuries. Some of them looked built to withstand hurricane-force winds, flood, fire. Armageddon. But this body, this dead girl, had been left unprotected, and the earth had returned her to its surface like a gift.

Evelyn wasn't feeling well, especially since the phone call with Libby, which, as usual, had not gone particularly well. She was nauseous and a little dizzy. The heat, lack of food, alcohol, and no sleep. She'd been mostly awake for what? Forty hours. Since the news came, at least.

Please call us back, Mrs. Adamsson. It's important.

She struggled to pull her handbag, which was easily the size of a small suitcase, from the backseat. She ought to clean it out. Most of its contents were buried so deep she'd forgotten about them days or weeks ago. Giving the thing a solid yank, it jerked free, nearly throwing her off balance, and she pulled it, along with her briefcase, out of the vehicle. Then she straightened and kicked the door shut with her foot.

She took one step toward the building, then another, wobbled a bit, readjusted the heavy bags on her shoulder, then took one more step and bit back a wave of nausea. Her peripheral vision grew dim, and suddenly she was peering through a narrow tube, like a hose. She squinted, which did not help. Then the dimming vision became no vision, and, as if with the flip of a switch, light became dark, and everything became nothing at all.

CHAPTER TWENTY-TWO

Nick | Eden

She arrived fifty-eight minutes late. Nick leaned one shoulder against the window frame, a mug of fresh coffee cupped to his lips, and studied the little rental car as it pulled into the lot. He lowered the cup slightly, absently running his thumb over its glazed surface. He hated this. To begin with, he did not know why Evelyn Yates had come to Louisiana. No way would the Sheriff allow her to view the remains, certainly not until the coroner released them, and a lab in California could have easily collected her DNA which they needed for comparison. But nobody asked him, so his opinion was not relevant. Nick didn't really care that the Yates woman was coming. He had to assume the higher-ups had a reason, even if he did not know it. What annoyed him was his boss, Chief Broussard, assigning him the role of chauffeur this morning. *Be there to greet her,* the Chief had said. *Take her up to the coroner,* he'd said. Blah blah blah. It was such bullshit. Broussard had an errand to run, wanted to meet with Nick later, promising to explain everything then. He needed this favor. Driving Evelyn Yates around. Of course, bosses don't request favors. They give orders, particularly in the Sheriff's department. Nick checked his watch again. He'd been hoping to get the Yates woman over to the coroner and then make it up to Broussard's house by six. Of course, now he'd be running late.

Nick watched as the car lurched and heaved a bit before stopping. The motor continued to run another minute, but the glare off the windshield blinded Nick. It was impossible to see the figure inside. A woman stepped out. Tall, athletic. Her back was turned, her hair drawn up into a knot, and he could see a few thick strands had come loose and lay in flat coils across her pale skin. She stretched and reached one hand around, rubbing at her neck.

She kicked the car door closed and approached the building, carrying both a briefcase and a huge leather bag. Her mouth was a tight line, but her other features were lovely, open. Vulnerable. As she walked, she shifted the bags to one hand and was yanking at the front of her blouse with the other. Abruptly, she lost her balance and dropped the briefcase. It hit the pavement, popped open, and exploded with papers that floated and scattered at her feet like leaves. Nick pushed open the station's front doors and took two strides towards her. He was just extending his arms to help. "Ms. Yates, hello, let me help you-" She did not meet his gaze when she looked up. Her eyes were unfocused, and she swayed once, then twice, back and forth a bit. Her eyelids drooped and her knees buckled. He took three long strides and caught her around the waist just as her knees brushed the asphalt.

She smelled of soap, jasmine, and breath mints.

•   •   •   •   •

The woman sat awake now, her long legs curved a little awkwardly around the edge of the too-short sofa in the back room. Roy Beaumont, the station's nineteen-year-old volunteer, sat on a stool next to her, holding a cup of water, beaming, a fierce blush staining his long face and large ears the color of a candied apple. He'd been assigned to watch her while Nick called Doc Carson, and he was taking the job extremely seriously. Nick suspected Roy had rarely, if ever, been in such proximity to a beautiful woman.

Nick introduced himself, feeling awkward. He said, "I'd planned on taking you up to the Coroner in Celeste, but if you'd rather not-" She'd been unconscious when Nick carried her in and lay her down. Now, however, she was fully awake, green eyes trained on him, hard and brilliant as emeralds.

She steadied herself, palm on the arm of the sofa, as she sat up. Fine, long fingers, no wedding rings. "I'm completely fine. I didn't eat this morning. That's all. Long week. But I'm ok." Her voice was deep, husky. A whiskey voice, his mother would have said. Her upper lip curved powerfully inward toward the middle, forming an exaggerated cupid's bow that might have been severe had it not been countered by the soft fullness of her lower lip. Nick supposed it would be possible to run a finger along that curve and know what she was saying through touch alone. "Look, I just want to clear this up and go home."

"Clear this up?" Nick asked.

She stared at him. "I guess your boss didn't tell you?" She raised her eyebrows in a question. "Yeah, well, look, I know you people think you have Carolyn, but you don't." Green eyes flashing with something that might have been anger. "I'm telling you right now, you don't."

CHAPTER TWENTY-THREE

Evelyn | Eden

Outdoors, the man was taller than Evelyn first thought. Cooler, too, like a color, the way green looks cooler than orange. The bones of his face drew shadows beneath his eyes, under his cheeks, his chin. He might have been sculpted; except he was moving.

She stared at him as the heat pressed in upon her and the sweat rolled down her back, creating an adhesive between her skin and the under-wire of her bra. Whatever makeup she'd applied hours earlier had either disintegrated or worse, melted, and was now puddled like rainbow sherbet under her eyes and in the hollows of her cheeks. She felt dirty, sticky, and stupid. She studied the hard lines of the detective's face, squinting into the glare. There was something sturdy about the way his bones held together, like cement reinforced with rebar. It irked her she found his masculinity appealing. His straightforward good looks reduced her to the level of adolescent insecurity she would have been loathe to admit to herself even as a thirteen-year-old.

As Eden receded behind them and watery vistas opened on all sides, Evelyn stared out the window at the bayou, gone hard and still after the rains. Flat and gray as iron sheeting. Even the clouds overhead had turned to rigid silver streaks across the white sky. There was a beauty in the landscape; like being inside a piece of quartz, everything sharp-edged and perfect.

She remembered this drive. How many times had she been up this road? Hundreds? Thousands, probably. They'd made it with Gwen, going up to the library, or shopping in Juliet. Other places too, places Evelyn couldn't remember as clearly.

Her mother had a million stories about the bayou, about the river, especially about the river, the fairies that lived there, the magic toads and singing angels. When the cicada and crickets grew so loud, Evelyn wanted to cover her ears; Gwen would say that the sound was the angels that lived on the waterways, singing their happy, forever song. Gwen would gently pry Evelyn's small hands from her ears and tell her to listen extra carefully for the special messages the angels were sending just for her. Singing angels. Evelyn hadn't thought about them in years.

By the time Gwen died, Evelyn was old enough to know that most of what her mother told her was an invention. Fictions spun like magic from nothing at all; when her mood was good, Gwen was the very best sort of storyteller.

Even when she shouldn't have been.

A little girl is pulling at her mother's skirts in the sunlight...
Evelyn is out back with Mama, helping to hang the laundry. She is small, and the sun is so large everything glitters. She shuts her eyes against the brightness of the white sheets. Mama is happy today. She hums and sings a bit. It's a good day. Some days she won't get out of bed. She doesn't eat, and she pretends not to hear anything. Not even her kids. She only talks about getting away from Eden. Daddy says this don't make sense since Mama is the only person anybody knows who grew up somewhere else and came over to Eden as a grown-up and stayed. Most everybody else fixes to leave soon as they can.

Evelyn is too small to reach the line. Mostly she's watching more than hanging, but sometimes she hands Mama a clothespin or runs to get something out of the house. Mama says she likes the company. She stands as near to Mama as she can without getting scolded for being in the way. She's so close she's inside the sweet-smelling folds of Mama's summer dress. There is no breeze, and mama's hair, so blonde it is almost colorless, moves in one smooth shimmery wave each time she leans back to fasten another clip to the line. It looks the way Evelyn imagines snow would look if the sun were to shine upon it. She has never seen snow. She is not sure it exists.

She asks Mama again about Clarksville.

"I told you that story, Lynnie baby. I told you that story so many times."

"No, Mama, you never did tell me. Please tell me." It's a game because Mama did tell the story lots of times, and they both know it. It's a big story, but on certain days Mama likes to tell it again, and Evelyn likes hearing it, however many times she's heard it before. She sits down in the dirt and dandelion weeds in front of a broken lawn chair. "Sit here, Mama," she says and pats the seat of the old chair. "Please. Tell me again."

Mama stops hanging sheets and looks at Evelyn, then she sits in the lawn chair and smooths down her summer dress for a long time. Evelyn crouches in the crabgrass and dirt at Mama's feet, looking up at her. She thinks about how beautiful her Mama is. She is impatient to hear the story and wonders if Mama will ever start, but she begins.

It is the summer of 1965, and her Mama, Gwen, is just fifteen years old. She is living up in Clarksville, a place Evelyn has never seen but her mother says is magical. Full of fairy castles and trees tall as mountains and sunflowers big around as pie plates. Gwen says the whole place, indoors and out, smells like lemon drops.

The night before Mama leaves, her family throws her a big party. Music and golden streamers and rainbow balloons and as much chocolate cake as she can eat. Everyone from the neighborhood comes and even some folks from the next county are over. They spend the night dancing and hugging and eating all the good food. Everyone wants to say goodbye to Gwen. Like she's a princess.

Evelyn imagines her mother wearing a gown made of pink satin with matching ribbons in her hair and a bejeweled princess crown like she's seen in picture books. Her beautiful mother glittered and sugared like a candy doll.

The next morning when it's time to go, Gwen's family helps her into a shiny white car, like a carriage, and they all stand on the doorstep waving goodbye and blowing kisses, like butterflies, in her direction.

Every time her mother tells the story, Evelyn closes her eyes and pictures her mother's mother and daddy and brother and baby sister, waving goodbye, smiles so bright the sunlight flashes off their gorgeous white teeth.

Her mother would be long gone before Evelyn was old enough to wonder why a princess might have left her kingdom so filled with magic and love.

CHAPTER TWENTY-FOUR

Nick | Eden

The Eden station disappeared quickly from the rearview mirror, and Nick sped up. He rolled the window halfway down and hit a dash button, hoping the internal fan would crank a bit. He rubbed his face, already wet with sweat, and reached for the cigarettes in his shirt pocket, the cigarettes he knew weren't there. Shit. He gave the steering wheel a resentful tap before gripping it with both hands.

The road narrowed, the bayou encroached, and, with the window down, the air in the car was soon heavy with the smell of moss, wet leaves, and rot. Outside the car, the heat got bigger, the air oppressive with humidity, and the car's interior gradually filled with the thickening atmosphere: it was like an expanding gel, nudging and pushing into every available space until there was no longer a boundary between inside and out. Nick ignored the oppressive heat, wiping at his brow now and then only to keep sweat out of his eyes. He knew this road, this future. He'd been here before. The pull of what was coming was physical, like tentacles. Nick drove on, his mind drifting back in time, over the borders of Eden and out into the vast landscape of his youth.

Nick MacCallum is ten years old and big for his age. He feels irritated at Lucas for being small and moving so slowly. It's muggy and hot. The air smells like rotten garbage, and the walk home from Neiderman Public School takes twenty minutes, even using shortcuts. They are already late, and Nick wants to get back before it gets so hot all the big boys come outside to smoke and hang around. "C'mon Lucas," he says, turning to grab at a hank of his brother's T-shirt, yanking him forward.

"Hey," Lucas said as he lurches forward, his frail six-year-old body no match for Nick. "Don't do that." His voice is whiny and thin, like a girl, which grates even more.

"Goddammit, Lucas, hurry up, you wanna get the shit kicked outta you by the Jenssen brothers? Plus, Mama is gonna be mad we're so late, anyway."

"Oh, I'm gonna tell; you can't say that," Lucas baits, grinning.

"Shut up, will you? Just shut up; you are an idiot. I'll leave you here." He turns and walks off fast, too fast for short, six-year-old legs to keep up.

"No," Lucas screams, running towards him to catch up. His scream holds genuine terror. A stab of something Nick cannot name shoots through his heart. He stops, turns. He thinks the little fucker is pathetic, but he can't leave him.

"Just quit freaking dawdling, okay? We gotta hurry." Nick turns and continues to walk a bit more slowly. It's not all the little guy's fault, anyway. There's something else bothering him. He shoves a hand down into the pocket of his Levi's and briefly fingers the bit of folded paper there. The suspension notice feels radioactive.

He hadn't planned to fight; Nick just lost control of himself. Like Daddy, he thinks. Tommy Fearnley is a blonde-haired sixth grader with watery blue eyes and broad features that make him look stupid. Tommy can't read, and they have already held him back two years, making him the biggest kid in the school. Nick thinks the teachers passed the kid to sixth grade because he was too mean to keep in the lower school. He steals lunch money, blocks the bathroom door, bullies' little kids for sport, and absolutely torments Rena Geller.

Rena and her brother Sam are the only two Jewish kids in the white, working-class school. All the other kids attend the *local First Christian church. Mama has reminded the boys many times how hard she works to pay the rent in this neighborhood, so they can "go to a good school." By good, she means white, and by white, she certainly does not mean Jewish.*

Rena and Sam are bullied constantly for their clothes or their food. Words like 'kyke' and 'big nose' and 'Jew girl' drop around them like litter. The school has a policy against this type of behavior, and Mrs. Geller complains, but nothing changes and the administration claims enforcing the policy is not possible. Nick thinks Rena is the strangest, most beautiful girl he's ever seen. Pale and delicate, with enormous black eyes and long auburn hair braided down her back, the girl is simultaneously angelic and fierce. He wants to catch her and protect her; keep her as a rare bird.

Nick glanced over at Evelyn. She was gazing out the window, but she seemed focused inward. Thinking. She leaned her head against the glass and closed her eyes. Sweat had mashed several locks of black hair across her cheekbone; it looked like a warrior's paint. He wanted to tuck her hair away from her face, fix her. He reminded himself that "fixing" was a problem. There'd been his brother. His mother. Then, he'd spent ten years trying to fix his ex-wife, and that had been a disaster for both of them. Kira was still looking for someone to glue her back together, and Nick was goddamn lucky she'd taken the search across state lines. It'd been three years after the divorce, trying to extricate himself from that relationship. Of course, Kira would say it was her trying to get away from him. Such bullshit. Sure, he'd been angry a few times, but who wouldn't be? She was nuts. Anyway, Nick was not looking for another mess to clean up.

He glanced through the window at the open wetlands to his right, just in time to see a flock of snowy egrets light upon the water for a few seconds before taking again to the air. He watched their wings spread in diaphanous curves against the sky and thought about angels. He knew it wasn't true, but from his current vantage point, the birds' lives looked peaceful. The thought made him smile. Nick supposed the daily fight for survival would be a challenge most humans could not endure. He looked again at this woman in the passenger seat. She had the look of a survivor about her. Could he help but be drawn to her? He squeezed the thought from his brain. Stupid, stupid, stupid.

CHAPTER TWENTY-FIVE

Libby | San Francisco

Libby got off the bed and walked to her window. Outside, the day had gone still and white. From her bedroom on the second floor, she could see over the eucalyptus trees' uppermost branches to the Palace of Fine Arts and the Bay beyond. Most days, the view was startlingly beautiful, but today it looked flat and washed out, like she felt. She dropped the silk drape and turned back to her room.

The punishment was a joke. It always went like this with her father. No matter what she did, however outrageous, he couldn't come up with anything more severe than grounding. And he couldn't even call it *grounding*. He couldn't call it *punishment*. He liked to use words like *redirection* and *contemplation time*. So, what he'd said was, "Libby, look, skipping school for the entire day and refusing to answer your phone so you can hang out with a friend is totally uncool, right? So... I have to do something parental here, and what I've done is give a redirect as some contemplation time at home. Cool?" Or something like that. She was sorry for him. He wanted so much to be her friend. He would have preferred to call her mother to come pick her up and deal with all this, but her mother had been unavailable. So, yeah, the punishment was trivial, but Libby still wished the housekeeper had kept her mouth shut. Libby couldn't really blame her. The poor woman was afraid of Stuart and petrified of his mother, who really ran the household. She'd have lost her job for sure, so she'd told Stuart about Libby showing up late, about the vice-principal coming out to say that Libby had been truant all day. Still, it would have been nice if she hadn't.

At least Evelyn was clueless about the whole thing. Libby was pretty sure her mother would have lost her shit over Conner and the fact that he was a twenty-one-year-old dude neither parent had ever met, but her father seemed to have forgotten to ask about it. He stayed focused on all the stuff the vice principal had written on the suspension paper. Things like "truant from school" and "lying to the administration." Her father was that way. He needed the important stuff written down. She hadn't lied to him when he asked where she'd been. She'd said she'd been at a friend's house. It wasn't her fault if Stuart did not ask the follow-up questions. Libby supposed it was a good thing her mother would never know about Conner.

She'd met Conner at her friend Celia's house three months earlier. He was a friend of Celia's older brother, and at first, Libby had avoided him. He made her nervous, but after a while, he started complimenting her thrift store T-shirts, he thought her hair was cool, and she had a beautiful smile. He still made her nervous. When Conner asked for her phone number, Libby handed it over and then waited anxiously for him to call. It took him a week, but he did. He had a car, lived nearby, picked her up whenever she could get away. Lying to her parents was easy. She could always say she was going to meet friends after school. Whatever. It thrilled her mother to hear she was socializing and never asked questions.

Yeah, it was better her mother didn't know about her truancy today. Conner was the only thing in Libby's life that made her feel anything. Not good exactly, but at least not numb.

She plopped down in an armchair, upholstered in velvet, the color of eggplant. Libby detested all things girlie, and her room reflected that. Her father's one concession to her, in exchange for her promise to stay at the house overnight once a week, was that she could decorate the room as she pleased. To her grandmother's dismay, she'd painted the walls dark blue-almost black, and furnished it in deep-toned velvets, purple and black and sapphire blue. Gam said it looked like a bordello. Libby wasn't all that sure what a bordello was, but she loved the look on her grandmother's face; lips pinched together so tightly it looked like her entire face might suck itself inside out.

Libby ran her palms over the curving arms of the chair, the fabric soft as petals. She turned her left arm over and ran one finger over the fresh cuts. She'd clicked out the blade from one of her disposable razors and used it to make three of them running horizontally across her wrist. Red, raw looking. They offered a comforting sting when she pressed on the skin around the slash marks. She leaned back. Closed her eyes. Images of an aunt she'd never met kept coming to her mind. She'd seen no photos of Carolyn, hadn't known she existed, so, of course, her brain left a blank where Carolyn's face should have been. Still, she could see her. Ivory-skinned, like her mother. Thin, she thought, delicate, with small bones like Libby's.

She opened her eyes and shook her head, trying to dislodge the thoughts. Stupid. It was dumb to think about some girl she'd never known, never would know. Why did she care anyway? Why did it matter what happened decades ago? She picked up her phone and checked the call history. She couldn't help hoping her mother would call back.

CHAPTER TWENTY-SIX

Nick | Celeste

Nick pushed open the staff entrance door at the back of the building, housing the Bonfante Parish Coroner's Offices, stepped back and allowed Evelyn to enter. The foyer space was small, brightly lit, and empty, except for a steel surveillance camera sitting high in one corner. It buzzed softly as it scanned back and forth. That's new, Nick thought, and pushed open a narrow door, revealing a small, sparsely furnished office behind.

"I'd like you to look at something for me before we talk to the medical examiner if that's okay. It'll help our investigation." He gestured for her to sit and told her he'd be right back.

A moment later, he was back holding a clear plastic bag marked EVIDENCE. He pushed it toward her gently. "Evelyn, can you please look at this without touching it and tell me if you recognize it?"

"Yeah," she answered almost instantly, chewing her lip slightly. "It was my sister's. It was Carolyn's."

"Can you tell me what it is?" He watched her stretch a finger toward the bag. He almost stopped her, then she caught his eye and stopped herself.

"It's a bracelet. I mean, it used to be a bracelet. My mother gave it to her. She wore it quite a lot." She wiped at her eyes, but he couldn't tell if she was crying. "That was a charm,"

Evelyn said and pointed to the metal chunk. "I think it said something like To Thine Own Self Be True. Probably still says part of that, anyway." She stiffened, looked up at Nick. "But so, what? They sent Carolyn away. That bracelet could have wound up anywhere. It might have been stolen. I don't even know if she still had it when she left."

"Ok, great, thanks. Can you look at one more thing for me?" He pushed the second bag across the table toward her. Waited.

She flinched, her eyes widened, then she shook her head, quickly and looked away. "No, I don't know. What is it?"

He picked up the bag, which held a square of fabric about six inches by four inches. "We're not sure. Some type of fiber, wool, maybe. But it's unclear if it came from a blanket or an article of clothing. The elements, heat, water, and whatnot, and of course time, caused a significant deterioration in most of what we found." Evelyn grimaced. "I'm sorry."

She waved his apology away. "It's fine, go on."

"Except for this. It was protected, so the lab could analyze it."

She nodded and sat staring at nothing, her hands folded in her lap. Why, Nick wondered, did he feel like she was lying?

CHAPTER TWENTY-SEVEN

Evelyn | Celeste

Evelyn watched as the Detective slid the evidence bag off the table and into a drawer. She caught him looking at her and let her eyes slide away. It felt like he knew what she was thinking. Knew what she was trying not to think.

It's late. A girl in her room. There's a girl in her room, searching for something. Pulling up the mattress, down on her knees, peering under the bed in the dark. Moving rapidly around the room, small and soundless, like a mouse.

Carolyn, is that you? Carolyn, what are you doing?

Shhhh, the girl says, whirling around to look at Evelyn where she lay in her bed. Shhhh, go back to sleep. It's ok. Just go to sleep, she repeats, and it sounds like a hiss. Dangerous and scary.

But what are you doing? Evelyn asks, feeling gooseflesh rise on the backs of her arms.

The girl does not answer this time. Only turns, her eyes flashing anger. Where is it? She says. What did you do with it?

"Hey," the detective's voice. "Are you ok?" he was reaching, fingers on her arm, his touch dry and warm.

"Yeah," she said. "Fine. Totally fine." She forced a smile, ignoring the rapid beat of her heart. How long since anyone had touched her gently? Without demand? She stood and pushed the chair back. "Can we go?" she said as images of Carolyn ambushed her brain.

It is 1986. Evelyn is ten years old. Carolyn is fourteen and sitting on the twin bed next to hers, calmly slicing her inner thigh with the blade she has removed from her plastic pencil sharpener. She has thirty-one marks already, and this will make thirty-two. Every slice is exactly one inch long and neatly parallel to the one before. Her leg looks as if it's been bar-coded. Evelyn does not know it yet, but there will be thirteen more marks, one each day before Carolyn stops. After Mama's funeral, Carolyn began keeping track of the days by cutting her inner thigh, and Evelyn guesses her sister means to cut her leg every day from now until forever the way things are working out. She wonders what Carolyn will do when she runs out of skin.

CHAPTER TWENTY-EIGHT

Nick | Celeste

Dr. Albert Finney was past seventy, but he looked only sixty, maybe less. A tall, thin man. Well-dressed. Some folks complained he dressed too well for a Bonfante Parish medical examiner. Besides that, who did he think he was, anyway? His reasonable looks and fashionable dress might have made him charming had he not lacked warmth, charisma, and a sense of humor. Instead, he appeared pompous and silly, and to some, arrogant and mean.

Dr. Finney invited Nick and Evelyn to sit at his enormous desk-curiously empty except for one stapler, one pen, and his computer monitor-and have a chat about the situation. Nick noticed there were no photographs, no diplomas, and save for one tiny Aloe Vera plant in the corner- apparently in the last stages of a terminal illness- no personal decoration of any kind. One window overlooked nothing in particular: a road, half the parking lot, a few failing shops. Nick could not recall seeing a doctor's office so depressingly devoid of personality.

Dr. Finney spoke, slowly, methodically. It was unnecessary, he said, for Ms. Yates to view the remains. They would make final identification matches based on DNA and other evidence, anyway. Evelyn interrupted him. She didn't care about what he thought was necessary. She knew her rights; she wanted to see the body.

Nick sighed, inadvertently meeting the doctor's eyes. They both knew she was right. Dr. Finney switched on his computer monitor and, after keying in a few entries, he swung it around on the desk, so Evelyn could see the screen.

CHAPTER TWENTY-NINE

Evelyn | Celeste

The small pile of material on the table did not look like anybody's sister. Evelyn could identify a few bones, tattered bits of tissue paper or cloth, and one horrible piece that looked suspiciously like a mouth with teeth still implanted. She studied the pictures on the computer screen forcing herself not to look away.

Carolyn has been angry all the time since Mama died. At night she screams and throws objects against the wall, and Evelyn waits for Daddy to come in and make Carolyn stop, but he never does, and she just goes right on.

There is a man from social services who comes to the house to help since Mama died. He wants the girls to call him Mr. Mike. Carolyn only calls him Mr. Clancy, and Evelyn doesn't call him anything at all. She doesn't like the way he keeps pushing his sticky hair up over his eyes. She doesn't like the big gold ring he wears on his fourth finger. It isn't a wedding ring. Once he tries to touch her head, and she growls at him. Then the man tells Daddy Evelyn might need the Special Kind of Help.

Mr. Clancy comes to the house four or five more times. He is supposed to be helping Carolyn, but things only get worse. Sometimes she refuses to get out of bed. She even stops going to the Back Field with Evelyn, although Evelyn thinks Carolyn goes alone sometimes, even at night.

The nighttime fits get worse, and when they happen every night, Daddy talks to Mr. Clancy, who says Carolyn needs Special Help and not just Special Help but Real Special Help, and he says she has to go live in Another Place. That is when all the trouble starts.

"Evelyn, Evelyn." A hand touched her shoulder. She looked up. The detective. He was looking at her strangely.

"I'm ok, really. Fine." She murmured the words, wanting him to leave her alone. She didn't take her eyes off the screen. "Just tired. That's all."

"I understand. I'm sorry about this." He gestured at the computer screen. "We know identification is impossible at this point. That's why we rely on other methods. DNA, dental records when available."

She bristled. "I keep telling you. She didn't..." Evelyn pointed weakly at the screen and added, "They sent her..." she paused, trying to ignore the tightening in her chest. "They sent her away, and then she died." The words came out thin and pressured.

Dr. Finney cleared his throat, then spoke. His words measured. The tone of his voice was patronizing, as if he was talking to a child or a crazy person. "Miss Yates, we will clarify identity once we have DNA, presuming we can collect DNA in adequate quantities. But I must tell you, based on the location, gender, and age of the skeletal remains, as well as the limited dental records we could find." He licked his lips. "We have presumptive identification that this is Carolyn Yates. Your sister." Evelyn narrowed her eyes at him, willing him to shut the fuck up.

"It's not possible," she muttered, mostly to herself. "Wait, age? You said, age. Carolyn died later. Years later. You said this is a child. How old?"

"Yes, my estimate is that this is the body of a twelve to fourteen-year-old female-"

Evelyn interrupted, "Well, ok, then. That's not right. She would have been at least seventeen or eighteen when she died."

"Ms. Yates," said Dr. Finney. His face and posture were stiff. "We presuppose she died well before that. Probably not long after the last time you saw her. There is other evidence supporting the identity of these remains." She spoke, then stopped. There really wasn't anything to say. He continued. "Like I said, will also run DNA. To be certain." He gripped the computer monitor and turned the screen away, out of Evelyn's line of sight.

"It makes no sense," she said.

He ignored her. "We also have preliminary results on the toxicology back from Baton Rouge." He pulled a sheet from the folder but did not hand it to Evelyn. Instead, he set it down, tapping at it with his pen. "We could get spongy tissue from some of the bone fragments. The only positive result so far is for chloral hydrate. That's a drug no longer used routinely in medicine. It is, however, known to cause poisoning sometimes, self-induced poisoning. We do not see any other cause of death, although the state of the remains makes it difficult to determine manner and cause conclusively.

Evelyn steeled herself. "What? What are you saying?" she asked.

"I'm saying, Miss Yates, that we cannot rule out suicide as the manner of death." He pursed his lips. Folded his fish-belly white hands across one another atop the desk.

She shook her head. No. That was it. She had to get away from this man. Both these men. Get away from them and their insane ideas. Standing, Evelyn smoothed some imaginary wrinkles from her slacks, and walked out of the room. They were wrong, she'd been there, and she remembered.

It is a Friday when they plan to send Carolyn away. Evelyn is sitting on the floor in front of the TV, eating sugar smacks out of a plastic bowl in her lap. Sometimes Carolyn eats cereal for dinner. She feels sad because Carolyn used to always watch TV and eat cereal with her. Carolyn used to do everything with her, but now she's always so mad. Sometimes Carolyn says mean things and tells Evelyn to go away. Evelyn worries that Carolyn no longer loves her. The thought makes her feel funny inside and not at all a good funny.

Daddy comes into the front room and says it's time for Carolyn to go, and does Evelyn know where she is? Evelyn shakes her head, no, and Daddy gets that frustrated look that sometimes means he is about to curse. He doesn't, though. He just turns and slams out the front door.

Evelyn is frightened to see Mrs. Coolidge from next door, standing at the door. The old woman is speaking, but the words fall out of her wrinkled mouth like pebbles and drop to the ground before Evelyn can catch them. Evelyn stands up, and the sugar smacks spill down the front of her T-shirt and out onto Mama's rag rug.

They keep asking her about Carolyn. Where is she? says, Daddy. Where is she? says Mrs. Coolidge. Where is she? says Mr. Clancy. He leans close and asks her again and again. Where is your sister? Evelyn puts her hands over her ears and screams. She screams again and again, but Carolyn does not come. Mrs. Coolidge's bony arms reach for her, and Evelyn watches the crepe skin and fat of the woman's underarms slither and shiver like snakes. Evelyn backs up hard against the front of the TV set. She keeps screaming.

She was in the ladies' room, rummaging in her purse for the flask she'd hidden away earlier that morning, just in case. Yanking it out, she unscrewed the little top and, with one eye in the mirror, she watched herself take several long pulls. Then she leaned forward and rested her head against the smooth glass.

She felt safe. Nothing in the world made her feel safe, like booze. Nothing was safe except booze. Thieves, murderers, rapists, cancer, bullets, and goddamn bad luck. Living was a sick game. Everyone crawling through a fucking minefield blindfolded and then, with dreadful foreknowledge, getting executed by some random means on the other side. Booze was like insulation. It didn't exactly take you out of the minefield, but it offered little bunkers along the way. You could crouch down and listen while bullets flew overhead. You could rest a bit. So, what if twice as many land mines lay waiting when your fickle bunker dissolved? The temporary respite was worth it.

"Ahhhh," she sighed, still leaning forward, her forehead on the mirror. The bullet sounds more distant now. CAPOW. Missing a dead girl. CAPOW. Hating a dead girl. She stood, took another drink, and set the flask down. In a minute, she'd meet back up with the detective, but for now... she'd rest. She let her eyes close. Ran her hands along the sink's edge. The porcelain was smooth and exquisitely crisp under her palm.

When Daddy comes back, he makes Evelyn sit down in the kitchen with him to talk. He lights a cigarette and hunches over the table and stares down at its surface like he's trying to memorize something there. He leans back, turns his chair away, and looks out the window, and just smokes. Then he talks. He tells her they have to find Carolyn. That Carolyn has to live at Another Place for a while, so she can get Real Special Help. He says that the Place has nurses and doctors who know how to deal with Girls with Problems, so that is the right place for Carolyn. She watches Daddy run his fingers through his thin hair repeatedly, and she follows his gaze out the window even though there is nothing out there in particular to see. He sits there and looks outside at nothing, and smokes. She doesn't look outside. She doesn't look anywhere but right at Daddy. She doesn't cry.

Evelyn stepped outside the building, rubbed at her eyes with the heels of her hands, and looked around for the detective. She found him waiting for her near the front entrance. They stood there in silence for a while, neither one looking at the other. There was a school across the street, but the children had all disappeared into the classrooms. The playground was empty, and the sticky blacktop looked poisonous. A half-empty, fast-food bag lay squashed against the curb, and ketchup oozed from the side, like roadkill.

"I'll get Finney's preliminary report by tomorrow morning. I'll call you."

"Okay. He's wrong, though. That's not her." she pulled her purse off her shoulder and fumbled around inside, coming up with a squashed cigarette pack. She removed one of the two remaining cigarettes, smoothed it with her fingers, and realized she had no lighter. "Fuck," she said. "You have a lighter?"

He pulled one from his pocket, flicked it, and lit the cigarette she held to her lips.

"Thanks. You don't look like a smoker."

"Not a smoker. Not anymore." He rolled the red Bic around in his palm. "Habit, I guess," he said. She nodded.

She inhaled deeply on the cigarette and blew the smoke off to her right. Avoiding the detective. Then she looked up at him. "I'm telling you, it's not her. I know what happened to her. I know where she went. Look, I was there." She inhaled the cigarette and took her time exhaling the smoke. "It's possible to get a private autopsy, right?"

"Yeah," he said. "Once you're established as next of kin, if that's what you want but," he hesitated. "But what do you mean? You were there?"

She took a breath. Studied him. "When they took my sister, I was there, I saw it. That's why I'm so sure. I tried to tell your Chief but maybe... I don't know... he didn't believe me. I'm not sure, but I know what I saw. The social worker who'd been visiting us for a while after my mother died. It was him. He came; he took her away to the hospital in New Orleans. I remember the whole thing. It was..." She threw the cigarette down. Crushed it out under the toe of her boot. "It was fucking horrible."

The ride back was long and quiet. The afternoon had grown dark and thick with humidity, the sort of weather that discourages movement. Just outside Celeste, the houses became scarce, and the front yards were mostly weeds or dirt. Plastic toys and trash lay scattered about, mixed with rusted-out car parts and old furniture. At intervals, cracks appeared in the blacktop, some of them wide enough to swallow a bicycle and rider whole. Beyond the last houses were trees grown older than people could ever hope to be. In spots, the tree roots had torn up the road like it was paper. The land, Evelyn thought, was devouring the road just like it had devoured her family decades earlier.

"My father," she said. Then, changed her mind. Stopped. No, she couldn't speak this part. Not to him. Maybe not to anyone. She wasn't ready to share the memories that were flooding back into her brain. Threatening, she thought, to drown her.

Later, after Carolyn has gone away, Evelyn slips out of the house. No one sees her. She goes out to the old barn and climbs through the small hole in the rotting boards that she and Carolyn found such a long time ago. She sits in the dark in the meadow, which spreads out to forever, and she waits for something to happen. Old Mrs. Coolidge always says the Back Field Will Eat Children, but Carolyn said that wasn't right, and they came out here all the time to build mud castles and make daisy chains and sleep and tell stories and sometimes just to hide.

Carolyn will come here to get her. She'll come, and she won't be angry anymore. She'll know that Evelyn didn't mean what she said.

Evelyn stays out in the meadow for a long time, but Carolyn doesn't come. It gets very dark, and she lays down on her stomach in the grass. She thinks it's true. The Field ate Carolyn, and the thought scares her. She buries her face in the earth; she smells crushed lavender, and she claws her fingers into the dirt and pulls up clumps of grass by the roots. She cries. Later, they come and drag her back to the house.

CHAPTER THIRTY

Nick | Eden

A spark of worry had ignited at the base of Nick's brain. Chief Broussard hadn't called to see what was keeping him. He was running twenty minutes late, and Broussard was a stickler for promptness. Broussard hadn't answered his cellphone, hadn't returned two text messages. Nick dialed the Chief's home; the call went straight to voice mail. Chief got like this sometimes, when he was busy, and he had let Nick know he'd be out of town all day on Tuesday, possibly even overnight. Nick was pretty sure Broussard had been out chasing down proof that Finney was barking up the wrong tree. It wouldn't be the first time those two went to battle over a case. Still... something seemed different this time. Too much silence.

The cutoff road over to Broussard's house was unlit. Cave-dark in some spots. Nick shifted in the driver's seat, leaned forward until his chest almost touched the steering wheel. He squinted into the black. Despite his earlier reservations, he was looking forward to discussing things with the Chief. The experience with Dr. Finney had been unnerving. If Nick had questioned Finney's sincerity before, then he had serious reservations about the man's professional trustworthiness now. Evelyn had been right. Even to a non-medical professional, Finney's conclusions seemed premature and inappropriate. Was it possible that Finney had his own agenda, that he needed or wanted this case conclusion to be suicide? Hopefully, Broussard could supply the missing pieces. It seemed unthinkable that an appointed official, a medical professional-even an asshole like

Finney-could be biased in his conclusions or even falsifying autopsy reports to push a personal agenda. No, Nick thought, there had to be another explanation.

A few minutes later, he pulled down the gravel drive to the old farmhouse Chief Broussard shared with his wife, Vera. Out here, away from town, on nights when the moon was slight, the stars were a million brilliant dashes across the clear, black sky.

He checked his watch. Dinner hour. Vera would want him to sit. Eat. Spend some time. He was pondering how he might get out of dinner with the Broussard's while still maneuvering a private conversation with the Chief when he heard a low whistling sound coming from inside the house. At first, barely audible, but as he climbed the steps and crossed the small porch, it grew louder, clearer. He pulled back the screen, the whining sound morphed into a cry. A woman. Then, a second later, stifled sucking noises.

He hesitated before the door, his right arm raised, hand curled into a fist. Were they arguing? Then another sob ripped through the door, louder and more distressed. Nick decided. Pounding on the door, he called out, "Mrs. Broussard? Chief, are you alright? It's Nick MacCallum, Mrs. Broussard? Chief? Are you there?"

Nick looked over his shoulder and noted that Broussard's car wasn't in the carport. The spark of worry blazed. "Mrs. Broussard? I'm coming in okay. I'm going to come into the house." He paused a few seconds, then stepped back. One shoulder turned towards the door, readying himself.

A weak voice answered, "Nick, I'm here, I'm coming." He heard light footsteps approaching. Mrs. Broussard pulled open the door. A small woman, her eyes soft and wet, her hands fluttering in and out of the folds of her apron, like tiny birds. She was pale, almost translucent, and her gray hair had come loose from its pins and hung in strands around her face. "Oh, Nick," she said. "It's Tom." Then she was clutching his shirtsleeves.

It took a minute to get her inside and seated at the kitchen table. She sipped at a glass of water, her hand shaking so badly droplets splashed her blouse, creating spots of translucency in the white fabric. When she spoke, it was in a whisper. "Nick, they... just called me... a few seconds before you knocked... you should call the station..." Nick checked his phone. No service. Goddamn cell phones.

"What is it?" Nick asked.

"They found his... car, Nick," she said, her voice trembling. "Blood. Lots of blood, Nick. But not him." She broke off and cried, turning her face away. Then she added, "Goddammit Nick, he wasn't answering calls. I... just assumed he was busy. He gets like that, you know. I should have..." She broke into sobs, unable to finish.

"Vera," he whispered. "I need to use your phone, ok? Can I get you anything?"

"No, no. I don't need anything," she answered, "just call the station Nick. Call..." She continued to cry softly, running her small, childlike hands back and forth over the tablecloth fabric. Searching for something she'd lost.

Sheriff Savoy arrived with a backup officer within twenty minutes, and Nick was relieved to step aside. Alice Savoy, a short, solid woman in her early sixties, had a warm smile and a certain musicality to her voice. She'd been the Sheriff forever and had a reputation for calm during chaos. Folks in Eden appreciated that about her. Savoy was their rock. "Vera, we will find him. You know that, right? We will find him, and whatever has happened, Vera, we will find the person responsible. I promise you that." Vera nodded at her. Said nothing.

Promises. Nick wondered as he stepped outside if making that promise was fair. He shouldn't have done it. He shrugged and sucked at the night air, pushing away the guilt.

Tommy Fearnley and his friends have surrounded Rena Geller, and Tommy is flipping at her long braid with a stick. She is standing, eyes downcast, clutching a small stack of books to her chest. Nick cannot tell if she is crying. "Hey, Tommy, cut it out, leave her alone," Nick says, approaching the group. His words sound like he's got a mouthful of Jell-O.

"Who's gonna make me?" Tommy says. He is sucking on a popsicle as he takes a step toward Nick.

"I am, that's who," Nick says, feeling ninety percent sure he is not. He raises his chin a little.

"Right." Tommy leans into Nick's face, squinting. "Go ahead, shithead."

Tommy's face is close. Nick can smell the cherry popsicle and tobacco on his breath. He stares into the stained and worn collar of Tommy's T-shirt, where it rounds the boy's beefy neck. Nick is now one hundred percent sure he will not stop Tommy. "Just stop picking on Rena, Tommy. Leave her alone. Okay?" The words come out sounding a great deal less threatening than Nick had hoped.

"Oh sure, no problem. I'll cut it out..." Tommy sings in a mocking falsetto while waving his hands in the air, one still clutching the red popsicle and dancing around on tiptoe. "I'm so scared I'll do whatever you say, beanpole." A group of girls nearby huddle together, tittering. Tommy drops the falsetto and pushes his face a few inches from Nick once more. "Get out of here. Mind your own beeswax, shit head."

Nick backs up a step, preparing to leave. Rena has quietly moved off anyway, and for the time being, is safe. He watches Tommy turn his back and raise his hands, fluttering them about in mock fear. A couple of boys who have been watching laugh nervously.

"That's it, loser. Run away." Tommy has turned around.

Nick feels anger course through him like electricity. He thinks about the nights he watched his father scream into his mother's face, the times Joe MacCallum shoved her or punched her. Sometimes Nick would rush at his father, small hands balled into fists, screaming for the man to leave Mama alone, but Joe was powerful, and most times he'd fling Nick out of the way with one hand and go right on.

"No, Tommy."

"Huh? Did you say something shit, head? Ah, c'mon, get out of here. Loser. You ain't gonna do nothing." Tommy turns away and is again laughing.

Nick propels himself towards Tommy's back, nearly knocking the bigger boy over. Nick flings his arms around Tommy's neck and squeezes hard. Tommy spins around, letting the popsicle fly, and Nick watches it catapult, like a red rocket, into the air as Tommy clutches Nick's elbows and shoves him to the blacktop. Pain shoots through Nick's back and shoulders as he hits the ground. Then, suddenly, Tommy is on top of Nick. They are rolling on the blacktop, limbs entwined, and Nick has a hold of Tommy's hair. Both boys are grunting and screaming, and all at once, Nick, the more agile, the faster of the two, is astride Tommy in one swift movement. He has one knee at Tommy's throat and is using both hands to pin the boy's head to the ground by the hair. Tommy's eyes are wide. He's afraid, Nick thinks. As he pulls harder at the bigger boy's hair and jams a knee into his throat, Tommy cries and begs Nick to let him go. Nick looks down at Tommy's face, streaked with tears and dirt, and feels nothing. Nick pulls his right arm back, clenches his fist, and slams it into Tommy's face.

Blood is spouting in several directions at once, and the big boy is making horrible squealing noises, reaching for his head. Nick's hand does not yet sting, but the fingers are swelling, and rivulets of bright blood cover his knuckles and run down the back of his hand. He is acutely aware of his own heartbeat as he looks down into Tommy's partially obliterated face.

"Boys, boys! Oh my God. Stop, stop this instant! What is going on?" Principal Wilkins is rushing toward them, her thick calves flashing, one past the other, beneath the hem of her navy skirt. Tommy is screaming and writhing beneath him, but the pain has made him weak, and Nick has no problem controlling Tommy's movements, using only the strength of his thigh muscles as he straddles the bigger boy. Nick looks around. To his right, just inches from his right knee on the asphalt, in a rapidly spreading puddle of cherry juice, he spies the discarded popsicle stick. He checks out Principal Wilkin, who is still twenty yards away. Nick snatches up the stick, snaps it in two, and leans in real close to Tommy Fearnley's face. He holds the jagged end of one-half of the stick just a few inches from Tommy's eyeball and waits until he is sure that Tommy understands.

By the time Principal Wilkins reaches the boys, Nick has thrown the broken popsicle stick back out onto the asphalt, and he's pretty sure Tommy Fearnley won't say a word.

CHAPTER THIRTY-ONE

Evelyn | Eden

Evelyn twisted the knob, shutting down the shower's limp spray of water. She'd convinced the water company to turn on the service as an emergency, but that did nothing to address the plumbing issues her father had clearly ignored. She stuck her head out of the curtain. Undergarments she'd rinsed out in the sink hung drip drying from the bathroom towel rack and miniature vanity, leaving no room for towels which, earlier, she'd moved hopelessly out of reach. Despite the heat outside, the inside of the house was remarkably cool. The idea of stepping out of the shower and skipping naked across the room was enough to make Evelyn give up and just wait for help to arrive. No choice, she decided, gritting her teeth. Careful not to hit her head on the metal frame, she ducked out and, teeth chattering, hopped across the floor and out to the bed, frantically snatching up one towel.

She rubbed her body vigorously, then dried her hair, and sat on the bed to survey the situation. The room lay in chaos. She'd dumped her suitcase that morning, searching for something appropriate to wear up to the coroners. What was the dress code for viewing remains everyone claimed were those of your dead sister? Trousers and blouses lay half out of the case, and underwear and t-shirts scattered, dropped wherever she'd last touched them. She bent to gather up a stray T-shirt and slipped it over her head, then stood, peered down at the floor, and kicked at a pile of clothing. A pair of sweats came loose, and she picked them up. Put them on, then snatched up the towel from the bed and wiped her face with it.

Something caught her attention. The smell. She pressed the terrycloth to her face and inhaled deeply into the fabric. It smelled earthy, dusty, which made sense but, beneath that came the scent of tobacco. Very faint. So delicate, she thought it would dissipate to nothing if she moved. She stood perfectly still, inhaling. Suddenly, she could see him. Clearly.

It is late 1988, and her father is tired. Evelyn is only twelve, but she can see his exhaustion because his skin has gone the color of old straw and there are black circles permanently gouged under his eyes. Like wax paint. It's been over two years since they lost Mama. Since Carolyn left. It seems like people have stopped saying he just needs time to grieve. Besides, Evelyn thinks, he's only getting worse. He shuffles more than walks, looking at the ground all the time. His long frame has become fragile and awkward under his clothes; so thin he practically disappears when he turns sideways. Evelyn thinks he looks like a lightning struck tree; hollowed out, ashy. Standing but no longer really alive.

The hospital has just released him. He left home in his truck three days earlier and didn't return. He'd gone on a binge and been picked up by the Sheriff two parishes over for belligerent behavior. Instead of jail, he'd wound up in the hospital to recover, the judge said, but Evelyn thinks he looks worse than ever.

Old Mrs. Coolidge came to stay while Daddy was away, and Evelyn spent those days locked in her room except for meals and bathroom breaks. Old Mrs. Coolidge scares Evelyn. Her hands are thick with blue and purple veins like ropes, and her sticky, sprayed hair smells like roses left too long in a vase. Evelyn has been mean to Mrs. Coolidge. She tells herself it's because the old lady is scary, but really, it's for no reason at all.

Word spreads around Eden; it's the drinking that's made Daddy sick, the drinking and the grief. The drink, people say, will kill him soon if he doesn't stop. Evelyn is also sure he will die, but she thinks it's shame, not whiskey, which will kill him.

Most residents of Eden still drive the long way around Road 12 to avoid passing by the house. Evelyn thinks it's because tragedy might be contagious. Suicide is a sin to most of the families around Eden, and Mama, of course, had been a mother, and that made her choice doubly unforgivable. Some people say Daddy's to blame. There are more than a few rumors going around that Mama's problems were spiritual, which, Evelyn knows, means whore.

Then there were the stories from the paper.

The local paper handled it gently, but the city papers were cruel, and sensational. The headlines read things like: Unstable Mother Takes Own Life by Drinking Acetone and Gruesome Suicide in Bonfante Parish. Some people around town even kept copies of the articles in scrapbooks or picture frames, which didn't help.

Everybody blames Daddy and Mama both for what happened to Carolyn. Kids at school say she went crazy after Mama died. Evelyn knows Carolyn wasn't crazy. Just sad is all.

Evelyn doesn't care much about the town or the people or anything else. She goes to school only enough to keep the teachers from coming to her house to see about things. She spends her time alone or taking care of her father, who seems sicker every day. He no longer works. As the work dries up, so does his will to work. He spends his days sitting in a chair staring at the TV, not taking notice if it's switched on or off. He drinks. When the old bottle is empty, he wants her to bring him a fresh bottle. Otherwise, he asks for little, but she brings him food and water, anyway. He doesn't eat much, sometimes he sleeps. All of this scares Evelyn. She worries Daddy will die, then someone will come and send her to Another Place.

The clock snapped forward, and the click shook Evelyn out of her reverie. 6:50 PM. She tried Libby's number. The call went directly to voice mail. Third time today. She'd try again later. Setting her phone to silent, she curled up on top of the bed covers and fell promptly to sleep.

A small person stood on a ledge inside Evelyn's brain, using a hammer to ping away at the underside of her skull. Thwick. Thwick. Thwick. She thought it didn't really hurt, but it couldn't be healthy. It would probably be smart to wake up and make the small person stop. She forced her eyes to open. Then she heard it.

Someone was picking at the handle on her door.

From the outside.

She lay awake in the bed staring straight up into the black night, unable to see the ceiling through the dark. She did not scream or move or even reach for her phone. She lay there, paralyzed, disoriented, terrified, and certain she was about to die. She listened.

Thwick. Thwick. Thwick.

Then there was no sound. No sound except the whirring of the old plumbing around the building and the continuous chirping of the cicada outside. Then, without warning, she felt her legs being yanked as if by some sort of industrial machine, and then her body, along with the bedding, was being pulled off the bed and down to the floor. Someone pushed her up against the bed and slammed her head against the iron frame, causing a sharp pain to spread across the back of her skull.

Suddenly, her arm was simultaneously caught behind her and twisted upward across her back. The pain caused white lights to explode behind her eyes. She still held some of the bed linen in her good hand, and she reflexively clutched it more closely around her torso. The result was that she found herself partially swallowed in sheeting, slumped against the bed in a half-sitting position like a mummified rag doll.

Then she saw him.

She opened her mouth to scream, and he slammed a thickly gloved hand over her face. She couldn't breathe. Panicking, her lungs burned. She was dying.

Slowly, he peeled his fingers away from her nose and then her mouth. As he pulled his fingers away, she took a deep, sucking, desperate breath, and then another, and pushed out a scream. Part of a scream before he slapped her across the side of her head hard enough to stop the sound as soon as it started.

He was straddling Evelyn with one knee in her gut and one arm around her back, yanking her elbow so hard it felt broken. When he'd hit her, he'd managed to hit with one hand and twist her injured elbow with the other.

He had some kind of kerchief or bandana over his nose and mouth and another covering his hair. Both were so filthy she couldn't tell the color. Evelyn studied his hard, lined forehead. He was so close she could taste the odors of whiskey and stale cigarettes coming off of him. His skin was the color of beeswax, and his eyes appeared like two black peach pits in his skull. Flat. Black. She would remember.

"Wh-what do you-" she sputtered, unable to form complete words. Her mouth was dry. Her tongue felt like sandpaper.

"Go, home lady, butt out of things that don't concern you." He leaned in closer. "If you tell anybody anything about this, I'll be back, and next time, I'll kill you," he hissed at her. She stared at his Adam's apple bobbing above the neckline of his stained T-shirt. He had a small mark. A badly done tattoo over his collarbone, black, blurry lines. What was it? A bar of gold? A book? Certainly not a book. She would remember.

Panic, immense and foul, stretched up from inside her, grabbed hold of her lungs, suffocating her. Libby! She forced the thought away, as if he could hear her brain. He might not even know she had a child. She nodded. Said nothing.

Then he was out the door. As quickly as he'd arrived, he was gone.

She sat partially slumped against the bed, legs outstretched, like a rag doll. Useless arm still pressed behind her back. For a time, she did not move. She stared into the darkness, silently repeating to herself what he'd said.

She believed him. Every word.

•   •   •   •   •

Evelyn took slow, ragged breaths and assessed the damage. She sat on the floor, back against the bed, right arm tucked awkwardly behind her and both legs sticking straight out in front, creating a disturbing L-shape. Her mouth tasted like she'd been sucking on pocket change, and there was a wretched unfamiliar ache emanating from her right elbow.

She tried twisting forward and pulling her arm around toward her chest. "Fuck," Evelyn said as she let her arm fall limp back toward the floor. Sweat rolled down her temples, down her back, her underarms. She stank of sweat. There was the smell of dust and Lysol around her and something like a mold that had been pushed out of the way, hidden itself in the dark. She could see up and out the window. The moonless night ink black as the interior of the room. She closed her eyes again. Tried to imagine she was shrinking, disappearing. Far away from the pain.

There was something she needed to do. If she could just focus for a minute, she'd remember what it was. She hauled herself onto the bed, clamping her lips shut, willing herself not to vomit from the pain. Suddenly, she remembered. Libby.

CHAPTER THIRTY-TWO

Libby | San Francisco

Libby was hot despite the arctic air conditioning. She'd given up on sleep, stripped off her clothes and sat in the dark. Naked under a thin sheet, pressing buttons on her phone. Conner had dropped out of sight again. Hadn't responded to her messages all afternoon. She'd wanted to tell him about the suspension. She was clicking through his Instagram account for the millionth time when her phone buzzed, startling her. It wasn't Conner.

"Hi Mom," she said, with no attempt to keep the disappointment out of her voice.

"Libby, hi," her mother's voice sounded breathless, strange.

"Yeah?"

"Uh, yeah, how are you, sweetie?"

"Fine."

"What? Lib, what time is it there?" Evelyn asked.

"Mom, I don't know."

"Yes, of course, sorry."

"Are you drinking, mom?"

"No."

"Good. Okay, whatever," Libby wanted badly to believe her, but believing Evelyn could lead to heartbreak. She'd been down that road so many times.

"I said I'd call you back. I'm sorry, it's so late. I got busy."

"It's fine," said Libby, wishing now she could just get off the phone.

"Look, Libby-" Evelyn stopped. Started again. "Are you ok, Libby?"

"Huh? Yeah. I'm fine," she lied. Then she added, consciously softening her voice. "Mom, I don't really like it here; nobody is around. I mean, Dad gave me his credit card to just buy whatever food and stuff, and grandma has her maid or whatever she's called drive me places. But there's nobody around. I hate it." And I'm so sad all the time, and I can't sleep, and I'm all alone, and the boy I love isn't a boy he's a man, and he won't call me, and I think I might lose my mind, Mommy, but she said, "Can you come home?"

"Not right now, honey, I'm sorry," Evelyn answered, and Libby could hear that she meant it. "I... I." Evelyn stopped without finishing the sentence.

"How long do you have to be there? Why can't I just stay home alone?"

"Not much longer," answered Evelyn, ignoring Libby's request to stay home alone.

"Mom, I..." she began, but let the words trail off.

"What is it, Lib? What is it?"

"Nothing. I gotta go to bed now."

"No. Listen to me, Libby. I need you to listen."

"Uh, ok. What is it?"

"It's just... it's just I really want you to be careful. Don't go with people you don't know that sort of thing. Okay? Please?"

"Um, okay."

"I love you, sweetheart; I love you so much. I miss you. As soon as I can, I will be home.

"Mom? Are you alright? You sound sort of weird." She did sound weird. Edgy. Not exactly sad, but something like sad. "You don't sound regular. Are you okay? Is it something else about your sister?"

"No. No, I have no more to tell you right now. Go on to bed, okay? It's fine. I'm sorry I upset you. I don't want you to worry. I only want you to be a little more careful."

"Uh, okay, I guess." Libby pulled the coverlet up around her shoulders.

"Libby, look. You need to listen to what I'm telling you. Please. I don't want you to take chances. Especially while I'm gone. Don't go places with people you don't know well."

"You said that already."

"I'm sorry. I just don't want you hurt."

"Okay, Mom, I got it. Don't worry. I'm fine."

"Okay. I love you."

"Okay."

Libby hit the END button, feeling deeply unsatisfied and even more irritated with her mother. It seemed like the more she talked to Evelyn, the more twisted and layered the secrets became. The more confusing their relationship. A knot of worry settled. Whatever was going on in Eden, whatever bad thing had washed over her mother's family, Libby was sure it was growing now. Like an infection ignored, it was spreading. The contamination had reached California and found Evelyn. Libby wondered if it would find her as well.

CHAPTER THIRTY-THREE

Nick | Eden

Blood pooled around the side of the car, rolling under the front tire, into its grooves like syrup, then fanning out several feet across the blacktop before it thinned and congealed. Nick had pushed his sunglasses up onto his forehead and was crouched down, peering under the axle. Fuck. No way had Broussard survived this. Whatever had happened, the poor bastard was dead.

"Sonofabitch," said Briggs, removing his outer jacket. Sweat stained his shirt and had left enormous damp circles under both arms. "Sonofabitch," he repeated. Nick only nodded. "Poor Vera," added Briggs. Nick nodded again, slipping his sunglasses back onto his face.

"Yeah, I'll call her," Nick volunteered. He was closer to Chief Broussard and his wife. Besides, Briggs was a good detective, but he had limited people skills. Nick let out his breath and pointed at a young man with a camera busily snapping photos of the car's interior, one of the forensic investigators. "Make sure he gets pictures of the backseat and the trunk, ok?" Nick was already pulling his phone out of his pocket, steeling himself for the call to Broussard's wife. A familiar sense of responsibility and guilt swept him. Broussard was certainly dead. If he'd pushed harder. Asked more questions. He should have been able to prevent this. To save this woman the pain he was about to inflict.

Nick and Lucas stay at school late because Principal Wilkins cannot reach their mother by phone. The principal makes Nick sit in the office until the school nurse says he is well enough to go. The nurse gives him a note instructing his mother to keep ice packs on his hand during the evening. Nick throws the note away. There's another letter as well. This one is in a sealed envelope. The principal tells him to be sure and give it to his mother. He opens the envelope as soon as they leave the school grounds. He reads:

TO THE PARENT (S) OF NICHOLAS MACCALLUM:

A PHYSICAL ALTERCATION WAS INCITED BY NICHOLAS MACCALLUM AND RESULTED IN SEVERE INJURY TO ANOTHER STUDENT. IT IS REQUIRED THAT A PARENT ENGAGES IN A PARENT-PRINCIPAL CONFERENCE BEFORE THE STUDENT RETURNS TO SCHOOL. IN ADDITIONS, HE IS TO SERVE TWO DAYS' SUSPENSION AND 12 HOURS' DETENTION FOR INVOLVEMENT IN THE PHYSICAL ALTERCATION ON SCHOOL GROUNDS TODAY.

The principal and vice-principal signed it, and, to Nick, it looks as official as an execution order.

At home, Nick puts his key in the lock but finds it unnecessary. The door swings open easily. Nick steps inside the doorway first. He feels Lucas slide a small hand inside his. A dark silence pushes in on them as they enter the front room. A sweet, sick smell envelopes them. Nick knows the smell. He sees her. She's lying on the sofa, snowy hills of tissue on the surrounding floor. The TV is on without sound. As Nick steps closer to her, the odors of fried food and tobacco pop off her body in fat clouds. She's still wearing her pink and white waitressing dress, but Nick knows soon she'll need to change into the uniform she wears to clean office buildings at night. She looks so tired. Nick's stomach twists itself peculiarly until he feels like he is falling from a great height. He forces himself steady and prays that she is asleep. He looks at her hair stuck to her cheek and the drool running onto the stained sofa cushion. He looks at Lucas, whose eyes are wide like dishes in his small skull, as he sucks on the fingers of one hand.

"Is that you?" she says without opening her eyes. Her voice sounds like she is speaking through a rubber tube. "Is that you, boys?" she repeats.

"Hi, Mom," Nick says.

"Hi," Lucas says so quietly Nick doubts their mother has heard him.

"Come over here," she says, which Nick thinks is strange since they are both standing right next to her. She opens her eyes, which are bloodshot, and Nick hopes it's not because she's been crying. She motions vaguely with one hand. Lucas slides his hand out of Nick's.

"Why, Nick? Why would you do this to me?" She sits up awkwardly, running a hand through her hair, not looking at them. She cries. "I do everything I can. I work as hard as I can. Why do you do this?"

"Do what, Mama? Please don't cry." Something inside him is coming loose, like someone has partially unscrewed a hinge and left it to fall apart on its own.

She sighs deeply and finally looks up at Nick, "You know what, Nicky? Tell me what happened today." Her eyes are black and deep in her skull. His pretty mother looks a hundred years old, and Nick thinks it's all his fault. Her misery, her unhappiness, her entire wasted life. A stone drops from his head to his heart, and he feels his body crumple under the weight. He sinks to his knees before her. Wetness streams down his face, and he buries his head in her lap.

She knows. He just doesn't know how she knows.

He tries to explain about Tommy Fearnley and Rena, and how she's like a beautiful bird, and he'd only wanted to help her, but it comes out all wrong, and his mother only seems angrier.

"Nick, you broke the boy's nose for God's sake. What is there to understand? He went to the hospital. Jesus Christ. I'm so disappointed. You are just like your father." She lets out a sob.

"Stop! Mama, please." Nick cries as something rotten blooms inside him. He wishes she could be like other mothers and yell at him, or hit him, or punish him with grounding, but she's nothing like other mothers. She cries a while longer and tells him it doesn't matter anyway because now everyone at school thinks he's a bad kid and there's nothing to be done about it. Later, she lies back down and turns away from him, and after a bit, it seems like she falls asleep.

Nick and Lucas sit at the kitchen table and take out their homework because they don't know what else to do. They make chocolate milk for a snack. They wait.

After a while, Mama gets up from the sofa, and Nick thinks she might come over to the kitchen to fix them dinner or just talk a little. Instead, she only stands at the sink, washing up a few dishes without a word. The rotten thing inside him grows larger. She turns around from the sink, and he watches her wipe a tear from her otherwise stony face. She picks up a dishtowel and dries her hands with it, then folds it neatly and hangs it on the rack. She shuffles to her room and shuts the door behind her. When she comes out, she is wearing her cleaning lady uniform. She kisses them both on the top of the head and says they should lock the door and she will be home as soon as she can. She always says the same thing. She's been working two jobs ever since their father left, which was so long-ago Lucas can hardly remember him. She always says she'll quit the second job when they have enough money. They never seem to have enough. Nick makes soup and toast for dinner and helps

Lucas get ready for bed. His little brother cries until he falls asleep.

In the morning, their mother is home, and she fixes them breakfast but does not look at Nick. He spends the day home from school on suspension, and his mother goes to work at the diner. He composes ten different apology letters to his mother. He gives her none. After that, Nick notices his mother seems more and more tired. She sleeps all the time when she's not working, and sometimes she even calls the diner and says she's too sick to come to work. She can't skip her cleaning job, though. She says they'll fire her for sure if she does. Nick thinks they are not very kind to his mother. He tells himself when he grows up, he will have a good job and make enough money to protect his brother and his mom, and he will make sure she does not have to work ever again.

Nick feels like he's floating through the rooms of a dollhouse. Like he might open a cabinet to discover a false front; pull on a fixture only to have its blind bottom yank free of the floor. The apartment has grown light, vacant, free of gravity itself.

Lucas has nightmares again, and Nick blames himself.

Nick's mother stops ignoring him. She smiles again, but things are never the same. When he tells her his plans to become a police officer, she warns him, "Now, are you sure they know all about you? Do they know you get angry sometimes?"

After the thing with Tommy, he never lays a hand on anyone again, but she is right; he gets angry, and the rotten thing inside him never goes away.

CHAPTER THIRTY-FOUR

Evelyn | Eden

Evelyn dropped the phone on the bed, frustrated with herself for being so obtuse with Libby. Not obtuse, dishonest. Why couldn't she tell Libby the truth? Why couldn't she tell anyone the truth? Lies came so much more easily than the truth. Lies felt safe. Her thoughts drifted.

> *Carolyn's face inches from Evelyn's, her eyes narrow. She's asking for something. Demanding. She's scaring Evelyn, who clamps both hands over her ears and closes her eyes. Leave me alone, she says. Just go away and leave me alone.*

In the bathroom, she kicked the door shut, glimpsing herself in the full-length sheet mirror glued to its back. A huge, bruised area the color of an overripe strawberry covered the back of her left hip, and another was evolving over her upper arm. By tomorrow, half her body would be plumb-colored and her elbow, mildly swollen now, would probably be the amount of a half watermelon. Her skin was sickly sallow, and fatigue had etched deep circles under her eyes. Her hair was filthy and tangled, four of her nails were broken to the quick, and three were bleeding. Her head, except for her face, wasn't so bad, she thought, examining the small amount of blood oozing from a cut near her temple. Might have been worse. That was always true, of course, until you were dead.

She averted her eyes and stepped into the shower, standing under the hot water for a long time.

Out of the shower, she slipped the biggest T-shirt she could find over her head, careful to avoid using her damaged arm. She stared at herself in the rusty mirror over the dresser, thinking about Eden, about Carolyn and Libby, about all the things she should have said, the lies she'd told. What the fuck was wrong with her? Leaning forward into the mirror, she peered into her own eyes, looking for some clue. *Go away, Carolyn. Go away and leave me alone.*

She gave up, shuffled to the kitchen. She'd left a paper sack of dry groceries and other supplies on the dusty countertop. Pulling out two bottles of liquor, she set them next to the sink. *You know what's wrong with you,* she thought. *At least you know part of what's wrong with you. You just don't want to know.* She picked at the label of one bottle. It was a pretty label, simple, elegant; the lettering printed in script across a cream paper. Seemed such a shame to waste it but fuck it. She picked up the first bottle, unscrewed the top, and poured the contents into the sink. She watched the clear liquid snake its way across the porcelain and into the ancient drain. She opened the second bottle, poured, then caught sight of something in the window above the sink. Her breath caught when, for a second, she didn't recognize her own reflection. She held the bottle up to the glass pane, wiggling her fingers, half expecting the image to be uncooperative. But it was her, the long nose, deep eyes, wisps of hair stuck to the skin of the forehead. She leaned in close, staring at herself and then beyond her own image into the darkness. *Carolyn, fragile in the pale moonlight, runs across the meadow, away from the house, up the path towards the barn, and into the darkness of the fields beyond.*

The low hoot of an owl shook Evelyn's thoughts, and she looked down. The bottle was nearly empty. She righted it, replaced the cap, and held it to the light; a few inches left. She placed it on a top shelf in the cupboard. Just in case, she thought, just in case.

PART TWO: WHERE DEATH REJOICES
Thursday, June 8
Present Day

CHAPTER THIRTY-FIVE

Nick | Eden

The road through the white cypress unfurled into the early morning like a snake. Nick drove on. Scanning radio stations pulling mostly static and gospel. The noise hurt his head. He shut it off, leaned back, exhaled, and began replaying the telephone conversation with Vera in his head. She'd wanted information, of course, and he had little to give her beyond the recovery of his car and the blood. She'd known he was holding back. He glanced in the rearview mirror at the cardboard box he'd pulled from Broussard's trunk and set down in his backseat. *No,* he thought, *he'd been right not to tell her about it. Not yet.*

He said, "Vera, we found his gun close to his car, by the river. I'm so sorry." He paused. When he heard only her breath on the line, he said, "Vera?"

He heard her stuttering inhale. She stifled a sob. "Yes, I'm here... thank you," she said. "Listen to me, Nick, I'm taking the phone into the bedroom; wait for a minute."

"Vera-"

"Shhhh," she interrupted him. "No time. I need to tell you something. Privately." Nick heard a door click shut. He held his breath.

"Look, Nick, I've been a cop's wife for a lot of years. I know what this means." A shuddering he could feel through the phone. "He would never willingly leave his car, let alone his gun. You and I both know that. They'll kill him soon if they haven't already. You know it too. So, there's something you need to know. You just have to listen to me." She was determined. Her voice was so steady, Nick thought she might be giving him a grocery list, but he knew Vera. He'd long understood the depth of her love for Broussard and seen the Chief's devotion to his wife. Nick had shared many meals with those two, spent holidays with them, and even a few vacation weekends. They were that rare couple who'd sustained not only love but deep respect and friendship over the decades. This was so profoundly unfair.

"Yeah, ok, I'm listening."

"This has something to do with that medical examiner. I'm sure of it. Look, I know they weren't fond of each other. I know they argued a lot about cases. Tommy complained about Finney all the time, but this, Nick, you must believe me. This was different."

Nick, along with everyone else in Eden, was uncomfortably aware of the long-standing contentious relationship between the Chief and the Medical Examiner. A few times, things had gone as far as Broussard dragging Finney into court over decisions the doctor had made. Mostly it came to nothing. "Vera, did he say some-"

"Nick," she interrupted. "Tom told me that man is dangerous. I can only tell you what he said to me. He said he was going to 'bring down that sonofabitch Finney.' That's what he said, Nick." She paused before adding, "And he said he had proof."

"Vera, look, we shouldn't talk about this on the phone. I'll come up there later-"

"No. Nick, whatever is going on, you need to know this now. I also know Tommy had an appointment in Baton Rouge with the Medical Examiner over there, someone by the name of Dr. Lee. There's a note about it on his desk. When I asked him if it was about Finney, he wouldn't tell me. You know me, Nick. I don't press. I trusted Tommy. But this time I was scared, worried, so I pushed him a little. I only wish," she said, and then her voice broke. "God, I wish I'd pressed him more."

"Vera, don't, don't do that," Nick said.

He heard her sniff back the tears. "He just told me to stop worrying. And, Nick, you know Tom. He's a realistic man. He's not one to just fly off the handle or get paranoid."

"No, no ma'am, he's not." In fact, Nick thought, Chief Broussard was strong-willed, stubborn, but practical, focused. The sort of man other men and women trusted.

She exhaled softly. "Nick. You will sort this out, won't you?"

"I will, Vera. Can you think of anything else he said?"

"No, but..." Her words faded.

"Yes?"

"It's probably nothing. Just..."

"What is it, Vera?"

"I don't know, Nick. It's just, well, it's funny, but when you've been married a long time, you just know things about the other person. Without them saying anything at all. In all the years I've known Tom, even before he was a cop, I'd never seen him look the way he looked yesterday morning."

"Look, how?" When she didn't answer, he tried again. "Vera, what do you mean, a *look*?"

Finally, she spoke. "Frightened, Nick... he looked scared." She cried, and Nick couldn't think of any words. She asked him to promise he'd find Broussard. He promised, even though he knew better.

•   •   •   •   •

At the station, Nick removed the cardboard file box from his car and carried it inside. Whatever happened to Broussard, whoever was responsible, the perpetrator hadn't had the foresight to search the trunk of his car and they'd left this box. A box Chief Broussard had apparently thought important enough to both collect and then transport in his trunk.

Nick placed the box on a table in one of the interrogation rooms. Why, he wondered, as he pulled out the folders inside and lay them across the surface of the table, did he have the feeling he should keep this to himself until he understood what exactly it was? Something vicious, icy snuck up his spine as the answer came. *Because Chief Broussard had felt the same way.*

The box held thirteen cardboard folders: pale green, faded, each one neatly labeled with a case number, stenciled in black block letters, across its cover. Beneath the number, a clerk had stamped: PROPERTY OF BONFANTE PARISH COURTHOUSE.

These were autopsy records. Broussard had collected thirteen specific and very old autopsy records from the courthouse. Papers stuck from the sides of the tattered cardboard. Some of the edges were folded and dog-eared; covers stained and torn. Nick ran a finger along one of the thinning pages and it occurred to him that soon these records, like the people they described, would deteriorate to dust. To nothing.

Autopsy records, hidden away in Chief Broussard's trunk. Why? And why had he gone to the trouble of retrieving the originals in the first place? He could have had a floater, or even Roy, go down and get copies for him, but he'd gone himself. Made the request himself and carried the originals back to his vehicle himself, without telling a soul.

Lying at the bottom of the box was a piece of lined paper. It looked torn from a cheap spiral notebook; the sort kids take to school. It was a list of names that matched the stack of folders. Beside each name, someone had written a list of dates and facts. Nick thumbed through the records quickly at first, then more slowly, searching for connections, looking for reasons.

Nick checked his watch and rolled his neck around trying to release some of the tension. He pulled out his notebook and pen, laid them on the table, and grabbed the first folder. Opening it, he read. The first page gave general identifying information:

Name Of Deceased: Jane Doe, Aka Crystal Bergeron, Aka Chrissie Spice, Aka Cristal.

Last Known Address: 1310 Marsh Street, Eden, La 70112.
Next Of Kin: Unknown
Date Of Birth: Unknown (Reported December 25, 1953, Presumed False)
Date Of Death: Approximately January 8, 1975
Time Of Death: Not Determined
Description Of Deceased: Caucasian Female Aged 14 To 16 Years.
Place Of Death: Unknown.
Body Found: Highway 119, Bonfante Parish, La
Cause Of Death: Overdose of Chloral Hydrate And Alcohol.
Manner Of Death: Suicide
Autopsy Performed: Albert Finney, Md
Autopsy Ordered: Judge Wesley Fulsome
Officer In Charge: John Picard, Sheriff Bonfante Parish

Jane Doe (aka Crystal Bergeron) had a thick file; it including police reports detailing the discovery of the body and autopsy findings, as well as legal case files and a burial disposition. Piecing it all together, Nick learned the story: Two poachers had found Miss Bergeron (a drifter, a homeless teen) in the early morning hours of January 8th, 1975. She was, according to the reports, partially dressed and at least three miles from any highway. Despite decomposition, one deputy positively identified her at the scene. She'd come into town without means of support other than prostitution. A local charity took her in and she'd run away before authorities could get involved. Someone (although there was no mention of who) had reported her missing a week prior to the discovery of the body. An autopsy report provided by Dr. Finney was less than one page long and included a brief statement about toxicology: positive for chloral hydrate. The name she'd used was an alias. Authorities never located family, the case was closed quickly, and officials sent the corpse for cremation and burial at public expense.

Nick moved on to the next report and the next and the next until he'd read every file. When he was done, the information he'd collected nearly filled his notebook with choppy, half-printed handwriting.

Of the thirteen files, nine made sense (at least to the degree any childhood death ever made sense): three were teenage girls killed in a drunken car crash in 1980; two were children under the age of three who contracted childhood diseases; there was a young woman born with cystic fibrosis who died at twenty; an eleven-year-old girl who fell into a ditch while riding her bike and died of a cerebral hemorrhage; a sixteen-year-old who committed suicide by hanging; and a girl, age twenty, born with mental disabilities, who wandered into the forest and died of exposure. Then there were the others. Those four made no sense at all. Nick read through their files until his head ached from the pressure of facts on the inside of his brain. Four girls; all teenagers, all drifters and all dead of the same thing. The same *rare* thing. The same thing that Albert Finney was claiming killed Carolyn Yates: *Suicide, an intentional, self-inflicted overdose of chloral hydrate.* Nick checked the other signatures on the four records. Curiously, Judge Wesley Fulsome ordered, Dr. Albert Finney performed, and Sheriff John Picard approved all four autopsies. Nick lined up the records and flipped the pages again, comparing them one to another. There were far too many similarities to ignore.

Judge Wesley Fulsome

Dr. Albert Finney

Sheriff John Picard

All dead between 1975 and 1981.

All the bodies found within the Parish, off the main roads. All Alone. No next of kin and no clear date of birth. They were all presumed to be using at least alias first names. They were runaways, drug addicts, prostitutes, and they'd all lived at the same local address just before death. No surprise, really. It was a halfway house or local charity of some sort. He'd check out the address later. He pulled a blank page from his notebook and copied down the basic information on these four.

> *Crystal Bergeron Age 14-16, body found*
>   *01/08/1975.*
> *Debbie Dugas Age 15, body found 02/14/1976.*
> *Tracy Wilkinson Age 17, body found 01/131978*
> *Wanda Rabalais Age 14, body found*
>   *04/22/1981.*

Chief Broussard believed these records were important enough to carry in the trunk of his car and, presumably, to speak to Nick about in person this evening. This had scared him, or at least worried him, according to Vera, and he'd certainly not trusted Finney. Somehow, all of this was related to the Carolyn Yates case. And someone had killed the Chief because of it.

The door clicked open, and Briggs appeared. "Hey Nick, can I interrupt?"

Nick looked up. Considered whether to share all this with Briggs. They'd worked together for three years. They were partners, and Nick had no reason not to trust him. Still, Broussard had trusted no one-at least no one in the department and Nick still didn't know why.

"You, ok?" Briggs looked concerned. Nick decided. Partners. That was that.

"Yeah, yeah, come in. I want to show you this, anyway."

A shadow fell across Brigg's face. "Nick, hey, we found him. I just got the call."

Nick didn't have to ask. He knew at once Broussard was dead.

CHAPTER THIRTY-SIX

Libby | San Francisco

Libby lay in bed watching dust motes dance in the sunlight. One of her own paintings hung on the wall opposite her bed. It wasn't one of her favorites, but now, as she looked at it, she understood why her mother had insisted she bring it over here, to her father's house. It was a large piece, painted on a scrap of plywood she'd found, and Libby did not know the exact dimensions. She guessed it was at least eight feet wide and six feet high. It covered much of the wall. She'd primed the word, then started by watering down an enormous quantity of aqua-colored paint and washing the entire piece in that color to make it look dipped in sea water. Then she'd painted ivory shapes across the surface, reminiscent of seagulls. She'd spattered it heavily with gold metallic automobile paint she'd found in the garage at their apartment complex and then run the whole thing through with slashes of acrylic, in colors of butter, yellow, sunflower, and fluorescent orange. All the hues made her think of sunlight. The effect was a preternaturally spectacular seascape. Libby had been happy the day she painted it, and some of that feeling came back to her every time she looked at it. Even now. Her mother had been right, Libby thought. Hanging the painting here was a good idea. It was the only painting of Libby's in the entire house.

Libby's thoughts drifted to the phone call with her mother. It had been weird. Of course, every call with her mother was weird lately, but this one was different. In the last few years, it seemed like every time she talked to Evelyn, they wound up having a fight, and half the time-more than half the time- her mother had been drinking, which made it worse.

This time, Libby wasn't so sure about the alcohol. Her mother's voice hadn't sounded *normal*, whatever that was. It was oddly delicate, far away. Like she was on the phone from the moon instead of just another state. Libby didn't like it. Evelyn in outer space.

And she'd said, *I love you, sweetheart, I love you so much. I miss you.*

Libby sat up in bed and checked her cell phone. No messages. She switched on her bed lamp and opened the drawer in her nightstand. Two perfectly proportioned joints sat where she'd left them, alongside the purple lighter she'd bought at the Wiz Khalifa concert. It was too easy to hide contraband at her father's house. It wasn't about hiding at all. She could practically wave it under his nose, and he wouldn't notice. Libby suspected over the last twelve months, she'd done everything on the list that should have precipitated parental action; engaged in all the nastiness that, in any normal family, would have qualified her for a trip to one of those kid jails, euphemistically referred to as "wilderness camp." At this moment, she ought to be chasing down her own food, or banging two rocks together to make a fire or whatever. She'd changed her wardrobe; pierced her nose, then her belly button, then her eyelid; dyed her hair; shaved her head; come home drunk; come home high; not come home at all. Finally, she'd started cutting herself. The first few times, she'd used a stretched paperclip and made light scratches across her wrist. Barely visible. But then, the pain inside had escalated, and the scratches did nothing to relieve the pressure. That's when she discovered blades from disposable razors. Then X-Acto knives. She started making slices deeper, longer. The sting took away everything inside. Loneliness, desperation, rage, fear. All of it. Gone. Until it came back. She tried to hide the scars from her parents, from teachers, from other kids. Unlike the piercings and hair dye and drinking, the cutting seemed private. Something worth protecting.

But her mother had noticed. Freaked out too. That was the problem. The inconsistency. Her father noticed nothing. Ever. He was too busy getting high himself, driving his expensive cars, and fucking around with girls not much older than Libby. Evelyn took note, but only sporadically, and when she did, she completely lost her shit.

What else had her mother said? *Don't take chances. Don't go places with people you don't know.* So weird. What was she talking about?

Libby ran a finger over one joint, picked it up and grabbed the lighter and rolled them both around in her palm and studied them. She could get high. Again. She'd feel a little better. For a while. Sleep maybe, for a while. Then she'd wake up, and it would start all over again. Just like every day of the past year. She'd wake up with a knot in her stomach and the feeling that something terrible was about to happen. She wouldn't eat. Then she'd drink and get high, and she'd feel better. For a while. Sleep. Wake up... start over. The same every day.

Only it wasn't the same because it was getting worse.

Whatever was wrong with her was feeling like a cancer in her head. She dropped the joint and lighter onto the duvet, buried her face in her hands, and let the tears come.

CHAPTER THIRTY-SEVEN

Nick | Eden

The corpse lay prone, neck twisted grotesquely to the side, head dipping below the waterline, legs set awkwardly on the shore. They'd found the body just outside town. About twenty yards off the main highway, in a small marsh isolated among the glades. Nick stood over it, feeling oddly numb. How could this *thing* be Chief Broussard? The right eyeball bulged like a poached egg, and what was left of the right cheek dripped gore from a wound the size of a silver dollar. Creatures of the swamp had pecked the face and neck free of flesh, and the remaining blue-white skin was pitted and torn. Another hole of a similar size to the one in the cheek was visible in the back of his skull, and, from his vantage point several yards away, Nick watched as something unidentifiable wriggled free from the space.

This stretch of highway, low and flat, bordered mostly by dense cypress groves and marshland, could hide a corpse for hours, days, or decades. Searchers discovered Broussard's corpse quickly because whoever killed him had not bothered to move him all that far from his car, and the car was in plain sight. Either they'd wanted it found, or the job was not professional. The scene was a tangle of yellow tape, patrol officers, orange cones, highway flares, and various official-looking vehicles.

Nick's feet sank into the gluey mud every few steps as he walked back up the bank, away from the body. He approached Sheriff Savoy, who had just arrived, and stood surveying the scene. She wore dark slacks and black rubber boots, and a yellow jacket with the letters "BPSO" stenciled on the back.

"Detective MacCallum," she said and nodded at him without turning her head.

"Good morning, Sheriff Savoy," he replied.

"How long, Nick? How long's he been here?" Her face was stiff. Unreadable.

"They'll know more later," Nick said. "But so far, it looks like since yesterday. He wasn't killed here. The lividity is wrong, for sure."

Savoy nodded her head in the road's direction. "And there are drag marks all the way back through the grove up that way. Right? Somebody dragged him down there; dead or dying."

"Yeah," said Nick. "Medical examiner will tell us for sure, but probably not conscious, no struggle, we can see. The path down to the waterline is clean, with very few broken branches. A man the Chief's size, if he was awake, he would've done some serious damage."

Savoy let out a quick breath, then pulled sunglasses from her breast pocket. Slipping them on, she peered at Nick over the top of the mirrored lenses and said, "We've got no room for personal here. I want you and Briggs one hundred percent focused on finding the bastard who did this."

"Yes, ma'am, of course," said Nick.

"Nick, he was my friend as well." She shook her head. "Poor Vera, you know." She paused, then said, "Nick, I'd like you to help me keep an eye on Vera. Would you do that for me? She's been told, but... you know. You can imagine how it is right now."

Nick nodded his agreement. "Yes, ma'am, absolutely." He thought for a moment and said, "Sheriff, Vera thinks this might have something to do with Finney. With the conflict they were having over the autopsy on the Yates girl, maybe?"

Savoy shook her head. "Oh, you know Nick. Those two argued all the time. They despised each other. I don't think they saw eye-to-eye even half the time. No, I doubt this was any different, but." She paused. Shrugged. "Talk to Finney. Look into it. We'll see."

Talk to Finney, she'd said. *Look into it.* Nick sat in his car, reviewing the notes he'd made earlier. He flipped back and forth through the pages. Names, dates flashed in front of him, ages. So young. Every one of them young. Broussard had known something. What had Vera said? *Tom told me that man is dangerous.* He'd known something, and whatever he'd known had gotten him killed. Nick turned back to the first page of his notes, carefully reading each line. Circling the most relevant information: Names, dates of death, last known addresses. Marsh Street. 1310 Marsh Street. He was circling *Marsh* for the third time when it hit him: 1310 Marsh. *He knew that address.* Not that address exactly. 1310 Marsh, he was pretty sure, was a vacant lot. But the one across the street. All those girls had stayed for a time at 1310 Marsh, and across the street, 1311 Marsh, lived someone Nick suspected was old enough, and interested enough, to remember.

CHAPTER THIRTY-EIGHT

Libby | San Francisco

Bruises. The first thing Libby noticed when Evelyn clicked open the FaceTime message was the deep purple mottling in the skin along her mother's lower lip and chin. The iPhone camera angle exaggerated the marks but still, Libby thought, who gets bruises like that? Libby had given in to her impulse and called her mother. She'd run out of things to do by 10 am and been unable to distract her mind from thoughts of Evelyn and Carolyn. This, she supposed, was why suspension was a punishment; time alone with your thoughts was hell.

Stuart left the house early *for an appointment*, he'd said. Whatever that meant. He hadn't returned, although he texted twice; once to remind Libby there was food in the fridge, and she had her credit card, once to apologize for not being home. She'd never really been a fan of television, and most of her video games and all her art supplies were at the other house. Her father didn't like what he called the *mess of painting,* so he didn't allow it at his place. That was one thing for which her mother deserved credit. Evelyn had set aside an entire corner of their living room for Libby's art, the spot with the best light. They'd covered the floor with tarps; set up an easel. Libby had spent a hundred hours there, producing canvases covered in acrylic paint. Libby was reluctant to call what she produced "art," although Evelyn loved them. Hung them everywhere in the apartment, over eight feet square. Libby rolled and dripped and brushed paint on thick in abstract forms, using unexpected color combinations like violet and gold and ivory with slashes of turquoise or charcoal. In recent months, she'd lost some of her enthusiasm for painting. She told herself it was because of Conner. The time he required. But mostly, it was because she was so tired all the time. The effort of painting, like everything else, seemed oddly pointless.

Evelyn answered the FaceTime call, looking sleepy as well as beaten. Libby could see the iron headboard and knew she was in bed. "Oh my God, Mom, what happened?" Libby blurted as the screen opened. She watched as Evelyn's eyes widened and her hand floated up to her face as if she were just discovering the injury. "What the fuck, Mom?" Libby added, feeling simultaneously angry and terrified.

Evelyn let out her breath and looked away from the camera. "Oh... nothing... It's fine."

"It's not nothing. What happened?" No way was she going to let her mother get away with another lie. Not about this.

Evelyn turned, looked straight at the camera, and sucked in her breath. "I got hit."

"No shit," said Libby, resisting the impulse to slam her computer shut. "By who? Why?" She wondered for a second if *why* was a fair question. Probably not. Who deserved to get slugged in the face? Still, somehow, Evelyn could easily have provoked this.

"It's... complicated," said Evelyn, sounding weary.

"Yeah?"

Evelyn bit her lip and looked into the camera as if trying to decide. Then she said, "Someone, I don't know who, came into the house and attacked me. Threatened me."

Libby's breath caught, her pulse rabbiting. Jesus fucking Christ. "Oh my God, Mom. Go. Get out of there." Libby gripped the laptop as if she were gripping Evelyn and could somehow shake her. Fear was now superseding anger.

"I know, I know, sweetie. I will. Soon but, I can't leave. Not yet."

"The police? Did you call the police? I mean... oh my God... you can't just... who? Who did this?"

"Yes, the police are aware. And I don't know. Like I said. A man. Libby, please, don't worry. I'm being watched now. The police here won't let anything else happen to me. Besides, I'm fine. This," she lifted her hand again to her face. "This looks much worse than it is."

"Are you... do you have other injuries?" Libby wasn't sure she wanted to know.

"No, I'm totally fine. I think the guy just wanted to scare me. You know, encourage me to... I don't know."

"Encourage what?"

"He wanted me to leave things alone. That's what he said."

"Then do that, Mom. Leave. Come home." Libby hated the desperation in her voice.

"Look, Lib, they're trying to say the body they found is my sister. And they're... saying things... drawing conclusions I know are not true. I have to stay and see this through." Evelyn was leaning toward the camera now, and Libby could see tears in her eyes. "There's something going on... something that I have to sort out."

"What does that mean? Something going on. That sounds sort of... crazy, Mom." She was careful not to use the word *paranoid*. "I mean, why? Why do you think that?"

"I can't explain it right now. I just have a feeling. I have these memories coming back, and what officials here are saying makes little sense, or at least what the coroner is saying. I think... I think people are lying to me, lying to each other. Covering something up, maybe."

"Why? Why would that be happening?" Libby asked, hoping Evelyn would backtrack. *Of course, that's not happening,* she would say. *That would be silly. That would be... crazy.*

Instead, Evelyn said, "I don't know, honey. I don't know why that would be happening. But I need to find out."

Libby just nodded in silence. Stuart was always saying that Evelyn was *nuts*, that the lies she told were part of her insanity and her drunkenness. What if her mother was truly mentally ill? Like actually diagnosable? Something cold crawled down her spine and she shuddered involuntarily.

When they clicked off, Libby buried her face in the cushions, grateful she was home alone. Gam and Stuart would have made things worse. *She's just so unstable,* Gam would say. *She's loony,* Stuart would add. *She won't take the medicines she's been prescribed. Prefers to drink instead.* What if it was true? What if her mother was delusional or whatever they called it?

Those bruises on her face were real.

Libby felt like her brain was on fire. No good answer. Either Evelyn was crazy or, and this was worse, she was right. She had to do something. Deciding, she went downstairs to the kitchen to find Jacinta.

·   ·   ·   ·   ·

An hour later, Libby back at the Sunset apartment she shared with Evelyn. She felt a little guilty for lying to Jacinta. *I forgot my history book, she'd said. It's critical. I have to get it, or I won't have my homework for tomorrow. Please, Jacinta. Please.* The poor housekeeper had resisted as long as she could. Libby nagged and begged until Juacinta had no choice but to defy the direct orders given by both Gam and Stuart to make sure Libby "stayed put." When they pulled up to the front of the apartment complex, Jacinta told her she could have ten minutes to run inside, grab what she needed, and come back out to the curb. She'd had to double park. Evelyn's car was in the one space allotted to their apartment. Jacinta sat in the car, the engine running while Libby raced up the stairs. Inside the apartment, she went to her mother's room. Darkness. Musty air. The usual clutter. Clothes on the floor, bed unmade. Wineglass next to the bed. Empty, of course. Evelyn *always* finished her wine.

She checked the small writing desk and emptied shoeboxes and searched between hanging clothes in the closet. Reached up high and pulled down boxes of scarves and gloves. She checked her watch. Eight minutes gone. She stood in the center of the room, spinning slowly. Looking. *Where? Where was it?* She heard Jacinta honk the horn. Fuck, she was out of time. Then her eyes fell again on the unmade bed.

Dropping to her knees, Libby pulled up the dust ruffle and peered under the bed. Nothing. She yanked the duvet to the floor, ran her hands over the bare sheets, down behind the headboard, between the mattress and box spring on one side and then around the underside of the bed to the other side. *Then she felt something.* It was stiff, like starched cloth, and she grabbed at it, pulling it free. She rolled back on her heels, nearly losing her balance, heart-pounding and breath coming fast and light.

A book. A diary. Bound in plain yellow cloth, it looked old. Bleached and dog-eared with age. She turned back to the front cover and read the inscription. Written in tall, elegant black script, lovely, curved tails under the *y*'s, a woman's handwriting on the foxed page.

> *April 10, 1986*
> *My Dearest Evelyn.*
> *Happiest of Birthdays, my darling. May you*
> *never stop writing your dreams.*
> *Love Mama*

This was it. Libby sensed it in her bones. The link. The connection Evelyn had been hiding all these years.

CHAPTER THIRTY-NINE

Evelyn | Eden

By the time Evelyn arrived at Marnie's Diner, the morning had already soured in the heat. The diner, however, was fresh and quiet, save for the whir of air conditioning and the crank of overhead fans. Evelyn pulled a pair of oversized, dark sunglasses from her purse and slid them onto her face as she entered. She was in no mood for small talk and loathe to be recognized.

She sat in a booth. In the back. Looked around before pulling off the glasses and setting them down on the table. An old man arrived carrying a mug filled with chicory coffee and set it down. Evelyn smiled up at him warmly. He smiled back, a gap where his right incisor should have been. She picked up the coffee cup with both hands and stared out the window at the street beyond. The soft, cool sounds of the diner folded around her and she tried to clear her mind.

She waited silently while the old waiter laid out the heavy China plates piled high with buttery white toast, fried eggs, grits, and gravy. *Jesus, when was the last time she ate grits and gravy?* Last, he pulled a tub of honey from his pocket and set it on the table as well. He smiled and nodded again at Evelyn, then shuffled away.

She sat for a long time, sipping coffee and poking the tines of her fork into the eggs, watching the soft yellow yolk run out of the center, spread in golden stripes over the white plate. *"Eggs,"* she's saying to her father. *"That's all we have in here, Daddy.*

Eggs." *Nobody makes groceries anymore, so they have to rely on Mrs. Coolidge to bring food.*

"Alright then," *he says back.* "Let's have eggs." *She cooks, frying the eggs because that's the only way she knows to cook them, and sets two plates on the table. As he eats, she watches him, noting the whites of his eyes look slightly yellowed. She wonders if it's the yellow yoke bringing out that color.*

"Daddy," *she says.* "Are you feeling ok?"

"Yeah, yeah, I'm ok," *he says, taking a long time to chop the egg into a mash.* "Why do you ask Lynnie?"

She shifts her gaze back down to her own plate and puts a forkful of fried egg into her mouth to buy time. She swallows and looks up at him. "I dunno, Daddy, you look just... tired, I guess." *She isn't sure why she doesn't mention the yellow color in his eyes, which is definitely not normal.*

"You don't need to worry," *he says, which makes her more worried.* "I'm ok." *He barely eats anything. Less than Evelyn, and she's only an eleven-year-old girl. He thanks her for dinner but says he can't eat another bite. Then he gets up and puts his plate in the sink, placing it carefully to one side of a long crack running laterally through the stained ceramic surface. He shuffles back out to his chair in the living room.*

She follows him, stands in front of the chair, staring at him.

"What is it, girl?" *he says, his voice sounding weary, cracked like old paper.*

"You ain't ok, Daddy. I can tell." *She waits for a second, and when he doesn't reply, she adds,* "Are you gonna die? Like Mama. Are you gonna leave? Like Carolyn? What's gonna happen to me if you die?"

He looks at her, then reaches out a bony hand and pulls her to him. This isn't like him, and it scares her more than anything else. He says, "Don't worry, Lynnie baby. I'm not going anywhere. I ain't gonna die. What happened to Mama? That was wrong, but it ain't gonna happen to me."

He doesn't mention Carolyn. He almost never does. Evelyn is only eleven years old, but that's old enough to notice what he doesn't say.

Evelyn paid the check and pushed open the glass door, exiting the restaurant. There were very few people about, and the street seemed both heavy and eerily empty. Like a ghost town. She thought about that. Ghosts. Wondered for a second if it had been the yellowing that had destroyed her father. Turned him to a dead-man-walking. It had started in his eyes and spread to the skin on his face and, later, his calloused hands and then even his feet. Had it been the poison in his blood, or had it been the other thing? The secret she knew he kept. *What was it, Daddy? What did you keep inside you all that time? What terrible thing did you know?*

•   •   •   •   •

Despite her promise to herself, Evelyn had downed a considerable amount of vodka by the time Sheriff Savoy called. She was on the front porch, or what weather and time had left of the porch, sitting in one of the ancient, low-slung, cedar deck chairs her father built so many years ago.

In the deep shade off Road 12, the morning had gone a brilliant green, sparkling, citrus-smelling, cool from all the rain. Two huge willows flanked the broken steps leading down to the driveway. Evelyn studied them, trying to remember how big they'd been the last time she saw them. The branches, black with moisture and a silvery Spanish moss hanging nearly to the ground, gave the trees a preternatural beauty. Evelyn recalled they had built the house around the trees rather than the other way around. They were that old. Older.

Beyond the willows, a grove of palmetto plants stood, thick and lush, their long-pointed leaves looking dangerous and vaguely prehistoric. As she watched, a tiny lime-colored lizard poked his head out of the shrubs, stood frozen for a moment, pink tongue lashing in and out, then turned with a jerk and disappeared into the weeds.

She remembered Mama was always trying to get light into the house, so thickly shrouded by plants and trees it remained shaded, dim most of the day. Mama hated it, but Daddy always said it was the only reasonable way to keep a house cool. *Running fans cost money,* he said a million times. Air conditioning was, of course, out of the question.

God, it got hot. Even with the shade. Even at night. In their tiny, cramped bedroom. She and Carolyn, kicking away the sheets, wet with sweat, and taking turns to fan each other. One lying flat out on the bare mattress, arms spread wide, and the other crouched above, waving back and forth, a piece of cardboard snatched from behind the Piggly Wiggly. There were times, in August, when sleep was impossible, and they'd stay up all night, just fanning and sweating and whispering to each other. The memory surprised her. Made her smile.

•   •   •   •   •

The call was unexpected but a relief. Alice Savoy was easy to talk to: her voice warm and open. She'd been a Sheriff's deputy when Evelyn was a kid, promoted to Sheriff by the time Evelyn was in high school, and Evelyn remembered her. She'd been kind, but not condescending, like some of the other adults in town. Once a year, Savoy gave the *drug talk* to the kids at the high school. The one where everybody went to the auditorium and nodded obediently as Sheriff told them to *Just Say No*, and then snuck out behind the Circle K to smoke weed and talk about how stupid cops were. But Evelyn liked her. She was smart, straightforward, and honest. A few times, it had been Savoy and one of her deputies, dragging John back home after a bender. She said nothing harsh. No judgment. She'd just tell Mrs. Coolidge to let him sleep it off, and it would be best if Mrs. Coolidge kept Evelyn at her house for the night.

Maybe it was the familiar voice, maybe the booze. Either way, within a few minutes, Evelyn told Sheriff Savoy about the assault, leaving out just a few details; Savoy didn't need to know how much she'd had to drink. Evelyn agreed to come in and make a statement. She'd refused medical attention with a lie but wondered now how it would look when she showed up at the station in her current state of disrepair.

"Are you injured?"

Yes. "No, I'm fine."

"Don't you think you should see a doctor, just in case?" asked Savoy. Her voice kind.

Of course, I should see a doctor. I'm a fucking mess. "No, I'm totally fine."

Clicking the phone off, Evelyn set it on her lap and leaned back in the chair, tilted her face upwards. Directly overhead, the sun slid out from beneath a whip-creamed cloud and, just for a moment, beat down, turning the back of her eyelids a bright orange, warming her skin. Beads of sweat collected at her temples. Hairline. For the first time, instead of cursing it, she was enjoying the moist Louisiana heat. All around the sounds of life. Chirping frogs, mosquito buzzing, and water bubbling at the creek down behind the house. Every now and again, from a long way off, she could hear the soft strum of a zydeco steel guitar. Someone else sitting on a porch. She sipped and listened. Her breathing slowed, and she welcomed the sense of well-being that accompanied the alcohol.

She thought about calling Libby and resisted the impulse. She'd know. About the drinking. Better to call her when sober. Whenever that was. She imagined Libby's face. Touching her. The feel of her heartbeat, her breath. The wild-animal strength of it inside that small body. Libby was a true thing, like the willows; Libby was real. Evelyn's one true thing.

She downed the last inch of liquid in the glass and pushed herself to a standing position. Wobbled a bit. Not drunk. Just tired, she thought. She pulled the huge chair back into its place on the porch and carried the glass inside.

She checked the bedside clock. An hour before, she'd agreed to be at the station and give her statement. An hour to get her head clear. She lay down on the bed, turning her head so that her cheek brushed the cool, cotton pillowcase-the one she'd brought from home-and, within seconds, fell deep into unconsciousness.

CHAPTER FORTY

Libby | San Francisco

Libby's hand trembled as she pulled the diary from her bag. She read the inscription again: *Happiest of Birthdays, my darling...* Laying a finger on each word, one at a time, as if she might feel the pulse of the writer. Beyond the ink, beyond the pen from which the ink flowed, up into the fingertips and the hand, straight to the heart of her grandmother. Then she turned to the first page. Puffy, girlish print sprinkled with childish misspellings.

> *April 10, 1986*
> *It's my birthday today. I am ten. Saturday, no school! I got this diary for my birthday from Mama. I already opened my other presents too. From Daddy, I got a leather belt decorated with flowers and swirls. He made it with a special hammer he has out in the shed. Mama gave me this book, like I said, and also sewed me a mini skirt out of blue denim I've been asking for. Daddy says it's too short, and Mama tells him to hush since I'm only ten. But I think ten is getting close to grown-up. Carolyn gave me one of her favorite stuffed animals-a pink puppy dog- as a present. She says she's too old for toys, anyway. Carolyn is fourteen already and thinks she's too old for everything fun.*

Mama is cooking spaghetti-my favorite-and we will have vanilla cake too. Mrs. Coolidge from next door is coming for dinner. Carolyn and I have a plan-don't tell anyone-we will stay up all night and watch the sunrise from Back Field.

Happy Birthday to me!

Lynnie-

Libby tried to imagine her mother as this cheerful, charming, ten-year-old girl. This Lynnie. A girl whose mother did not die when she was a baby. Whose father wasn't an abusive alcoholic and a girl who was not an only child? This child, this diary version of Evelyn, was an illustration in a fairy tale. Water-colored shades of rose pink and lavender, and periwinkle. Full of optimism. Magic. The grown-up Evelyn-at least the Evelyn of recent years seemed rinsed in gray paint.

Libby turned to the next entry. And then the next and the next. More light, childish chatter:

April 12-When I grow up, I will never do math ever again. Mrs. Carson is the meanest teacher in the whole world, and she has giant ears like a donkey.

May 2-The asters are blooming, and today I made a chane as long as me.

May 9-Carla Purcell got a new puppy, and his name is Dixon, and he bites.

May 11-Today, Carolyn got into a fite at school and got suspended, and now Daddy is so mad he won't even talk to her. Carolyn says she

doesn't care and Joey Gernhauser dezerved to get
punched, which I think he probably did.

She'd decorated a few pages with curlicues and doodled flowers. The sort of thing little girls like to draw when they are thinking deep little girl thoughts.

Libby turned pages, mesmerized, searching for a clue. When had Evelyn gone from a chatty, happy child, whose biggest problem was a teenage sister who was, occasionally, a pain in the ass, to a grown woman who had made an entire life of lies and secrets and drink?

The more she read, the less it made sense.

CHAPTER FORTY-ONE

Nick | Eden

Mary Sonnier, proprietor of the Eden Motel, perched on a stool behind the registration desk, skinny elbows propped up on its Formica surface. A heavy amber ashtray sat next to her, overflowing with the butts of her menthol cigarettes. The place reeked of stale tobacco and rose-scented air freshener.

She was leaning forward, muttering to herself, and appeared to be writing figures into her ledger book. The neckline of her worn, cotton housedress slung so deep, it invited a clear view of her breasts resting on the counter. Two small pools of wrinkled flesh, like desiccated twin pork chops. She looked up as Nick entered, grinning to display two rows of false teeth so white they were almost blue. She looked, Nick thought, like a thousand-year-old Cheshire Cat. He could imagine a million places he'd rather be, but he reminded himself, right across the street, in Mrs. Sonnier's direct line-of-sight, was the vacant lot at 1310 Marsh, and Mrs. Sonnier, well known for self-righteous nosiness, knew something about everything that had ever happened on that piece of property. So, right here was where he needed to be.

"Morning, ma'am." He tipped his hat.

"Well, hey Nick," she said, still smiling. Her teeth slipped and made a clicking sound, and she slurped and pushed at them with her fingers. "I ain't seen you round in a while."

"I heard about the body y'all found, Nick. Shame about that girl." She made a clucking sound. "You know what I say, though?"

"How's that?"

"Well," she said, scratching her head and sniffing. "A whore's a whore, right Nick? Girl gets what's coming." He said nothing. She continued. "Not saying anything about that girl in particular or nothin', but you know what I mean." Raising her eyebrows, she rolled her eyes. "Ah, Nick, don't listen to me." She closed the ledger book, slid it into a drawer under the counter. Then folded her arms across her withered chest and stared at him. "What do I know, anyway?" Her smile was defiant. "Anyway, how can I help you?"

"Ma'am? Do you know something you need to tell me?"

"Oh, shoot. I don't know nothin'. You know how it is around here. People are talking and saying that it's the Yates girl, right? I mean, especially now that the other one is back. You can tell me, Nick. Is it? Is it that Yates girl?"

He ignored her question. Asking instead, "Ma'am, did you know the Yates family? I mean back then?"

"Well now, Nick, I been here 'bout as long as the hills, so I guess you could say I knew everybody, but my people had nothin' to do with them, people. That woman, Gwen, was her name; she was crazy, some folks said. I don't like to speak ill of the dead, you know, but she was *from away*." Mrs. Sonnier said *from away,* as if it explained everything that had ever happened to the Yates family. "Anyway, she kilt herself, so that's that. Such a shame. That family had troubles. That's all I'll say."

Nick was quite certain Mrs. Sonnier would say plenty more, and sure enough, after a brief pause, she went on. "You know, I always told my boy to stay away from them people." Mrs. Sonnier's *boy* was Tom Sonnier, Jr., and he was a middle-aged man now, but Mrs. Sonnier always referred to him as Junior or her *boy.* "That was before all the mess with the mama and the girl, too. I just never felt right about them people."

By *them people,* Nick suspected Mrs. Sonnier was referring to poor people. That the Yates family was both poor and afflicted (mental illness, suicide, and teenage behavior problems) only made ostracism worse. The Sonnier family, although uneducated and decidedly lacking in all characteristics genteel, was well-off by Eden standards. The late Tom Sonnier, the elder, had amassed a small-scale fortune beginning with one used-car lot and a sleazy motel left to him by his father. By the time he died, the senior Sonnier had owned two more sleazy motels and multiple check-cashing joints scattered around the parish. There were rumors the family was involved in other, even less savory, and less legal businesses, but rumors, Nick reminded himself, were not facts. Several of Tom Sonnier's brothers managed various business interests, but the consensus in Eden was that Mary was really in charge. Junior, with his large, soft face, slightly high-pitched voice, and awkward loping gait, had certain *limitations* and spent his time *supervising,* according to Mrs. Sonnier.

Besides being rich by Bonfante Parish standards, the Sonniers were also connected. They'd been around so long and knew so much about so many that people were reluctant to counter them for fear of social, political, and economic ruination. Even in the mid-1980s, rejection by the Sonniers would have had significant implications for the Yates family. Nick took a step forward and rested a hand on the countertop. "Mrs. Sonnier, do you recall a building that was across the street there?" He motioned toward the front door. "It would have been some kind of charity maybe, or halfway house?"

She wrinkled her already wrinkled brow. "Well yeah, back in 70s I think-now that's almost before my time." She winked at this. "A church, I think it was over there. Some kind of *Methodists,* maybe?" For years Methodists were little better than Satanists in Eden, and she said the word as if it left a foul taste in her mouth.

"Do you recall them putting kids up for the night? Or a few nights? You know kids on the road, coming in off the highway, that sort of thing."

"Well, now I don't know about that. We didn't have much to do with those folks. Them being, well... Methodist and all. I recall a few young people coming and going, but I can't say for sure."

As sharp as she was now, Nick knew Mrs. Sonnier would have been a ferocious neighborhood spy forty years ago. No way would she have ignored the comings and goings at the church, Methodist or otherwise. She was lying. Or at least withholding. He was sure of it. He pressed her, and her answers became increasingly vague. Finally, he gave up. Thanked her and asked her to call him if she thought of anything else that might be helpful.

"Sure, you come back and visit me again soon, Nick," she said, leaning forward so that the neckline of her housedress opened further, revealing an expanse of skin so decayed Nick imagined it coming away from the bone. He looked away, tipped his hat, and backed towards the door, exiting before she could extend the visit.

CHAPTER FORTY-TWO

Evelyn | Eden

The interview room was small, like a jail cell, and Evelyn had been there thirty minutes before it occurred to her she could leave. Thankfully, she'd popped four Xanax on her way over, and she found the enclosed space wasn't bothering her much. She sat in a hard metal chair jammed up against one wall with a table before her. Steel bolts ran through the chair's feet into the concrete floor. Evelyn supposed those bolts would be unfortunate should she wish to pick up the chair and bash in the skull of a security guard or unfortunate bystander during her jail break. She checked around for another weapon.

She shifted her gaze from one spot to the next in no particular order. Stared at the gray walls, then the concrete floor, and then the ceiling tiles-there were twenty-four or twenty-seven. She'd lost count. The room smelled of cleaning products and body odor. Just faintly of mold. She checked her watch but did not note the time. Continued waiting.

Sometime later, she might have been asleep, a silver-haired man who could have been forty or fifty-hard to tell with the military short haircut and ruddy complexion pushed open the door with more force than necessary, causing her to startle uncomfortably and resent him instantly. He had a small mouth, sharp blue eyes, and a long serious face that made him look as if he ought to be very intelligent or very cruel. He carried a thin, manila folder, which he dropped on the table between them before taking a seat. She studied his hands, noticing the ring he wore: a chunky piece of gold, not a wedding ring. She was aware of her body leaning into his personal space. The pills had blunted her inhibitions, and she started to ask why Detective MacCallum wasn't interviewing her but stopped herself. Too personal.

"Hello, Ms. Yates," he said, sticking out his hand. She stared at his hands and thought his fingers were very wide and paddle-shaped. "I'm Detective Martin Lambert. I'll be taking your statement." It made no difference who took her statement, she thought. *Trust no-one.* Besides, she'd already forgotten his name.

She repeated what she'd told Sheriff Savoy, silently thanking alprazolam for helping her keep emotional distance-*chemical padding*-from the words. They came out sounding as if she were reading from a newspaper. An old newspaper. Goddamn microfiche. He took notes, recorded everything. Asked her more than once if she'd recognized the man who attacked her. Anything? Clothing? Smell? No, she said she didn't know him. Never met him and nothing about him was familiar. *Nothing. Nothing. Nothing.*

He was leaning forward now. Asking her again if she had recognized the man. Maybe he'd followed her home or something? Maybe she'd met him somewhere before? She was shaking her head. No, no. Nothing. But then... something. Not a memory. More like an impression, a shadow.

Dark eyes, hard, lifeless, like flint. In her face, in the night, and the stink of smoked cigarettes and sour breath. She shivered. Fuck she should have taken more Xanax. Had another drink. She thought about the flask in her purse.

"Ms. Yates?" Lambert was staring at her. Waiting. "Are you alright?"

No. "Yes, yeah. I'm sorry, I just... just..." She let the thought trail off.

"You just?"

She pressed her eyes shut, opened them. "For a second, something about him seemed... I don't know. Familiar, maybe?"

"You know him?"

Maybe. "No, I don't think so." Letting out her breath, she repeated, "No." Whatever the memory had been, it had passed now. Floating over her mind and dissipating like a fine mist, almost before she sensed it. "I have to go," she said and stood.

"Just a couple more questions, Ms. Yates. Please," he said and gestured toward her chair. Reluctantly, she sat back down. The medication was wearing off. She could feel the swell of its effects ebbing now and all the sharp edges of her thoughts poking through. She tossed about in her mind for an excuse.

"It's fine. But I have another appointment, so..." she checked her watch. "I have to go... soon."

•   •   •   •   •

It seemed like a long time, but she did not know. Might have been ten minutes. Ten hours. By the time he switched off the recorder and pushed the paperwork towards her for signature, Evelyn's heart was thudding in her throat, and the enclosed space seemed much less benign. She snatched the pen, scrawled her signature, and pushed the door open without shaking his outstretched hand.

She spotted the fire exit just ahead and, ignoring the alarm warning sign, pushed the door open. Sunlight flashed so brightly it blinded her and she stood, one hand cupped over her eyes, waiting for her vision to adjust. Silence. So much for the alarm. Leaning against the closed door, she slid the flask from her purse. The relief was immediate.

The glare diminishing, she noted the space was oddly peaceful for the middle of the day. Too quiet. *Shouldn't there be vehicles pulling in and out? Sirens or at least radios going?* She turned back to the door she'd just exited. Twisted at the steel doorknob a few times. Locked. *Of course, they kept it locked.*

She screwed the top on the flask-now empty-and dropped it into her bag, then rummaged in her purse for her car keys. The air was hot, sticky already. Still feeling around the bottom of her bag, she wiped at her brow with the back of her free hand and scanned the parking lot. *Not a car. Not one.* No people either, and the outer gates to the lot appeared closed. *Goddamn,* she thought, *was it possible to be trapped out here?* She pulled out her phone. Battery dead. No way. It was working an hour ago.

Working an hour ago. Gates locked. Nobody here. Trapped... Nobody here...

"Fuck, fuck," she said. Pills and booze catching up with her; she was woozy, and tried a deep breath to clear her head.

Then it came. The rustle and click of a boot heel and toe-tap on the pavement behind her. She turned to look, glimpsing... someone... something. A shadow, maybe? Before she could process what was happening, an unseen force shoved her forward, then downward, and the pavement barreled up towards her as she stretched her arms out into nothing, her hands grasping helplessly at nothing but empty space.

CHAPTER FORTY-THREE

Libby| San Francisco

Nine words. At first, she missed them. Then, peeling back the diary pages, one at a time, even the blank ones, Libby found the entry toward the back. It was penciled in small print across the middle of one otherwise blank sheet. Just nine words. Libby ran a finger across the letters. Dated but not signed. No salutation either. No sweet doodles. Nothing to embellish the stark print.

> *August 11, 1986*
> *I did something bad, and now Carolyn is gone.*

Libby closed the book and sat back. *I did something bad. Something bad.*

Hadn't Evelyn said they'd sent Carolyn "away." She was "sick." Yes, that's what she said. In 1986, right after their mother's suicide, Carolyn had gone to a psychiatric hospital for troubled adolescents and died there. Died years later of something; what was it? An infection. A brain infection. That's what Evelyn had said. No mention of *Evelyn's doing anything bad.* No mention of anything at all involving Evelyn. But here it was in black and white. In Evelyn's own ten-year-old hand. *I did something bad, and now Carolyn is gone.* She was admitting culpability, or at least responsibility for something. This made no sense. Unless, of course, her mother's story about the social workers, about Carolyn being sent to the hospital, contracting an infection, was just more lies. Libby supposed, that was the simplest explanation. Yes, Libby thought, feeling sick with the realization this made sense. Lies. It was all lies. The body they'd found really was Carolyn's. It had always been there from the beginning. She'd never gone away. Never left Eden. Everything Evelyn said about the hospital was a fabrication. She was not crazy, just a pathological liar. What was it Libby's psychology teacher had written on the board at school? *The best predictor of future behavior is past behavior.*

She read the words again, willing them to say something different. But there they were. Exactly the same: *I did something bad, and now Carolyn is gone.*

Oh, God. What did you do, Mom? What the fuck did you do?

In the bathroom, Libby sat atop the toilet seat and pondered the razor in her right hand. It was a new blade. Extra sharp, and it glinted in the ray of sunshine streaming through the narrow window above the shower. She twisted the blade around between two fingers. Then she grasped it and drew a long line across the inside of her left arm just below the elbow. A stripe of bright red blood appeared and, with it, the sharp, sweet sensation that wasn't really pain. It was relief.

CHAPTER FORTY-FOUR

Evelyn | Eden

Evelyn lay face down on the asphalt, sucking air through her one available nostril, the smell of hot tar and car oil flooding her senses. A procession of ants crossed the pavement just beyond the spot where her left cheek pressed into the pavement. She heard a single sound. A car horn miles away. The pounding of her heart worsened the pain in her ribs, and she was too terrified to move. What if whoever pushed her was still nearby? Watching. Waiting. Her eyes fell suddenly on her purse, which had opened as it hit the ground, spilling its contents in a wide arc to her right.

Her keys were right there.

Without thinking, she grabbed them, rolled onto her back, and sat up, keys clawed in She screamed. Feeling more rage than fear. *Fuck, fuck, fuck.* She lashed her head back and forth, looking around. For someone. Anyone. *Breathe... breathe... where is he? Where the hell did he go?*

But he was gone. *Into thin air,* she thought. Was that possible? Rising to her knees, she squinted into the sun. Checked the perimeter again. There was nothing. Just air and sunshine and parking lot. Empty stillness and silence that, beneath the roar of her own breath, was absolute.

●   ●   ●   ●   ●

A few more bruises, scrapes, a little more emotional trauma, but otherwise, she told everyone; she was okay. *Whatever that meant,* she thought.

The man, whoever he was, disappeared. Despite the search, nobody could find anything. *Did she get a look at him?* They had asked. *Any look at all? Was she sure? Really sure?* They asked her about this at least three times. *Trust no one.* The words kept flashing across her brain, unbidden but as bright as a neon sign. *Trust no one.*

•   •   •   •   •

It was Nick who showed her the tape. "I need you to look at something," he said. His face grave. Concerned. Like a doctor delivering bad news.

He had her take a seat at his desk, stood next to her, and played the surveillance tape from the parking lot. She made him play it twice all the way through and then once more, stopping at various points. When finally, she sat back in the steel chair, her mind had gone hazy. Vague. The way it feels to wake up too early in the morning. She couldn't quite put the pieces together.

"It's there, Evelyn. I mean," he looked at her apologetically, leaning back against the desk, hands jammed into his pockets. "It's not there, I guess."

"I don't get it," she said, staring at the computer screen. "It's not possible. Not fucking possible. Someone was out there. I... saw him." *But had she?* "He pushed me. I'm telling you; I was pushed." *Wasn't she pushed? Yes, she'd heard him. Seen him. Hadn't she?* She tried to remember. What did she recall exactly?

"Evelyn, it's on the tape." He spoke softly. "There's no one there. You just stumbled. That's all."

There's no one there.

She sat, not breathing, in his desk chair, staring at the frozen screen. Nothing but a black-and-white image; her own body sprawled, prone across the asphalt, one arm reaching out toward her key ring. Alone. Completely alone. "Play it again," she said.

"Evelyn, you've seen it three times."

"I don't care… please." She looked at him. "Please, just play it again."

It was no different. There she was appearing from the fire exit door… leaving the building… pulling the flask from her bag… leaning against the wall… a few shaky steps before… it happens. No attacker. No mystery, man. Just a pathetic drunk stumble, followed by a terrifically ungraceful fall to the pavement.

"Jesus Christ," she blurted.

What was going on? Is this what it felt like to go crazy? She'd felt it. The push. The shove. She'd seen him. Seen something. She was sure of it. Wasn't she? She looked at Nick. Could he be lying? Could they have doctored the tape? No, not in ten minutes. Was that even possible?

"No," she said, shaking her head. She could not allow this to be true. It couldn't be real. She noticed her hand trembling where it rested on the desk and quickly snatched it back, hiding it in her lap. "There was someone out there. This is… crazy. I don't know what's going on, but this makes no sense." Nick didn't argue. He just shut down the computer.

Nick gave her a clean T-shirt from his locker. Her blouse, if not her body, had sustained a mortal injury in the attack-or whatever it was. "You can change in here," he said, opening the door to a small private office. "It's Sheriff Savoy's office, but I don't think she'd mind." He looked at her as if waiting for her to excuse him.

"Thanks," she said, reaching out to take the shirt, careful not to get blood on the clean fabric. "Shit," she muttered, then looked away.

"What?" he replied, staring at her. "What is it?"

"Nothing, it's… fine." She was holding his T-shirt now, clutching it to her breast. Her clothes, all of them, were filthy, stained, torn, ruined. Her cheek was scraped raw, and she still carried the wounds from the night before.

He raised his hands, palms out, in a gesture of surrender. "Ok, got it."

He smiled. She saw no malice in his eyes. She smiled too. He reached out, nearly touching her scraped cheek. "Let me get you something for this." He moved his fingers down towards her chin. "And this." Then the spot under her eye. "And this too." His fingers lingered a fraction of a second longer than necessary. She caught herself almost leaning towards his touch.

"Thanks, yeah." She stepped inside the door and closed it behind her.

Slipping the filthy, blood-stained blouse over her head, she thought about Nick. Handsome, solid, smiling Nick. She unfolded his crisp, white T-shirt and held it to her nose. It smelled like laundry and like something else. Something earthy and tangy. Awkwardly, using only one arm, she slid it over her head. God, her body hurt.

This place was trying to kill her or drive her crazy, or both. Literally. Yes, literally, one of Libby's favorite words as in *You are literally the worst mother in the world.* And *I literally hate my entire life.*

Catching a reflection of herself in the window over Savoy's desk. Broken, bruised, hair has gone yarn stringy. Wild. She looked feral. Insane. *Could she be crazy?* She'd learned long ago not to trust her memories, but present reality? Was that becoming suspect as well? This place, she thought, was more dangerous than she'd imagined. She'd escaped twenty-five years ago. Coming back had been more than risky. It had been stupid.

Suddenly, a memory came. Like a wave, choking her, pushing her down... down. She leaned against the corner of the desk, willing herself to keep breathing... *Lying on her back, dress pushed up, and the feel of cold steel beneath her thighs. She's pushing at him, both palms on his chest. Please. Don't. Eyes like peach pits. Too close. Nowhere to go. Darkness shrouding the back of his head. The moon above, in a silver sliver, too narrow to give off much light. A gentle swaying underneath her back. Swaying. Shifting. He says he'll kill her if she talks, and she knows that it's true.*

A knock came. "Are you ok?"

Absolutely not. "Yeah," she answered, straightening up as if Nick could see through the door. "I'm good. Be right there." She re-capped the flask and was putting it into her bag when she caught sight of her cellphone. Libby. She needed to talk to Libby.

As she dialed, her brain flashed again to blank, dark eyes, hovering over her in the night. *I'll fucking kill you;* he'd said. *If you tell, I'll come back, and I will kill you.*

CHAPTER FORTY-FIVE

Gwen | 1965

August 3, 1965

Dear Diary,

"If you tell, I will kill you." That is what he said.

For a long time, it's the only thing I can remember from everything that's happened to me in the last month. I suppose that's why it's taken me such a long time to write it all down. July 7. The man with the tattoos comes back. On the way downtown, he takes a shortcut. At least that's what he calls it. I don't think I believe him but, by the time I'm sure he's lying, it's too late.

He's steering the truck in-between the white cypress pressed so close together I think for sure he'll run the truck up to one side or the other. I start asking him to turn back, but he won't answer me, and the smell inside the truck- stale cigarettes and something moldy or dead even-is making my eyes water, and I feel sick. He just keeps staring straight ahead, into the forest, and I think his eyes don't look so nice anymore. I'm scared, and I just started blubbering like a little kid. Like little Katie.

When he parks the truck off the road, I can't tell where we are. He slides over on the seat, and he's real close. I can smell the cigarettes, and he's breathing too fast. He reaches an arm around my shoulder, and I reach for the door handle. That's when I see the knife. He's pressing it into my side, and he says if I don't take my hand off the handle, he'll shove it up into my heart. That's exactly how he says it, up into my heart.

He keeps the knife on me the whole time. Makes me get out of the truck. Lie down in the dirt. The knifepoint is so sharp it cuts me a little just by touching my skin. I watch the blade down by my left side. I can't move, and I can barely breathe; I'm so scared. He says he'll kill me if I fight, and I believe him, so I just lay there and try not to make him angry. It hurt terrible, but I barely make a sound.

Afterward, he says he'll kill me if I tell anyone. I believe that too. He tells me to stay where I am until I count to two hundred, then he gets back in his truck and drives away. Leaves me laying in the dirt Like I'm nothing. I feel like nothing, and I hope I'll just disappear. I lay there for a long time. I don't count, but I don't move either. I'm in the dirt, and then I hear the cicada and think it'll get dark soon. I'll die if I don't move, so I do.

I'm by the side of the road when he finds me. Limping on account of losing one of my shoes. My dress is torn down the front, and I have to hold it together with both hands, so I won't be naked to the world. He slows down his pickup, and at first, I think it's the tattoo man, but then I see it's not. It's a boy, not much older than me, I think. Still, I try to run anyway, but the pain between my legs and all the bruises on my arms make it impossible. So, I turn around and stare at him. Trying to look really fierce. I've heard somewhere that works with bears. And wild dogs.

When he parks and gets out, I see he's thin, with a baby face, and fine, lank, brown hair, and gigantic eyes like a puppy. Still, I don't trust him. He comes toward me, and I can hear myself screaming. He freezes right there on the side of the road, puts up his hands, and keeps apologizing.

I feel so cold. I'm shivering. Just shivering and screaming. He lays his jacket on the ground and backs away. He says his name is John Yates. He's going to get help.

It's a long time before John returns, and when he does, he doesn't bring the police. I'm relieved he doesn't bring them. What if they sent me home? Back to Clarksville? I can't go back there. And besides, what happened it was my fault. I shouldn't have gone with the man in the truck. I couldn't tell anyone about it. Not a stranger. My cheeks feel hot, even as I write this.

Instead, he brings his mother, and she is kind to me. She tells me it's the right thing not to go to the police. They wouldn't understand, she says. They would blame me for what I did. I'd be in trouble, and everyone would know. She wraps me up in a blanket and talks and talks about nothing at all. I think it's the chatter that makes me feel less afraid.

They bring me home, to their house, and let me stay. I'm here now, with Mama Yates and John, who it turns out is twenty - nearly five years older than me- and they say I can stay as long as I like. I'm learning about cooking and sewing, and Mama Yates has a little garden. Each day I am more grateful. Just once, I told Mama Yates about the man with the tattoos, and she told me to hush up. She knows that man, and he's powerful, she says. It's best not to think about it, she says. It's best to let it go. Then, she says men won't want to marry a girl who's had that happen, so it's real important I keep quiet. She never asks me anymore about it. Just like she never asks about my parents. Where I came from. She says sometimes it's safer to let bygones be bygones.

I think about that word a lot. Safer.

-G

CHAPTER FORTY-SIX

Libby | San Francisco

When the phone buzzed, and Libby saw the caller ID, her heart sank. It was late in Louisiana. Three hours later than California, where it was also late. And with Evelyn, late calls meant drunk calls.

Libby was already in bed, curled around a U.S. history book, open to a chapter on the Boston Tea Party-which, despite tomorrow's scheduled final exam, she had yet to finish reading. Her phone balanced on the binding. She'd run through all her social media connections: Snap Chat, Instagram, Facebook, Tumblr. Hunting for signs of Conner. The idiot had posted a handful of pictures of himself on his own sofa, hitting the Juul with two of his loser friends. So, she knew he was home. Just ignoring her. She'd finally given up stalking him and moved on to online shopping at Urban. Her father's credit card had its uses.

Evelyn was definitely drunk. Libby could hear it in the spaces between her mother's words. In her breath. As if the whole ugly betrayal of drunkenness had shot, at the speed of light, straight across two thousand geographical miles, leaped out of the cellphone and smacked Libby square in the face. For once, she felt nothing about it. Not angry. Not resentful. Not sad. She didn't know if she cared. She didn't know this woman. Maybe she'd never known her. She wasn't even sure why she answered the phone.

"Libby? Are you there?"

"Yeah. Yeah. I'm here. I..." *I read your diary. You lied. About everything.* "Nothing, never mind." She couldn't say it. There was no point. She'd only get more lies in response.

"Look, Libby, please stay away from anyone you don't know? K? Promise me? Promise." Her words were running together, drawing out and blurring at the edges.

Libby sighed. "How can I believe anything you say? I mean, is this even true? What you're saying about danger. Is this bullshit? You know, to get me to do whatever? Stay home?"

"Lib, please. Please listen. Just be safe. K?" Her lips sounded wet, too close to the phone now.

"Then tell me the truth. Stop lying to me, or I won't believe you. About anything." She heard Evelyn's sharp intake of breath.

"About what Lib? The truth about what?" Evelyn whisper-slurred into the phone.

So badly she wanted to ask the question that hung between them. She needed to know. *I did something bad, and now Carolyn is gone.* Evelyn had committed some unspeakable act as a child, and now, they both knew it. *They both knew it.* Their relationship could not tolerate the secret any longer. But Libby suspected their fragile connection also could not tolerate the truth.

Suddenly, the entire conversation seemed too hard. Too big. Everything... "I have to go, Mom. It's late. I have school." She clicked the phone off and slid the DO NOT DISTURB button to the right.

CHAPTER FORTY-SEVEN

Evelyn | Eden

"Cigarette," Evelyn said as they left the station.

"Cigarette?" Nick turned to her.

"I want one. Let's get some." Evelyn eyed him closely for signs he recognized she'd been drinking. Saw nothing. It was funny, really. The more she drank, the less she thought other people could tell she'd been drinking.

"Uh, ok. Sure. I'll take you to get some before I drop you off. But... I quit. A while back."

"Nah, you didn't quit. Not tonight." She grabbed his arm. "And beer. Let's get a beer." The night was thick and warm. Comforting. Familiar. The smell of magnolias and jasmine rushing in from the trees and bushes bounding the fractured walkway. An unusually fine rain, mist, more spreading than falling. The sounds of tree frogs clamoring for attention like excited children.

When they stopped at a red light, the windshield shimmered like Christmas. Nick rested his right hand next to hers on the center console, his skin brushing over hers. A pulse of electricity pin-pricked a hole in her gut. He was saying something about the deputy vehicle detail at her house all night. She drew a finger to her lips. She did not want to think about being watched or about the attack. The whole thing had receded into some closeted part of her brain, and she'd shut the door. For now, anyway. Evelyn eyed his hands, now resting on the steering wheel. Strong fingers. Clean, square nails. Better things to consider, she thought.

· · · · ·

Standing on the porch, Nick behind her, Evelyn fumbled through her purse for the key-*makeup bag, old credit card, wallet, mini hairbrush, crumpled gas receipt, old boarding pass, shit where is it, office key, another crumpled receipt, ah, here it is*-and pulled it out. She squinted in the semi-darkness and tried to insert the key. Missed. Tried again. Missed again. Nick moved up behind her, slid his arm around her waist, barely grazing her body. She could smell him. All of him. He took the key from her hand and slid it easily into the lock, leaned forward to push the door inward.

They sat in her front room, side-by-side on the ancient sofa, windows open to screens, to drive away the stuffiness, listening to the cicadas and bullfrogs. Evelyn watched as one roach, then another, climbed up the screen on the outside. She'd forgotten how big they got down here.

They drank the beers, although Evelyn drank three or four, and she was pretty sure Nick was still nursing his first. She'd lost count. She heard herself babbling but seemed unable to stop. Every time she paused for breath; the memories came: *Hard eyes. Flinty. Cold.* Memories trying to bang their way out of the closet into which she'd stuffed them. *Carolyn's body hunched over, searching under the bed. Small hands pulling at sheets and blankets. Her eyes, frantic. Where is it? What did you do?* Memories threatening to insert themselves despite Evelyn's best efforts. So, she talked. About California, about Stuart, about Lanterman Causey. Nick listened, laughed. A few times, she allowed herself to think he was genuinely interested. Finally, she said, "What about you? You've always wanted to be a detective?"

He smiled. Shook his head, looked down at his beer. "Nah, no way. I wanted to be a race car driver." His tone was too serious, and she laughed, then stopped herself.

"Wait," she studied him. "Seriously?"

His face cracked. "Hell no. I always wanted to be a cop. But the race car driver is way more impressive. Right?" Then they were both laughing and, despite herself, Evelyn liked this man.

They talked for a while. About everything. Nothing. Family. Pizza. Movies. Books. First jobs. First dates. Evelyn felt lighter than she had in a long time. Not lighthearted, but certainly less burdened. And that was good.

He slid closer on the couch. It was ok. When he turned towards her, reaching to touch her hair, then her cheek, she welcomed it. Then it was her, leaning into him, kissing him, and he was kissing her back. Softly and then harder and deeper on her mouth. Her head swam a bit, and she thought he was resisting, but she stood suddenly, then sank back down, straddling him, and he caught her hand with his and pulled it down, pushing it onto him. She thought briefly she might be in danger, but the thought passed. Then she was lost, swept out to sea, far from safety. His hand was up under her blouse and bra, and he was touching her, cupping her breast, softly and then harder until she was unsure whether she was feeling pain or pleasure. She leaned her head back, and he pulled at her hair, gently at first. He was kissing her neck, her shoulders, pushing at her blouse until she ripped it open herself. He licked at the flesh, and suddenly he stopped, and she cried out at him not to leave her. His fingers in her hair again, pulling too much pulling. She buried her face in the roughened skin of his neck. Salty, drenched, like the ocean. "I'm not going anywhere, Evelyn." He picked her up and lay her back down on the sofa, pulled her down with him. He leaned over her face, kissed her chin. Pulled off his own shirt and pressed his chest to hers. "Not now, not tonight."

She let go of the moorings, let the waves take her further and further out. His mouth was everywhere until, finally, there was no land in sight.

CHAPTER FORTY-EIGHT

Nick | Baton Rouge

Friday, June 9
Present Day

The text from Dr. Lee had come early, and Nick was on the road before dawn. Windows open, he drove toward Baton Rouge, the air charged with something edgy and dangerous. Morning crackling with heat and humidity. The case, having evolved in complexity with Chief Broussard's murder, now warranted Nick's request to move the remains out of Bonfante Parish for a second opinion by the Medical Examiner at the state capital. Sheriff Savoy had agreed and signed the transfer order. Finney would be unhappy, but Nick figured that was Savoy's problem. Lee wanted Nick up in Baton Rouge as soon as possible. The medical examiner had "information to share" already and preferred not to discuss it over on the phone.

He'd left Evelyn sleeping, and a twinge of guilt hit when he thought of her. She was a grown woman; he reminded himself. Not his charge to rescue. Besides, he'd texted her twice. No response. Probably still asleep. It had been a mistake. The sex, the night, the whole goddamn thing.

So many mistakes he'd made in his life. Too many to count. He would not add this woman to the list. Anger bubbled in his chest. Unfounded, he knew, but somehow familiar. The unfairness of the situation, the frustration. He'd gotten better at handling his anger after Lucas. Hadn't he? He hadn't had a choice.

Nick is twenty-seven and has been a detective for nearly two years when Lucas goes missing for the third time. Nick tells Mama not to worry; he's done it before. But this time he's gone a long time. Finally, toward the end of May, a body is found under the I-10, a young, unidentified male. Another team gets the call.

Nick stands on one side of a thick pane of glass while, on the other side, a coroner's assistant pulls back a sheet to expose his dead brother's face. Nick doesn't cry; he doesn't even move except to nod his head that, yes, that's Lucas. That's my brother.

In the parking lot, the muscles in his legs go lax, and he finds himself on his knees in the weeds, retching until only bile comes up. Still, he cannot stop. When he finally stands up, he staggers to his car, yanks open the door and falls inside. He has to spend a long-time pulling cat-o'-nine-tails out of his hair, face, and clothing before he can drive away. Nick avoids his mother after that. Her grief makes him angry. He cannot sleep or relax, and his body grows tense and achy from insomnia.

Nick refuses bereavement leave, thinking it'll make everything worse. A month later, he is in the interrogation room with his partner, Simpson, a forty-two-year-old veteran detective, who has been saying for months Nick needs to get his shit together. The piss-ant drug dealer they are questioning is no more or less repulsive than the thousands of others they've interrogated and yet Nick can feel his irritation rising every minute as they try to ring the truth from the piece of shit.

"I didn't do nothing. I ain't seen nothing, and I ain't gonna help you with nothing. Okay?" says the suspect, grinning to expose his four remaining teeth. Laughing, he makes a comment about dead crack whores, and Nick loses it. Snatches the boy (and that is what he is-a boy) by the scruff of his shirt and yanks him out of his chair. Drags him to his feet and slams him up against the wall behind the table. Nick holds him there for a few seconds, one hand around the guy's throat, scrawny

as a twelve-year-old's; then he balls his right hand into a fist and slams it into the wall next to Jimmy's face with a sickening crack. As Nick pulls his arm back, Dale Simpson is behind him, grabbing Nick around the waist and by the arm and pulling him away from Jimmy, who has stopped laughing and looks like he's about to cry.

Two uniformed officers drag Nick from the conference room. Nick is aware he has broken his hand, but the pain does not reach his brain. So clouded is his consciousness by anger, he is not aware of anything other than his rage. His chief will tell him more than once that, had he punched Jimmy Larabey's face instead of the wall, the mistake would have been career-ending rather than just massively stupid and inconvenient.

Nick gets three months suspension and mandatory counseling. Simpson says he ought to feel grateful they did not terminate him. But he does not feel grateful. He only feels rage.

CHAPTER FORTY-NINE

Evelyn | Eden

He was gone. She knew it before she opened her eyes. Evelyn lay still, allowing the colorless space in her brain to settle into place, then she rolled to her side and sat up. She ran her hand over his pillow, feeling the dent in its surface where he'd rested his head during the night. She paused, then shoved the pillow, hard, off the bed, kicked off the covers, and got up.

In the bathroom, she flipped on the shower, let it run, shuffled back into the kitchen, pulled open the cupboard, and reached up to the shelf for the half-full bottle of vodka. She poured a half-inch into a plastic cup, held it to her lips without drinking. Carried it back to the bathroom and set it down on the sink edge. The shower water was still only lukewarm, but she stepped in and stood under the water a long time before getting out.

Afterward, Evelyn snatched up the cup, looked into it for a few seconds, and let her eyes drift upward to the mirror over the sink. She'd let go of the towel and was standing naked. She stared at the tearful, disheveled-looking woman who looked back at her. Covered with bruises. Too thin. *Nobody's sister, nobody's daughter.*

Shaking her head at her own image, she thought of Carolyn, Mama and of Libby. In the tiny bathroom, she dumped the vodka in the sink and threw the cup in the trash. Then she lay back down on the bed and let her mind drift back towards sleep.

Evelyn is small and alone in the house. She's calling out for her mother, already chatting about the day. Telling Mama about Miss Barton, the new teacher, and how she's letting each child grow sunflowers from seeds in a big pot in the classroom. Mama doesn't answer, but Evelyn doesn't feel worried. Only frustrated. Where are you, Mama? She calls out into the darkness.

She wanders for a long time, which is strange because the house is very small. Finally, she pushes open the door to the bathroom. It's hot in there, like outdoors, and humid. Huge palmetto plants are coming up through the floor, and bright red hibiscus has grown through the walls and is dangling from the roof. Evelyn stares at them and realizes they are growing as she watches.

She sees Mama standing at the sink, still. Too still, while everything around her is moving. It's hard to see Mama's face because a palmetto leaf is blocking Evelyn's view. Now she's afraid. She screams and sees the vines are wrapping around Mama, squeezing her like snakes. Still, she doesn't move.

Blood pounding in her head woke her. Nauseated and temporarily disoriented. *Not her bedroom. Not her apartment.* Evelyn sat up, rubbed at her forehead. The bare window through which she could see sunlight pushing past the thick leaves of a live oak. *Eden. Road 12.* Her face was sticky with sweat, and she'd kicked the sheets to the floor.

Peeling herself out of bed, she considered another shower, then rinsed a washcloth under the tap and used it to wipe her face and underarms instead. She dressed in shorts and a cotton tank top, leaving her feet bare, and padded into the kitchen where she filled a pot with water, and placed it on the stove. She spooned Nescafe into a mug that was missing its handle, propped open the back door to allow air circulation, and sat down at the table, waiting for the water to boil. She rolled her head around, trying to ease the kinks in her neck. The bed was unbelievably bad: short, stiff, and creaky, smelling of dust and mold despite the fresh linens she purchased at the new Wal-Mart. She decided to blame her achy body and head on that. The bed. Not the booze.

She let her eyes drift over the cracked tiles of the kitchen countertops, grout brown with grease and accumulated dirt. The painted walls were dented and peeling, and the screen door which led out to the patch of dirt Gwen had used as a tiny vegetable garden was hanging by one hinge. She eyed the door for a moment, then moved toward it and lay both hands, palms out, on the broken screen. Sunlight was already warming the metal mesh. She pressed her cheek onto it and tried to remember.

She's ten. They'd been out much of the day. Carolyn and Evelyn and their father. Shopping maybe. She is the first to the door when they get home. The sensation of the screen door's metal mesh under her palms as she pushes it open. Hot from the sun. The loud creaking sound it makes.

Calling out for Mama, once or maybe twice, and suddenly anxious because of the dark and the quiet in the house. Mama hates darkness. She keeps the shades open, the lights on. All the time. She hates quiet, too. Unless she is having one of her bad days, she's always moving, singing, and talking. But, today, the shades are pulled down. The house is so dark, Evelyn can barely see. She stumbles, falls forward, smacks onto her hands and knees. Pain shoots up through her elbows and thighs, and the impact knocks the wind out of her, leaves her gasping for air.

Then, everything continues in slow motion. She's on the floor. Her eyes adjusting, and there's a laundry basket, and that's what caused the fall. A dumb laundry basket sitting right there by the backdoor, and it's all full of clean laundry. Or it was until she knocked it over. Now the sheets are all wrapped around her legs like ropes. She's thinking how much her leg hurts and how strange that Mama just left the basket sitting there in the way. Evelyn looks up and sees Daddy and Carolyn passing her before she can get up off the floor, and she already knows something is wrong, very wrong, and she's already scared. But only a little.

A terrible scream. Evelyn thinks a wild animal is in the house eating her family, and there she is, all tangled up in sheets, unable to help. She is fighting with the sheets to get free, and she hears the scream come again and again, and she's getting mad, really mad, that she can't move. She can't do anything.

The odor of hot metal pulled her out of the memory. Something was burning. She turned around. Smoke drifting up from the bottom of the pot she'd left on the stove. The water must have boiled off. Now bone-dry, the bottom was scorching on the heat. Protecting her hand inside her T-shirt, she pushed the pot off the flame, then shut off the stove.

She went back to the door. Running one finger over the broken screen, she stood looking out into the gray-brown dirt of the former vegetable garden and tried to remember what happened next. Another blank inside her brain. The memory not faded. Broken.

Hours must have elapsed because there are lots of people in the house. Some she knows, some she doesn't. She is sitting in the kitchen, and she has the sense of waiting, but she cannot remember what it is she is waiting for.

CHAPTER FIFTY

Nick | Baton Rouge

A thick mist hung over the city as Nick pulled into the Baton Rouge coroner's parking lot. The oak trees lining the lot hung heavy with Spanish Moss, and, in the pre-dawn light, they took on a translucent, haunted appearance. Nick had pulled the reports surrounding the death of Gwen Yates and now sat in his car waiting for his appointment with the medical examiner and reading the witness statement and police files by the dashboard light.

According to official records, on June 12, 1986, while the rest of the family was out, Gwen Yates made the beds, straightened the house, did the dishes, took the sheets off the line, and left them folded in a basket by the back door, much as she did on other days. Then she took a shower, combed out her long hair, and, after some indecision- multiple outfits lay scattered here and there around the bedroom-she dressed in a blue skirt and new wedge sandals. Next, she went into the bathroom, sat down on the floor next to the toilet, emptied a medium-sized bottle of acetone nail polish remover into an over-sized, glass tumbler already half full of gin, and drank most of it before dropping the glass to the floor, where it shattered around her spilling the remaining contents and burning a hole into the floor the size of a half-dollar. As she died, she fell sideways, her head coming to rest, left cheek buried in the linoleum. The small puddle of vomit just outside her lips showed she'd been alive when she fell.

Officials ruled the death a suicide. Nobody argued. Gwen had a history of psychiatric problems and she'd been in the mental hospital at least once for a *breakdown.*

According to the official reports, Evelyn Yates, age ten, had witnessed the gruesome scene. She'd responded by retreating so quietly that her absence went unnoticed for over an hour. Someone found her under a pile of folded laundry near the back door. Mute and curled into a fetal position, she became violent when a neighbor tried to collect her and move her to a more appropriate location.

Nick had seen poisonings. He knew the effects of death by poison on a body. Evelyn's lack of memory had to be a blessing.

•   •   •   •   •

Dr. Lee, a small man in his early forties whose mellifluous southern drawl seemed at odds with his efficient sentences, sharp, bird-like features, and peripatetic movements. He walked ahead of Nick, leading the way into the morgue without a backward glance. A row of surgical steel operating room tables occupied the center of the autopsy room. A series of tubes stretched like snakes down the length of each table before terminating, open-mouthed, into red buckets attached at one end. Only one table had an occupant. Nick imagined he could hear the plop and squash of blood and organs dropping into the plastic containers, smell the odor of human decay and see the purple mass of a liver dropped unceremoniously onto a silver scale. In his mind's eye, every table held a corpse, and every red bucket over-flowed with biological bits and pieces; *parts,* already removed, examined, measured, weighed, and recorded. Several basins lined the walls, all of them extra deep to prevent blood and other human detritus from splashing up over the edge and onto the tile floor. Fluorescent bulbs were recessed into the ceiling, and over each table hung an additional light, huge and circular, that reminded Nick of movie house spotlights. The entire space smelled of formaldehyde, rubbing alcohol, and death.

"Here," said the doctor, reaching for the one gurney that had a body. Without warning, he pulled back the sheet. "Here," he repeated. "Look at this, please."

What lay beneath the sheet was not the pile of debris Nick had viewed previously with Finney. This was more disturbing. Pieces of bones, indeed entire bones, were shattered, missing, and eaten. However, enough material was present that even a layperson could tell what the thing might once have been. Most alarming was the skull. Fine pieces of the skull had been carefully fitted back together and now rendered much of the face- eyes, nose, chin, and mouth-clearly distinguishable. It was but a small leap to imagine the delicate features of a living young girl.

Dr. Lee pointed at the skull. "I realize you've seen these remains, Detective, but this," he said and ran his long, gloved finger just above a thin crack approximately four inches long which ran across the surface of the skull, "this is what I wanted you to see today. This injury is clearly significant. See here," he said as he brushed his finger further along the crack. "Also, here and here." He pointed and then looked up at Nick and appeared to be smiling slightly. "You see what I mean, Detective MacCallum?"

Nick shook his head. "No, not quite Dr. Lee," he replied.

Lee picked up a miniature baton-shaped surgical object and showed Nick how its rounded end, about the length of a half tennis ball, fit perfectly into a dent along the center of the crack. "Here, this skull would have been injured just here with this action," he said and demonstrated by hammering the device downward toward the skull, stopping just short of the surface. "And the injury would no doubt have been fatal." Nick winced.

"Are you saying someone hit her before she died?" Nick asked. "Could it have been the butt of a gun?"

"Hmm, maybe, or some other blunt object."

"How do we know that didn't happen after death in the last three decades, for example?"

"So," continued the doctor, "when an injury occurs before death, broken fragments of bone remain connected to each other. We call these bone flakes. Live bone breaks along distinct lines, different from dead bone. The patterns are unique. I can tell this bone was alive when it was fractured. No doubt. Also," he was pulling off his gloves now and shoving them into a biohazard container. "I can tell you now that the skull fracture, which might have been inflicted with anything from a lead pipe to the butt of a gun, was certainly fatal. Surviving an injury of that magnitude would have been impossible."

Goddammit, Nick thought, *a child, Evelyn's sister, with a hole in her head big enough to pass a tennis ball, and Finney had been ready to let the bastard who did this get away with it.*

"What about the drugs? The chloral hydrate. The Celeste medical examiner seemed to think that killed her. You're saying she did not die of an overdose and then sustain those injuries later?" Nick asked.

Lee shook his head. "What I am saying is that whether she had ingested enough of any substance to kill her became irrelevant as soon as she incurred that head injury," Dr. Lee answered. "She was dead anyway. We know the preliminary toxicology results are positive for chloral hydrate only. It's possible she ingested that, or even another substance voluntarily, just as its possible someone drugged her to unconsciousness and then bonked her on the head to make sure she was dead. The head injury killed her. When I get the final toxicology report, I'll let you know."

Lee finished scrubbing and rinsing his hands, then used a paper towel to turn off the water and dried himself. "If you have time, Detective, I'd like to look at the photographs with you," said Lee.

"Photographs?" Nick asked with genuine surprise.

Lee looked at Nick with curiosity. "Yes. I thought you were aware. The photos that Chief Broussard brought me. That's why he came to see me."

Nick spoke, trying to sound calmer than he felt. "Did he tell you where he got the pictures? Did he say anything else?"

"No, no, he didn't actually," said Dr. Lee. "I assumed Chief Broussard took them."

"Broussard?"

"Yes, they are photos of-" He stopped talking and went to unlock a cabinet nearby. "Well, here, just look yourself. I think it will be easier than my trying to explain."

Nick held up the first of the three photographs so that he and the doctor could view it together. It looked to be a photograph of the remains Nick and Lee had just examined. *The same remains Nick had seen the day before at Dr. Finney's.* In this photo, however, the bones (all the bones) were arranged as a human being. A slightly built human being.

"This photograph," Dr. Lee said, pointing at the third and final picture, "is perhaps the most disturbing." Clearly shot from above over an autopsy table, Nick had to agree it was a disturbing image, although he guessed Lee was not referring to the overall gruesome nature of the subject.

"Is that... is that the Bonfante Morgue?"

"I assumed so," said Lee. "Although I'll admit, I didn't ask Chief Broussard."

The photograph focused on two bones of the lower right arm. The bones looked as if they might curve together perfectly if they had not both been badly fractured near the lower end. "These bones," Lee said and pointed to the right arm, "these should not be in several pieces. They should look like this." Lee moved to a poster on the wall, a skeleton drawn in anatomical detail. He pointed specifically to the bones of the lower arm.

"Ok, so what does that mean?"

"So, we only received the actual remains late last night," Lee said, and motioned for Nick to follow him. "However, Chief Broussard dropped those photos with me on Tuesday morning, indicating they were pictures of the remains he was trying to get transferred. I assumed he'd shot a few photos for me to study the remains. I thought little of the pictures until... well, frankly, until the recent events."

Nick knew that by recent events, the doctor meant Broussard's murder.

"I pulled everything and made a comparison," Lee continued. "Near as I can tell, those photographs match these remains." He gestured to the corpse on the table. "Almost perfectly. They come from the same individual, which, of course, is to be expected."

"Okay," said Nick.

"Well, often remains, especially old remains are incomplete, so, at first, I assumed it was just deterioration or animal activity."

"What was?" asked Nick. Irritated by his own confusion.

"No radius and no ulna," Lee said, pointing first at the corpse's right side and then the left. "Compared to the photographs, the actual corpse lacks a radius and ulna bilaterally. Someone has removed this child's lower arm bones."

CHAPTER FIFTY-ONE

Gwen | 1972

September 23, 1972

Something is wrong. With me. With the baby. I don't know, but there's blackness in the house. I've been in bed since we got home. John brings the baby to me, but I can no longer look at her. My hands tremble under her tiny body. I worry I will drop her, just let go, and she'll fall down and down beyond my grasp. I fear the creeping dark. The look in her eyes scares me.

John's mother is here. I didn't want her, but John says he can't manage without her. I can hear them out in the kitchen arguing. Mostly, it's Mama Yates telling John that we should never have moved out of her house. That this wouldn't have happened if we'd stayed put. I heard her say there's something awfully wrong with me. A weakness. I shouldn't have been working so hard in the garden while I was pregnant. I didn't take the right care. She blames me. I think she's right.

John asks her to stop clattering around in the kitchen since the noise wakes the baby. Mama Yates just tells him to hush, and she'll keep right on clattering until she has everything set to rights. She calls him ungrateful, and I know how sad that makes him.

Still, I can't seem to help him.

My body has become weighted to the bed like I'm carrying a flour sack on my back. The energy it takes just to think about rising is too much. Makes me feel dizzy. I don't want to eat, but they keep bringing me food.

I only want to sleep. Why won't they just let me sleep?

-G

October 10, 1972

John tries to bring me the baby. He reaches out to hand her to me, and I'm so scared I try to bite him. I put my mouth on his arm and taste blood. Then he's screaming, and I'm screaming, and Mama Yates comes in and takes the baby and looks at me like I'm a wild dog, which is what I feel like. She tells John something needs to be done. I know they are talking about me.

I'm afraid to write this down, but it needs saying.

There's something wrong with the baby.

CHAPTER FIFTY-TWO

Libby | San Francisco

Libby sat on her bed, popping orange Tic-Tacs into her mouth at a ridiculous rate and clicking through the search screens. Things didn't fit. What Evelyn told her didn't fit. The mother, dead before Evelyn, was old enough to remember her. The abusive father. And now, a sister conjured into existence out of the ether.

Web pages clicked past, and Libby wondered why internet investigation had not occurred to her earlier. Maybe she'd known what she'd find.

It turned out the story, the first story, had made news at least at the state level. Libby found articles online from both the Baton Rouge Gazette and the Times-Picayune. Gwen Yates had committed suicide. Another lie, and a heinous one. Comparing the date of Gwen's suicide with Evelyn's diary, Libby realized Gwen died eight days after Evelyn's last cheerful entry on June 4, 1986.

That was it. The turning point. Following Gwen's suicide in June of '86, the little girl of curlicues and doodles had disappeared. Then, nothing but blank pages until... Something else must have happened. That one entry, one forlorn line, dated August 11, 1986:

I did something bad, and now Carolyn is gone.

What could that mean? Evelyn had been ten. Not a baby, but not old enough to commit a truly horrible act of her own volition. She was a liar. She could be selfish, but she was kind. Libby knew that. *Didn't she?* She wouldn't have meant to harm her own sister. *Would she?*

But so many lies. So many dodged questions. She'd been plenty old enough to remember. And old enough to know lots of things about Gwen. Things Libby had asked a million times, and every time Evelyn had replied with a vague shrug and a sad expression.

The thing was: what if Evelyn, as a child, had done something unintentionally? Something accidental? What if she'd made a choice, a childish choice that had turned out to have disastrous, even tragic consequences, and she'd spent the rest of her life running from what she'd done? Burying her past with booze and drugs and lies. *Was that possible? Yes*, thought Libby. *That was possible*. More than possible. It made Evelyn's insane life make sense. In a really scary way, it made Libby's life make sense, too.

Jacinta was calling from downstairs. It was time to leave for school. Libby slammed the laptop shut and shoved it into her backpack. Just before leaving the room, she turned back, and from the drawer in her bedside table, snatched up the lighter and both of the joints.

CHAPTER FIFTY-THREE

Gwen | 1973

January 4, 1973

I've been here almost three months. The hospital. They won't let me see Carolyn. Dr. Lavie is my doctor. He's kind, but his eyes float away when I speak to him. Makes me feel like he's not really listening. John doesn't listen either. He tells me it's just for a little longer, but I know he's lying.

They give me medicine every day. Three times a day, I swallow pills from a paper cup, two small red ones and a big yellow one. The nurse makes me open my mouth and show her the pills are gone. Like I'm a child. At first, I don't mind so much, because the pills make me sleep and take away the pain. But now, I need to stay awake to see my baby. Every day I ask. When John comes, I beg him, and he says he'll try, but I don't believe him.

Tuesday is Arts and Crafts. We are all in the day room working on macaroni jewelry boxes when they come and get me. Two young men in white uniforms. Faces blank. They say nothing. They put me in a wheelchair and strap my arms to the sides with leather straps, like belts. I don't know why they do that since I'm not struggling.

They roll me into this room, like an operating room, like I've seen on TV or in movies. Clean, shiny. Steel bed in the middle with complicated machines all around. They make me sit up and slide over to the table. My bare bottom feels cold against the metal. Something sharp-a needle, I guess- jabs into my arm. Someone covers my mouth with a plastic cup. They tell me to breathe slowly. After that, it's blurry. More straps. Seems like hundreds. One on my forehead. Heavy. Something in my mouth now, making it hard to breathe, making me gag.

I look around at the faces over me, and I see Dr. Lavie, and I feel ice water in my veins, and I think for sure they are killing me.

CHAPTER FIFTY-FOUR

Nick | Eden

Nick studied the remains again, forcing himself to look slowly over the entire body, first one side, then the other. It was true. The corpse in the picture revealed the child's arm bones in place, although disarticulated from one another, and one set fractured, but the remains on the table before him did not have bones of the lower arms at all. He did not need to be a forensic pathologist to see it.

"Why would anyone want to do that, take the arms like that?"

"Ah," said Dr. Lee. "See here. These fractures are of a rotating type." Dr. Lee demonstrated. His fist clenched, Lee wrapped his surprisingly powerful hand around Nick's forearm and gave it a forceful twist, jerking upward at the same time. Nick grimaced and snatched his arm back.

"Hurts, yeah?"

"Yeah," replied Nick, still rubbing at his arm.

"This is what we call an NAI. Non-accidental injury. Typically, we would see something like this in a younger child, a preschooler, or a toddler. An angry or abusive adult will grab a child by the arm, twist, and yank, causing a spiral fracture of those bones." Nick had seen this type of injury more than once and always in children too small to fight back. Babies. Goddammit.

"But this girl was older, right?"

Lee nodded. "Yes, this girl was older, but she's small, her bones light. A powerful adult could have inflicted this injury easily. The lack of healing tells us these fractures were relatively fresh, occurring not long before death." He hesitated, then pointed at the photograph. "Also, here. Someone removed these arm bones after completing the first autopsy. Someone," Lee added, "did not want us to find the broken bones in that right arm."

Finney, thought Nick. Finney had taken those bones, and Chief Broussard knew it.

"What about an accident?" Nick asked. "Could she have been intoxicated, fallen and hit her head, that sort of thing?" As soon as he asked, he knew the answer.

Lee sighed. "No, no way. People don't fall and get a single injury to one spot on their skull in the shape of a man-made object. No other head injury, facial, no facial lacerations, plus there's the twisting injury to the forearm. That is an inflicted injury. No way, not an accident. Someone did this and there's something else. When someone dies after an intoxicated fall, they more typically wander around town or at home. They fall down, hit their head, face, other parts of the body, and die slowly of a subdural - a brain bleed - which does not even result in an actual skull fracture."

Nick nodded. "Of course, young kids do a lot of stupid things. Our thinking was that she went willingly. You know, goofing around, got too high, had an accident, and whoever was with her took off."

"Yeah," said Lee, "that would work, except for the injuries. So, no, it doesn't work. Somebody took her out there and killed her. She was unconscious when she got out there or fully conscious. No matter. Either way, somebody killed her."

Conscious or unconscious? Nick thought. *Of course, it mattered. Imagining a terrified young girl fully awake while she's being yanked so hard her arm breaks towards what she must have known was her own death.*

CHAPTER FIFTY-FIVE

Evelyn | Eden

The Bonfante Parish Main Library was unchanged. Evelyn remembered the red brick building on the corner near the center of town. The library was a testament to Bonfante's more optimistic, if not more prosperous, times. The privet, which Evelyn guessed had to be older than her father would be, lined the front walk, and the same heavy giant oaks stood sentry out front.

The tiny parking lot's perimeter was edged with patches of crabgrass and overgrown honeysuckle. It was empty save one car, probably the librarians. The air was acrid with the smell of hot asphalt. Sweat droplets quickly accumulated on Evelyn's neck, then rolled downward, pooling at the small of her back where they caused an unpleasant tickle. A small gecko, nearly invisible between blades of grass, scooted onto the blacktop and across her shadow, before disappearing under the car's front wheel. It made her smile.

It was in the year after Mama died Evelyn began appearing at the library. She bummed rides from teachers who lived in the town. Sometimes they'd give her dinner, let her sleep over, and bring her back to school the next day. Other grownups would bring her up and back for no reason at all, except she asked.

Following the summer of 1986, Evelyn discovered she was no longer *Evelyn*. She had morphed into an exotic creature known by locals as *That Poor Kid*. Teachers, parents, town gossips would huddle together and discuss her plight. Not even Lynnie Yates. Now she was: *That Poor Kid. Did you hear about what happened to her family?* Or *That Poor Kid, she has nobody but her father and he is in no condition to raise a child.* Or *That Poor Kid, she's all alone, you know.* To other kids, she was a freak, but to adults, she was royalty. Rides to town, lunch money, movie tickets. If they could afford it, any adult she asked would oblige. Sometimes even when they couldn't afford it. She hated them all for their superiority, for feeling good about being kind to the kid with a dead mom and a gone sister, and a drunk dad. The more she hated, the more she took, and the more she took, the more she despised them all.

Someone had tended the library's entryway; at least they'd trimmed the wisteria vines and cut the grass along the path. The brickwork was old, and the concrete pathway chipped and buckled in places where the oak trees pushed up from underground, their roots as big around as a man's thigh.

Evelyn stopped to look at the iron scrollwork over the front entrance: *Bonfante Parish Library, Est. 1897.* She took a few deep breaths and waited until she was calm before pushing open the big double doors.

The library was one open, sunlit space. Inhabiting as it did, the corner of the building, it had the advantage of light, even on a day like today. It poured in through two walls of double-paned windows, which stretched the full height of the room. The floors were oak, worn, and refinished so many times that the tiny nails used to hammer each narrow slat into place over a century ago were smoothed flush with the wood. The space was thick with the scent of old paper and lemon oil. Mismatched chairs cushioned in faded brocade and flowery pastels, contributions to the library over the years, sat empty around the perimeter. To one side, three surprisingly modern computers stood alert, humming eagerly at the ready.

The library internet either had no security password, or someone without guile had preloaded it into the system. Evelyn found the Bonfante Parish website in a few seconds and started with the medical examiner's official bio. From there, she searched for Albert Finney and then Finney in all the combinations she could think up: *Albert Finney and Celeste; Albert Finney and medical examiner; Albert Finney and forensic evaluations.*

She found nothing particularly surprising. Dr. Finney was born Albert James Finney seventy-three years earlier, in Biloxi, Mississippi. The only child of parents who emigrated to the U.S. from Europe as young children. Born late, his father was already an established dentist and mother a pharmacist with her own shop in Biloxi at the time of his birth. The father continued to practice dentistry until his death from a massive coronary while Finney was in high school. His mother never returned to her career. Nothing grossly atypical in his childhood. He attended college at Dartmouth and medical school at Vanderbilt, graduating with honors. He went on to a medicine residency at Vanderbilt. Following residency, he lived and worked briefly in Nashville, but moved to Bonfante Parish, settling in Eden in 1973. He was appointed Medical Examiner shortly after his arrival in Eden.

He'd held the position continuously ever since. Over forty years. He had been Medical Examiner, Evelyn realized, the day her mother died. *Was he one of those faceless adults she remembered at her house that day? Had he been there? Why had he not said anything about it? Why was it she had no memory of the man?*

Evelyn sat staring at the computer screen for a few minutes, tapping the table with the eraser end of her pencil and listening to the clock overhead tick off seconds with an intrusive "bick... bick... bick" sound she thought might make her head explode. Then she leaned back in her chair and shut her eyes, trying to imagine Finney's life as a timeline. Like the geological timelines she'd learned in elementary school, only in reverse: the latter parts squished together, the earlier dates spread wide for detail.

Something was missing, she thought, scanning her mental timeline. *What wasn't there? Everything was so ordinary. The Finney family life, Albert's childhood, was so ordinary, but then some things were not there.* She re-read the record several times. Born in Biloxi, successful parents, settled in Nashville... college... med school... residency. So clean, it was almost boring.

Except it wasn't.

That was it. The logic broke down, looking at the timeline. City kid... private schools... Dartmouth... Vanderbilt... Eden. *Why would any physician with an Ivy League resume like that move to Eden in the first place, let alone stay for the rest of his life?*

Money? Bonfante Parish had even less financial clout in the 1970s than in the present, and she suspected Finney's family was at least moderately affluent, given his parents' backgrounds. So, no way, not for money. *Altruism?* The profound desire to give back to the world through lifelong service to an impoverished township. One meeting with Dr. Finney was enough to convince Evelyn that was not possible. He was an arrogant, entitled narcissist, not Mother Teresa. *Relationships?* He didn't seem to have any. No photos in his office, no family, no kids. Nothing to tie him to the area. So why, she thought again, had Dr. Finney chosen Eden?

•　　　•　　　•　　　•　　　•

Evelyn was walking. The air smelled sweet with summer, and the walkways were lined with old Magnolia trees for shade and beauty. The few people Evelyn passed seemed pale, recessed, like shadows. She didn't recognize anyone, which was a relief. Still, she peered into shop fronts, over her shoulder, down alleyways. A flock of blackbirds swelled from an elm as she passed by, rising into the air with a winged clatter, and she jerked away in surprise. Her breath quickening. Palms wet with sweat.

She had no appetite but was suddenly lightheaded. Stopping at a deserted sandwich shop, she ordered a salad and a glass of chardonnay at the counter. That was the thing about Louisiana. The food anywhere would be good. As would the wine. She carried the items outside. The small patio, covered by a green tarpaulin, featured a ragtag collection of cafe tables and delicate chairs. She took a seat at a corner table; her back up against the wall, just in case. She ate, cutting the lettuce into tiny shreds, and drank in measured sips, and watched as dark gray clouds moved in from the east. The air was thickening and smelled of earth and electricity.

Her phone buzzed. Nick. She declined the call, already aware of what he would say. *It had been a mistake... They'd been drunk. Or at least she'd been drunk.* It shouldn't happen again. A chill caught her, and she shivered despite the heat.

Trust no one.

The storm grew until sheets, and then slabs of water crashed into the sidewalk around the little cafe, threatening to crush the concrete beneath its force.

If you tell anyone, I'll come back and kill you.

She drained the glass of wine and motioned to the counter clerk for another.

Evelyn's thoughts turned to her past as she watched the water come down hard. *Flinty, black eyes in the night. Sour breath. I'll come back and kill you.*

Suddenly, she knew who he was.

She remembered him. The eyes. Thirty years later, she was sure that the voice, deeper now and ravaged by tobacco, belonged to him. The coffin tattoo at his collarbone. Not a bar of gold, not a mistake. It had been a coffin. Self-inflicted with a ballpoint pen, as a joke, although Evelyn couldn't see that it was funny.

He'd been several years older than Evelyn, in the same school year as Carolyn. Tall, and handsome in an off-beat, sinister sort of way. In grade school, he'd made Evelyn uncomfortable, but after Mama died, she'd found him appealing. He broke the rules. Snubbed authority. He didn't care, and he never seemed worried about consequences. In retrospect, Evelyn thought she wanted not so much to be *with* him as to actually *be* him.

The year she turned thirteen, he had a license and a car. He'd driven her up to the library a few times as a favor. Teased her about being a bookworm. He seemed harmless enough. When he handed her a beer one night on the way back from Celeste, she took it. Without thinking, she took it, and she drank it. When he pulled into Eden and drove to a tiny, abandoned park, rather than taking her home, she did not feel afraid. She felt giddy. Lightheaded by the beer and excited by the attention. It was late. She was out with a boy.

In the playground, they lay on their backs, side by side on the steel roundabout. The thing creaked and moaned, lolling back and forth as the boy pushed at the sand underneath with his boot heel. He gave her another beer and then, after a while, another. The night was moonless, but thick with stars. He leaned over her, bringing with him the smell of sweat and beer, and when he leaned in to put his mouth on hers, she wriggled aside, feeling dizzy and a little sick.

"I need to go home," she said, trying to sit up. He pushed her back, two hands heavy against her shoulders. He silenced her with his mouth. His tongue inside her mouth, probing, insistent, made her gag. She tried to push him away, but he was on top of her, his body weight pressing her backward into the corrugated surface of the roundabout. Her skirt was up around her waist, and the back of her thighs pressed painfully into the steel. She tried to scream, but he slapped a hand over her mouth and told her to shut up. Suddenly she knew exactly what he was going to do, and afterward, she thought, he'll kill me. She could see the sky beyond his head; the entire world had gone still and black. The stars now looked tiny. Pitiful, helpless, and far away.

She started to cry and then wail, and he put his hand on her mouth again and told her to shut up. His blank, dark eyes bore into hers, and she froze. "Just shut the fuck up."

"I'll fucking kill you," he'd said. *"If you tell anyone, I'll come back and kill you."*

CHAPTER FIFTY-SIX

Libby | San Francisco

They called for her after lunch. One of the office volunteers, an older woman with stripes of gray in her blond hair and deep creases around her eyes, came into the classroom with a summons. Libby's pulse quickened, even before her name was called. Her throat was dry as she followed the aid up the corridor. Being called to the counselor's office was never good, but today it might be anything on a spectrum of *dreadful things*, ranging from mildly annoying to completely fucking disastrous. She kept her eyes on the office worker's thick back. The woman wore a tunic patterned with miniature squares and pink flowers, a bit like a tablecloth. It was probably supposed to be upbeat. To Libby, it just looked sad.

"Libby, hello, please have a seat," said the counselor as she entered. Libby suspected Ms. Mabel-the girls called her Miss Maybelline for the eye makeup she wore-lacked formal training in psychology. She was a petite woman in her twenties, with deep blue eyes and thick, dark hair she wore in a shiny ponytail at the nape. The heavy mascara made her look perpetually concerned but about the wrong things, like a Barbie Doll.

Libby sat down in the visitor chair, staring at her feet, avoiding the woman's gaze. "Libby, I'm so sorry to have to bring you in and discuss this, but." She was pushing something across her desk. "Is this yours?"

Libby glanced up. The weed. They'd found it, and the only way they could have found it was by searching her locker without her consent. She felt her face flush with embarrassment and rage. "Libby?" the pert counselor was asking.

She nodded. Said nothing. Held her mouth tight to avoid an explosion that would make things worse.

"Can you explain this to me?" Ms. Mabel was tapping a long, tapered finger against the plastic baggie that held the joint.

"Uh," Libby said. "It's marijuana."

Ms. Mabel smiled blandly at the sarcasm. "I realize that Libby. Can you tell me where it came from? And why it's here? At school."

Libby thought for a moment and finally shook her head. "Nope."

"Ok," said the counselor. Her voice was full of false patience. "You should know that our principal wanted to contact your parents first, but I requested a chance to speak with you." Libby shrugged, resisting the urge to offer Miss Maybelline a cookie for her efforts. "But if you won't talk to me, then we have no choice. I'll need to call your parents."

"You'll do that, anyway. Besides, I don't care. My mom's not here, anyway."

Ms. Mabel leaned forward, her expression of concern deepening. "What do you mean your mom's not here?"

"She's just gone. You'll have to call my dad." As Libby said the words, she realized she cared. If the school called her father, that would mean both Stuart and Gam getting involved. Gam was on the school's Board of Trustees, and she would not handle this well. She took a deep breath. "How'd you find it?"

Ms. Mabel cocked her head. "Libby, you know we may search the lockers, it's in the contract your parents sign."

"Yeah, but you don't. Someone said something, right?" She knew Mabel would not admit it, but someone had tipped off the administration. Libby was fairly sure she knew who it was. The anger flared thick and hot in her chest. She wanted to scream.

"Libby, we are all concerned about you. We are all on your team." Libby, who did not have and did not want to have "a team," barely suppressed an eye roll at that one. She pictured the counselor as a drill team of one valiantly chucking spirit flags into the air, rooting for Libby's success even as she crashed and burned. "You've been having a tough time lately, right?" the counselor added.

Now that surprised her. Libby thought she was hiding it better than that. Her grades were ok. Not great, but ok. She'd have to be more careful. "I'm fine, really," she said, failing at the insertion of a light tone into her words. They came out sounding stiff and brittle.

Ms. Mabel nodded, and they sat in silence for a while, the counselor waiting for Libby to speak. She said nothing, even when Ms. Mabel nudged a bowl of hard candies towards her, prompting Libby to wonder if she'd learned in counselor school stoners liked to eat sweets.

"Well, ok then. You know you'll be suspended for this? But we can discuss it further when your father gets here. You and I will meet again when you return to school, ok?" Libby still said nothing, but tears were welling in her eyes.

Unable to sit still, Libby was up and pacing around the office, where she'd been instructed to wait. They'd left her in the Vice Principal's office. Fucking nightmare. Her grandmother's angry squawks were coming through the wall from the office next door but could not make out the words. It didn't matter. She knew what Gam would be saying. Something about the school's responsibility for this disaster and something else about how she was certain they'd agree keeping it quiet was in everyone's best interest.

Why couldn't they just suspend her and get it over with? She looked at her phone, made a decision and clicked out a text message.

Me-I fucking hate school.

Her mother's response came a few seconds later.

Mom-hi sweetie, what's up?
Me-in the vice principal's office.
Mom-oh no, what happened?
Me-this fucked up place has no respect for privacy.
Mom-Libby, what happened?
Me-they went thru my locker. Found stuff.
Mom-what? what did they find?
Me-u know.
Mom-no, I don't know.
Me-weed
No response for a minute. Then finally, her mother's text
    reply.
Mom-you need to call me.
Me-can't
Mom-why?
Me-they won't let me. not supposed to text even. dads
    here w gam.

Gam's presence would get to Evelyn. She hated Gam. She'd never admit it but, it was true. To be fair, Gam treated her like shit. Condescending and rude. The way she was with most people, only worse.

Mom-what is the school going to do?
Me-fuck them probably nothing.
Mom-come on. what happened?
Me-suspension at least this week. No dance, but I don't
    give a shit. I hate my friends. She hesitated then
    added, *they said expulsion, but I'm sure Gam will give*
    $$$ and that won't happen. Gotta go. I fucking hate
    school.

Libby set the phone down on her lap and swallowed hard. She had no idea why she'd done that. Texted her mother.

The phone dinged. Message indicator.

Mom-Libby. I love u. this is hard-i get it. Do u hear me? the weed is obviously not ok. but we will talk.

After a minute, without a response, Evelyn sent another text.

Mom-lib, really. call me as soon as you can—I'm so sorry I'm not there. we will sort this out together. I Luv u.

Libby stared at the phone until her tears blurred the words.

CHAPTER FIFTY-SEVEN

Gwen | 1973

July 1, 1973

I'm better today. Better than yesterday, anyway. I can get out of bed, move around a bit, but not for long. Still, I'm so tired. My arms and legs don't feel like my own. I keep telling John it's the pills, but he says I have to take them. For me. For the baby. I sleep all night, and then I sleep half the day again.

I tried to tell the doctors at the Orleans Clinic but have trouble forcing my mouth to make the words. A few times, I think I've fallen asleep right there in the exam room. It's been months since the hospital since those awful treatments. I think I should be doing better by now.

Mama Yates is here. Living with us. Ever since the hospital. I don't have the energy to fight, so I let her take care of most things. Groceries, cooking, cleaning up. The house smells like something chemical all the time. Ajax, I think. Bleach. Like she's trying to clean every bit of me out of here.

I think Carolyn doesn't know me now. I'm with her just a short time every day, and then they take her away. Watching all the time. Circling me. Like vultures.

The doctor says I've been ill. He says I didn't know what was real and what wasn't. It's confusing because I remember being afraid. Before the hospital. Before the medicine. I was afraid all the time. Of the baby. Of John. But I'm not now. What's real is what I can touch, see, and hear. I know the difference. Still, five pills a day. That's what I have to take, and Mama Yates makes sure I take all of them.

The weeds are strangling the garden. Except for the foxglove, which I can see, standing deep pink and strong from my bedroom window, all the other flowers are dead.

Next year will be better, I think, as I look out into the dying garden. But then, Mama Yates comes in to close the curtains, tells me I need to rest, and I have to wonder if next year will be any better at all.

-G

CHAPTER FIFTY-EIGHT

Nick | Baton Rouge

The rain began as Nick was leaving the medical examiner's office. Huge, ash-colored clouds were gathering in the east like armies. The air was thick and thunder growled across the landscape. Getting into the car, he cursed himself for a thousand things. He should have listened to Chief Broussard; he should not have been seduced by simple answers; he'd been angry and lazy. Broussard knew they were lying and Nick should have known the Chief was onto something.

Nick turned the key, shifted, hit the gas too hard, and felt childish when the car tires squealed rubber into the pavement. He thought about the box of files. Where did Broussard get those names? Crystal Bergeron, Debbie Dugas, Tracy Wilkinson, Wanda Rabalais. Four homeless teenagers. Four dead teenagers. Not just dead, murdered. If it was true, if all those autopsies were lies, then the cover-up dated back forty-plus years, and someone had killed Broussard or had him killed for crimes that were decades old.

The drive back down to Eden from Baton Rouge could be pleasant on some days - dry days. Straight, flat, wide-open most of the way. Views of the bayou broken only by clumps of bald cypress here and there. He used the time to work through cases in his head, or clear his mind, or just relax. On some days, this familiar stretch of highway was a comfort, offering respite from a life that so often left him feeling disoriented and alone. Today was not one of those days. The air seemed intentionally oppressive, and the road before him was infinite. His irritation grew with each curve of the highway as he watched the blacktop unfurl with no end in sight.

Fat raindrops plopped against the windshield in twos and threes and then fours and sixes. In a rapid crescendo, the rain turned to sheets, and a curtain of water blocked his view. He flipped the wipers to ON for the fourth time since starting out. Rain in southeast Louisiana came like that. Without warning, thunderclouds could split the sky, and, because of being near or below sea level, entire communities might watch their lives wash away with floodwaters in a matter of minutes. The result was a murky, sodden world that appeared always precipitously balanced at the edge of obliteration.

Other things washed away in this part of the world, too, Nick thought. Things like sins. Down here, folks buried their dead in vaults above ground to keep the water from bringing the bodies back to the surface and washing them away. The hopelessness of finding a child killer after thirty years of filth and flood seemed overwhelming.

The wipers were having trouble keeping up, and Nick had to slow the car to pedestrian speed just to stay on the road. "Shit, shit," he blurted, hunching over the steering wheel, trying to peer through the rain and see beyond to the road. It was twenty minutes later when, as suddenly as it had begun, the rain ceased. Nick let out his breath in a long sigh and sat back in the seat.

His phone buzzed, and Briggs's voice came through the dash. "Hey Nick, listen, we finally got in touch with someone from NOAH, that psych hospital up in New Orleans."

"Yeah? Let me guess. Nothing right?"

"Actually, less than nothing. The records administrator, if you can believe it, is still alive, retired but still living in New Orleans, and guess what? He remembers the case."

"No shit."

"Yeah. Thirty-plus years and the guy remembers the fucking case. It was a big deal. After the mother's suicide, social services were heavily involved. Caseworkers were at the house. They completed all the paperwork. They planned the admission for the kid, Carolyn, but then, and this is the weird part, she never showed up."

"You mean she got picked up by social services but never transported?" asked Nick.

"Nope. I mean, according to this guy, they canceled the whole admission; he says no way would social services or hospital personnel have picked her up without an admission. So no, nada, nothing. It never happened."

"Wow. Any explanation why?"

"Nope. That's the other weird thing. Although I guess that happened sometimes. Parents changed their minds or whatever, but not without paperwork. There was no paperwork to follow-up. This guy remembers the whole thing being peculiar."

"Yeah," said Nick. "But in this case, we have a sister who claims she remembers the girl being hospitalized. Spending years up there, maybe even dying up at that place."

"Yeah, right. I asked the guy about that. He couldn't figure it out. There are no records. So, that's where we are as of now, anyway. It could be the wrong hospital, I guess, but according to this retired administrator, adolescents from Eden wouldn't have gone anywhere else. Not back then, anyway. You want me to talk to the Yates woman about it?"

"No," said Nick. "I'll check it out with her. Thanks, Briggs."

He rolled his head from side to side, rubbed at the back of his neck, and hit the button to release the driver's side window. He thought about confronting Evelyn on this hospital thing. She seemed so utterly positive her sister went up to the psychiatric facility. Explanations whirled around in his mind. Was Evelyn lying? But why? What would be the motivation? Confused? Deluded? She'd been so young. Children misremember all the time. Then there were those things the psychologists talked about a lot in the '90s. False memories? Could that be it? Or was it possible someone had really taken Carolyn?

He leaned his head outside and glanced toward the sky. A slice of sunshine cut through the cloud cover, and he could just make out the beginnings of a rainbow.

CHAPTER FIFTY-NINE

Evelyn | Eden

Evelyn set the phone down on the café table, pushed the wine glass away and shut her eyes. Her daughter's face came to mind. Not her daughter now, but Libby at five on the beach with sunlight in her hair and innocence and hope in her eyes.

Opening her eyes, she glanced up in time to see a man watching her from across the narrow street. *Was he watching her?* No. Yes. She thought so. She had no idea. She looked in the man's direction again. His face was turned toward her, confident, chin firm, like he knew her. Lanky with acne scars on both cheeks. She couldn't see his eyes behind dark glasses, but she pictured them. Wet stones. She picked up her bag, preparing to make her way back inside the cafe. Perhaps they had a back door. Escape.

He's tall. He'll be fast. He could outpace her two to one. He'd grab her from behind and guide her away. Even if she screamed, he could drag her off before the lone waiter could call anyone.

She left a bill on the table and stood, holding her handbag in front of her; it was a weapon if necessary. She thought about the hard metal flask inside. Stepping off the curb, she monitored the man as she made her way back toward her car. She watched him as he checked his watch, probably pretending he was waiting for someone, she thought. Sly. Then he took a few steps in the direction she was moving. He was following her. She sped up. Her car was right there, less than ten feet away, but she had the terrible feeling the man would break into a run and snatch her before she made it. She glanced up and down the street. Deserted, except for a couple of boys who looked to be ten or eleven, sitting on the sidewalk, huddled over some sort of handheld game device. Distracted. For an insane second, she wondered if they were part of the plan to abduct her, although she couldn't see how they'd be helpful.

At the car, she fumbled with the key, finally getting the door open. Inside, she hit the buttons to lock everything, then glanced out the windows, looking for the tall man. He'd disappeared, and she had a momentary panic. Somehow, he'd made it to her car ahead of her and was waiting in the backseat. She turned sharply and peered over the seat. Nothing.

She turned the key, half expecting the engine to stall, horror movie style. It turned over smoothly, and she pulled out of the parking space, trembling, sweating, and shaken. After a minute, her heart calmed, and her breathing slowed. She was irritated, and confused, even a little embarrassed. Was she crazy? Paranoid? No, this guy was following her, she was sure.

•   •   •   •   •

Back at the house, Evelyn pushed open the front door, checking behind it before she went inside. Dark thoughts tangled her mind. Attackers. Rapists. Murderers. Kidnappers. There was nothing behind the door, and, although she felt a little stupid doing it, she propped it open before searching the rest of the space. The bathroom door hung open, and she could see it harbored no intruders. The master bedroom was empty, save for the mess she'd made, cluttering clothes and papers across the bed and floor. She flipped on the kitchen wall switch and blinked as harsh white light flooded the space. Nobody waiting in there either. Finally, she approached the door to the second bedroom. The one she'd shared with Carolyn and been unable to confront. Hand on the blackened brass doorknob, she twisted it and inched the door open.

The smell hit her first. Mold. The room must have been shut up since before her father died. She wondered if he'd ever gone in after Evelyn left home. Over twenty years' worth of dust and accumulated moisture from leaky windowpanes and a sagging roof.

The little twin beds sat, headboards against the far wall, positioned as they were the last time Evelyn had been in there. The two mattresses were bare. Someone must have stripped the sheets off at some point. Mrs. Coolidge. The cotton curtains her mother had sewn still hung from the single window, the lining destroyed by the sun, and the red cotton unevenly faded to a pinkish white.

She hit the wall switch. Nothing happened. The bare bulb was dead. There were no lamps in the room, just the dresser she remembered, now flaked and filthy, in the corner. The walls were as bare as when she'd moved out. The wallpaper now buckled and peeled away, the glue underneath probably liquefying with the heat and moisture. Evelyn sat on the bed nearest the window. Her bed. She let her eyes close and forced down the lump in her throat.

Carolyn is searching for something in the dark. On her knees. Pushing aside the bed linens. "Shhhh," she says. "Go back to sleep." Evelyn watches, wide-eyed and awake. She's afraid to speak. To breathe. Finally, her sister turns. An angry light in her eyes. "Where is it?" She demands. Carolyn hisses, "What did you do with it?" Evelyn covers her ears and shuts her eyes. Go away. Leave me alone. She only thinks these words, but when she opens her eyes, Carolyn is gone. The room is empty. Silent except for the ticking of Mama's clock in the hall and her own breath coming short and hard. She props herself up on her knees and watches out the window. The moon is full, and its silver light, scattered by the trees, falls like jewels to the ground around the girl as she runs away into the night.

CHAPTER SIXTY

Libby | San Francisco

Libby was pacing. The whole day had agitated her, left her wanting what she could not have. Gam searched her room after school and had, predictably, found the razor blades and taken them along with everything else. Even the little X-Acto knife Libby kept in her desk drawer. *For emergencies.* Stupidly, she'd shoved it in there and forgotten about it. Computer, credit cards, social life. This time her father actually said *grounded.* Gam lectured her all the way home. Told her stuff she already knew. Using words like *family, potential, pathetic,* and *disappointment.* Drugs were a "last straw" for Gam. Which was, of course, ridiculous, given Stuart's daily habit. Libby glared at him in the car as he stayed silent while Gam went on and on. Hypocrite. Libby tried to shut her out, but they'd taken her headphones too. For whatever reason, they'd forgotten to take the phone.

It didn't matter. Tomorrow was Saturday. By noon, her father would be high as a kite and off somewhere with his newest hottie. He'd leave the maid or Gam in charge, and Gam would be asleep by eight-thirty. Libby's phone buzzed. She checked it. A text from Celia. She didn't really want to talk to Celia, but she'd been avoiding her much of the day.

> *Me: Hey.*
> *Celia: what are you doing?*
> *Me: Nothing. Loving suspension. Not.*
> *Celia:* 😞

Me: joke, it's fine.
Celia: Are you going tomorrow?
Me: can't
Celia: today?
Me: grounded for today.
Celia: Does that matter? ☺

Celia, well aware of Stuart's inconsistent parenting techniques, was referring to the overnight after-party they'd planned to follow the dance. Both Celia and Libby knew that, as long as Evelyn was not involved, "grounded" meant little. Half the time, it meant little, even if Evelyn was involved. The thing was, and Libby would not admit this to Celia (or anyone); she didn't even *want* to go anymore. She didn't really *want* to do much of anything.

Me: LOL, yeah. Don't know. Will have to see.
Celia: I'm sure it will be fine.
Me: I hope so.

Celia had a perpetually optimistic outlook, and sometimes it annoyed Libby. Nothing terrible had ever happened in Celia's life. At least, nothing Libby knew about. She had a bratty little brother and parents with high expectations, but that was about it. It wasn't Celia's fault she was so fucking optimistic. Celia was Libby's oldest friend, and Libby felt a peculiar, sisterly loyalty towards her. Libby thought for a moment, then typed.

Me: wanna come over after school?
Celia: gotta finish homework first. My mom checks it. Ok?
Me: sure. I'm stuck here, anyway.
Celia: K. Be there later. TTYL.
Me: K. Bye.

She checked her messages, hoping for Conner. Nothing.

She stripped out of her clothes and padded to her bathroom to take a shower. As the hot water ran, she studied her reflection in the mirror. Pictured Celia doing homework that her mother would then check before allowing her to leave the house. *What would that be like? To* have a parent so involved with your life, they actually knew you had homework, let alone were willing to check it before setting you free to pursue your social life. The idea was so foreign; Libby could not even sort out if she would like the arrangement.

She thought about her own mother, thought about the text conversation they'd had earlier, still struck by the strangeness of it. Her mother had not freaked out today. What was it she'd texted? *I love you. I get it. This is hard.* Something like that anyway. That was the first time Libby could remember her mother handling something serious without losing her shit. It wasn't too late. The thing in Libby's head was ballooning. Soon it would be too big to handle on her own. Suddenly, she regretted inviting Celia. She shook her head at her own image in the mirror. *Fuck it*, she thought and got into the shower.

•　　　•　　　•　　　•　　　•

Libby checked the clock next to her bed. She still had time before Celia arrived. Lots of time. Too much damn time. She dressed in sweats and a UCB T-shirt, then changed her mind. Celia would notice the stain on the shirt. The sloppiness. She'd ask *concerned* questions. Libby did not want to answer *concerned* questions. She pulled off the sweats, shoved them into the closet, and pulled a pair of black legging off a hanger. Tried a cardigan over the T-shirt. Looked at herself in the mirror. She looked homeless. Shook her head and started over.

Finally, back to the sweats but with a minor upgrade in T-shirt (at least this one was clean), she sat in the big chair in her room and thumbed through the history book she hadn't read. God, she couldn't wait for school to let out. Five more days and freedom. Not that she was looking forward to doing anything over the summer. It was more that she was looking forward to *not* having to do anything. Ever. She suspected this thought was unhealthy.

She tossed the book to the floor and picked up her phone. Scrolled absently through Instagram and Snapchat, looking, of course, for Conner. Fucker. She texted him exactly that: fucker. Changed her mind and deleted the text without sending it.

Getting up, she crossed the room to the closet. On her knees, she dug Evelyn's diary out from where she'd hid it in the corner, under a pile of old runners. She opened it to the first page and then flipped through to the very last entry: *I did something bad, and now Carolyn is gone.* She tapped at the page, considering, then she picked up the phone.

CHAPTER SIXTY-ONE

Gwen | 1973

July 17, 1973

Mama Yates is dead. Yesterday morning I'm in the kitchen with her, and she's telling me I need to let her alone to do what she needs doing and as usual, I'm feeling too worn down to say much. She's reaching over the sink to shut down the faucet, and she turns to me, and her eyes have gone wide and wild, like a cornered dog. Her face is pale. More than pale. Bluish, sickly, and I ask if she's feeling alright, and she doesn't answer. Just stands there for a few seconds like she's lost. Then she clutches at her face, looking like she might scratch out her own eyes, and she falls down screaming. John is gone for the morning, and I'm so scared I'm not sure what to do.

I kneel beside her, and she's sort of flopping around on the ground, like a fish, making a terrible sound I've never heard before. Then she just stops. She lays there staring up at the ceiling, but I know right away she's dead.

Her screams have woken the baby, and I can hear Carolyn whimpering in the next room. And up in the sink, the water is just running and running.

The doctor says it was a blood vessel in her brain that did it. He says it was just sitting there, swollen, and thin and ready to go at any moment, only she didn't know it. The doctor tells John it's nobody's fault. These things happen, he says. But John can't stop thinking he should have been home. Should have been here to help. I think, no matter what the doctor says, John blames me. At least a little.

-G

July 31, 1973

John is drinking more. Ever since the funeral. When he's not drinking, he's so sad and distant. It's like he's not here at all.

He forgets to check up on my medication. Hasn't asked me about it in weeks. I tell Mrs. Coolidge she doesn't need to come anymore. I don't tell her I stopped taking all that medicine, and I feel much better, but I think she knows. She smiles when I tell her we're doing fine on our own.

I spend three days out in the garden, weeding and planting for late summer. Giant sunflowers and marigolds and red anemone. There is pink moss rose spreading under the weeds, and I find them as I pull away debris, like tiny treasures.

John gets worse every day. He mentions my treatment at the Orleans clinic just once. I tell him I don't have to go anymore. He says nothing. Just takes another sip of his beer.

-G

CHAPTER SIXTY-TWO

Nick | Eden

Saturday, June 10
Present Day

Twenty-four hours. He'd been calling her since yesterday morning and she'd not been answering for exactly that long. Obviously, she did not want to talk to him. At first, he'd been calling out of guilt, some misguided sense of responsibility for what had happened between them. But now... things were different. She had to talk to him... or at least listen. He'd see her in person. No choice. He'd decided.

As he pulled up to the house on Road 12, he felt suddenly, profoundly, less sure. He didn't know this woman. What he knew was messy. Worse, what he had to tell her, the information he needed to pass along, would be unsettling or even emotionally traumatic for Evelyn. He thought for a few moments about turning the car around. She hadn't seen him drive up. He turned off the engine and sat for a moment, the key still in the ignition.

Then he saw her. In the kitchen window, her dark head bent over the sink. He watched as she rubbed at her forehead with the back of her wrist, water running off the ends of her fingers, glistening droplets in the morning sun. She looked up. Their eyes met. She cocked her head, trying to reconcile his presence in her front yard. Her eyes narrowed, and he thought she looked annoyed. Too late now, he thought as he got out of the car. She was at the door, pulling it open as he climbed the front steps.

"What?" she asked. Definitely annoyed.

"Hi," he said, aware he sounded sheepish and stupid.

"Yeah?"

"First, I just wanted to apologize. I'm... I'm sorry. For the other night."

"Ok, you said it. Is that it?" Her mouth was a dark line, but her eyes were soft.

"Uh," he stuttered, hesitated. "Uh, no. Not really. Can I come in?"

She stared at him, and for a moment, he expected her to turn on her heel and disappear inside. Then she shrugged, stepped back, and let him pass.

She poured them both coffees, and they sat opposite each other at the tiny kitchen table. He tried to tell her again he was sorry, but she cut him off. "Look, it's fine. We're both adults. It was... a mistake. The beer. You know. Whatever." She waved her hand in the air in a gesture of meaninglessness. He felt hurt instead of relieved. He let it go.

"Ok, well, there's something else. The preliminary DNA results are back. The comparison with yours." He watched her for signs of resistance. She looked away.

"And?" she almost whispered.

"It's her, Evelyn. It's Carolyn." He started to say something else, but she held up a hand. He quieted. Waited. He could see her processing what he'd just said, folding it into her belief system. She chewed at her bottom lip.

After a minute, she looked at him, inhaled deeply. "I don't get it. She... left... They took her... I saw. They took her to the hospital..."

"We checked it out. The hospital, I mean. We looked into it. The hospital up in New Orleans and... she wasn't there, Evelyn. Carolyn was never there."

She shook her head, staring at him. "You're wrong; that's... just wrong."

"No," he said. "It's not wrong. I'm sorry. There are no records. She wasn't there."

Evelyn pushed herself out of the chair, and went to the sink, looked out the window for a long time. She wore an old-fashioned sundress of yellow cotton, and her feet were bare. Finally, she turned toward him, dark eyes shining. "What do you mean, anyway? She wasn't there? Of course, she was there. I watched them take her there. I watched them drag her away. She fucking died there. My father told me. What are you talking about?"

"I'm sorry, Evelyn."

She shook her head. "No, no, don't tell me you're sorry. You're wrong," her voice was calm, but her hands trembled where they rested on the counter behind her. "You're just mistaken. Maybe the records were lost, right? It was a long time ago."

"No. We spoke to a man who remembers." He tried to explain, but she'd stopped listening.

"Just stop, I don't want to hear anymore. Ok? Not now. Just. Stop. I need to think." She looked up at him. "Look, I know you're trying to help, ok? I need to... I just need to think. Be alone right now. Ok?"

"Yeah, sure, ok. I'll go." He stood and carried his coffee cup to the sink. "Look, one thing. One other thing you should know. You were right, or at least I think you're right. We've had a second opinion on the autopsy, and the findings are inconsistent with Dr. Finney's conclusions." Her back stiffened, and Nick could see the muscles in her neck tense. She said nothing. "Dr. Lee, the Baton Rouge ME, had a different conclusion."

"She was killed wasn't she?"

"Yeah. It was murder, likely by a blow to the head with some type of blunt object."

Evelyn looked deflated. Exhausted. Her eyes welled with tears.

"Evelyn, I am so sorry. We all are. Please know that we are doing everything we can to investigate."

She tilted her head; her eyes suddenly focused on him. Warm. "And your Chief? He knew something, didn't he?"

Nick nodded. "We think so."

"And they killed him for it." Her face was softer now. Her cheeks flushed. She turned and reached for Nick's hand. "I'm sorry too, Nick. I'm so sorry, too."

CHAPTER SIXTY-THREE

Evelyn | Eden

The box sat on the bed, staring at Evelyn. Daring her. She ran a finger around the rim of the plastic cup she held on her lap and considered. She needed answers. Nick's visit had raised so many new questions, and she didn't know where else to turn. She could open the box and review its contents. A proposition that seemed much less palatable now that she'd gotten the thing out of the bottom drawer. Evelyn took a long drink, emptying half the cup. It was a tumbler, if she was being honest. Not her fault she was drinking from an enormous vessel; there were no actual wine glasses in the house, so she'd been reduced to a trip to the Circle K for red plastic party cups everyone remembers from frat parties. Circle K also sold screw top wine, so it was a double win. The tumblers served nicely; they didn't need re-filling as often. She'd have to remember that for home.

She looked at the box, unable to lift the lid. To empty the contents. She'd thought it was a shoebox when she first saw it the day she arrived, but it wasn't. It was a cardboard box, pale green, about twice the size of a shoebox, and on the lid faded lettering and delicately drawn flowering vines. It was a seed catalog box. One of Gwen's. Suddenly Evelyn remembered Gwen would order these seasonally. She'd let the girls help open the box, and they'd marvel at all the colored packets of flower and vegetable seeds. Little packages of promise. She couldn't believe she'd forgotten about that. This was Gwen's box. The things inside belonged to her.

It took a long time to go through everything. She'd made herself a deal. One slug from the plastic tumbler for each document. There were many photographs, primarily pictures of Carolyn and Evelyn as babies and young children. Holiday pictures. Birthdays. Several children were seated around a small table, Evelyn in a highchair, an oversized birthday cake in the middle, thick with icing a shade of pink no food should ever be. Five candles. Carolyn, wearing a golden paper crown looks into the camera as if she's surprised all this is happening. Evelyn picked up each photo, and studied it, trying to summon an associated memory. It was like viewing a slideshow of someone else's life. She had no recollection of birthday parties or happy holidays or friends coming over to the house.

There were letters from her father, written while he was on the road, working. More informational than love letters, really. A few postcards. Mostly local and blank. Her mother had collected them, sometimes pinning them up on the walls as artwork. Evelyn had forgotten that.

She'd downed the first bottle of wine and was working on the second when she finally reached the bottom of the box. There it was, a leather journal, red and worn and tied up with twine. A homespun lock. Gingerly, she lifted it from the box and lay it on her lap. The twine was old, crispy. It would have disintegrated if she'd yanked at it. But, somehow, it seemed essential to keep all of it, everything, intact. She was carefully untangling the twine when her phone buzzed. Not a text. A call. Libby.

Libby had found the diary. Evelyn's goddamn diary. And, weirdly, she'd chosen that exact moment to call Evelyn about it. If Evelyn had been a spiritual person, she might have found it touching or even profound; her daughter finding her diary at the moment she's discovering her dead mother's old journal, but Evelyn suspected this situation would be more complicated and stressful than spiritual and profound.

Gwen gave her that book for her tenth birthday, although Evelyn's commitment to journaling had been only sporadic. She tried to remember what she might have written; what secrets might Libby have discovered? There were probably a handful of entries during the months before Gwen died, light, stupid, childish stuff, when Evelyn's biggest problems had revolved around hating math, impatience with not yet being a teenager, and not liking whatever was in her lunch sack. The few times she'd looked at those early pages (and she'd only looked at the early pages) as an adult, the experience had been like viewing the photos in this box. Like looking into someone else's life, someone else's *happy* life. What had she been thinking about keeping it? She hadn't been thinking. She hadn't even considered the diary's existence since they moved into the Sunset apartment eight years earlier. She'd shoved it under the mattress and successfully forgotten about it. Jacinta, the housekeeper, changed the sheets weekly and must have just tucked the thing back every time.

Of course, Libby went looking, and, of course, Libby didn't believe that she'd forgotten it was there. Evelyn could hardly be angry with her for it. Given everything going on. Poor kid just wanted information, needed some kind of grounding, and she deserved the truth. Or at least as much of the truth as Evelyn could stomach and remember. That was the problem. She hadn't lied about her memory. It really was shit. Enormous holes where days and months should be. If she hadn't been a kid then, she'd swear that back in 1986, she'd been blacked out drunk. It was the same feeling. Like her brain did not lay down the tape during certain parts of her life.

Yes, she admitted to Libby, she had lied about her mother. Gwen didn't die when Evelyn was an infant. That had been a pure fabrication. In response to the admission, Libby refused to believe anything else Evelyn said. *It's bullshit,* Libby hissed into the phone. *You are totally full of shit. Everything you say is a lie.* Evelyn thought that was a little harsh. Not *everything* she said was a lie. Just much of it. Most of it.

Gritting her teeth, Evelyn concentrated on making sure the words coming out of her mouth were truthful to the best of her recollection. She felt like she was on a witness stand. She'd never been in court, but that's what it looked like on SVU, anyway. It felt like the truth was being squeezed out of her. Yes, she told Libby, my mother lived until I was ten, and then she committed suicide (true). No, I don't know why (true). No, nobody ever speculated why (sort of true). Yes, she was sad sometimes (true), but no, we didn't expect suicide (true). I lied about Carolyn, and yes, I know what happened (sort of true). She had problems after Mama died. Well, she always had problems, but they got worse (true). My father, I guess my father, and some social workers sent her to live in a special hospital. I never saw her again. (Sort of true. Sort of true. Sort of true.)

John was another story. Evelyn couldn't tell Libby about John. She honestly couldn't remember. He'd been a drunk, that was true, but was it fair to call him abusive? Probably not. He was ill, grieving, pathetic, but never cruel.

Libby had said, *It's not good enough, Mom. You need to tell me what's happening. What the fuck is going on? I need to know.*

So do I, thought Evelyn. *I need to know what the fuck is going on, too.*

Then Libby said it. "You wrote something in your diary, Mom. Something in August, after your mother died, after Carolyn left, or whatever. It was the last thing you wrote. Do you remember?"

"What, Libby? What did I write?" Evelyn's heart pounded. She did not know what Libby was about to say. Another blank in her memory. She couldn't blame the childhood stuff on alcohol. She wasn't drunk at ten. Was it possible she'd done some sort of damage to herself during the intervening years? She'd read somewhere that childhood trauma could cause lots of... what did they call it? Fragmented memories. But that was the thing; she didn't feel traumatized. Pissed off, but not seriously traumatized. She was more numb than anything else; that was not good.

She could hear pages turning, then, Libby recited the words Evelyn had penned over thirty years earlier: 'I did something bad, and now Carolyn is gone.' Evelyn's breath caught. She held it, afraid to move, wishing the next moment would never arrive. She glanced down at the red leather journal still in her lap. Outside, she heard the knocking of a woodpecker in the stillness. "What did you do, Mom? What happened to Carolyn?"

After a long pause, Evelyn said, "Lib, I... I don't know."

"What is that supposed to mean? You don't know? That's not even an answer."

"Oh, God. I'm sorry. I know." She tried again. "Look, Libby. I swear. I don't remember writing that. I don't even know what it means." She could hear Libby breathing on the line, but she was saying nothing. "I'm sorry, sweetie. I wish I did, really I wish I did."

Libby sighed. "Mom, stop, just stop. When are you going to learn to trust someone with the truth?"

Evelyn needed time to think about the last question. The truth. What exactly was the truth? Was it what she remembered? Was it the pictures in the box? Or was it the stories people told her? "Libby, for now, I just need you to believe I don't remember that diary entry. I wish I could tell you for sure I did nothing wrong, but I... I can't. I just can't." It would be so simple. She could make up a million reasons for that stupid diary entry. All of them plausible. None of them true. "Give me some time. Ok? I'm trying to figure it out. What I remember is that Carolyn went away. They came and got her and took her, and she went to a hospital in New Orleans, and years later, she died there. That's what my father told me, and I had no reason to believe otherwise."

"I want to, Mom. I want to believe you." Evelyn could hear the sniffle of tears in her daughter's voice, and it broke her heart. "I think I believe that's what you think happened. I just wish... I don't know. It's all so... so messed up. That's all."

"I know. I know. Just give me some time. I'll figure this out. I love you, Lib."

She'd finally ended the call. Some excuse about an appointment. Another lie. God, bullshit just slipped out of her mouth, as easy as breath. It was such a messed up habit, but the words were often out of her mouth before she knew she was doing it, sometimes before she realized they weren't true. It occurred to Evelyn it might be possible to tell an untruth so often that it became a fact in your mind. Was it possible that's what had happened with Carolyn? Had she manufactured a story about Carolyn and repeated it to herself tens, hundreds, thousands of times until it became so embedded into the fabric of her consciousness that the lie became virtually indiscernible from the truth? How would that be any different from insanity?

She collapsed back on the bed, staring at the water-damaged ceiling; huge, yellowed splotches discolored the ivory paint. She thought for a moment about her father. Who was he protecting with his lies? Himself? Evelyn? And the way he'd died. Alone, sick. His corpse rotting for a week before being found. If he weren't the monster she'd convinced herself he'd been, what did that make her?

It's 2001, and Evelyn goes to Eden for her father's funeral. She has no desire to attend but supposes she goes anyway out of something like guilt or obligation. Instead of contemplating her reasons for going, she stays drunk the whole time. They cremate him. The afternoon of the burial, it is so quiet that the entire world seems dead. Only a handful of people show up. The Sheriff, Doc Carson, and a couple of guys from the bar who look rented for the part. Except for the minister, nobody speaks.

Evelyn supposes she should but cannot think of anything to say. No one says anything about John Yates being three sheets when he falls down, but she knows. He hadn't had a sober day since Carolyn left.

A man she's never met before sits Evelyn down in a strip mall office that smells of menthol cigarettes and vanilla air freshener. He talks and talks to her. He tells her how John died intestate, how he had only one descendent, and how that is her. She stares out the window. People drive up and park beat-up cars at Blockbuster or the Chinese takeout place or the beauty supply store. They go in, and after a few minutes, they appear, sometimes carrying packages, sometimes not. Nobody smiles. Some with grimy little kids. Some drag them or holler at them or both. Clerks shuffle in and out on smoke breaks. Most of the stores have dusty windows and garish signs in need of repair. The whole place is depressing and vulnerable.

The lawyer snaps his folder closed and says, "Ms. Yates?"

"Huh?" She looks at him. "Sorry, distracted."

"Hmm. I said, do you understand what I've said?"

"Uh, yes."

"Yes, okay, well then, the last thing is the house. What do you think you'll want to do with it? And its contents, of course?"

"The house." A statement, not a question.

"Yes, Ms. Yates, the house. The estate is fairly small, but there is the house and its contents."

"Right, the house," she repeats.

"Would you like me to have someone go over there with you? I know you are in town alone."

"That's okay. No."

"Fine then. You can let us know what you want to do. If you choose to sell the house, I can help you with that. Just let me know." She looks at the keys he pushes toward her, and a wave of nausea rolls over her like a freight car. Shaking her head, she pushes the keys back to him, and tells the lawyer to arrange for *a real estate agent to sell the house and furniture. Donate what's left. He says he'll have the few personal items boxed up and shipped to her. She says she doesn't want them, and he says he'll send them, and she can dispose of them.*

As she leaves the lawyer's office, thinking that when she leaves Eden this time, she will not be back. She will never see that house again.

Evelyn found a dull knife in the kitchen and used it to finish picking apart the twine that bound Gwen's little journal. As it came apart, she found there were three books, nearly fused together by time. She pulled them apart and lay them out on the kitchen table. Made of identical red leather, gold ink inscribed each cover. Her mother's handwriting, long, lovely curves under the small *Y*'s and *G*'s, like calligraphy: *Diary of Gwen Yates.*

It had grown dark since she'd entered the kitchen, and she got up to switch on the light. One bulb popped and burst; Evelyn's heart thudded against her ribs, and her whole body jerked involuntarily. God, she was edgy. The remaining bulb threw the room into a half-light, accentuating tree shadows that moved over the floor like ghosts. Outside, a nightbird called plaintively, invisible somewhere in the darkness. Evelyn sat back down at the table, and opening the first book, she read.

> *June 1, 1965*
> > *Dear Diary,*
> > *So, I'm out in the barn with one of Daddy's straight razors when they find me...*

CHAPTER SIXTY-FOUR

Nick | Eden

The Yates case had attracted little attention until today; there'd been a few brief articles, mostly local, nothing national beyond one blurb in the crime section of a minor paper. The department had been careful not to release any details about the investigation. But, surveying the scene, it was clear to Nick that things had changed; someone had leaked information either late last night or early this morning. News vans jammed the parking lot and several reporters buzzed around the front doors.

Nick made a quick U-Turn in the street and headed to the back entrance, avoiding the crowd. He was stepping from his car when a young man rounded the corner of the building and jogged towards Nick. The boy was too thin for his height, with small, close-set eyes, a slightly upturned nose, and thick lips, which gave him the sort of stupid appearance peculiar to inbreeding. Nick knew him. Billy Saveneaux. Nick could not imagine what Billy might want, but any interaction with this boy right now would be remarkably inconvenient. However, the kid belonged to the town, and the town, Nick believed, was his charge. He sighed to himself. "Billy, what the hell are you doing back here? You ought to do something productive right now, like school, maybe?"

"Uh, summer."

"Aren't you old enough to get a job yet?"

"Uh, no, sir, I just made fifteen last month, sir," Billy said.

Nick softened. Billy was not a smart boy, and he was prone to petty criminal activity, but he was always polite and had a sort of sweetness about him. "Yeah, right, well, something then," Nick said and started looking through his keys. "Last time I brought you over here for stealing from the Piggly Wiggly, and you were what? Twelve or thirteen?" He gave up on the keys and looked at Billy. "So, what do you want, son? What have you got there?" Nick gestured at the manila envelope the boy was clutching to his chest. Sweat soaked his white T-shirt at the neckline and underarms, and a few of his ribs were visible through the nearly transparent fabric.

"Uh, I got this for you, uh, sir," Billy said and held out the envelope.

"Is that right? From whom?" asked Nick.

"Can't say." Billy passed the soggy envelope to Nick, who held it between three fingers. "Open it when you're alone. The man said, give it to Detective MacCallum and tell him to open it when he's alone."

"What man Billy? You need to tell me." Nick's thoughts were ticking by quickly. "Come on inside. Let's sit down, okay?" *Could he hold this kid? He couldn't arrest him for delivering a message, at least not yet.* Nick looked down at the envelope, weighing his options. He peeled at the seal.

"Gotta go," Billy said. He turned and sprinted back down the alley before Nick could say another word.

Inside the building, things were calmer than Nick had expected. Sheriff Savoy was on the premises to address the media, whose numbers, Nick could now see, were escalating at an alarming rate. *What the hell had gotten out?* He'd deal with that next.

Nick grabbed an evidence bag and rubber gloves and sat down at his desk. He dropped the envelope into the bag, placed it on his desk, and slipped on the gloves. He held the clear plastic bag up to the ceiling light and examined the envelope it held, twisting it back and forth to see it on all sides before setting it back down. Then he picked up a thin steel knife, slid it inside the bag, pried open one edge of the manila paper, and slid out the contents using two gloved fingers.

Five photographs. That was all. Reprints from digital images, it looked like. Poor quality. Nick spread them out and studied each individually, then all five together. Using a magnifying glass, he spent a long time examining various objects within each photo, and then he put down the glass and pushed the images together so that they were sitting edge-to-edge.

It was like this before a nasty car accident, he'd heard. The oncoming car, the wall, the cliff, or whatever is clearly visible, but the victim cannot comprehend the total disaster, and cannot quite wrap his brain around the accident's inevitability, until just before the end when reality hits. Nick had never understood that before. Now he did. He stared at the photographs on his desk, the terrible facts laid out like pieces of a jigsaw puzzle, feeling nothing beyond mild confusion. "No," he said aloud, "this isn't right." He didn't understand. Then, a half-second later, he did.

CHAPTER SIXTY-FIVE

Gwen | 1974

January 3, 1974

I've met a man. As I write, I feel ashamed and excited at the same time. It happens like this:

I am downtown with Carolyn, buying groceries when he bumps into me, spilling one of our bags. The next thing I know, bean cans roll every which way, and he is lurching around the sidewalk, trying to catch them. We both laugh as he hands me one of the dented cans. We speak on the sidewalk for a few minutes, and he reminds me we've met before. I feel flattered, he remembers, but also embarrassed. It was at the community center last year and I wasn't at my best. He's a professional man. So good-looking and young with clear, intelligent eyes and the smile of a boy. I feel sure he doesn't drink.

We said our awkward goodbyes, and I turned to leave, pushing the stroller ahead. As we go, I can feel his eyes on me.

-G

January 10, 1974

It's been a week, and I see him again downtown. I pretend it's a coincidence, but I've been visiting the grocery nearly every day, hoping to bump into him. When he shows up, I wonder if he's been doing the same.

This time I've left Carolyn with Mrs. Coolidge. He asks if he can buy me a coke or a cup of tea. We sit on a park bench across from the grocery, sipping sodas and talking.

Never in my life has anyone listened to me the way he does. Curious. Gentle. Honest. He tells me he has a wife and a child, and, for a moment, I feel as if the world has ended. Then he smiles and asks if I'll be back next week, and I tell him maybe, but I know I will.

-G

March 12, 1974

We meet every week now. Sometimes twice. We are careful. I tell him about John, the drinking. His desperation. I tell him about California, about the barn, and the night I left. I even tell him about what happened when I got to Eden. The tattooed man. At first, I am afraid. I remember what Mama Yates told me. But he only touches my hand when I tell him, and he says he is so sorry that the terrible thing happened to me. When I finally dare to look at him, I see he is crying. He tells me I did the right thing to let it go. He says that Mama Yates was right about that. It's safer to let the past stay in the past.

He says he loves me, and I believe him.

-G

CHAPTER SIXTY-SIX

Nick | Eden

By the time the deputies found Billy Saveneaux, not forty-five minutes had passed since he'd given Nick the envelope. Rounding the corner of an alley two blocks from the station, Deputy Gernhauser noted a small window cracked open just wide enough for a thin teenage boy to get through if he'd had occasion to scale about six feet of a brick building and fling himself inside. At six feet, four inches, Gernhauser was just tall enough to stand on tiptoes and get a peek into the tiny utilitarian bathroom on the other side of that window.

Billy Saveneaux lay on his side, crumpled on the floor; his underfed body was so pale it was almost translucent, his legs bent at a vulgar angle, arms outstretched. The kid's face, along with with most of his skull and brains, had been blown off and up, and much of it now adhered to the wall behind the toilet.

•　　•　　•　　•　　•

"They knew each other." Nick's voice was louder, more urgent than he'd meant it to be. Sheriff Savoy looked up from her desk, where she sat reviewing what looked like a year's worth of files. "I'm sorry, ma'am. Sorry to interrupt, but I think you'll want to see these." He was holding the evidence bag with Billy Saveneaux's photos.

"Actually, Nick, I'm glad you're here. I guess you've seen the mess outside?" Her voice was low and calm. It never wavered, making it impossible to tell when she was angry or anxious. *Maybe,* Nick thought, *she wasn't either of those things. Ever.*

"Yeah, yeah, I saw it when I came in. Something's out."

"Oh yes, you could say that. What I need from you is an explanation. I suppose, however, an update is forthcoming. Am I right?"

"Yes, ma'am," Nick said.

"Well, that's good," Sheriff Savoy said, squaring the papers on her desk. "I'd say we have about five minutes, and then I need to say something to these people. Otherwise, they are going to come straight through those front doors and tear us apart."

They sat across the desk from each other; the photographs laid out next inside their plastic sleeves. Nick pointed to the first one. "So that is a photograph of Dr. Finney's parents," he said, pushing the picture closer to Sheriff Savoy. The image was black and white, a couple in old-fashioned wedding clothes. They were smiling stiffly. Captioned at the bottom was OUR WEDDING, 1940. "The date is right," Nick said. "And this guy looks exactly like our Dr. Finney, don't you think?" Sheriff Savoy nodded without taking her eyes off the picture. Nick turned the photo over.

Sheriff Savoy read out loud, "Our wedding, 1940, Lucy and Albert."

"So, I didn't make too much of that until I saw this." Nick tapped a second photograph. In this image was a copy of a birth certificate. "It's Albert Finney's birth certificate. Albert Finney, the second to be exact, was born to Albert Finney, Sr., and Lucy Picard Finney of Eden, Louisiana, in 1944. Dr. Finney doesn't use the suffix, but I'm not surprised. I don't think he wants any connection to his past. That also explains why he has no photographs, mementos, nothing personal in his office."

Savoy leaned close and read aloud, "Albert C. Finney, II born to Lucy Picard Finney and Albert C. Finney, I, DDS." She looked up at Nick. "Huh, we know that name Picard, don't we?"

"Right, we sure do. And this photo." He slid it over to the Sheriff. "Two teenagers you might recognize."

The Sheriff smiled. "Oh my," she said, studying the picture. Two teenage boys, shirtless, in cuffed jeans and crewcuts leaning against a gleaming 1950s Chevrolet. Both boys looked almost giddy. She turned it over. Printed on the backside were the words *JoJo and Ace*. "No date?" she asked.

"Nope, nothing," Nick replied. "But I'll bet that car dates the picture no earlier than the mid-'50s, and that one," he said and pointed to the tall thin boy on the left, "bears a striking resemblance to Dr. Albert Finney."

"He does, I agree," said the Sheriff.

"So, I believe that Ace and our doctor are one and the same. That's a photograph of Dr. Finney as a kid."

"And this guy, JoJo," Sheriff Savoy said, indicating the short, scrubby-faced boy in the photograph with the Chevrolet. "Is the late Sheriff Picard. Am I right?"

"Yes, ma'am," agreed Nick. "That's right. Those two knew each other as kids. More than that, they were first cousins. Then there's this," he said, pushing the fourth photo towards her. "Please, look closely; I believe they took this at the Yates' place." She picked up the plastic sleeve and held the photo to the window light.

The scene was dim. It was evening, and the image was grainy black and white, obviously digitized from another source and copied many times, yet there was no mistaking the location: the dark patch of dirt flanked by a small grove of pecan trees and four ancient live oaks laid heavy with Spanish moss. A light perched on the roof of the big barn (a barn Nick knew had burned down not long after Carolyn's disappearance) illuminated the patch. A tall fence surrounded the barnyard, and an enormous gate had been left swung open. Two men, partially shrouded in darkness, appeared to be carrying something across the patch of dimly lit earth. One was small, thin, what might be called wiry. He was wearing jeans, Doc-Martin-type boots, and a work shirt, all of which seemed too heavy for the time of year. It was easy to tell it was summer, given the rich moss on the trees. The other man was taller but still thin, his facial features almost impossible to make out. A bundle lay on the ground, partially unwrapped from what appeared to be a blanket or tarpaulin. The taller man stood with his head bowed and hands to his face in what looked like a gesture of distress. In his arms, he held something soft. A blanket or some item of clothing. There was a hole in the ground next to the bundle, and it looked like nothing else but a grave. She studied the photograph for a long point then looked up. "Jesus, Nick, we know who they are, don't we? We know who those sons of bitches are."

Nick nodded. "That's right," he said. "We know the little guy, at least. That's John Picard, for sure. The tall guy, I hope to God he's not who I think he is. Also, we don't know who the hell took these pictures and why anybody would want to record something like this."

Sheriff Savoy sat back in her chair and leveled her eyes at Nick. "Well, okay, so our late Sheriff Picard and somewhat elderly medical examiner, Dr. Finney, are first cousins and, they knew each other decades past and," she said, tapping the photograph. "Picard was involved in something seriously sketchy with a man who looks suspiciously familiar." She glanced at Nick over the top of her glasses. Eyebrows raised. "More than familiar, right? You know who that is, don't you? You know what they're doing?"

Nick nodded. "Yeah," he said quietly. "I do."

CHAPTER SIXTY-SEVEN

John Yates | 1986 | Eden

The night is sickly sweet. The scent of old magnolias wafts in over the sills of the open windows and fills the rooms. John hates the smell. It reminds him of his mother. He is unsteady on his feet, and his hands shake so badly it's difficult to tie his shoes, but he's sworn not to take a drink tonight. The thought, the sober idea, of what he is about to do sends waves of nausea crashing through his belly and brain. He sets his jaw and squeezes the wetness from his eyes.

He turns on the tap in the bathroom and leans into the sink, splashing water (lukewarm from sitting in the pipes) onto his face. He straightens and looks at himself in the mirror, now rusted around the edges and cracked. *Something about bad luck*, he thinks. The image in the mirror - desperate, piteous, lost - he does not recognize. He studies his own eyes as they search the image for something tangible to which he can grab hold. As if he's been dropped over the side of a cliff into a void, he sees himself reaching out desperately into nothing.

•   •   •   •   •

Outside, the night stench claws at his skin, and he shivers despite the heat. He holds his breath. In the distance, he sees a figure unloading something from the truck bed. He changes his mind about not taking a drink, reaches into his breast pocket, and then remembers he left the flask upstairs. In his mind, he can see it on the bedside table, and he thinks for a moment about turning around. He looks back over his shoulder in the house's direction and then dismisses the thought. *Goddammit,* he thinks, *how has it come to this?*

He reaches into his pack and runs the pads of his fingers over the soft material. *She'll need this,* he thinks. *It might get cold.* Tears spring to his eyes, and he jams the heels of his hands into the sockets.

•   •   •   •   •

They don't speak, the two of them with their spades. Repeatedly, they lean and heave, and drive the shovels deep into the earth. An owl hoots once, twice. Somewhere in the distance, a dog howls and sets others to squealing. After a minute, the sounds stop, leaving only the cicada and the river frogs.

John watches the pile of dirt as it grows and becomes a hill, a mountain, a continent. He sees earthworms wriggling in the moonlight. The thought makes him gag.

When it's done, they return to the truck bed, and John watches as the other pulls back an orange tarpaulin, which, in the starlight, has gone the color of hell itself. John picks up the blanket-wrapped bundle, and his palm accidentally runs along the hard, rounded edge of something. He remembers placing a hand over his wife's pregnant belly. *An elbow,* she'd said, smiling, *a knee. Do you feel that John?* Holding his hand on her cool skin. *That's the heel of her tiny foot.* They place the bundle down on the ground, and John falls to his knees beside it. This time the tears come unglued from his eyes, and he cannot stop them.

"Shut the fuck up," says the other. "You want to wake the goddamn world?" What world? John wants to say. His world lies there on the ground, wrapped in a blanket, waiting. *Like a dead dog,* he thinks.

He pulls the sweater from his pack. It's a butter-yellow color muted by night. He peers at it in his lap as if it might give him answers. If only he knew what question to ask. He clutches it to his breast, turning his face upward into the moonlight, and he prays to God, not for forgiveness, but for punishment, swift and sure. Then he buries his head in his hands and sobs.

CHAPTER SIXTY-EIGHT

Nick | Eden

Savoy stared at the photographs. "And this one?" she said, picking up the fifth and final photo.

"That," Nick said. "Gives someone leverage for blackmail. Or at least it did back in the day."

Savoy examined the photograph. A younger version of Albert Finney appeared with a boy, possibly nineteen or twenty, strolling hand-in-hand across a lawn. Possibly in a park. The picture, a long shot possibly taken with a telephoto lens, looked slightly distorted.

"You think someone knew Finney was gay and blackmailed him?" she asked.

Nick nodded. "I do."

"I don't know, Nick. Being gay in the south in the 1970s wasn't popular, wasn't even acceptable by most people's standards, but it was happening. Quietly, but it was happening. That photo isn't lewd. The young man looks of age."

"He was a doctor. No way would he have wanted this community to know about his personal life," said Nick. "I think the threat of exposure might have been enough to force him to do almost anything. Plus, we have a connection, a blood connection, between Sheriff Picard and Finney. It's especially suspicious because Finney has kept it a secret all these years. Don't you think with all the harassment he's taken for being an outsider, he might have used the fact that he was born here and had connections with a Sheriff going back to the 1950s? Wouldn't that have made sense to improve his reputation? But he didn't. He buried it. There must be a reason. And I believe it's connected to the lies he's telling now."

She set down the picture and looked at Nick. Studied him. Then, "Ok, look, Nick, we need that final report from Dr. Lee. Accusing Finney of making a serious mistake is bad but accusing him of intentionally falsifying data is another thing entirely. Just be careful."

"I will. Look, someone is threatening people to stop this. They've threatened Evelyn. Billy Saveneaux. Whatever it is, it's big enough to hurt someone powerful. Someone else is helping us. Sending hints, information." He pointed down at the pictures.

The Sheriff sighed and rose. "Well, I need to face the death squad out there." She nodded toward the front of the building. "What do you think I should tell them?" She was asking Nick.

"I still haven't heard what they know."

"Oh, well, it's interesting, actually. Apparently, early this morning, somebody contacted the media with information about the death of Gwen Yates, mother of the missing child."

"About the mother?" Nick asked.

"Yep, just to add fuel to the fire," Savoy replied. "According to the gossip, not only is this office withholding information confirming the identity of the remains found last week, but according to sources," she made quotation marks with her fingers, "we now have information linking those remains to the death of Gwen Yates around the same time in 1986 and, you will love this part, both deaths are being investigated as unsolved murders. The press would like confirmation or denial of those allegations." She looked tired as she said the words.

He shook his head. "What a mess; I'm sorry you have to go out there, Sheriff," he said. "I'm sure you have better things to do."

"All part of the job," she said. "Now you do yours and get me some proof. Something I can use." Nick pulled the door open and was nearly out when the landline on Savoy's desk rang. She answered it, listened, held up a finger for him to wait, and then jotted down a few notes. Hung up. Nick could see in her eyes; it was bad.

"That was Lambert. It's Billy Saveneaux." Her voice was gentle. "Someone got to him Nick. He's dead."

"Oh shit," he said. "Who?"

"So far, we don't have much." She looked down at her notes. "Lambert gave me ballistics. Nothing there. No matches. So far, no prints at the scene. Professional job, I'm sure. One thing, though."

"Yeah?" he asked.

"The money. The killer didn't have the smarts to take the money out of Billy's pocket. He was still carrying an envelope with cash somebody gave him. His fee, I suppose, for delivering that envelope to you. Check with Lambert on it."

"Yes, ma'am." Nick nodded and pulled the door open.

"Nick?" she called to him, and he turned, one hand on the door handle. "Why do you think someone would have sent Billy to us with those photos?"

"Ma'am, I don't know, but my best guess? Someone is helping us. Why? I have no idea."

•   •   •   •   •

When he got back to his desk, Nick found an envelope with a sticky note attached: *Fax from Tech.* He sank down in his chair, picked up the envelope, and slid out two stapled sheets of paper. He read the genetics report slowly, then re-read it more slowly, then slid the sheets back into the envelope and leaned back, let out his breath, and looked up as Briggs approached. "You've seen this?" he asked. Briggs shook his head, reaching for the report. He scanned it and then looked at Nick.

"Wow, this will be hard for her to hear. Poor lady. Been through so much, and now... this. How do you think she'll take it?" Briggs was making a face, part grimace.

"Not well."

"Yeah, can I ask you something, Nick?"

"Uh, yep." Nick stood to meet Briggs eye to eye, although he (Nick) was a head taller.

"Is she... uh... you know? I mean, you seem to... know her a little better. Is she right?"

"Right?"

"Yeah, I mean right in the head?" Briggs pointed a twirling forefinger at his temple and rolled his eyes around, demonstrating crazy.

Nick shifted uncomfortably. He didn't know how to answer the question. He suspected Evelyn was not entirely right in the head, but he felt oddly disloyal reporting that fact to Briggs. Still, he had a duty to be honest with his partner. "No, I don't think so, but look, I'm not a fucking doctor, Briggs. Jesus, I mean, come on, look at what she's been through, right?"

"Right. I mean, she believes a lot of wacky stuff, right? It don't make sense."

"Right, that's our job. To sort it out."

"You think she knows something she's not telling us?"

Nick shook his head. "Nah, I think she's confused. Maybe not all there. I don't think she's withholding; I think her motives are good, she wants to know what happened, that's all." He picked up the phone. "I'll talk to her about this. I'll let you know how it goes." He tapped the report. As he dialed, he hoped to God what he'd just told Briggs was true.

CHAPTER SIXTY-NINE

Evelyn | Eden

Nick was on the phone. He was saying something, but Evelyn drifted. Somewhere. She'd missed it. "What? I'm sorry, can you say it again?"

"The DNA, Evelyn, we got the final genetics report. It's just come through. It's a match like I told you; we know it's Carolyn, but." He hesitated, she heard him inhale, "There's something else."

"Ok," she said, but the word came out elongated. *Okaaaaaaay.* She wanted to be in a room with him, to grab his face and make him look at her.

"The DNA sample they got from the remains matches yours, but they call it an incomplete match. It's only partially identical to yours."

"Partial?" Evelyn's thoughts raced as she tried to put this information into perspective. So, it was Carolyn, and this made sense, they had some identical and some different DNA. Or maybe that was wrong. Maybe partial meant they weren't sisters. She couldn't remember from her google search. "Just tell me what it means." She was fighting to clear her thinking. "I don't get it. So, it's not Carolyn? Is that what you're saying?" *A mistake? Was it possible? She allowed a tiny kernel of relief to settle in the pit of her stomach.* Maybe her world hadn't been turned on its head; she hadn't fallen down a rabbit hole; Carolyn would still be dead but only regular dead, not murdered dead, and Evelyn wouldn't have completely lost her mind.

"No. No," he said too quickly. "It's definitely Carolyn." *So much for not falling down the rabbit hole,* Evelyn thought. "But apparently, there is a third-party DNA involved." Two beats. "You share one parent with her, but not both. Evelyn, it means," another uncomfortable silent beat, "It means Carolyn is not your full sibling."

For a moment, Evelyn froze. The room felt smaller, darker. When she spoke, the word came out in a whisper. "No."

"Yes, Evelyn. It looks like Carolyn is your half-sister."

Half-sister, what the fuck? Which half? What did that even mean? "How can they know that? How can they be certain?"

"I don't know all the science behind it but, it's definite according to the lab."

She asked Nick to give her a minute. Hung up the phone. Sat at the kitchen table and tried to catch her breath, which was coming in short, hard pants. Her vision dimmed at the edges. She had to calm down, or she'd hyperventilate. She dumped out the entire contents of her purse and fumbled in a mess, finally coming up with a pill bottle. Popped the top and swallowed two of the tiny white pills. Then one more. Breathe... one... two... three... four. She reminded herself. Breathe. Ten minutes later, she called him back. "Look," she said when she reached him. "I don't know what's going on with your DNA person or department or whatever it is, but now I know you've made a mistake. I mean what are they saying? My mother was fucking around. Not possible. Forget it." *There's a man.* "No way. She was extremely conservative about that stuff." *There's a man.* She squeezed her eyes shut. "I have to go. But look, you need to figure this out. Re-run the DNA or something. I don't know. But this is not making sense." She hung up without saying goodbye.

•　　　•　　　•　　　•　　　•

She's in the water. Floating in a pool wrapped in silence. Like a tomb. Sky the color of beach glass. Surrounded by a forest that scents the air, pine and earth, and smoky wood. She lays like a child on the surface, looking up into the sky at the pale moon's edge and beyond it to where all the secrets hide. She reaches up and up to touch the moon from her floating place, but, as she does, the thing beneath pulls her back. It sucks her down into blackness. She pulls in at the air, great aching gulps, chest heaving, but nothing will come. She is drowning. The water is all around her and inside her and claiming her, and she knows she will die.

Then Mama is there, skin pale as marble, hair dancing silver snakes around her face. She reaches to touch Mama's hands, and she can see blue veins beneath the skin, and she sees the filth under every oval fingernail. She raises her eyes to look at Mama's face and sees the eyes are solid, likes blue stones, and they do not see the child. She tries to scream, but no sound comes except the lonely hiss of water rushing in.

Evelyn opened her eyes, disoriented, sticky with sweat and humidity. The dream woke her, and she could not resettle. Libby was right. It was time to trust someone. She'd traveled too far down the road to turn back now, she needed answers. Her daughter needed answers. Her mind raced. Was it possible? Carolyn, dead and buried on Road 12 all these years. Evelyn went over the words in her mind as if, by repetition, she could force them to make sense. *You are my half-sister. Half. Half. Half. Half-sister.* Breathe... one... two... three... *my sister... my half-sister... my dead half-sister... my murdered half-sister.* Her eyes fell on the little red journal, still where she'd left it open, but turned down on the bedside table. She pulled it towards her, turned it over, and flipped back through, looking for the words she remembered... *There's a man.*

Who? Could this man have been a lover? Her soft-spoken, modest, almost prudish mother had a lover? Carolyn's father? It seemed impossible. She checked the dates, turning the pages; bile rose in her throat and she struggled to keep it down. No sense wasting good Xanax. She scanned the entries again. When was the first mention of this man? She pulled at the pages with the tips of her fingers, back and forth, faster and faster. Words and dates flew by and her heart, the beat slowed by the medication, pounded in her chest. Where was it? Where was the entry? She came to the page and read the date:

January 3, 1974
There's a man.

Dated, sixteen months *after* Carolyn's birth. *After.* The mystery man, Gwen's secret lover, was not Carolyn's father. She pushed the book away as if it threatened to bite. The thought came again: The mystery man was not Carolyn's father.

He was Evelyn's.

CHAPTER SEVENTY

Nick | Eden

This woman was making him wonder if he was the crazy one. Her attitude, along with her perspective, seemed to change faster than Louisiana weather. One minute she seemed reasonable and open to examining the evidence; the next, she rigidly adhered to preposterous claims that defied all logical arguments. Like this thing about her sister's DNA. Why would she be so adamant that the DNA was wrong? It was DNA, for fuck's sake. Everyone in the twenty-first century knew DNA didn't lie. Everyone with at least an eighth-grade education, anyway. And what about this issue with psychiatric hospitalization? Clearly, Carolyn Yates never went to the hospital. No records: the administrator had no memory of it; nothing. It didn't happen. Period. The body in the ground was Carolyn Yates. That's all there was to it. Why was Evelyn so set against accepting reality? And she was throwing mini-temper tantrums along the way as well.

He thought about the conversation with Briggs. *She believes all this wacky stuff,* he'd said. Or something like that. It was true. For a smart woman, she believed in wacky stuff. She drank a hell of a lot, too. She was moody and dishonest at least part of the time, and she'd told him about these lapses in her memory. Her mother had been mentally ill, and wasn't that stuff genetic? The entire story had too many holes. He couldn't let his rapidly evolving feelings for her cloud his judgment. She was intelligent, funny, beautiful, complex, sensitive, passionate, and weirdly kind, but he had stopped focusing on all that. He had a case to work on, and he was just following this dangerous woman down her own rabbit hole. He had to analyze carefully and coolly what she told him. Stop taking it at face value. She might be lying, but even more likely, she might be fucking delusional. What if Evelyn Yates was just as crazy as her mother? As unbalanced as her sister. He decided, going forward, that everything she said went under the magnifying glass. Period.

CHAPTER SEVENTY-ONE

Evelyn | Eden

"I know who it was." Evelyn was standing over Nick's desk in the squad room, spitting the words before he had a chance to stand up. "The man who attacked me." He looked up. Deep grooves had settled across his forehead, and there was a crevice between his eyes Evelyn hadn't noticed earlier. He looked ten years older.

"Ok," Nick said, getting slowly to his feet.

"I'm sorry," she muttered, rubbing at her forehead from which spears of pain were shooting back across her scalp and down into her neck. She needed water. She looked around. The room was constructed of gray metal points and sharp corners, with pictures of the wanted and the missing pasted to bulletin boards like advertisements for a circus freak show. The pounding in her head grew worse. "I mean, I'm sorry to interrupt you. I just wanted to tell you as soon as possible. God, this place, how can you stand it?"

Everywhere crowding into her personal space, were the dead. The recently found dead, the long-lost dead, the dead and gone dead, the beloved dead, the unidentified dead, the suspected missing and the presumed dead. The open cases, the closed cases and the ones with no solution, like Carolyn. She pushed the fingers of her right hand harder into the skin above her eyebrow. "Can we... talk somewhere?"

Nick took her into an interview room, brought her water and coffee, and asked her to explain. She imagined he could smell the booze leaching from her pores. He wouldn't believe her. She couldn't blame him. She wouldn't believe her either.

Slowly. She told him what she could, leaving out the part about the park when she was thirteen. The playground. The feel of corrugated steel on her bareback. Could she even rely on that information buried so deep in her brain it might be little more than random neurochemical connections, anyway? But his identity? Of that, she was certain. "His name is Franklin," she said, the name sharp and bitter on her tongue. "Franklin Molinaro. I knew him. Back then. He was a few years older than me, Carolyn's year in school. It was him. He's the one who broke into my house and... threatened me."

"I thought you said he wore a mask." Fuck, she knew it. He didn't believe her. She sounded crazy. Or drunk. Or maybe he just thought she was lying. Why wouldn't he?

"It was his eyes. I knew his eyes." *His words. She knew his words. I'll come back and kill you.* "Please, believe me." She waited for him to ask how much she'd had to drink. Instead, he just nodded, excused himself, and returned a few minutes later with a thick notebook full of pictures.

Evelyn looked at the notebook, then looked from the notebook to Nick... then back again. She slid the book closer so that the edge of it was flush with the edge of the table and leaned in closely, studying the first page. "I don't know Nick; I don't see him." Desperation clouded her thoughts. Make her feel less sure. She turned the page and ran a finger down the center of the next one, letting her eyes drift lazily from left to right. Twenty-five years. More than that. Nearly thirty. How could she know the man who attacked her was the same boy who had pinned her down on the merry-go-round all those years ago? She couldn't even be sure what she'd had for dinner last night. "I don't know," she repeated, feeling like the bottom of the world was dropping out. She turned a page, then another. Why had she come here? It had been a mistake. Whatever chance she might have had at salvaging her credibility after the disastrous phone call earlier was eliminated now. Why couldn't she have kept this crazy idea to herself?

He's there, you see him. Look at his eyes. The eyes.

She felt her heart heave inside her chest.

You can't pass him by again. He's really there don't leave him.

Her breath caught, and she was momentarily disoriented by a sense of tipping in a weightless environment; up was down and left was right, then up was left and down was right, or was it up was right and... it didn't matter. Gray light enfolded her and it was warm and down and around she went... the smell of jasmine wafted past and cigarettes and something else very clean. She caught herself, shook her head, sat up straighter in the chair and took a few breaths to steady herself, then flipped a page.

She scanned it, using her finger as a pointer.

This time, she saw him for sure.

•   •   •   •   •

Franklin Molinaro had never left Eden. Like so many others of the generation, he'd grown up to be a drinker, druggie, chronic petty criminal, a troublemaker. He'd been arrested most recently for stalking an ex-girlfriend who also claimed repeated physical and sexual abuse. How did he get out of jail? Evelyn wanted to know. Reduced bail, Nick told her. Molinaro's legal history was no more remarkable than any other chronic criminal, with one exception. *Judge Wesley Fulsome had ordered his bail reduced from $100,000 to $10,000 one day before the attack on Evelyn.*

"Are you saying," Evelyn asked, "that this Judge had him released so that he could come and, um, visit me?"

"We don't know that yet. All I can tell you is the bail was reduced, but we don't have any evidence Fulsome was complicit in the attack on you. Or on Broussard. I don't know. It doesn't seem likely." He looked at her. She didn't like his expression, although she wasn't sure what it showed. "And, Evelyn, don't forget, we don't know for sure this is the guy. Not yet." He didn't believe her, but she was too tired to be angry. She felt nothing.

Evelyn looked toward the row of windows lining the building's east wall. The sun streamed through the glass in ribbons, and the sky was clear. The room had brightened considerably, and her eyes stung. She watched as Nick grabbed the books and started down the hall to put them away. Briggs was coming from the opposite direction, and the two stopped together just at the entrance to the detective's area. Nick's back was to Evelyn, but his voice carried, the words choppy and sharp. "... another warrant... this scumbag, Molinaro... might be... how do we know... don't give a fuck what Savoy says... need to make her...."

The two men walked away, their backs to Evelyn, making it difficult for her to hear.

"-talk to Fulsome-"

"-yeah-"

"-have enough to get Finney... I'm getting... warrant-"

"... good luck-"

What had she just done? Fear picked at her brain. How did she know they weren't all complicit? What if the only reason she was still alive was that she hadn't named Molinaro? God, the implications of that. Trusting Nick MacCallum had led her way down this path. It was too late to reverse direction. She'd already told him too much.

●   ●   ●   ●   ●

Nick returned fifteen minutes later, apologizing for the delay. She studied his face, tried to see inside him. The eyes were not the window to the soul; she saw nothing in his eyes, nothing but exhaustion. She gave up, either she'd trust him and he'd help or she'd already fucked up beyond repair. Either way, she was going to go all the way.

"Look, there's something else I remembered. I'm not sure how it fits, but I should tell you. Carolyn had this photograph. She'd been hiding it between her mattresses. It... it was meaningful to her. She had it right before she went away." Speaking the words out loud was like pulling away a carpet to expose the filth beneath. Light flooded the secret, and her thoughts gained a sudden ugly clarity.

Without warning, a picture appeared in her mind. Unbidden. Unwanted.

Mama on the floor in the bathroom, blood, or liquid around her face. There was a hole in the linoleum floor, and her eyes were open. And there was something else. Evelyn touched her own face. Ran a finger along the mark on her jaw. Still tender. There was something else. Then she saw. Bruises. Purple, almost black. On Mama's neck, around her neck, like jewelry. Mama's eyes were open. Too open. Bulging. They looked... what? Terrified.

Evelyn shuddered. "Hey," Nick said and touched her arm. "Are you okay?"

No. Possibly. "Yeah. I'm ok. Look, I don't know why I didn't tell you. I... I didn't remember, I guess. Not until now."

"Ok, so try to remember. What was in the photo? Why do you think it was important to Carolyn?" She studied him. He looked interested, genuinely.

"I... I don't know. I can't remember. I don't even know when I saw the picture. Maybe I never did. Maybe I only remember her freaking out about losing it. She was... I don't know... scared, maybe? It must have been the day she left. Or the night before. I'm not sure."

He blew out his breath. "Ok, so you said she seemed afraid. What does that mean? Was she often afraid? Was that unusual for Carolyn?"

"Never. She was never afraid, not of anything." Evelyn's voice broke. She wanted to run or sink into the floor. "Goddammit," she said. She turned to Nick. Studied his face, his eyes, his angular jaw, the long line of his nose. She noticed he had a deep scar over one eyelid as if it had been split open once. She'd somehow missed it before. *Such a strange man.* Hard features that should have made him intimidating, but just now, she found comfort in his presence.

"Try to remember if you saw the photo. Close your eyes and think," he said. "Take your time."

"I've tried. It's just not there. The way some of my memories are just... absent. I've been trying."

"Ok, ok," he said. "But I want you to try again. Just take a few deep breaths. Like I said. Close your eyes. Let's just see what happens."

She did as he asked, unsurprised when the exercise went nowhere. *Where is it? What did you do with it?* She imagined Carolyn's words. Her face. *The photograph. What did you do with the photograph?*

Then it came. From nowhere. It was from the past. From Carolyn.

"A man," Evelyn said, eyes flying open. "It was a man in the photograph. Maybe wallet sized. Small, you know. Black and white. A man. I remember now."

"Ok. Great. What did the man look like?"

She shook her head. The image blurred in her mind. Had it been a blurry image? Maybe one of those taken at carnivals, in a twenty-five cent photo booths? "There was writing on the back, but I... I don't remember what it said. Maybe I didn't even read it. Just I remember letters. And numbers."

"Numbers?" Nick asked. "Like phone numbers? Addresses?"

"No, more like dates." She closed her eyes, trying to see the photograph in her mind's eye. It kept coming into focus, then drifting away again. "I don't know. I'm sorry."

"It's ok. Try to remember where you saw the picture. Or when? Do you recall when you saw it?"

"No," she whispered. "Nothing else. There's just nothing else." She inhaled deeply. Wished badly for a cigarette. "I just know it was important-" She paused, shrugged. She was trying to fit the pieces together.

Carolyn's face on hers in the night. Where is it? What did you do with it? Carolyn's deep blue eyes. Full of fear. What did I do with what? Just leave me alone, Carolyn. Leave me alone. Evelyn backing away, huddling in the corner of her bed, hands over her ears. Carolyn pulls her hand away. Leans hard into her face. The photograph? What did you do with the photograph? Evelyn shakes her head, staring into Carolyn's face. Her eyes are ringed with worry. Deep gray circles of worry.

Carolyn in their room, crouching next to her bed, pulling something from under the linens. From between the mattresses. She turns. Small fingers snatching at the edges of her sweater. Shhhh, she says. It's ok. I'll be back.

CHAPTER SEVENTY-TWO

Libby | San Francisco

Libby yanked a diet coke off the shelf and slammed the refrigerator door closed with a loud slap. She squelched a childish urge to shake the can and explode the contents all over her father's pristine stainless-steel kitchen. He'd lose his shit, which was almost worth the lecture that would inevitably follow. Instead, she pulled the top back and walked outside to the broad deck overlooking the garden. From that spot, she could see over the city, all the way to the bay bridge. Cloudless, pale blue sky and quality of light so energizing that it could only be described as effervescent. A breeze blew in off the water, and she tilted her face to catch the cool, moist air. Libby plopped down in a chaise lounge and listened to the bleating of harbor boats and the distant sounds of people and cars crowding on the city's streets. She let her eyes close and focused on the feel of the chaise's sun-warmed mesh pressing into the skin of her thighs, below her short.

Her phone buzzed. She squinted at the Caller ID before answering. Evelyn.

"Hi Mom," she said.

"Libby, are you busy?" She sounded sober.

"Not really."

"I've been thinking about what you said. Trusting someone. Honesty. All that."

"Uh-huh."

"I have more to tell you. You're right. You're not a baby."

Had she said that? Had she called herself a baby? Libby didn't think so. "Uh-huh," she repeated.

"Look, something is going on here in Eden. Something terrible. I think it's all connected with what happened to my family, and I need to stay here until I figure it out. Does that make sense?"

"No." Irritation growing.

Evelyn let out her breath. "Ok, look, I'll try to explain. At least what I know, ok? But first I want you to know I'm ok. Really. I'm careful, so I don't want you to worry."

"Fine, ok. Mom, just tell me." On the other end of the line, she heard her mother inhale deeply, pause and then begin.

•　　•　　•　　•　　•

Insane. The story was almost too much to believe. Not *almost*. It was definitely too much to believe. Conspiracies involving sheriffs, judges, and doctors? They sent Carolyn away to some hospital and never saw her family again. Or maybe not being sent to the hospital. *But maybe being killed*. But nobody knew why or how.

Why? Libby tried asking. *Why would anyone kill a fourteen-year-old girl?* She didn't add *a crazy* 14-year-old girl, but that seemed obvious. Evelyn hadn't even addressed the question. It had taken Evelyn the better part of an hour to tell everything. The more she spoke, the crazier it all sounded. Not like lies, so Libby supposed that should be an improvement. Just crazy. Libby wished her mother would go back to lying. Lying, at least, was familiar.

What was Evelyn's proof, anyway? A photograph she could hardly remember, of someone she didn't know, she vaguely recalled seeing once. Diaries written by Gwen, who had been certifiably insane, even hospitalized, on and off powerful medications. She'd had shock therapy, for fuck's sake. Who could tell if what she said was reality or psychosis? Libby felt sick. Her father had been right. Evelyn was insane, too. This whole thing sounded like a paranoid delusion. And wasn't that stuff inheritable?

Then there were those episodes Evelyn liked to call sleepwalking, but it was so not that. It was much worse. Most of the time, she reeked like booze, and Libby wrote it off to blacking out. She had friends who did it. They'd be walking and talking, doing stupid stuff, like peeing in the bathtub or peeling off their clothes at a party, and the next day have no memory of the event. With her mother, it was weirder. Once Libby woke up to find Evelyn in bed with her, curled up like a baby, crying, babbling in a voice that sounded high-pitched and raspy; she was saying all kinds of freaky stuff. Apologizing over and over for being such a *bad girl*. A *mean girl*. She kept asking Libby if she was *still mad*. Stroking Libby's face over and over. It scared the shit out of her. She'd read somewhere that waking a sleepwalker could be dangerous. They might kill you or themselves or something, so she just lay there frozen until finally Evelyn got out of the bed and padded out of the room. But before Evelyn left, she pulled open the blinds and stood at the window, sort of pawing at it, like she wanted it open but couldn't figure out the mechanism. The whole time Libby lay there too petrified to move, she was just as terrified her mother might get that third-floor window open. That time, Libby remembered, Evelyn didn't smell like liquor, she hadn't been drinking. Still, Evelyn denied all of it the next day. She'd accused Libby of inventing the story. Libby quickly dropped the debate. There was no point.

Libby did a google search: PARANOIA. She founds lots of causes. Lots of genetic causes, which were scary. But alcohol and drugs could do the same thing. And combined? Who knew? Evelyn had been drinking and drugging for years. Was she just spinning out of control now? Making up stories to fit the way she felt inside? Maybe someone from her past had reached out, attacked her for something she'd done. It was possible. Evelyn had pissed off a shit-ton of people over the years; it made sense that she'd have angered someone from her hometown. *Enough for the guy to hold a thirty-year grudge.* Maybe.

And what had Evelyn said about that one line in her diary? *I did something bad, and now Carolyn is gone.* Nothing. She didn't remember. Evelyn seemed so confused, paranoid, and panicked. Maybe, Libby thought, she had been paranoid way back in 1986. God, it was too much to think about. Her head hurt. She wanted this to stop, all of it. She wanted a normal life, whatever that was.

Libby pulled out the drawer next to her bed. One joint remained. She snatched it up along with the lighter and took both outside to the balcony.

CHAPTER SEVENTY-THREE

Evelyn | Eden

Nick handed Evelyn a soda and sat down next to her on the concrete bench near the station's front doors. They sat far apart like bookends. A gentle breeze, the kind Mama called fairy's *breath*, was pushing around the bushes behind them, and the weather had cooled slightly.

"Did you get her?" asked Nick.

Evelyn stared down at the phone in her hands. "Yeah. I did. Thanks."

"She's, ok?"

Evelyn nodded. "Yeah, she's good." She looked at Nick. "I mean, not really. She's scared, I think. Angry, worried. I can't blame her." He nodded and looked at her. She'd been wrong before. There *was* something in his eyes. Compassion. Evelyn had seen so little of it in recent years, she'd not recognized it at first. "Thanks," she said again.

The sun had come out from behind a cloud, and the skin on her face and neck was feeling the sting of sunburn.

"Do you think it's all connected, Nick?"

He nodded, took a sip from his soda can, then set it down on the bench beside him. "Yeah, yeah, I do. I think Finney and Picard and Fulsome and Molinaro are all connected somehow. And I think Chief Broussard knew too much, and someone killed him for it."

"And Carolyn?"

He nodded. "And Carolyn."

Evelyn sensed something like the crumbling of a wall inside her brain. Something was giving, making way for something else. The truth perhaps. "Listen, I need to tell you something," she said.

"I'm listening."

"That first day. When you showed me the bracelet, remember?" He nodded. "That other thing. The one I said I didn't recognize?" Again, he only nodded. "I lied. Right away, I knew it. I knew what it was. I guess I just couldn't believe it. Didn't want to believe it. I'm sorry."

"It's ok. Just tell me."

She picked at the aluminum tab on her soda can, bending it back and forth until it broke. "A sweater. It was part of a sweater." She felt tears. Blinked her eyes. A siren blew in the distance. A welcome distraction.

"Carolyn's sweater?"

"Yeah, but more than that. My mother made it for her when she was little. By the time she, uh, went away, it was way too small. Had holes." She gave a slight smile. "It looked ridiculous on her, but she loved it. Wore it all the time. So anyway, when she, after she was gone, I took it from her drawer and started wearing it. I wouldn't take it off. Not even to wash it. I don't remember how long I had it. Days, I guess. Weeks maybe. Then, one day, it was just gone. I freaked out and looked everywhere. Eventually, I gave up, forgot about it, maybe, until I saw it that day, the day you showed me that little piece of it in a baggie. In a fucking baggie." She wiped at the wetness on her face. "I can't remember a lot of things but I remember that sweater. I remember I still had it after Carolyn was gone. I still had it, and then, suddenly, I didn't."

Nick thought for a long time, then he said, "So, that means either Carolyn came back to get it or-"

"Or," Evelyn interrupted him. "Someone came and got it from the house, from me, and buried it with her." *Someone who knew what it meant to her.*

CHAPTER SEVENTY-FOUR

Gwen | 1975

January 10, 1975

I first hear about it from the clerk at the Stop-n-Go on Main Street. He tells me they found a girl in the woods just outside of town. A young teenager, he says. It's a child, a drifter without a family. It makes me think about Tara, the little friend I met at the halfway house years back when I first came to Eden, although I know it's not her. Tara was a teenager back then. She'd be a grown woman now, and this girl, this child, she's not been dead very long. That's what they're saying.

I meet him in the park. He only has a few minutes today. I'm so cut up about the dead girl, but he tells me not to worry. It's ok, ok, he says. He touches my face, but we both look around. Nervous that someone might have seen. I love him so much, but this can't go on. I don't know how to tell him. The way he looks at me makes me forget my words.

-G

January 12, 1975

They're saying her name is Crystal, the dead girl, I mean. I try to stop thinking about it, but my mind goes back to 1965, like a rubber band snapping into place. The man with tattoos haunts my dreams. My days. He's still in town. People around here like him. The halfway house is still in Eden, too. It's got a new name now. I can't remember.

I try to make the memories make sense, but it's foggy. I see the tattoos and feel the sharp sticks scratching the skin of my back as he lay his whole weight on top of me. I remember the pain, the feeling like I can't breathe, but none of it is in order. It comes in streaks, like bright flashes of light shining into a black room through tiny, moving windows.

Sometimes, it seems like none of it really happened. Like it's not connected to anything. The memories float up and away like balloons.

-G

June 12, 1975

My fear and guilt seem to grow bigger right ' along with my love. He keeps telling me to stop thinking about Crystal, about the man with tattoos, about what happened. But it's hard. His strength and kindness overwhelm me. We talk about all sorts of things, and sometimes we say nothing at all. He makes me laugh more. He is part of me, and I am part of him. He feels like my breath, I don't think I can exist without him. I found someone who takes away the loneliness. Sometimes, I take Carolyn with me into town when I meet him. But she's growing fast. Not long until she tells John what's going on.

-G

PART THREE: BLOOD BONDS
Sunday, June 11
Present Day

CHAPTER SEVENTY-FIVE

Libby | San Francisco

A rave. Libby had never been to one. She'd found the concept intimidating; the heavy drugs, the older crowd. But she didn't feel intimidated today, only numb; she felt nothing when she thought about Mitch. It was weird. Not anger. Nothing. When Celia texted to invite her, she'd said no. Celia had complained that it was the first week of summer, and Libby *never* wanted to do *anything* anymore. Libby thought that was mostly true. What was wrong with her? A slow sludge was smothering her heart, squeezing it down to nothing. She was no longer capable of emotions such as elation, excited anticipation or passion. What was left was only a thin layer of apathy. Conner was out of her life, and she didn't think she even cared about that anymore. She had to snap out of this somehow. She texted Celia back quickly before she could change her mind, her fingers clicking out the words almost of their own accord. *Ok, she'd go to the rave.*

She lay on her bed and stared at the ceramic beads of her chandelier. Immobilized. She rolled her cell phone around in her palm, looking at it now and then as if it might magically produce instructions, and tell her what to do. Finally, she pressed the speed dial number for her mother and, reaching Evelyn's voicemail, Libby was both disappointed and relieved.

"Hi, Mom, it's me. Just calling. I'm thinking about going out to a party. With Celia, I mean, she's someone I know. Right? I know you would say not to go, but I just have to get out of here. I got invited to this party and I just want to go for a little while. I will be safe. Don't worry. Okay. I love you."

She hit the end button, confused. She had not intended to call, much less to tell her mother she was going out. *And then I love you? Where in the fuck had that come from?* Maybe she felt guilty for ignoring all her mother's calls and texts lately. Maybe it was the fact that she couldn't get the episode with Mitch out of her head. She wanted to tell someone. She wanted to tell her mother.

Whatever, she thought and swung open her closet, searching for something to wear.

•　　•　　•　　•　　•

Libby's feet weren't working properly, and she was having trouble coordinating her mouth with her brain. Her vision tunneled in and out. She couldn't see where she was going. *What's the time? Was she making the sounds, or had she just thought the words?*

"Three baby, it's three, and you're fine," someone answered. Laughing. Something unpleasant tickled under her arm and she told them to stop, but they wouldn't stop. Pulling away, trying to walk, but her feet. Something was wrong with her feet. *What time is it? Why wouldn't they tell her the time? Is it three? What day?*

She could smell Conner. Hair gel and aftershave and weed. Next to her, holding her, while they took the stairs to his house, or at least she thought it was his house. She was having trouble holding her eyes open. So tired. Maybe those were someone else's stairs. Then there was another boy or several other boys. She couldn't see them clearly, but she heard them laughing and talking. Yes, she thought, Conner. *Conner,* his name, floated across the surface of her brain, a brief sweetness, a smile in his voice, and it made her feel better. She'd heard him, his voice, he was here; she lay her head against his shoulder, only the shoulder wasn't Conner's, didn't smell like Conner. She tried to remember. She had had nothing to drink... or... or had she? She couldn't remember. *Where is Conner?*

"Don't worry, he's here, baby. You're fine." She thought maybe she was crying. Her eyelids were getting heavier, like those fat rubber shades her mother used to black out the bedroom on hangover days, unrolling them with a *smack*.

Mommy?

You're ok, just sleep now.

She lay her head down.

For a second. Just a second. To rest.

•   •   •   •   •

Darkness. Not even moonlight. She couldn't see the outline of her own hands held up before her face. She pushed around with her hands, trying to feel her surroundings. Sheets. Bed. The room was stuffy. Smelled heavily of weed. Conner's room. She shut her eyes against the dark and tried to remember. A party? She and Conner were at a party. His friends. Stumbling as she tried to climb the stairs, then nothing.

The dance. She'd missed the dance. And the after-party she'd fought about so hard with her mother. Celia would be pissed. *Fuck it.* Her head hurt like hell, and she was still so sleepy.

Suddenly, someone standing next to the bed, in the dark. "Hello?" she said into the void. "Who is that, hello?" She was more fully awake now and afraid.

"It's me, Lib, don't worry."

"Me?" She did not recognize the voice. "Who? Who the hell are you?"

"You're kidding, right, Lib? It's me, Mitch, you know me." He sat on the bed and the mattress slanted heavily in his direction. She struggled to roll away. Stale beer. More weed and the sort of cheap aftershave sold in supermarkets. It was Mitch, Conner's best friend, and resident drug dealer. She knew him. Closer to thirty than twenty, he gave Libby the creeps.

"Turn on the light, Mitch. Where's Conner?" She felt around on the bed for her bag and found it lying next to her. Reaching inside, her fingers lit on the new X-Acto blade she'd bought to replace the one Gam took. She let her hand rest there. "Goddammit, Mitch, turn on the light," she repeated. Her mother's warning flashed through her mind. *I need you to be careful,* her mother had said. Mitch had done nothing to threaten or frighten her in the past, nothing beyond being the creepy, middle-aged drug dealer he was. She wrapped her fingers around the handle of the blade inside her bag.

"Aw, come on, Lib," Mitch said, ignoring her request about the light. His hand was on her bare thigh and she scrambled to the other side of the bed. Still clutching at the X-Acto.

"Leave me alone, Mitch. Turn on the fucking light, or I'll scream."

She heard him laugh. A low, intoxicated-sounding chuckle. Fucking creepy. "So what? We're in the basement. Scream all you want." Now his hand was reaching for her again.

"Get away from me. Turn on the light, Mitch." Her voice was high and squeezed, sounding.

"Oh, come on, Libby, you know you like me." His hand was on her thigh again. She yanked the blade from the bag as he slapped his other hand over her mouth, muffling her as she thrashed about, trying to get away from him. The blade of the special knife. Tiny but brand new and extremely sharp. She raised her hand nearly over her head and slammed the knife into the back of his forearm. *Motherfucker.* He screamed. She drew it forward, slicing the skin open, elbow to the wrist.

Blood gushed from the wound, the warm liquid drenching her thigh and the bedclothes. The coppery stench was overwhelming. And she thought maybe he'd pissed his pants. He screamed again, more of an animal squeal, really. When he recoiled, she drew back her leg and sent her knee hard into the general vicinity of his scrotum. She must have connected because, this time, he hunched forward and let out a horrible wail. A moment later, a flash of light as he shoved open the door, making his way into the stairwell. She could hear him squealing and blubbering as he mounted the stairs.

In the dim light from the hallway, she collected her things, crept out of the townhouse, and escaped into the freedom of the night.

CHAPTER SEVENTY-SIX

Gwen | 1976

June 13, 1976

Another one. They've found another one in nearly the same spot as the first. Mrs. Coolidge came to tell me. She said she thought I should know. The girl's name is Dugas, it's Debbie Dugas, and she is young, like the last one, but folks are saying she's been dead longer.

I can't reach him or he doesn't want to be reached. I'm so afraid. I wonder about my pills. I've not taken them since Mama Yates died. What the doctors said about reality. How I don't know what's real and what's not. I know that can't be true and the pills make me tired. More tired than I am already. And the doctors, I'm not sure I trust the doctors.

-G

CHAPTER SEVENTY-SEVEN

Finney | Eden

Albert Finney was livid. He raked long fingers through his thin hair until it stood straight out all over his head, then went on pacing nonstop, first the width and then the length of his jail cell, sporadically calling out expletives to no one. Or at least to no one who cared. He muttered to himself like a psychotic, wondering how things had gotten so quickly out of control. *Meticulous. They had all been meticulous; that was the word. For such a long time. How could one tiny thing unravel everything they'd done?* Panic rose and fell within him like a tide over which he had no control. This angered him further, and he called out again to no one in particular, "Goddamnit to hell, goddamn all of you." He leaned his left shoulder against the wall, closed his eyes, and counted, forced himself to breathe. He placed two fingers across his left wrist, feeling for his own pulse, willing his heartbeat to slow. He opened his eyes, righted himself, and looked around, and began pacing again. He checked his wrist and saw the white mark where his watch had been and cursed. They'd taken his watch, the bastards, taken his Patek Philippe. For what? They were calling him something he was not. The accusation was too preposterous to even be offensive. It was ridiculous. Someone planted that crap on his computer, pedophile. Thinking the word to himself made him shudder. No matter. Of course, they couldn't prove he had a thing for kids because it wasn't true. The thought calmed him, but only a little. They might be idiots, but right now they were idiots who had him locked up. He stopped pacing, forced himself to calm his breathing. *Patience. Need a little patience.* Finney sat down on the lower bunk and picked up the small hard pillow with two fingers and tossed it to the floor. Disgusting. He lay back, placed both hands behind his head, and closed his eyes.

CHAPTER SEVENTY-EIGHT

Evelyn | Eden

Evelyn sat at the bar inside Luke's Barbecue, eating a chicken sandwich and thinking about ordering a drink. Thinking about ordering a *second* drink since she'd already finished the first. To her right, a middle-aged woman wearing polyester leggings, track shoes, and lots of fake gold jewelry sat nursing something pink in a martini glass and staring up at the television mounted behind the bar. "Y'all see this fiasco?" she said and pointed her cigarette up at the screen. "Just terrible. And him a *doctor*. Now, what is wrong with some people? That's what I want to know." Evelyn, who had not seen the fiasco, glanced up at the television. On the screen, a neatly dressed young woman with hair football helmeted over her skull stood outside a two-story, brick colonial speaking into a microphone. Behind her, a line of yellow police tape warned the public not to cross. Beyond that, uniformed officers appeared to be removing a series of cardboard boxes from the house. Pink martini lady said, "Hey Scooby, turn up the damn tv, will you? I can't hear a damn thing." The bartender, whose parents had apparently had a unique sense of humor and named him after an animated dog, snatched up the remote control and hit a button. Immediately, the reporter's slightly nasal voice filled the bar. "... *arrest today of Bonfante Parish Medical Examiner Dr. Albert Finney on charges of child pornography has shocked the local community. Dr. Finney may face added charges linked to the recent recovery of the remains believed to be those of fourteen-year-old Carolyn Yates, who disappeared from Eden in 1986. A source tells WWPP News*

*that among articles removed from Dr. Finney's home today
were his computer, telephone records, and bank statements,
possibly linking Dr. Finney to another person of interest in the
case. Stay tuned, and we will keep you..."*

Evelyn stopped listening. What was happening? Finney was
an asshole. A liar. Maybe even a murderer. But a pedophile? No.
She slid a twenty across the bar, stood up, and was pushing
numbers on her cellphone as she headed for the exit. By the time
she let the heavy, wood doors of Luke's Barbeque slam had shut
behind her, it was another sixty seconds before she realized that
she'd forgotten to get that drink.

"We got him," Nick's voice leaden. He was tired.

"What does that mean?" Evelyn asked, holding one hand
around the phone and the other over her eyes to block the sun as
she tried to remember where she'd parked her car.

"It means, Evelyn, that we got him, at least for now. We got a
warrant from another judge. Found what we needed and picked
him up."

"I don't get it, Nick. He's not a pedophile." She dropped her
hand away from her eyes, momentarily gave up on her car. "Or...
Jesus Christ, is he?"

"We can hold him on what we have. Meanwhile, I've got
Briggs out tracking down Franklin Molinaro." Nick hadn't
answered the question. "Hey," he said.

"What?" she replied.

"Are you alright?"

No. Yes. "What do you think?"

"I don't know, Evelyn. You are impossible to read."

"I'm sorry," she said, and she was.

The sun was big and cruelly bright overhead now. It filled the
sky and beat a ferocious rhythm. By the time she found the car,
her back and underarms were wet with sweat; her long hair stuck
in clumps to the back of her neck and around her face. Endless

hours of light and heat could be spectacular if you happened to be a kid, out of school, with nothing to do but turn barefoot fairy circles in the grass and steal sugar from your mama's kitchen. Or skip off to the backfield with your slightly loony older sister to dig secret tunnels and catch fireflies. But today was not spectacular. Today, the sun only made her pain seem infinite. She drove a while, thinking. Tried calling Libby, then Stuart. No answer. She didn't leave a message; she had nothing to say. When Libby's phone kicked over to voicemail, Evelyn told herself not to worry, then swiftly panicked. Libby could be anywhere with anyone. Doing fucking anything. Stuart was useless. The thought she'd left Libby alone with him made her stomach lurch. She was headed back to town, down the outer loop road, intermittently fiddling with the near-useless air conditioner. settling for rolling down the windows. The air flowing inside the car was crazy hot, but at least it was moving. A road sign flashed in her rearview mirror. Small, but she'd seen it. Pulling over, she made a three-point turn and drove back to the sign. Without shutting down the engine, she stepped out of the car into the sticky air. One hand on the halfway-open car door, her head cocked back a little, she squinted to see the faded lettering more clearly. On a pale green background, a giant alligator appeared to be happily drinking a beer. Painted words, just below the alligator's beer glass:

IT'S ALWAYS 5:00 AT O'HARE'S!
O'Hare's Irish Pubs
LOCATIONS THROUGHOUT SOUTHEAST LOUISIANA

She stood, staring at the sign, reading and then re-reading the words trying to process what she was seeing. She'd seen it before. A photograph. Three teenage girls. A white sundress. Giant peonies. Blood red. Like wounds.

"*Mama,*" she whispered.

It made sense. Nobody ever actually *came* to Eden. People *sprouted* in Eden, carelessly, hopelessly, like weeds. They spent childhoods trying to figure a way out. Believing that by transplanting elsewhere, they could bloom into something better. Some, like Evelyn, got away. Most, like Mrs. Coolidge and John Yates, stayed behind, becoming ghosts. It was different for outsiders like Gwen. An outsider could live in Eden forever without ever becoming part of the place. They could *see* things. Invisible things. And no matter how long an outsider lived in Eden, even if they died in the town, they never became ghosts. That made them different. That made them *dangerous*. Yes, thought Evelyn, it made sense. *Gwen lies on the bathroom floor, Eyes unnaturally wide open. There are marks encircling her neck.*

This story hadn't started with Carolyn at all. It was Gwen's story. *It was about Gwen and the ghost she had refused to become.*

CHAPTER SEVENTY-NINE

Gwen | 1978

January 20, 1978

There are three dead girls now. Three in Bonfante Parish. All teenagers, all homeless. All accidents. That's what they're saying. Accidents. I keep trying to explain to him how I need to go to the police. I know that something is wrong here. Somehow, this is connected to what happened in 1965. He says it's too dangerous. He says I must stay out of it, for my girls' sake. He reminds me that getting involved won't bring those dead girls back.

He says I should maybe take my pills again; he doesn't understand why I won't. What they do to me. I keep my necessary secrets. I don't think he's telling me the truth. I love him, but part of me doesn't trust him. -G

February 12, 1978

I won't let up, even though I know it's making him angry. He says there are people keeping secrets here in Eden. Of course, I already know that. He says these people are dangerous. Powerful. But he won't tell me what he means. He doesn't know who they are, he says.

I'm so tired of the lies.

I want to talk to John about it, but he's drinking almost all the time now. Twice I show him the newspaper. I show him where they found these girls out in the woods. But his eyes go vacant. Distant. Like he's thinking of something else. I tell him I need to do something. Tell someone. He begs me to leave it alone. For the girls' sake, he says.

-G.

CHAPTER EIGHTY

Nick | Eden

Sheriff Savoy sat at her desk, as Nick entered, intermittently clicking the tip of a ballpoint against her teeth, then tapping at her keyboard. She held the pen in the air like a finger. *Wait.* Then used it to point to the guest chair. He sat. Watched the pen, wondering if it would leave a blue mark on her tongue. After a few seconds, she stopped typing, dropped the pen to her desk, and leaned back in her chair. "So, Lambert called about five minutes ago."

"Yes, ma'am?"

"The envelope in Billy Saveneaux's pocket? The one with cash? We got a hit on the prints. Interesting hit, actually. It's definitely more than one set of prints for sure, but only one match, and you will never guess."

"Don't think I want to guess."

"Fulsome, The Honorable Judge Fulsome."

Nick shook his head, "You've got to be fu-," he stopped himself. "Kidding, ma'am, seriously?"

"Do I look like I'm kidding?" Savoy never looked like she was kidding, but Nick said nothing. "So, here's the deal. He's involved, somehow, but he might actually be helping us."

"You think maybe he's helping us?"

"Maybe," she nodded. "Given what was in that envelope." Her eyes narrowed as if she were studying him. "Or he's crooked, and what he's doing is leading us away from-"

"The real perpetrators," Nick said, finishing her sentence. He blew out his breath. "I don't see it... but maybe."

"You don't see it? Sure. He's smart, old, connected." She shrugged. "It's possible."

"Right." Nick couldn't believe that was true. He barely knew the old Judge, but he was aware of the man's reputation. Hard on criminals with a low tolerance for laziness and lack of follow-through. But straightforward and ethical. People respected Fulsome. He seemed like one of the good guys. Nick was wondering if anything in Eden was as it seemed.

"And Finney? What's the DA saying?" Sheriff Savoy asked, interrupting his train of thought about Fulsome. He cleared his throat, collecting his thoughts.

"No history of anything related to kids. Still, the DA will charge him. But that stuff on his hard drive? Completely obvious. I don't buy it. Finney would have had to be a total idiot to leave it there. I mean, he had a lot of stuff in a folder right there on his desktop and it was labeled in big caps PRIVATE, for gods sakes. Who does that with child pornography? You might as well put a sign on your front door 'Pedophile Lives Here,' right? You can say a lot of things about Finney, but he's not a moron. I'm pretty sure he'd hide his crimes better than that." Nick glanced out the window. Sheriff Savoy had a view, or at least what passed for a view, in this building. Sun dappled the weedy grass patch that surrounded three enormous live oaks. "It was too convenient," he said, looking back at her. Surprised to come down on the side of Fulsome and now Finney, Nick hoped he wasn't naïve. Or just stupid.

"So, you think they set him up? That's what you're saying?" Sheriff Savoy said and squinted her eyes. "Okay, so let's say for now, he's not a pedophile. What else? Bank records?"

Nick shrugged. He didn't like the way Savoy was only half-agreeing with him; it sounded like she was humoring him. "No way was he being bribed. Finney's loaded. Slightly over five hundred grand in two local banks and investments in the millions." Nick shifted in his seat and continued, "I talked to him this afternoon. Jail has shaken him up a bit. He's looking at prosecution for possession of child porn, maybe worse. Thing is, he said a few things, and seemed ready to talk but then he lawyered up. We didn't get much."

"So, before the lawyer? What did he say?"

"Admitted to writing illegal scripts in the 1970s. I'm sure he's aware the statute of limitations has passed on those. Claims he had no choice but to write those scripts. They blackmailed him with exposure of his homosexuality."

"Who? Who exactly blackmailed him?"

"Yeah, that's where he gets a lot of faulty memory, right? Claims he doesn't recall who he wrote scripts for, vague about which drugs. Maybe chloral hydrate, maybe not. Has no records, of course why would he keep records blah, blah. So, he couldn't give names."

"You mean wouldn't."

Nick nodded, "Yup." Nick rubbed his eyes, suddenly tired. "He's lying, of course."

"Right," said Savoy, her expression unchanged. An initial *A* hung from a chain around her neck. The gold glittered in the sunlight. *A*, for Alice, he thought absently. Just behind the *A*, another initial peeked out. It was smaller, and more elaborate. Nick wondered what the delicate, scrolled *T* stood for. Tom? Taylor? Tina? God, his brain was derailing. "So, what else, Nick? What else do we have?"

"I asked Briggs to check out Molinaro for Broussard. He ran the DNA and fingerprints on the Broussard's car."

"And?" She stared at Nick; her expression was unreadable.

"Well, it's a cop car, you know. It's a mess. But, so far, we have two prints that match Molinaro, one from the index and one from the thumb of the right hand. On the outside. It may not mean much. Franklin was in trouble all the time. He could have leaned on or touched Broussard's car in any of a hundred different ways. We're still waiting on the DNA fibers. Not much to go on there."

"Fulsome?" The entire question in a word.

"Nope, so far. No luck getting in to see the judge. Full calendar, out of the office, indisposed, things like that. Still working on it."

"Ok," she said. "Listen, Nick, I want that judge interrogated. We need to look at everyone. I'll get you the warrants you need." She picked up her pen and turned her eyes back to the computer screen. "Everyone," she repeated, without looking up.

· · · · ·

Briggs' voice on the phone sounded strained, and if Nick hadn't known better, he would have said Briggs sounded a little tremulous, almost scared. "It's a fucking mess, man. They got him in bed, and the place isn't that big. We're talking brains and blood splattered on the inside of a fucking shoebox. I mean, you know I've got no love lost for this asshole, but man, this is bad."

"I'll be there in ten." Nick ended the call.

This would be bad, really bad, Nick thought, as he put the car in reverse and backed out of the parking space, then made a wide turn and pulled out onto the road.

· · · · ·

Franklin Molinaro lived with his elderly mother in a rundown trailer to the west of town. Weeds pushed up through the dirt, and crabgrass grew in patches around plastic steps up to the front door. Several patrol cars were parked haphazardly near the trailer, and the front door stood open. A coppery blood smell mixed with excrement hit Nick as soon as he got out of his car, and, as Briggs had promised, the scene inside was a fucking mess.

Briggs approached as Nick stepped inside. He was already talking, running a hand through his thinning pate. "We've got cash withdrawal and deposit sheets, more cash taped to the underside of the sink. Total moron, man. Kept his payoff right here, and what he didn't keep, he deposited into his goddamn bank account. It looks like more than $10,000."

"From?"

Briggs shook his head. "Don't know. All cash."

Franklin lay spread-eagled on his small bed. He was naked, which Nick supposed was the way the killer had found him. Someone shot him through the throat, leaving his face intact and an expression of surprise and horror frozen just inches above the wound. The bullet had caught an artery and, before his heart had stopped, tremendous sprays of Molinaro's blood had decorated the walls and ceiling of the tiny trailer. Briggs had been right. It looked like someone had exploded a blood balloon inside a shoebox.

They found Molinaro's mother in the toilet. She hadn't been shot, but she was dead. Her eyes bulged like boiled eggs, and her tongue protruded from her mouth at an impossible angle. The wrinkled skin around her neck had gone the color of eggplant. Someone, Nick could see, had wrapped an electrical cord around the woman's throat, compressing the tissues to the diameter of a baby's arm. He wondered if she'd been hiding in the bathroom, forced to listen while they killed her son. "Jesus fucking Christ," he muttered to himself, surveying the scene. *High stakes,* he thought, *meant no mercy.*

CHAPTER EIGHTY-ONE

Libby | San Francisco

The sun's rays burning her cheek stung her awake. Libby opened her eyes, stickiness over her hands, arms, and stomach. The smell, like rot and copper, was nauseating. She struggled to sit up in the bed, her own bed, thank god, and rubbed at her eyes. She looked around the room, blinking several times as her eyes adjusted. At least she'd made it home. Then she saw it.

Blood. Everywhere. Color-blocking her white sheets, rolling across her duvet in rivulets and staining her hands, her arms, her T-shirt. She bolted up and out of bed, panicking. Pulled her T-shirt over her head, closing her eyes and holding her breath as the sodden cloth pushed past her face. In the bathroom, she examined herself in the mirror. Spinning to see all angles over her shoulder. Her back, buttocks. Crimson smears marked her neck, and finger swipes of blood ran down one cheek. Again and again, she ran her hands over her body, chest and stomach, hips, thighs, turning around and peering into the mirror over her shoulder, buttocks, back. But there was no wound. No pain.

Not her blood.

She let out her breath, slumping against the side of the bathtub, sat. Then she remembered. Mitch. *Asshole.* Noting at her bloody hands, she must have cut the crap out of him. She didn't think she'd made more than one cut, but who knew?

Conner had taken Mitch to urgent care. Everybody said he'd need stitches. Libby hoped so. She'd hoped he'd need stitches and a fucking heart transplant or whatever to stay alive. She'd hoped he'd turn into one of those vegetable people and spend the next ten years on life support, having his diapers changed until he died a horrible, lonely death. She'd even allowed herself to imagine she'd killed him although death by X-Acto blade was highly improbable. She wondered what story Conner and Mitch had concocted to tell in the ER. Certainly, they hadn't told the truth. They hadn't said Mitch sustained those injuries when he tried to rape a teenage girl. *Rape.* The word appeared spiked and ugly in her mind.

Conner had returned from urgent care to find Libby on the steps out in front of his townhouse. She hadn't known what to do, so she'd just sat there in the darkness, letting the bay-cooled air brush across her face. Calling her father at that hour was out of the question. He wouldn't answer, and besides, she could never explain this heinous fucking situation.

Conner drove her home, but he was angry. *Mitch didn't mean anything by it,* Conner said. Besides, he'd been high. Libby shouldn't have cut the shit out of him like that. And what was she doing with a knife, anyway? Was she some kind of freak? Libby didn't have answers for him. No answers she wanted to say aloud, anyway.

In the shower, she soaped her body three times. Afterward, she took a bath. She tried to feel bad for hurting Mitch. She did not.

CHAPTER EIGHTY-TWO

Nick | Eden

Nick left the Molinaro scene feeling, for the first time, like they were making progress. Maybe this case wasn't just a series of depressing dead ends after all. He was back at the station when he got the call from Briggs.

"We got the gun." Briggs's voice on the phone was high and excited.

"Yeah?" Nick asked.

"Idiot perp dropped it close to the crime scene. Tracking the serial number now. Perp didn't rub it, believe it or not, it looks like a legal weapon. Unfuckingbelievable."

Tracing the gun that killed Broussard might be extremely helpful. Nick was pleased. "Great, thanks."

"Ok," said Briggs. "What about Finney?"

"Still not talking. But I figure he screwed himself years ago giving in to blackmail. Once they had him writing illegal scripts-especially scripts that wound up killing teenage girls -he was on the hook for good. Of course, he's denying all that but, we have enough to hold him a while longer."

"Ok," said Briggs. "So, the title search came back on the Marsh Street address. It's a vacant lot now, but it wasn't always." said Briggs.

"Yeah, I know. So, who is it?" asked Nick.

"You'll never guess," said Briggs, sounding too cheerful for Nick's mood.

"Not in the mood, Briggs."

"Sorry, partner. The Sonniers. Well, Mary now, I guess. The old guy has been dead forever. Mary Sonnier owns Continental Properties, and Continental owns 1310 Marsh Street."

"Shit," said Nick. "For how long?"

"Forever. As far back as I can find records, and she still owns it."

"Lying bitch," said Nick. "She owned the halfway house. She owned the last place those girls lived and never told a soul."

•   •   •   •   •

"Take back up," said Sheriff Savoy.

"I can go talk to old Mary Sonnier alone, Sheriff," Nick insisted. He didn't want a backup. He wanted to do this one on his own, although he wasn't sure why.

"No. No, you can't. I want you to have a backup.

"Briggs is busy right now, out with the floaters," Nick said.

"Take Lambert," she said. No room for discussion.

Nick looked away from her, hoping to hide his irritation. Fucking Lambert. Of all people. "Yes, ma'am," he said.

•   •   •   •   •

Nick and Lambert pulled into the tiny, barren lot in front of the Eden Motel. One of those ancient, low-slung, flat-roofed, roadside motels that, if it had any style, would have been called mid-century classic but was just a paint-peeling, wall-crumbling wreck of a place in the middle of a town nobody visited. The place was a shithole. That was for sure. A vacant shithole, Nick thought. The Eden Motel couldn't be self-sustaining; he should have noticed that earlier.

A low-pitched moaning sound floated across the dirt path leading away from the parking lot. Nick and Lambert looked at each other, then around the perimeter of the property. It was coming from behind the aluminum doors of a storage shed at one end of the lot. The sound grew louder as they approached the chained doors..

"Hello, who's in there? Are you ok? Sheriff here, open up." Nick rattled at the chains. No response. Nick stepped back to make room for Lambert, who had retrieved a pair of bolt cutters from his car. *Snap.* They were in. Through the darkness, the smell hit them first. Blood, shit, piss, and something else. Fresh kill. Like hunting. A stream of light from the doorway shone down on the figure. Shriveled and curled in the corner, it was making weak burbling sounds, more animal than human.

The perpetrator had cut Mary Sonnier fifty, maybe a hundred times with something sharp enough to take out neat, small pieces all over her body, then left her to bleed to death. She was missing one eye, a few fingers, and toes as well. The temperature in the shed had to be over a hundred degrees. "Hmmm, preese," she said through broken, bleeding lips, swollen to twice their normal size.

"Jesus, God," murmured Lambert, who turned his face away and stepped quickly back out of the shed.

"Shit, they tortured her. Call backup, get an ambulance," said Nick, and then he kneeled beside her. "Mrs. Sonnier? Who did this to you?" She couldn't answer. Only squirmed a bit. Was she trying to get away? The moaning sound escalated and Nick repeated the question. "Mrs. Sonnier, please, who did this to you? Help is on the way; you'll be okay," he lied, "but you need to say who did this."

She opened her mouth slightly and murmured something that sounded like "laladimplehrt," but Nick thought it might have been, "don't know, lips hurt."

"Okay." He leaned in towards her, trying not to inhale too deeply. "Did you know the person?" She nodded almost imperceptibly. "Mrs. Sonnier, did Junior hurt you?"

At this, her eye widened, and she shook her head with more energy. "No, not him," she said her speech suddenly clear. Then, she added, "Nah, nah, Juna." She closed her eye.

"Okay, okay. Good, that's helpful. Thank you," said Nick. "Can you tell me anything else?"

She only shook her head. Her skin rapidly lost its color, shifting from gray to milky white to bluish. Her lips went lavender, and Nick could see a pool of blood fanning out underneath her skull, like a tiara. He carefully reached behind her but could not find any single wound to apply pressure. She'd been cut so many times, so many places. It was impossible to stop the bleeding. He searched for a spot free of injuries and settled his hand lightly, using just the tips of his fingers, on her right shoulder. "Mrs. Sonnier, can you tell me why? Why did someone do this? What did they want?"

"File," she said with surprising clarity and then a word that sounded like, "wandiles." She raised her right arm an inch, trying to point at something, although the direction was ambiguous.

"Please don't move, Mrs. Sonnier, just rest. I hear you." Nick understood. "You said file. Whoever did this wanted something in your records. Right?" She closed her eye. He asked a few more questions, but she had lost consciousness, which was a mercy. He told Lambert to stay with her until the ambulance arrived and then went to have a look inside.

The door to the front office stood ajar. Nick drew his gun and called Junior's name. No answer. Called again and announced himself. No response. Finally, he nudged the door fully open with his foot and stepped inside. Same smell as out in the shed.

"Junior," he repeated. "You in there? Come on out. We have your mom. She's alive. It's okay." He waited a moment, silent, then tried again. "Look, Junior, come on. She's alive. You only injured her." Despite Mary's protestations, Nick thought there was a high probability Junior was the one who'd done the number on her. "You can still turn this around. Come out. Talk to me a bit, that's all." Nick slid past the reception desk and into the quarters the Sonnier's occupied behind the motel, down a narrow hallway, back up against the wall, gun down. He listened. Silence. "I'm coming, Junior, okay. Talk to me." Still nothing. Nick raised his gun and crept around the first corner.

The room was dim. Shades pulled. Nick could make out Junior's large frame on the floor, lying prone, his right arm outstretched, much of the rest of his body soaked in a pool of blood the size of a fishpond. He'd been shot in the upper back, at close range. The wound was gaping and ragged. A second wound in the back of his head was sticky with hair, blood, and brain tissue. They had hunted the poor dumb bastard down before they killed him.

•   •   •   •   •

Backup arrived within ten minutes, and shortly after that, a team of forensics people had descended. Nick was crouched down next to Junior Sonnier's body, examining the fingertips of his right hand, dark with bloodstains, although the rest of his arm was clean. "Detective?" came the voice of a young deputy. "I think you'd better come to see this."

Nick peeled off his gloves and followed the deputy into the hallway separating the living room from the two back bedrooms. They stood together, staring at the blood-stained wall. "Shit," Nick said, and let out a whistle.

"Yeah, that's what I thought too," said the deputy. "What does it mean?"

Nick cocked his head, studying the wall, which was smeared with bright red, sticky blood. Junior had apparently run or stumbled down the hall in an attempt at escape from his murderer, wiping his hand along the walls as he went. Several framed photographs had been knocked to the ground, and glass fragments lay strewn across the carpet. "Not sure. Looks like it took Junior a while to die," said Nick. "Poor bastard." Nick crouched down. "And it looks like while he was dying, he did this."

"Did what?" asked the deputy.

Nick pointed to a section of the wall where the smears seemed to take on a more organized shape. "See that?" Nick said, pointing to the wall. "Those are numbers. Looks like he was trying to write a series of numbers. He got to the number six before the killer shot him in the head."

"Jesus," said the deputy. "Jesus H. Christ."

"Yeah," said Nick. "This explains the blood on his fingertips." Nick looked up at the deputy. "I think our buddy there was trying to leave us a message."

CHAPTER EIGHTY-THREE

Evelyn | Eden

Light poured in through the double-pane windows of the reading room's south wall. Dark mahogany bookshelves lined the wall on the opposite side, and the wooden tables were the old-fashioned heavy sort, with fat legs that looked as if someone had carved each one from an individual tree trunk. For a courthouse, Evelyn thought, the ambiance was oddly spiritual. She chose a table in the back, setting the narrow folder down gently. On its cover, in plain black type: *Yates, Gwen Carolina, DOB 05/01/50, DOD 06/05/86*. Evelyn ran her fingers over the words. Then, with a breath, she lay her palm on the top of the folder and, in one instant, swung it open and read.

Evelyn looked hard at every word, even the ugly ones. Words like *rigor mortis, chloral hydrate poisoning*, and *time of death*. As she read, there came inside her a sense of stripping away. *Blood toxicology preliminary results: positive for chloral hydrate and alcohol*. The bits of sparkly lies were being yanked down one by one like so many decorations from a Christmas tree.

... all other tested substances preliminarily reported negative.

And, finally, what was left was something else altogether.

... substances negative.

A kind of naked grown-up truth.

... final toxicology lab report dated 08/10/86.

Maybe, Evelyn thought, turning the page, grown-up truth was only hanging up the sheets on the line because you couldn't afford an electric dryer, rocking a sick baby into the night, or going back to a difficult job because it paid the rent. Maybe it was facing the truth about someone you loved because you finally understood that, otherwise, life had a way of setting the rot inside you lose upon the world

... *report dated...* and you'd been left the responsibility of cleaning it up. *Final toxicology report negative for acetone.* Evelyn read that again.

... *report negative for acetone.*

Acetone, the key ingredient in nail polish remover. The meaning of the words hit her full force like a fist punch to the gut. Her breath became short and her chest hurt. She thought about Gwen lying on her side by the toilet, a pool of vomit next to her mouth, so toxic it had burned a hole into the linoleum floor. The chemical smell of nail polish remover was so strong in the room it made Evelyn's eyes water; she'd forgotten about that. And those marks on Gwen's neck. Reddish-purple bruised marks around her neck. It wasn't a dream; she hadn't imagined the marks on her mother's neck, she'd seen them. She *remembered* them. *Gwen hadn't died of an acetone overdose.* Evelyn flipped through the file to the end. Reading the official signatures.

Albert Finney MD, Medical Examiner
Hon. W. Fulsome,
John Picard, Sheriff.

All three were dated June 15, 1986, just days after Gwen's death, but nearly two full months passed before someone had added the final toxicology report (a lab printout with no signature) to the file. That meant the record was signed and closed without examination of the toxicology report.

Only one other official name appeared in the record. Macy LaPlace, MD typed in tiny font, at the bottom of an otherwise blank page: *This forensic autopsy report was prepared for John Yates by Macy LaPlace, MD, Forensic Psychiatrist on this 25th day of November 1986.* Evelyn flipped forward through the pages and then back again. Nothing. Other than the doctor's name, Macy LaPlace, and that brief statement, there was no evidence of a forensic autopsy report. Whatever a forensic autopsy report was, someone had removed it from the record. Evelyn stared again at the other signatures. Then the words: *negative for acetone. Positive for alcohol and chloral hydrate.* Finney had lied. Here it was, proof. Gwen never drank the nail polish remover. She didn't kill herself. Someone staged the whole thing, pouring the liquid onto the floor to make it look as if she'd ingested it. That same someone would have had to trick her to get her to ingest the chloral hydrate.

Someone had drugged Gwen and after that, either the same person or someone else had killed her.

•　　　•　　　•　　　•　　　•

Evelyn stepped through the courthouse doors into the late-morning sunlight. Now she knew. She knew and, maybe for the first time in her life, the next right thing seemed clear. The day was already dew-heavy and hot; honeysuckle thickened the air with its sugary perfume. She called Nick and asked to see him without telling him what she'd discovered. It would be better to explain everything in person. He insisted on picking her up, and she reluctantly agreed. Evelyn sat down on the stone steps to wait, and closed her eyes, thinking about the possibilities. Then she tilted her face, already moist with perspiration, up and up and up, like a hungry sunflower.

•　　　•　　　•　　　•　　　•

"Hey," Evelyn leaned in as he rolled his window down. "Thanks for coming."

"Hey," he said. "What are you doing?" He gestured across the lot at the rental car, engine running.

"Letting the car cool, although I think the A/C might be shot. Black interior. I can't even sit on the seats until it cools."

"Let me drive you," he said.

"No, no. I thought about that. Just follow me. It'll be fine. I think I was just paranoid earlier."

Nick got out of his car, shaking his head. "No, you weren't par-" The earth gave a violent shove. Something like a gunshot punched through the air, simultaneously deafening Evelyn and slamming her to the asphalt. A cloud of smoke and debris enveloped her, so thick that her eyes and mouth involuntarily slammed shut. For several seconds, Evelyn couldn't move. A thousand tiny pebbles were digging into her cheek, tearing into the already wounded flesh. She was face down on the macadam. Terrified, she sensed, but could not hear, her own rasping breath and vibrations coming from her chest as she moaned. The weight on top of her was Nick. He must have covered her with his own body when the explosion hit.

Oh, God. Oh No. No, no, no. "Nick," she pushed at him, but he was too heavy. "Nick?" She couldn't hear her own voice. Couldn't see his face. She wasn't sure if he wasn't responding or if the explosion had made her permanently deaf. "Nick," she was screaming now as the smoke cleared. "Nick, please, please don't. Please wake up." He only lay there upon her. Unyielding. Still, like a stone.

CHAPTER EIGHTY-FOUR

Evelyn | Metairie

In the silence, squashed into the macadam, Evelyn had only a narrow view between her arm and Nick's chest through which she could see shoes and lower legs coming towards them. Then there were people rushing over, mouths gaping open, arms waving. Terrified, she couldn't hear them. She concentrated on breathing. Sucking air into her compressed lungs. One... two... three. They pulled Nick off of her, and she scrambled away, gasping. Sucking at the air as if she'd been drowning. Faintly at first, then louder, she could hear sirens. And voices as well. She pushed away the hands trying to help her and scrambled back toward Nick, who lay still and silent on the pavement. *Please, please, please god, please god,* she heard herself saying. She bent over him and stroked his face, his lips, his eyes. *Don't die,* she told him. *Just don't die.* Tears had sprung to her eyes and she couldn't stop them. It had seemed like forever. Hot air. The crackle of a radio. Paramedics. Smoke. The smell of burned metal as she waited and watched the paramedics pulling her back, working on him. *Breathe. Breathe. Don't die, please god, god, god.* His eyelids fluttered open. *Not dead,* she thought, *you're not dead. This matters, so much, you matter, don't die.* After a bit, he sat up, rubbing at his face. His eyes. The paramedics ordered him not to stand right away. They pummeled him with instruments and devices. Told him he needed to go to the hospital. Get checked out. He refused. But promised he'd see a doctor later. They insisted. *Not now,* he repeated, and she watched him push his way toward her. The relief was overwhelming. She'd cried harder. How was it they'd come through this uninjured, or at least mostly uninjured? It was hard to tell for sure looking at Nick; he was filthy, covered with dirt and debris from the explosion. She guessed she looked the same. She didn't care. He was walking and talking, smiling as he approached her, he was ok.

They embraced for a long moment, then Nick made her promise to stay close. *Absolutely*, she told him. She promised from now on. Except for one more thing that she had to do on her own.

•　　　•　　　•　　　•　　　•

Macy LaPlace, MD, was smaller than Evelyn had expected, nearly elfin, mid-sixties with neatly cut silver hair, delicate features, and intelligent blue eyes. He'd been easy to track through Google once Evelyn had his name. And finding his name in the records had been an astonishing stroke of luck. He opened the door wide, grabbing Evelyn's right hand in both of his, and shaking it vigorously. "Welcome, Evelyn," he said. "I'm so happy you found me."

"You know who I am? I mean, you knew when I called earlier?" asked Evelyn.

"Of course, I do," the small man replied, beaming. "Even if I hadn't known you before, your family has been in the news lately." He looked at her, eyebrows raised. "Or perhaps you were unaware."

"Yeah, I guess I am unaware." Evelyn thought about it. She'd been avoiding the media, mostly. Of course, the story was huge. Digging up dead children was big news, for a while anyway. It would drift. People would lose interest.

"Evelyn, I know you," he continued. "I knew your family. We even met once, you and me. You don't remember?"

"No, I'm sorry I don't." *Don't feel bad. I don't remember much of anything from my childhood.*

"You were about ten," he said. "Your father brought you with him after your mother died. The first time I met with him."

His words made her sad. Another missing piece of her past showing itself. Another place, event, or some human being she could not recall. The experience always created the same ache in her gut. She recognized it now, maybe for the first time. It was grief.

She followed him through the old house with its polished wood floors and high ceilings to a large sunny kitchen in the back. He gestured for her to sit, and she pulled up a chair at the big farm table. The doctor took a small tray of shortbread cookies from the counter and set it down on the table. "Store-bought, I'm afraid. My wife was the cook, but I lost her last year."

My wife, Evelyn thought, touched that the doctor told her something so private. He didn't even know Evelyn. His words, "I lost her," made Evelyn think of Nick. Alive, he was alive, they both were and they shouldn't be. She'd been terrified to lose him, what did that mean?

The doctor asked a question and Evelyn nodded, smiled empathetically, and took one of the store-bought shortbreads. "Thank you," she said.

He smiled, revealing a row of small, perfectly straight, white teeth. "Coffee?"

Her eye fell on one counter where several crystal decanters sat winking at her. Nearly full. Booze. In the South, people kept liquor on hand. Just in case. As in *just in case visitors stop by*, or *just in case I can't get to the store before Sunday*, or *just in case I accidentally sober up*. She'd forgotten how much she loved that. Eden had blue laws when she'd lived there. Bars closed, and stores didn't sell liquor on Sundays. Of course, every real drinker just stocked up earlier in the week, and real, real drinkers thought nothing of driving a few hours to another parish to get supplies if it was the Sabbath. But the *just-in-case* policy made it easy to buy obscene amounts of alcohol under false pretenses, avoiding the mortification of admitting your alcoholism to yourself.

"Sure, coffee, thanks."

He started the coffee, then sat down at the table and peered into her eyes. "Evelyn," he began, "I know why you're here."

"You do?"

He nodded. "I was in practice nearly 40 years before I retired. But I will tell you: I remember your mother's case."

"How?" Evelyn asked. "It was over three decades ago."

"I remember her for the same reason that you are here," he answered. Evelyn watched his eyes carefully. "Because something went terribly wrong." A lump formed in her throat. She gazed out the window toward his garden.

He went to a built-in desk on the opposite side of the kitchen and opened a small drawer. From it, he pulled a moleskin notebook and then shut the drawer, and softly padded back across the kitchen to take a seat at the table. "I reviewed my records, making a few notes today before your arrival," he said, smiling at her and opening the notebook. "It's been a few years after all, but I keep everything, including all my appointment calendars, so I could reconstruct the events." He plucked reading glasses from his breast pocket and settled them on the end of his nose. Then, using his index finger as a pointer, he reviewed his notes for a few seconds before looking up at her. "Are you sure you want to know all this?"

No. "Yes, please, tell me."

He took a deep breath. "Ok," he said, checking his notes once more. "So, in July, about six weeks after your mother's death, I received a call from your father. At the time, most of my work was in forensic psychiatry, specifically psychiatric autopsy. I was writing a lot, teaching at Tulane. I assumed your father got my name in connection to that work."

"He said nothing," Evelyn remarked.

"Of course not," said the doctor. "You were a small child, Evelyn."

"Yes, but he said nothing in later years. He never said a thing, ever."

"Hmm, perhaps he felt it would be too upsetting?" LaPlace said sounding tentative. "In any event, we spoke. Talked about your mother, and he gave me some background information. I was debating about taking on the case-I was terribly busy at the time-but something he said startled me." Evelyn wasn't really breathing now. More like sucking at the air.

"He told me that, despite all the evidence, despite how ill she was, he was certain she would never have killed herself. At first, when I asked how he could be so sure, he was vague. He said he just *knew* it. But I pressed him, and he added something. I wrote it down in my notes." He glanced down at the notebook in his hand. "He said that your mother always planned to leave Eden one day, but your father did not believe she would have left without her children." Of course, thought Evelyn, forcing herself to stay calm. She'd known all along they killed her. She closed her eyes briefly, to ward off the impending tunnel vision.

"So that phone call," continued the doctor, "was on July 30th. We scheduled a meeting for August 9. Then things changed."

"How?" Carolyn asked. That's how.

"So, typically, when I do this type of work, families are desperate for answers. They are hoping for miracles they want, or need, to know. Often, it's not possible, and knowing isn't always the panacea they think it will be. Often, the truth is more devastating than mystery. Still, they seek answers. When I spoke with your father at the end of July, he was like that. He agreed to pay my fees, meet with me, and supply records, but then a few days later, he calls back. Completely different. He didn't want me at the house; he didn't even want me to come to town. Things were fine, he said." The doctor removed his reading glasses and laid them on the table. "Then, out of the blue, he shows up at my office. Brings along a box of papers. Records, journals, notes, and reports, and asks me to take them, read them, make what I can of them, but, and this is the strange part: he doesn't want to know what I find out. He can't be involved, he says. Said it just like that, in those words. He couldn't be involved. He seemed terrified, desperate for me to have those records, so, against my better judgment, I took the box,"

"Where is the box now?"

"It's here, Evelyn. It's here, with me." She felt a terrible, unexpected ache in her chest. Laplace continued. "I went through it and put it all back, just as it had been. One can piece together much of your mother's story from her psychiatric records and her journal."

"Journal?"

"Yes, she kept a journal. You didn't know?" He was pulling open a large plastic box, shuffling papers around off the top.

Of course, she knew. She thought about the three little journals in her bag. The last dated entry 1981, over five years before her death, Gwen already sounded unstable. Non-compliant with her medications, increasingly consumed by paranoia. But this man was referring to something else, another diary, another window into Gwen's life. Why not? Why wouldn't she have continued to write? She had no one else to confide in. A sharp ache, loneliness, and guilt stabbed at Evelyn's gut. She knew how Gwen must have felt. "I guess... well... not exactly."

"Ah, here it is. The entries are sporadic over about four years," said Dr. LaPlace. "1982 to 1986. Would you like to read it?"

No, she thought, and nodded *yes.* He handed her the book. Another one. Small, red, labeled in the same smooth, gold script as the ones she had with her. Evelyn imagined herself standing at a crossroads, two paths, neither defined, and both running off into identical infinite distance, into the darkness, into the night.

CHAPTER EIGHTY-FIVE

Gwen | 1982 to 1986

January 6, 1982

There is a fear I live with all the time. It's like a shawl around my shoulders that I can't remove. Today has been a hard day. Gray skies and a chill in the air that bites like razors. Clothes refuse to dry on the line, and a particular angry whistle passes continuously through the house.

He was in town with his family, and I saw him across First Street, heading to lunch maybe or shopping. My mind raced in all the directions he might have been going. The pain was excruciating, but still, it made me happy to see him looking good. He was smiling, reaching down to lift his smallest child to his shoulders. The last time we spoke, it devastated him. I think in my life there will never again be such a love. I am now resigned to it. When I think of the damage our love has caused and the responsibility we bear for others' lives, I feel ill all over again, and yet, I am again fortified against my weakness for him.

I've not been right since I got home this afternoon. These pages are where I will say the truth. I can't trust myself to speak it aloud or maybe it's that I can't trust others. An icy terror sits within me. A feeling, or more than that, a certainty that something terrible is about to happen, or has already occurred. Some form of destruction, an unraveling. I see shadows following me; I find objects in my house no longer where I left them—sometimes things are moved and lost for good. Yesterday, I went to get the mail, down to the box, a five-minute walk, and found the box empty. When I came back, the mail was stacked neatly on the kitchen table. John says I must have forgotten I'd gone to fetch it. I'm sure I would remember if I was the one who'd put it there. I tell my doctors someone is watching me, but they only want to give me more medication, so I stop telling them. This is not a sickness. This is real. Why will no one listen?

-Gwen

May 26, 1986

I see a new doctor today. Young, just out of school, I tell her she looks much too young to be a doctor. She laughs and says she is twenty-nine, which is quite old enough. I like her right away. Her name is Dr. Alyssa Carter. I see it on her name tag. She's not from here. I can tell. She asks lots of questions I've not been asked before. Who is president? What is the day of the week? She makes me do math equations in my head. That gives me particular trouble, and when I'm not able to count to ten by twos, I think she gets worried. I'm sleepy too, and she wakes me up once or twice.

In the end, Dr. Carter frowns at me. But she's not angry. She says she's worried about my lethargy. That's what she calls it. Lethargy. She also tells John that I seem unresponsive, which is confusing since I'm listening to her and answering the questions.

Dr. Carter says I'm on too much medication, which is also confusing since I've not been taking it. Although I cannot say anything to the doctor because John doesn't know, I don't take it. He doesn't know I just dispose of the pills when he's not looking. John argues I need to stay on the medicines. He tells Dr. Carter that I've been on the treatment for four years and how she might know what is best after just a few minutes. He is angry, which surprises me. But I think it's just that he's worried I'll have a breakdown like I did after Carolyn was born. I wish I could tell him I've been doing fine without the medication for a long time now, but I'm afraid he'll never trust me again.

Dr. Carter tries to tell John that I'm doing well, that it's unlikely I'll have another episode like I did so long ago. They argue, but then she explains that it's my choice. When she asks if I want to stop the medicine, I tell her yes, and she says ok, and she won't write any more prescriptions for the pills. I can tell John is unhappy, but I try not to look at him.

-G

June 3, 1986,

It's been a week since my last visit, and today we go back to the clinic. Dr. Carter wanted to see how I was doing without the medicine. I feel different. Awake, alert. Less sluggish. This time, I tell the doctor she is a beautiful woman and an excellent physician. She blushes a little.

I ask to speak to the doctor alone. She agrees, but John says we have to go, we are running late, he says, but I don't know why.

Dr. Carson promises to allow extra appointment time next visit, and I decide this is ok. We make another appointment for two weeks.

When I get home, I pull out a photograph from the newspaper. It's a photo of him. The man with tattoos. From his obituary. I'm not sure why I kept it, but now it's useful. On the back, I make notes so that I'll remember to tell the doctor next time. I write:

CB 1975
DD 1976
TW 1978
WR 1981

Then I tuck the picture into my journal, and stuff it into the bottom drawer where John would never look. Then, II go out into the garden to pull weeds. I'm feeling happy that a plan is in place. The sun is shining, and it warms the earth, where I dig my fingers in around the pink peony plant. Everything is going to be fine after all.

-G

CHAPTER EIGHTY-SIX

Evelyn | Eden

"And that's it?" Evelyn asked, closing the diary and looking up. "She never went back did she?" She wiped tears from her eyes and then ran a finger over the delicate pink flowers that decorated the edge of her coffee cup.

"No, Evelyn, she didn't. Your mother died two days after that visit."

She was silent for several seconds, willing herself to stop crying. Keep breathing. "She knew, didn't she?"

"Yes, I think she did," said Dr. LaPlace. "And I believe she planned to tell that young doctor about it."

"And someone stopped her," said Evelyn, pulling a tissue from the box perched on the table.

Dr. LaPlace nodded. "Her journal in the weeks and months leading up to her death had no indications of depression or suicidal ideation. She was optimistic, relatively clear-thinking, cheerful, enjoying activities, sleeping well. On the morning of her death, she made an entry that included plans for her garden. That would be entirely inconsistent with suicidal ideation."

Evelyn pictured Mama in the garden among the delphinium and peonies. She hadn't thought about that in years or maybe she hadn't remembered until now. This memory was genuine. She knew it. The tears came too suddenly to stop them. "Shit," she sputtered. "I'm sorry." She slapped at her eyes, annoyed. "Can I ask you something?"

"Of course," he said and pushed a silver tissue box toward her. She plucked another one and pressed it to her nose, wiped her eyes.

"Sometimes," she hesitated. "I... I can't remember things, or I remember, but my brain is mixed up, you know. Maybe what I remember isn't even real. Does that make sense? Is it possible? Things from my childhood especially. Nearly everything about my mother is like that. Hazy, fragmented. Do you think it's possible that she was... you know, really crazy, and I just don't remember it that way? I remember her as gentle, tolerant, reliable, and always so present for us, for me and my sister. She was a better mother than me, for sure. Most of the time, anyway." She dried her eyes and straightened her posture. "Oh, I don't even know what I'm saying. Not really."

He nodded, his face so full of compassion, she had to look away. "This is difficult, Evelyn. It's understandable. You've been through so much. Children who've been through trauma often find themselves confused, their memories fractured, lost, and conflicted. You probably have strange dreams, flashbacks, and sleep issues as well." She said nothing, uncomfortable with the intimacy of the moment. He waited a moment before continuing. "So, diary entries alone are certainly proof of nothing except that a person is literate. Documenting thoughts and feelings one does not actually have for many months would be difficult for anyone, and it would be impossible to conceal actual psychosis if it had been present."

"Wait," Evelyn said, shaking her head. "So, are you saying she was not psychotic? She was sane?"

"Right. Her entries are healthy. Every month or so, there are a few entries where her handwriting becomes scant, forced, and small. For several days, she writes only a few very dark words. But I went back and compared the entry dates to clinic appointments. There is a correlation."

"I don't—I don't understand." Evelyn felt confused and sick.

"I think someone was drugging your mother, giving her medications in high doses before appointments, leaving her unable to say anything significant or incriminating to the doctors. If she said something, she'd have been ignored because of her unstable mental state. I think the residual effect of the overdosing caused depression, probably lethargy and extreme sedation for several days following the overdose."

Evelyn put a hand to her mouth. "Oh, god. I remember the days she couldn't get out of bed. She ignored us. She seemed so far away. You're saying that wasn't psychiatric illness?"

"Well, your mother had at least one episode of documented mental illness when your sister was born. It appears she suffered from severe post-partum depression and became psychotic, at least for some time. Doctors made that diagnosis in the 1970s but it was no longer relevant to your mother in the 1980s. Whatever was happening in the 1980s resulted from inappropriate medication management by her caregivers and, likely, intentional poisoning."

A pause while her brain resisted this information sinking in. "Who? Who would do that? And why? I—I don't..." Evelyn's voice trailed off. A needle in her brain. Poking. She couldn't ignore it. "My father," Evelyn said the words flatly. "Oh my god, it was my father."

"Maybe."

"Bastard."

"Evelyn, I think he might have believed he was protecting her. Perhaps drugging her was the only way he could think of to keep her quiet or, at least, to damage her credibility with the doctors. People get desperate when they feel hopeless. Especially some men. Especially very traditional men. Maybe he didn't know how else to protect her."

"Oh no, it's too... too... awful," she said, burying her face in both hands.

"I'm so sorry, Evelyn."

After a long time, she looked at him. "So, what does this all mean? What were your conclusions?"

He said it plainly, but there was compassion in his eyes. "On the record, I can only answer the forensic question put to me."

"Which was?"

"Does the evidence support suicide as the manner of death?"

"And?"

"No, no, it doesn't."

"So, they killed her?"

Slowly, he said, "Off the record, I'll tell you that yes, I believe someone killed your mother, and I'm so sorry."

Her pulse quickening, Evelyn said, "But I don't understand. If you knew, all these years, why didn't you tell them? You just said she was murdered."

"I said that's what I believe, Evelyn. That's different. I have no basis for my opinion. No medical basis." She sat looking at him, trying to put the pieces together in her brain. "Evelyn, your father gave that box to me at that very brief meeting in August 1986. He was frightened, desperate, and I took it from him despite my better judgment. I authored a forensic report on the findings and gave my professional conclusion. But I never met your mother, I wasn't her doctor, and I never evaluated her." Dr. LaPlace looked into space for a moment, considering something. "And Evelyn, I don't think I fully understood the impact of my actions until your phone call today."

She glanced out the window, trying to make this all make sense. Sun shone brilliantly across the expanse of lawn and fell in shafts through a row of elm trees, turning the coleus to neon shades of magenta and fuchsia. Gwen would have loved the doctor's garden. She let her gaze slide back to the doctor. "What did you not understand?"

"Something was going on in your family for years, for decades. Then suddenly, in 1986, your mother dies, and your father knows Evelyn; he knows why, but he can't do anything about it. So, he comes to me. He wants it exposed, even though he's frightened. Then, just as suddenly, a few days after your sister goes away, he changes his mind or seems to. He's still willing to let exposure happen, but now he doesn't want to be a part of the process. He's scared out of his wits when I see him. I do not know why he's so afraid, but I want to help him, so I take the box."

"So, what? What made him change his mind?" Evelyn asked, but she already knew. The truth seemed suddenly clear as the sparkling picture window out to the doctor's garden. The real truth. The truth for which Carolyn had been searching the night before she left. The truth Evelyn had been running from ever since.

•　　　•　　　•　　　•　　　•

The sun was setting over the bayou as Evelyn left Metairie. Great swaths of sky, the color of fired brick and blood orange, touched the water in all directions, and cloud shadows looked like demons silhouetted against the preternatural backdrop. She glanced at the box on her passenger seat. Gwen's life, at least her adult life, wrapped up, stuffed away, forgotten. A thousand thoughts swirled in her mind. The 1986 diary. Her father had kept it, passed it along after Gwen died. *After Carolyn left.* The other three, the ones she'd found in the dresser, John hadn't known about those.

Think. What had Gwen written about her rapist? Blue eyes. Tattoos. Elaborate and specific tattoos of women. She'd seen a man like that before. Where? When? What had her mother said? His eyes, she'd liked his eyes. She'd trusted him because of his eyes.

Real nice blue eyes... he has tattoos covering the muscles, which are thick.

Then she knew.

Where is it? What did you do with it? Carolyn frantic in the bedroom. Tearing things apart. Searching. What did I do with what? Evelyn screams. Leave me alone. Go away. Evelyn's hands over her ears. Carolyn in her face. Her breath sweet and hot. The photograph? What did you do with the photograph?

You're crazy, Evelyn hisses at her. You're totally crazy, and everyone knows it, and they are sending you away. Did you know that? They're sending you away to a place for crazy kids. A crazy house. Evelyn is saying all the things she's been holding inside since Mama died. I hate you, Carolyn! I hope you go away and never come back.

Then she is on her knees, on the bed, propped up to look out the window, watching as Carolyn runs away under the moonlight. When her sister finally disappears into the blackness, Evelyn crumples into a heap in her bed. Her fingers stretch into the black space down between her mattress and the wooden headboard. For a moment, she panics. Her mouth is dry. Is it gone? Then her fingers brush lightly against the crinkled surface, and she gently slides it free. It tears, but only a little.

Evelyn lays in bed for a long time, clutching the photo to her chest. She is ten years old. She does not know what Carolyn wanted with it. Since Mama died, Carolyn has been mean and crazy. Her sister stopped watching TV or going up to the Back Field or anything else with Evelyn and she says she hates everyone and Evelyn wonders if Carolyn hates her too.

Evelyn is glad she stole the photograph. Carolyn up one night, late, under her sheet, reading something with a flashlight. It's not for babies, Lynnie. That's what she'd said. It's private. Leave me alone, she said. Shhhh, she said. So, Evelyn lay awake, watching, even though Carolyn thought she went back to sleep. Evelyn watched as her sister took something from the book and looked at it for a long time, then slipped whatever it was in-between her mattress and bed.

When Evelyn heard Carolyn's breathing go steady and soft, she peeled back her bedcovers-just a thin sheet on account of the heat-then set her feet down gently on the wood floor, wincing when it creaked under her weight. Carolyn slept on. Evelyn crossed the narrow space between their beds, slipped a hand under the mattress, and withdrew the paper.

It is a small square photograph. Black and white. Cut from a newspaper-old and yellowed- with printing on the back. A sailor in a white uniform stands on the deck of a ship. Small and wiry, both forearms tattooed with anchors and pictures of women with flowing long hair. His eyes are notably pale, even in a black-and-white photograph.

And on the back there are marks written over the newsprint. Numbers and letters. Dates and initials, maybe. The handwriting is tall and elegant. Long tails beneath the G's and Y's. Her mother's writing. Evelyn hid it carefully behind her headboard.

She thinks about how Carolyn looked. Sad and afraid and angry all at once. Good, she thinks. She wanted Carolyn to be sad. Good, good, good.

The road between Metairie and Eden was long, flat, and open to the wetlands on all sides. In the fading daylight, fatigue settled over her heavily, fogging her thinking, and pushing her towards sleep. She'd read somewhere that shock could manifest as nearly unbearable exhaustion. Several times, Evelyn shook herself to keep from drifting. She turned up the radio and sucked at the water bottle on her lap.

Abruptly, a truck appeared in her rearview. No headlights, but she could see its outlines clearly in the last light of the day. It was approaching too quickly, much too quickly. He'll slow down, she thought, immediately wide awake. Glancing around. No shoulder on the road. She pulled as far to the right as she could without driving into the marsh ditch. The truck came closer. Closer still. Enormous. She briefly considered driving into the ditch but realized it was more of a terrifyingly deep trench. Likely a wet one as well. Before she could finish the thought, the truck was on her, looming within a few feet of her bumper, headlights switched on. Bright enough to light a fucking football field shining into her car's interior, blinding her. She blinked several times, tried slowing her car, and heard the truck rev its engine behind, coming even closer. Then, without warning, it swung around to her left and drew parallel to her car.

She heard and then felt the sick scrape of metal on metal; the collision pushed her car sideways, and the force wrenched her head and neck to the left.

The metallic scraping stopped, and both cars skidded in parallel for a few seconds until the truck veered over the center line and hammered into the side of the little rental car. She pulled frantically at the steering wheel but felt the vehicle careening hopelessly out of control. Evelyn looked up in time to see the truck slowing, its brake lights illuminated, just before her car went off the asphalt, and she felt the front wheels slam into something too hard to be dirt.

Then, she and her entire vehicle left the earth.

Spinning and turning in space, the shoulder harness strap which had been digging vice-like into her chest and abdomen loosed itself and they whirled together, she and the car once, twice, in a weirdly calm slowed motion that seemed to go on forever and then, without warning, the glass in all four windows exploded and the car crash landed into the marsh grass on the side of the road. Immediately, as in a special effects film, the scene rewound itself. The previous several seconds rolled up and condensed into nothing, and everything had happened in the same instant.

CHAPTER EIGHTY-SEVEN

Nick | Eden

Nick arrived by the time the paramedics had pulled Evelyn from the wreckage. Other than a nasty gash to her forehead, she seemed unharmed. The paramedics bandaged the wound but Evelyn refused the trip to the hospital. She'd had worse, she said, glancing at Nick, who smiled despite his concern. Of, course she had; this woman had been through hell but he wasn't convinced she knew how lucky she was that the truck hadn't come back to finish her. Evelyn agreed to let Nick drive her back to Eden. Not really a choice, looking at the ruined rental car. The second ruined rental car. Her name would go into the DO-NOT-RENT database now. She'd probably never get another rental car in this parish or anywhere in Louisiana for the rest of her life, maybe anywhere in the country.

As they drove, she was silent, rubbing at her neck, her injured arm, her bruised face. She chewed at her bottom lip, then said, "I have some things to tell you. I've... I've sorted a few things."

"Ok," he said cautiously. She'd been run off the road, he told himself. At least that's what she said. And there were the enormous skid marks to prove it. Evelyn's imagination did not make those. So far, she'd been attacked in her home, nearly blown up by a car bomb, and now, run down by a vehicle bigger than an SUV. Something beyond her control was going on. Someone was trying to scare the shit out of her and might be trying to kill her. He had to listen to what she had to say. Crazy or not.

Evelyn told him what she'd learned. "Nick, as I read her diaries, my mother's diaries, I thought she was just paranoid, or, if not out of her mind, at least, exaggerating."

"But?

"But now, I think that's wrong. The man who raped her, I can't believe I missed it the first time."

"Wait," said Nick. "I'm not following."

"There's a man with tattoos on his arms. He'd have been maybe fifteen years older than my mother. Does that sound like anything to you?"

Nick shook his head. "I don't think so. A lot of men around here have tattoos, these days the women too. That was long before my time, so, I don't know. Who is he?"

Evelyn closed her eyes and lay her head against the seatback. She said, slowly. "That's the man who raped my mother." He reached across and touched her hand. She'd struggled so hard for so long. He wanted badly to do something for her, but he needed to exercise caution. "I don't want to go home tonight, ok?" she asked.

He tried to protest. If what they'd done was a mistake the first time, it would be beyond idiocy, beyond professional misconduct, to let it happen again. But then he felt her interlace her fingers with his and lost his resolve. Fuck it. She needed him and taking care of her felt good. He'd give her a place to stay. Protect her. Nothing more. This one last time.

At his place, she took her time showering, finally padding out into the living room in one of his T-shirts. Somewhere upstairs, a baby cried. A man and woman spoke to each other in voices that were loud, without anger. The baby settled. The cicada sang, and the night air seemed to thicken. They sat on his sofa in semi-darkness. Evelyn said, her head hurt, and asked Nick to switch off the lights. Then she lay with her head on his lap, on a small pillow, and closed her eyes. He bent forward to kiss her lips and inhaled her scent; he felt intoxicated by her sweetness intermingled with the smell of Magnolia drifting in through the windows thrown wide open to the summer night.

CHAPTER EIGHTY-EIGHT

Nick | Eden

Monday, June 12
Present Day

It came to Nick in the night. He opened his eyes in the darkness. The image in his mind was clear. He'd seen the man in a photograph, or at least he'd seen the same man in another photograph. Where? Sailor... black-and-white photo... tattoos on both forearms. The broken glass had distracted him on the carpet. The blood on the wall, the numbers written in Junior Sonnier's blood. A series of mismatched family photographs, some in color, some fading black-and-white. Several were on the floor, knocked off the wall as Junior ran-or possibly crawled away from his killer. Chubby, smiling boy, with lank hair and a vacant expression. Elementary school photos. A few pictures of Mary, years ago. Smooth, brown hair falling over one shoulder. Wide-bottom jeans. Not a beauty, but not the wreck she was today. And there, lying on the floor in the hallway where they'd found Junior dead, among the shards of glass, three young men in navy uniforms, grinning, standing on the deck of a ship. The one in the middle, short, pale eyes, forearms muscled and tattooed. And there'd been a caption: TOM SONNIER WITH FRIENDS, 1957.

Evelyn was right. Nick knew this man. Gwen Yates's rapist was Tom Sonnier.

He sat up in bed, mind racing. It made perfect sense. The Sonnier's owned Continental Properties, and Continental owned 1310 Marsh St, the location of the halfway house. Tom Sonnier.

Junior Sonnier. The number sequence Junior had written, or tried to write, in his own blood on the hallway wall. Someone wanted it or wanted something it unlocked. They had tortured Mary to get it. Killed Junior. And Junior had left it as a message. A goddamn message. Nick should have seen it all before. He should have seen how all of this fit together.

Who alive would know its meaning? So far, Nick had every forensic tech team available working on it. He'd pulled in resources from Baton Rouge, and he had floaters pounding the pavement to local banks and credit unions. So far, nothing. He rubbed at his eyes as if that might provide clarity. Swung his legs out of bed, planting bare feet on the cool wood floor, he leaned over and picked up his phone, checking the time. Think, he told himself. Who could know the meaning of that sequence? The answer came as easily as his next breath.

Finney.

•　　•　　•　　•　　•

The two men sat in the interview room across from one another, a bag of greasy breakfast sandwiches and two plastic cups of orange juice between them. Finney stared at Nick without speaking. Perhaps, Nick hoped, Finney's willingness to give up information would improve in the early morning when his lawyer was not available. Finney was to be moved over to Parish Jail within hours. This might be Nick's last chance. He'd explained to Evelyn he had to return to the station, and she'd been too sleepy to ask questions, so Nick had pulled the blanket up around her shoulders, kissed her cheek, and silently hoped she'd sleep a long time; she so needed to rest. He'd taken the police vehicle and left her the keys to his car so she could drive herself home if she woke up, only because he knew how much she would hate being stranded. Now, he wondered if that had been smart. God, he hoped she wouldn't do something reckless.

He was trying not to think about it. He was starting to care about this woman. Scratch that. Not starting to care. He fucking cared, and it was too late to stop the feelings.

"So, I thought you might want some food that wasn't heated in a microwave," said Nick, gesturing at the paper bag. A bribe. "Or at least I didn't heat in our microwave." Finney sighed and shifted slightly in his chair. He looked at the food with disdain. "You don't like it?" Finney offered no response but kept his eyes on Nick, who did not look away. "Well, if you tell me what you want, I can try to get it for you." Nick grinned.

"So, are you the good cop?" Finney said, each word heavily weighted with sarcasm.

Nick cringed, his dislike for this man escalating. "Not really, Finney." Nick leaned over the table just a little. "I'm the cop who is running short on time. We know you are in this thing deep. Your friends are dead. Mary Sonnier and Junior?" Nick shook his head and made an exaggerated grimace. "Dead, in the most awful way. I don't think you want to see the pictures, but I'll tell you, Finney, I'm pretty sure if the wrong sort of rumors got around the jail, you'd be in the same shape. Isn't that right?"

Finney flinched and sat up straighter. The man knew how to control himself, that was for sure. "What happened to them? What's going on?" His eyes flashed with fear, but his words were cool, and easy.

Nick cocked his head. "Well, let's see. The folks you helped all those years ago are back, Finney, and they sure as hell don't want anybody finding out what happened. It looks to me like we," Nick gestured around the room, "are not your real problem. Unless you talk real soon, I think your problems will get, uh... solved." Nick drew a thumb across his throat. Then slid a piece of paper toward Finney. "That's a gift from your friends. Specifically, Junior Sonnier. That's not the original, of course. This is." Nick pushed forward a photograph of the bloodied wall at the Sonnier house. Finney made a face of disgust and turned away. "No, no," said Nick. "I think you need to look at this, Finney." Nick's voice was hard. "Now I'm assuming Junior Sonnier did not give those numbers out to the person who tried to turn his mother into meatloaf." Nick paused, but Finney just stared at him. He continued. "And unless the killer saw this message Junior left for us, which I doubt since he did not bother to wipe it away, I'd guess he, or they, will move on to the next likely candidate." Nick pointed his pen at Finney. "I mean, from what I could tell, whoever went after Mary and Junior really, and I mean *really*, wanted this information."

Finney glanced at the paper. "I think I need my lawyer."

"That's fine, but I don't think your lawyer will make it here before you move over to central jail, and," he paused for emphasis. "Who knows what will happen once you get over there? I'm pretty sure the people who cut Mary Sonnier to ribbons and hunted down Junior will have people on the inside, too." Nick widened his eyes and frowned. Mock concern. "Could be bad for you." Nick got up and started toward the door. "So, I'll see you later."

"Wait," Finney said, suddenly looking pale, bloated, and, for the first time, as old as his years. "I'll talk to you," he said. "But you have to promise you'll help me."

Nick sat down. "That depends." He pointed at the paper with the numbers. "Talk."

CHAPTER EIGHTY-NINE

Evelyn | Eden

Evelyn sat in Nick's kitchen with a cup of coffee and her mother's last journal, the one Dr. LaPlace had provided. She'd considered spiking the coffee-she rarely drank coffee except as a mixer for booze-but, as she held the bottle over the cup, she changed her mind. Perhaps, she considered, when one's life is threatened more than once in twenty-four hours, a clear head is the better choice. She opened the book, smoothing back the thin pages. Some entries had been written in pencil and were now so faded she had to squint to see the words. Her mother's handwriting was elegant and familiar. She re-read the words:

> *January 6, 1982*
> *There is a fear I live with all the time... Perhaps it is only the memory of seeing him this morning... pain was excruciating...*

Evelyn closed the journal. Sipped at her coffee and stared again at the words on the page... *memory of seeing him...*

Him, she thought. Evelyn read the words slowly, almost sounding them out... *In town with his family... the pain was excruciating...*

Could it be? ... *seeing him....*

She closed her eyes, clutching the journal to her chest. Trying to imagine Gwen's love for this man. She could smell the age in the paper. She inhaled deeply, imagining her mother's scent still lingered between the pages. *This man. Her father*. The thought hit her: *Gwen would not have been the first woman killed by a lover.* And this man, she'd told her deepest secrets. Confided everything. Was it possible? *Could he have had her killed?*

This secret lover, this mystery man-if he'd killed her-he would have been someone powerful, rich, connected. And corrupt. Someone old enough to have seduced her mother as a young girl. Someone married. Kids. Prominent in the community. In her mind, Evelyn ran through the list of known and possible players. One at a time. Then went through them again. It hit her then, the thing she'd been aware of all this time and, yet, somehow also unable to see.

Evelyn straightened in her chair, then stood, looking around for her jacket and shoes. She borrowed the keys to Nick's car, and in less than ten seconds, she was gone.

CHAPTER NINETY

Nick | Eden

Nick arrived at the Bonfante Parish Home Loan and Credit Union, followed by three Sheriff's vehicles. He requested the numbered deposit box and, escorted by two uniformed officers and two bank officials, opened it inside the bank vault. A goddamn safe deposit box code. That was it. Nothing spectacularly clandestine about that. Finney had given up the information easily once he considered the options. Punishment by the guards for being a cop killer, prison rape by other inmates for being a pedophile, and, of course, the possibility of death at the hands of either party.

The box was empty, save for one small key and a scrap of lined notebook paper.. More numbers; two strings of eight digits, written one over the other in ballpoint pen. It took Nick only a few seconds to recognize their meaning. "Coordinates," he said. "These are geographical coordinates; let's go."

•   •   •   •   •

La Rue Cemetery. Outside of town. Dozens of above-ground graves. Varying in size and ostentatiousness-some bigger, more elaborately decorated than small houses- dependent upon the wealth of the dead. Narrow grass-lined paths in-between for the living.

The coordinate strings were long enough to establish a precise location within eleven centimeters. A medium-sized marble vault, the type rich families bought in advance so they and all their loved ones could be buried together. This one appeared to hold no human remains. At least there were no epitaphs indicating human burial. There were no markers at all, no nameplate, nothing. Nick slid the key into the iron door, heard a click, pulled, and watched it swing open. The deputies' flashlights bounced off the dark, stinking tomb walls and repeatedly lit on the stacks of clear plastic boxes. Papers. This was some kind of storage room.

Nick, holding the flashlight between his teeth, approached one box, removed the lid, took the flashlight from his mouth, held it in his left hand, and reached a gloved right hand inside. Among the canceled checks, financial and occupancy records, and ledger books, there were pictures, so many pictures. He stepped back and focused his light on the vault. From one clear plastic box to the next, stacking the full height of the vault and lining the walls, there were so many of them, dozens, maybe. And staring out from the inside, were the children; their expressions plaintive, or pleading or vacant. There were hundreds of terrible images and decades of stolen children.

•　　　•　　　•　　　•　　　•

"Jesus fuck," Briggs said. Nick looked at him, noticing he'd gone pale. Nick had never seen Briggs react in such a way to a crime scene. "Jesus," he repeated. "It's sickening."

Crime scene investigators had arrived in force. White suits and brilliant floodlights. They carried out the contents of the vault, one box at a time. Bank records, account numbers, even addresses on some statements. Dating back decades. And photos. Hundreds. Thousands maybe. Young girls, and a few boys, dressed or undressed. Some alone. Some with adult male partners-the face always obscured. "What the fuck is all this?"

Nick took in a deep breath and said, "Trafficking."

"What the fuck?" said Briggs. "Fucking kids?"

"Yeah, I think what we'll find is that the Sonniers were collecting and selling kids. Maybe pictures of kids and the children themselves, probably for years. Using that halfway house as a... I don't know... warehouse, I guess. Maybe until the old man died in eighty-two."

"Motherfucker," said Briggs, going an even whiter shade of pale.

"Yeah, that about sums it up," said Nick. Nick thought about his morning's interview with Finney. He'd finally given up information after he got scared enough.

There was a mole, Finney had said. *A mole on the inside.* Someone with access to criminal records, personal records, socials, driver's licenses, addresses, whatever. Information that can blackmail, or sometimes bribe, just about anyone. Finney, Picard, John Yates.

Yes, Finney had admitted, he'd started out giving sedative drug prescriptions to Tom and Mary Sonnier. They threatened to expose his homosexuality, which, in 1973, would have been career destruction. Picard, Finney's cousin, had provided that ammunition to the Sonnier's. According to Finney, his first cousin sold him out, forced him to take the position in Eden, and then sucked him into the illegal prescriptions. But, *no, Finney insisted,* he never knew the real purpose of the drug prescriptions. "I knew it had something to do with sex. But, you know, I honestly believed it was for... parties. All consensual. Party drugs."

Finney was lying about that, of course, Nick thought. Looking around this vault, that much was clear. None of the victims in these photographs were anywhere near the age of consent, and Finney would have known that. Sonofabitch. Finney may not have been in charge, but he'd been willing to go along with anything as long as it kept him out of trouble.

CHAPTER NINETY-ONE

Evelyn | Eden

The house was dark, low slung, and melancholy-looking in the afternoon sun. It carried a peculiar slant as if it were sneering. Set so far back, the expansive lawn might have been a golf course. Parking the car, Evelyn fumbled with the key, and it bounced to the floorboard beneath the steering wheel. "Shit," she said to nobody and bent to search for it. Groping along the mat, her fingers contacted metal, and she snatched it up. Calm down, she told herself. Calm the fuck down.

She yanked the door handle and kicked open the door; it swung open with too much force, lodging firmly in the grass at the curb. Climbing out, she went around the back of the door to give it a shove. It slammed closed with a loud *thwack* sound. "Shit," she said again, looking around to see who she might have disturbed. There was a neighbor on his porch across the street. He didn't look up. Evelyn shoved the key into her pocket. Struggling to breathe evenly, she made her way up the path toward Judge Wesley Fulsome's house.

The front doors were huge, heavily carved, and sinister looking. Making Evelyn think of fairytale castles, not the good kind, but the ones that were guarded by trolls and housed witches.. Ivy stretched around the front of the house, and the leaves, grown halfway up the porch wall, covered most of a small speaker that sat above what Evelyn assumed was a doorbell. Evelyn hated ivy. She'd heard once ivy was like a rat hotel. She shuddered and moved several tendrils aside to push the button. It appeared the judge received few visitors. The bell emitted no audible sound. No answer. She tried again. Nothing. She raised her fist and was about to knock when the door swung back away from her, and she toppled forward a few feet into the doorway.

"Hello, Evelyn." Judge Fulsome said. He looked unwell. He was tall but stooped, his skin the color of dishwater and his blue eyes watery and dull. "I hoped you'd come." He knew her. The bastard knew her.

"Uh... yes... I don't know... I mean. Yes. I need to talk to you," said Evelyn. *Get it together*. The stakes were too high. She could not and would not screw this up.

"Ah," he said and stepped back, motioning for her to come in, his hand trembling. She noticed both his thin hands trembled even as he let them hang to his sides. He was sick, she thought. "Let's talk in my study," he said. Over his shoulder, the paneled hallway was dark, and still. A chandelier hung in the foyer. Made of so much iron, it resembled a medieval torture device more closely than a light fixture.

"We can talk out here," she responded. No way was she going in there. This man was dangerous. Sick. Maybe desperate.

"Okay." He pointed to a huge wicker porch chair. She took a few steps toward it and sat. She felt swallowed by it. Ridiculous. But struggling up out of it would be more humiliating than staying put.

"Can I get you a drink?" he asked.

Yes. "No."

"Okay." He didn't sit down but folded his arms across his chest and looked down at her.

"Okay." Evelyn inhaled deeply, trying to catch enough air. "My mother. What happened? I need the truth. What did you do to her?"

Judge Fulsome shook his head slowly. "Nothing, Evelyn. I did nothing to your mother."

She took another breath, forcing out the words, angry at herself for finding this so difficult. "That's a lie." She glanced over the banister across the street at the neighbor, who appeared to be paying them no attention. She wondered what would happen if she screamed. "You killed her," she said, forcing herself to slow her voice, remain calm.

"I didn't," he said. "I didn't kill anyone." His voice was soft, beaten. He ran a hand over his head, fingers stroking a few thin, gray hairs. She saw beads of sweat on his forehead. His eyes glistened.

"You did." *You killed all of them, you murdering, lying bastard.*

"No, but I understand why you think that." His voice was steady, softer than she had expected.

"I don't think it. I know it," Evelyn said. Tears were coming, despite her efforts to keep them back. "I know what happened." Evelyn inhaled again, held her hands one within the other, willing them to stop shaking, and began again. "My mother did not kill herself."

"Evelyn, you are right. Your mother didn't kill herself. But you are wrong about me. I didn't kill her." Judge Fulsome hung his head. *Was that shame?* "I have no reason to lie to you," he said.

Evelyn pushed herself up out of the stupid chair and stepped towards him, matching his gaze. "You have every reason. You've been lying for years. To protect yourself. To protect," she waved a hand toward the house. "All this."

"I'm sorry. I'm so sorry." There was compassion in his voice.

"Don't do that," she said, shaking her head. "Don't pretend to care about me. You do not give a fuck about me. You care about *you*, and that's it. Just have the decency to tell me the truth about that, at least. Why? Was it because of what she knew? Or what she suspected?" She was feeling less terrified. Maybe stupidly so, she thought. The neighbor across the street was now standing. He had walked out onto his lawn and was peering at them. He looked curious, more than worried.

Fulsome appeared to be considering what she had just said. He pulled an envelope from his pocket and handed it to her. Dropped his gaze to the floor. He looked a thousand years old. "Evelyn, I am guilty many times over through both my actions and my lack of action. I convinced myself I was protecting you. I failed. I.." He said something else, and his voice faltered.

"Don't, just don't..." She did not have any other words. Staring down at the delicate envelope in her hands, she turned it over and ran her forefinger across the tiny butterfly printed in the corner. She recognized the stationery. Gwen's gift to Carolyn on her birthday. Carolyn kept it precious. Never used it. From the convenience store bargain bin, it was beautiful. Evelyn tore open the envelope and unfolded the sheet of paper. The writing was not Carolyn's. There, in her mother's elegant script, it said:

April 11, 1981

Dearest Wesley,

If I were to look into your eyes, I would be unable to speak these words. And so, I write them.

You and I both know that our love cannot go on. I need you to let me go now, and for Evelyn's sake, I am sure you will understand. My fear for her is so great it cuts my heart like a blade. She deserves a life that makes sense, Wesley, a life without the dangers we have created. She will never know. You and I will never speak of it. But we will have her in our hearts, and she will bind us together, always. Do what you have to do to keep her safe, my darling. I will not forget you.

Yours forever,

G

It was true, Evelyn thought. This sick, pathetic old man who'd been complicit, through inaction if nothing else, in unspeakable crimes. This man was her father. The last vestige of hope crumbled and Evelyn felt herself floating away from her body as if she were watching herself through a camera lens. She read the page again and then again, looking for something familiar. The smell of magnolia blossoms and jasmine, perhaps. She watched her own fingers retrace the words over the soft, sloping cursive on the page. It was as if she were playing the voyeur, pulling back the wrapping to peer inside a package that did not belong to her. Whatever had existed between her mother and the Judge had been half-dead for over more than thirty years; it's dwindling light kindled by nothing more than the flickering memories in this old man's brain. This letter was between two lovers Evelyn had never met. As unreal as a fairytale.

She looked up at the judge, hollowed and dry; this was not the man her mother had loved. "I wanted you to be safe. I wanted your mother to be safe. Do you understand?" He was pleading. "They would have taken you both. So, I did the only thing I knew to do. I went along with it. I know now it was wrong, and I'm so sorry."

Evelyn shook her head, confused. "You knew? All along, you knew. Tell me." She was nearly whispering. "What did you know?"

Fulsome hesitated a long time, and then he told her. She watched as the words tumbled from his dry, thin lips. Spittle accumulated at the corners of his mouth, and she noticed tiny reddish blood vessels road-mapping across his nose and cheeks. He kept talking. She told him to stop. *Trafficking,* for God's sake. Is that what he just said? Selling girls. Selling boys. How could that possibly be true? Her stomach churned. She stared at him, silent, lips clamped together over clenched teeth, as the pieces fell into place.

"Oh my god... are you saying... that you knew? You knew they were—what they were doing?" She had to force the words. Revulsion in her voice. She wished she could paint her words black so he could see as well as hear how this made her feel. "Oh, god, you knew about the deaths too, didn't you? You knew those bastards killed all those girls back then? Jesus."

"No, no. Not at first." He didn't look at her. "At first, I thought... I hoped the deaths were accidental. And I suppose they were. In a way. That's what I told myself, anyway." She said nothing. "I don't know, Evelyn. I... I guess I wanted to believe those girls had done it to themselves. Too much partying, maybe in with the wrong crowd. Something goes wrong. Someone gets scared and tries to hide the evidence."

"Bodies," she said. "Not evidence. Say what it is, they hide bodies, sometimes children's bodies."

"Yes, that's what I mean. I signed the autopsies; I looked the other way. But I did not know the details. I swear to you."

"Too much partying? They were children, those girls. Only kids." They were Libby's age. "Someone fed them those drugs. Why? To keep them quiet. Docile? What the fuck? Why would you help those monsters?"

"It was for you, Evelyn. For you and your mother."

She held up her hand. "No, stop. You don't get to do that. Blame my mother. No."

"Please," he said. "They've been threatening you for years. They said they'd take you, hurt you if I said a word. So, I said nothing, and did nothing. Hoped it would go away, I suppose. And it did after a while, as far as I could tell. When Sonnier died in eighty-two, everything stopped, even the threats, but then your mother, Gwen," he looked as if he might collapse as he said her name but steadied himself against the railing,. "she knew. She knew, or at least suspected, what was happening, and she wouldn't let it go. I tried to convince her of the danger, but she wouldn't listen. Oh, god." His voice broke slightly, and tears appeared. She watched him cry, feeling nothing but revulsion. In the distance, something squealed and whined. An ambulance, maybe. A police car.

"You son of a bitch," Evelyn spat. "You knew about my mother? You knew those fucks murdered her." It wasn't a question.

"I knew Evelyn. But I didn't know who. I still don't. Someone didn't want Eden's history exposed, and they got wind that your mother had suspicions. Maybe even proof."

"It doesn't matter," Evelyn said. "You knew. You knew, and you just let them get away with it." *How dare he cry over this. How dare he feel a goddamn thing?* His shoulders slumped more deeply; he looked like a man with a mountain on his back as he leaned heavily on the railing. "And Carolyn?" Evelyn asked. "You knew about her as well." When he remained silent, she knew the answer. "You knew what they did to her as well." Thoughts ricocheted in her mind. The photograph Nick had shown her. He'd asked her to identify her father in the picture. Her father burying- "You were there when they buried Carolyn, weren't you? You took that photo." *An anonymous source,* Nick had said. They'd received the photograph, along with others, from an anonymous source. Evelyn took a step back, away from Fulsome. "Did... did you kill her?"

"No," he sputtered. "No, no, no. I had nothing to do with it, I swear." She didn't believe him.

"Then what the fuck were you doing there?"

He hesitated. "Evelyn, look, your father came to me. He told me what happened. He told me Carolyn was dead. Murdered. He... he found her out there."

"Out where?"

"I'm not sure. But on your property. He needed help. He knew what they'd do to him if he went to the authorities about Carolyn. More than that, he knew what they'd do to you."

She stared at him. It wasn't possible. She'd been there. Seen Carolyn dragged away. Watched as her father handed her over to Mr. Mike. She'd *seen* it. Could it be? She'd believed her own version of the events for years. Decades. It had been so real. But then, her memory had shown itself to be unreliable. Worse than unreliable, it was riddled with glitches. Could she be wrong? Nick said so. Now Fulsome was saying so. She closed her eyes, shaking her head, trying to block out the image of her damaged father discovering the body of his dead daughter on his own property. "So, what did... you... do?"

"I helped him. I got him help. Picard helped him bury her. That's all. Your father was too distraught to do it alone." *Too drunk,* Evelyn thought. *Too fucking drunk.* "And, yes, I was there," Fulsome added. "I took pictures."

"Why?" She was struggling to keep her voice down. He was lying. He had to be lying. "Why would you do that?"

"Insurance. That's all. Nobody knew what was going on. We didn't have all the pieces. It seemed prudent to document Sheriff Picard's involvement." He pulled a handkerchief from his shirt pocket and wiped the sweat from his brow. "Evelyn, I sent the photographs anonymously in order to protect you. If they'd known I was helping, they would have hurt you. I knew you were in terrible danger, Evelyn. As soon as you arrived in Eden. So many secrets in this town, Evelyn. So many people with terrible secrets."

She studied him. The tremble around his mouth and the way the tendons in his neck quivered as he swallowed dryly. His hunching shoulders. His weakness. He was telling her the truth. Motherfucker. "Who? Who would hurt me?"

He shook his head. "I don't know, Evelyn. None of us know."

Evelyn sat back down, no longer afraid of this man. This weak, cowardly man. After a bit, she said, "Wait. What about Molinaro? You reduced his bail. You let him out so that he could attack me. And you've been following me, planning this. That man I saw-"

"God no. No, Marcus works for me, I asked him to keep an eye on you. So, yes he's been following you, but only to try to protect you." She recalled the tall man outside the cafe that day.

Had she seen him more than once? Probably. "I got an order to reduce the Molinaro bail, and I did it. Nobody said a thing about why, there was no way for me to know they'd use him to hurt you." He sighed. "I should have known. I'm sorry." She wanted him to stop apologizing. She wanted to slap the sorry out of him. Instead, she stood up.

"I have to go." She moved past him quickly to the steps.

"Evelyn, please forgive me. I've not been a father to you, but I'd like to be... something if you'd let me."

She turned around. "No. You're not my father. I had a father once, but he's dead. My family? They're all dead." *Except that's not true,* she thought. *There's Libby.*

CHAPTER NINETY-TWO

Nick | Eden

"Party drugs." Nick slammed a photograph down on the table in front of Finney. "Fucking party drugs? That's what you call the lethal concoctions you turned over to a group of child rapists and killers. Is that what you told me this morning? Look at that." He pointed at the photo. "There are dozens, hundreds more in that vault. Naked children, Finney. Naked children being raped by adult men." He was back in the interview room with Finney. He'd get the information he needed if he had to kill the guy to do it.

"You don't get it," Finney mumbled.

"No," Nick said. "I really don't. How about you explain it to me? How do you rationalize handing over poison to people you knew were buying and selling children? How, Finney, are you not committing murder when they use those drugs and some of those children die?"

Finney shook his head. "Look, once I was in, I was in. That's how they operate. After I started falsifying autopsies on top of supplying those drugs, they had me. It went way beyond social ostracism. I could have lost my license to practice medicine. They'd have sent me to jail. They could have killed me."

You are definitely going to goddamn jail, Nick thought. He couldn't care less what Finney's sexual preferences were but couldn't help wishing someone had killed him for being a psychopathic asshole who helped rape and murder women and children.

"So, what choice did I have?" Nick had heard that before. Every piece of shit he'd ever arrested used some version of that excuse for committing a crime. They kept in a safe place, ready to use at a moment's notice tucked up their sleeve right next to: "Hey man, it wasn't me, it was this other dude."

"So, you did what? You hooked up with Mary Sonnier for protection?"

Finney grimaced. "No, it wasn't like that. After old man Sonnier died, I thought the whole thing would go away. It did for a while. Mary was no longer involved in the business." Nick winced inwardly at the reference to child trafficking as a business. "The demands for drugs, for autopsies, stopped. Then in 1986, something happened."

"What, Finney, what happened?"

"I don't know. That's the truth. Things were pretty quiet, and then suddenly, we were getting threats from an unknown source. Typewritten notes. Then with what happened to Gwen-"

Nick interrupted him. "Nothing just *happened* to Gwen Yates," Nick said, feeling that old rage rising in his chest. "Your people murdered her, and then you killed her 14-year-old daughter." Finney protested, but Nick put a hand up. "I don't want to hear how you didn't kill them. You did."

"Look," said Finney. "I took part in Gwen Yate's death only after the fact. I agreed to sign the autopsy. That was it. I didn't kill her, and I don't know who did. After that, I was just as scared as anybody else. This person was serious. Or these people, I guess. I mean, I didn't know. The way I saw it, anyone who crossed them got killed. And it wasn't Mary Sonnier. She was being hit for cash like crazy and playing the game to stay alive like the rest of us. It was my idea that she and I pool our resources. We didn't know who was orchestrating the threats - an old john or someone else. But we figured if we kept all those records under lock and key and kept our mouths shut. Yeah, we really believed we'd be okay, right?" He said it like it was a question. Nick said nothing. "And with all that transparency, we were safe from each other. Sort of mutual deterrence."

Nick had to resist the urge to say something he'd regret. He bit it back. "Why not burn the records?"

"Yeah. Well, what do they say about hindsight? I wish I had. But, insurance," said Finney. "We figured if things got bad, we had enough to make threats right back. Only we never did." He shrugged. "We wouldn't have known whom to threaten. Or how to go about it. I guess—we hoped by hanging on to all that old stuff we'd be, I don't know, safer."

"Too bad that turned out not to be true for Mary and Junior," said Nick. "I guess someone tired of you sitting on a time bomb, right?"

"Yeah, well, after 'eighty-six, for years, it worked. Things were quiet. We made payments, but that was it. Cash drops every month. Same place. For years, it went like that. Thirty goddamn years. We paid, no one talked, no one got hurt."

"Nobody, meaning *you* didn't get hurt, Finney. Plenty of others got hurt."

"I know that now. But it seemed okay until..."

"Until?" Nick asked.

"Until the girl's body showed up. That's when everything came... unraveled."

"Ok, Finney, so here's where you can turn things around, help me out a bit. Who?" said Nick. "Who would have wanted the information you had in that vault? Who wanted it bad enough to kill Mary and Junior for it?"

Finney shrugged, and Nick wanted to punch his ugly face for his indifference. "I don't know. Could be anybody, nobody."

Closing his notebook, Nick stood to go. "That's a shame, Finney. I guess you'll be looking over your shoulder for a while. I've heard that's not so easy in prison."

CHAPTER NINETY-THREE

Evelyn | Eden

The phone rang, and Savoy started speaking before Evelyn said anything. "Look, Evelyn, you're in danger, okay?" She stood in the street, car door open, phone in one hand. "Real danger," continued Savoy. She glanced back across the lawn to the Judge. He still stood on his porch. Watching.

Getting into the car, she slammed the door closed. "I know, Sheriff; I mean, that's been true for a while, right?"

"Evelyn, I don't think you realize how much danger. Right now, Evelyn, you are being hunted, pursued - right now." Evelyn dug a finger into the plastic stitching in the bucket seat, digging her fingernail into the pleather until it bent and ached. Hunted. Could that be true?

"Wait, Sheriff, I don't understand." Evelyn glimpsed herself in the rearview mirror. Scared, pale, drawn. She looked like an animal. A sick animal.

"Evelyn, you need to trust me," Savoy said, her voice almost harsh in its intensity. "Your life is in immediate danger. Stay where you are. I'm coming to pick you up. Try not to worry."

Not worry? What the hell did that mean? Evelyn had a thousand questions, but all she said was, "I'll be here. Thank you."

"I'll be there in less than three minutes, and Evelyn?"

"Yes?"

"Whatever you do, please do not call anyone."

"What? Why?"

"We can trace your location through your phone. Make no more phone calls. Not to anyone, okay? It's not safe." Evelyn agreed and quickly wished she had not.

Clicking off, she checked her messages. Heard Libby's voicemail, and, despite the Sheriff's warning, she immediately returned the call. No answer. Voice mail greeting. She was frantic. Who could she trust? Who could her daughter trust? No one. According to the Sheriff, someone knew about Libby, about Evelyn's life in California, and someone was hunting her. Prey, she was prey. And now Libby might be as well.

She couldn't think of a better solution than having her child with her. Once they were together, they could sort out their next move. Her hand shook as she held the phone. "Please don't go out, Libby, please. Look, call me as soon as you get this. It's important. You could be in danger. Libby, I want you to come to Eden. To me. Right away. I'm buying you a ticket right now. I'll text and email you the details as soon as I hang up. The ticket will be waiting for you, and I want you out of there tomorrow morning. I'll call your dad and tell him what's going on, sweetheart. Please, call me." She was about to hit the end button when she added, "Libby, do not go to that party; just come to me." She hung up the phone, texted Libby and Stuart, and dialed the airline.

Sheriff Savoy arrived just as Evelyn finished the calls, and she stuffed the phone into her bag, feeling a bit like a guilty child for defying the Sheriff's request. As she transferred herself and her few belongings to Savoy's car, she wondered if Savoy noticed the old judge still watching from his porch.

It would be hours before Evelyn realized Sheriff Savoy had never asked her for her location.

CHAPTER NINETY-FOUR

Nick | Eden

Nick was at his desk, running files on the internal database. He tapped his foot rapidly against the chair leg as he watched numbers and names scroll past and tried not to think about Evelyn. She wasn't returning messages, and he was becoming increasingly anxious while telling himself not to worry. He shifted in his chair, thought about getting a cup of coffee, rejected the idea, and went back to staring at the screen.

They had a mole, Finney had said. *Someone on the inside.* It could be anyone, Nick thought. Hackers were everywhere. Texas, Idaho. Fucking Canada. Ok, not Canada. He'd queried the database. Searching for anyone who'd accessed records inappropriately. Illegally. Nothing. All access appeared legitimate. All entries were appropriately logged and electronically signed. The mole was someone who knew what they were doing, had no intention of being caught and covered their tracks well.

He tried it another way. Pulling the queries through the audit log rather than straight reports. The audit log was a permanent record of every action by anyone who touched the computer database. It was the fingerprint left behind and, by definition, immune to editing. Unlike a regular access event, which could be deleted, duplicated, and edited, they could not alter an audit log event. Not unless the programmer responsible for writing the original code had left a back door in the software. But, Nick reasoned, you'd have to be some expert computer hacker to find that, and he doubted anyone in the department had that level of expertise.

He started by viewing audit reports on those with high-level access to the computer database. He felt a little guilty pulling records on Sheriff Savoy but did it anyway. Found nothing. He'd have to explain his query to her later. Then he worked his way down the list of department employees. Names flew past, and he hit pause now and again to double-check something, then scrolled again. Nothing. Nothing. Nothing. *Shit.* Then, suddenly, there it was. He leaned forward and read the words on the screen several times.

One particular detective (according to the security access code listed) had recently logged into the arrest record on Franklin Molinaro. Someone had access and presumably read the file three days before the attacks on Evelyn, and the access code did not belong to anyone involved in Molinaro's case. *It belonged to another detective.*

Nick pulled up that detective's name and started a review of his activities day by day, hour by hour, for the previous month. As he did so, the pieces gradually fell together in his brain like a jigsaw puzzle. Standing, he scooped his keys off the desk, grabbed his jacket off the back of his chair, and was gone.

CHAPTER NINETY-FIVE

Evelyn | Eden

Evelyn and Sheriff Savoy drove along the River Road for what seemed like hours. The day was waning, and the evening noises were escalating along the banks of the bayou. Evelyn found it strange that Savoy had shown up alone. She'd gone along, too terrified to refuse. She was being *hunted*. That's what the Sheriff had said. *Hunted.*

A safe place, Savoy said. A place nobody knew about. As the evening grew darker and the road narrower, the Sheriff seemed to loosen up and speak more freely. At least more freely than Evelyn had heard her speak in the past. "You know," she said, turning her broad face toward Evelyn. "You and I have a lot in common. Were you aware of that?"

"Uh, no, Sheriff, I didn't know that." The hairs on the back of Evelyn's neck stood up. She noted how the moonlight made the Sheriff's grin look more Cheshire Cat and less Betty Crocker.

"Yep, we do." She nodded as if to herself. "You and I both come from nothing, had nothing, and folks probably expected us to amount to nothing. Am I right?" Another disturbing grin.

"I suppose." Evelyn rubbed her damp palms on her jeans.

"Yeah, I know all about you and your family. I remember y'all. Of course, you probably don't remember me much?" It was a question, but Evelyn said nothing. "Anyway, the point is, I know how poor your family was. And I know how sick your Mama was."

The sun was setting now, and the road would soon be lit by moonlight and starlight alone. The night creatures sang so loudly that Evelyn found it hard to hear what Sheriff Savoy was saying. She wished mightily she'd stayed in her car. She glanced at her cell phone. No service. Not a surprise. "Sheriff, how much further do you think it is?"

"Not too far. Don't worry." Her voice was becoming a singsong. "So, as I was saying, the thing about Eden that I know, and that I know you know, is the sickness. It's full of sickness, isn't it, honey? And it's a man sickness too." The Sheriff stared straight ahead into the night as she spoke. Lost somewhere in her own thoughts.

"I don't know, Sheriff," Evelyn said. Increasingly anxious. What in the hell was man sickness? Savoy hated men. So what? Lots of women hate men. Evelyn stared out the window and watched as the countryside disappeared and the cypress forest leaned in, encroaching on the road, the car, her brain.

"Well, I do, and it is. Tom Sonnier, Doc Finney, Judge Fulsome, even your father, bless his sad soul. All of them were sick. Most of the other men in town, too. Torn apart by lust and greed. Unable to control their impulses." Evelyn watched the Sheriff's thick fingers clutch the steering wheel more tightly. Strangling it.

"Sheriff," Evelyn said, "do you think it's wise to drive out this far, so late at night?" She slowed her breathing and looked around for a way out of the moving vehicle.

Savoy ignored her. "Pathetic hypocrites if I'm feeling generous, and criminal, deviant, rapist murderers if I'm not. You see something had to be done? Someone had to take charge?" Evelyn stared straight ahead, but her fingers fumbled about for the door handle. "One of those sons of bitches attacked my mama. That's another thing you and I share, you see. John Picard, the nasty old bastard, raped my mother. I was there. I saw it, so I know it happened. Tried going after me but, by then, I was too big, too strong. I beat the shit out of him. Got my sisters, though, and got away with it. Protected by the Tom Sonnier. And

Picard in return? Protected the Sonniers, redneck shits they were. They could do whatever they wanted in this town, and no one could touch them." Savoy's eyes were shining in the moonlight, and a soft growl overflowed her teeth. "But I guess they got it in the end. Right?" Evelyn was watching closely and did not see her lips move. Her look was almost erotic.

Murder. She'd killed them. All of them and how many others?

Evelyn bit back a shudder and looked away. Her fingers moved over the inside of the door panel.

The goddamn handle. Where was it?

CHAPTER NINETY-SIX

Nick | Eden

Nick knew the man would be running. He was a coward. That's why the traffickers had chosen him. For his weakness. Nick felt almost sorry for him. Almost. As he pulled up to the curb, he wondered at the neatly trimmed lawn, well-kept fence, and garden. What sort of person could, for so many years, live two lives, separated by only a tissue-thin membrane of lies?

He knocked and found the door partially open as if someone had left in a hurry. He pushed it open and called out. Nobody answered. Walked into the entryway and called again. Nothing.

At the stairs, he tried again. His voice was loud. "You forgot about the audit logs. I've got your name in the audit reports connected to illegal searches on Franklin Molinaro, every Sonnier family member, every member of the Yates family, and Evelyn Yate's in-laws. You hear me?" No answer. He clenched his teeth to quiet his breathing and took the first few stairs back against the wall. "I also have your bank records showing cash deposits you couldn't justify if you were a fucking brain surgeon. There are phone records between you and every other piece of shit involved in this thing. I know what you've done, and, as for Mary Sonnier, I know that was you too. And I know about Billy Saveneaux." Nick winced as he said Billy's name, trying not to think about the kid's last few minutes. "You fucked up there. I mean, you had to know we'd trace that gun back to you, right? So, you can talk to me, or I can call it in. So far, it's between you and me, and that's it." Nick waited. Still silence. At the top of the stairs, he stopped, waited for a few beats, then slid down the hall, both hands gripping his gun.

"Look, I get it. Temptation happens to everyone." Nick felt sick saying it. "This has been going on forever, right? I know it's not just you." He waited again. "Better to talk to me, man. Come on." Nick started up the stairs. "Just me, okay." Hand on his gun. "Just me." A few steps down the hall. The silence was so thick he heard his watch tick, the blood coursing through arteries in his neck. At the top of the stairs, a door was slightly ajar. Nick pushed it open.

Suddenly, it swung open all the way, causing Nick to startle back in surprise. Standing in the doorway, slightly unsteady on his feet, naked from the waist up, wearing wrinkled trousers and holding a bottle of something alcoholic, stood Detective Martin Lambert. He had the bottle aloft, and Nick could see rivulets of sweat pouring down his pale flanks from under his arms. His less than perfect belly sagged slightly over the waistband of his trousers; he looked twenty years older than he had last time Nick saw him. Lambert grinned grotesquely. "Sure, come on in, Nick. It's a party."

•   •   •   •   •

The thing about Eden, Nick would think later, was that it did not allow for a simple escape. With one road in and one out, a criminal would need to take off on foot to have a chance. Perhaps Lambert knew that, so he just went home and got drunk. *Laladimplehrt.* A dying Mary Sonnier hadn't meant *lips hurt.* She'd been trying to say, *Lambert.* He must have known it was only a matter of time. That's why he'd allowed Nick to come inside, upstairs.

He'd shuffled back away from the door, pulled his gun from the back of his pants, lay it down next to his thigh, and sat on the unmade bed. His back curving as if under enormous weight, head hanging heavily, he stared at the bottle in his hand. "Fine," he'd said. "It's all fine, right Nick?" He'd looked up then, and Nick could see the red-rimmed eyes, the wetness on his cheeks. He'd been crying.

"Look, Lambert backup is on the way. This is over. Give me the gun." Lambert stared at him. Nick wondered if he was so far gone he wasn't understanding. More slowly, Nick said, "Give me the gun, Martin. This is over."

Lambert shook his head. "No, no, I don't think so."

"Ok, ok, look, just talk to me. Tell me what happened," said Nick. What had he learned in school about standoffs? Hostage negotiation? He'd never had to use those skills. Not yet anyway.

"It wasn't my fault, Nick. You gotta believe that. I never wanted to do those things. But—I have kids. I have two ex-wives. Expenses. You know a cop's salary is fucking worthless." He shrugged. "Fuck. I never—never wanted to hurt anyone." Nick forced himself to nod, smile, agree, and listen.

"Can I sit?" asked Nick. Lambert nodded, and Nick took a chair next to the bed. Hand still on his gun. Lambert's weapon sat less than two inches from his fingers. And he was an excellent shot. Better than Nick. "Tell me, Martin. Tell me how it happened. I can help you."

"Yeah, that's bullshit," he smiled weakly. "Nobody can help me. You know that. Not after—everything." He was right, of course. Lambert was utterly screwed. He'd committed conspiracy, larceny, torture, murder, and probably two dozen lesser crimes, the names of which Nick did not even know. It didn't get much worse.

They sat like that for nearly an hour. Lambert talked. Confessed. Cried. Blubbered. Drank. It was sickening. Finally, Nick convinced him to hand over the gun. He slid it off the bed and handed it over. Nick took it slowly, shoved it into his waistband, and stood. "Come on; it's time."

When Lambert stepped out of the house, Nick at his side, he appeared calm, his expression weary, complacent. He raised his hands as two officers approached to cuff him and read him his rights. The late afternoon was one of those rare jewels of the Louisiana summer when the breeze seems to blow all the heaviness out of the air, leaving only light and a life-giving dew behind.

Lambert's face never changed. He stared at Nick as he grabbed one of the officer's guns, stuck it into his mouth, and blew his brains right out into the clear, blue sky.

●　　　●　　　●　　　●　　　●

Nick stood with Briggs as twenty officers swarmed. CSIs had been called, and there were officers in white spacesuits seemingly everywhere.

"Motherfucker," said Briggs. "Just, motherfucker."

Nick nodded. "Yeah. I agree."

"How could he do it?"

Nick shrugged. "Money. Power. The promise of advancement. Same as most crimes."

"Yeah," said Briggs. "I guess I can see some of it. You know, passing money, messages, even weapons. I guess he could have told himself that whatever was happening behind the scenes wasn't his business. But, motherfucker," he said again. "He fucking tortured and killed that old lady."

"He did. Said he was following orders. To get information from her. But Mary Sonnier was a tough bird. She gave up nothing. She probably thought all she had to protect her and Junior was in those hidden boxes. She didn't figure Lambert would kill her. Anyway, he mistakenly believed that she was dead when he left her in the shed. Shocked the shit out of him to find her still breathing when we went over there."

"So, he finished the job."

"Yeah. Smothered her when I left him alone with her. Goddammit." Nick paused. Squinted off into the distance. "Goddammit, Briggs. I should have known."

"Hey," Briggs said, resting a hand on Nick's shoulder. "It wasn't your fault, man. You couldn't have known."

"You know the really fucked up thing?" Nick looked at his partner "Lambert insisted, right to the end: he was only following orders. Not his fault, you know. Someone else was always in control, deciding, calling the shots, and supplying passwords, access codes, and database entry. Burner phones. Cash drops. That's all he knew. He took the money, he said. The promotions, the favors. He kept denying any responsibility."

"Sick fuck," said Briggs.

Nick envied Briggs his ability to categorize the world so cleanly. Good vs. Bad. Sick fucks vs. Not Sick Fucks. Us vs. Them. "You know what he told me?"

"What?"

"Who could blame him, that's what he said. Two kids and two ex-wives to support. Who in the fuck could blame him?"

"Jesus Christ."

"Yeah, the thing is. Whoever had him by the balls, that's who we need to find." Nick turned to Briggs. "By the end, Lambert was scared enough to do anything he was told. Car bombs, assault, murder. Whatever. Even this." Nick gestured at the blood-soaked sheet that now covered Lambert's body on the pavement. "Whoever controlled him is way more dangerous than Lambert."

A search of the premises turned up four burner phones and fifty thousand dollars in cash hidden in various bundles taped to the backsides of dresser drawers. Not professional.

"Detective." It was one of the forensic guys. A young one. New. Nick couldn't remember his name. "We just pulled this off the underside of a desk drawer. Thought you might be interested." He held a piece of lined notebook paper between two gloved fingers.

Nick took the page. "Thanks." He examined it for a few seconds. Security key codes. All starting with the letters CFXDND, for *confidential file/, do not distribute*.

"You know what those are?" asked the forensic officer.

"Yeah, I do. They're CFX codes. Computer passcodes issued by the governor's office and only to high-level law enforcement; Chief Deputy or higher."

"So... not Lambert then?"

"No, definitely not Detective Lambert. It's database access. Administrative level, he got these from someone a lot more powerful than him. With these codes, Lambert could have erased and manipulated data he created in the computer databases. He would have been able to erase his visits, covering his cyber tracks."

Except for the audit log, Nick thought. *He would not have been able to alter the audit log.* But Lambert was likely not smart enough or tech-savvy enough to know that.

"Someone wrongly convinced Lambert, he'd be safe from detection as long as he used the CFX codes to erase his online activity," said Nick.

"So, we'll find he's been accessing confidential information for years and feeding to... someone," said Briggs.

Nick considered this. "Yeah, someone who considered Lambert ultimately expendable was using him. That's who we have to find."

A person who was both politically savvy and emotionally unreadable, a person who could lie convincingly and on a grand scale for a decade.

•   •   •   •   •

It took four rings for Tracy at dispatch to answer the call. What the hell was she doing? When she picked up, he interrupted her greeting.

"Tracy, I need the Sheriff. Right away."

"I'm sorry, detective. She's not in right now. She got a call and took off fast as a jackrabbit. She's not here. Can I take a message?"

Nick squeezed the phone hard and swallowed. "Where did she go, Tracy? She's not answering her cellphone."

"Well, all I can tell you is that she said she'd be unavailable for the next few hours. I heard her on the phone with Evelyn Yates. I think she was worried about her. Went to fetch her maybe."

Nick swallowed hard. He said, calmly. "Think Tracy, where might they have gone? Tracy, where? Where did they go?"

"Oh, I'm sure I don't know." Tracy was fiercely loyal to Sheriff Savoy, and she held onto information like it was diamonds.

"Tracy, where do you think they might have gone?" repeated Nick, trying to keep his voice down. "Where would Sheriff Savoy go if she wanted to keep someone safe?"

"I'm sorry, Detective, I have no idea." Nick could hear the eye roll in her voice.

"Tracy," he said, his voice sharp now. "Yes, you do. You've known Sheriff Savoy for what? Twenty years? Longer? Come on

Tracy, where does she go for privacy?" No response. "Look, Tracy, the Sheriff's life might be in danger," he lied.

A long pause. Soft breath in the phone. Then finally, "Um, I don't know. The woods, maybe. Her dad's old cabin, probably. I mean, she wouldn't go to her house, right?" The words came out rushed. Anxious. "You really think she's in danger?" Genuine concern.

"I don't know," Nick said, impatience crowding his voice. "I need the address of that cabin."

"It's some old place off River Road. Somewhere. I've never been."

"Right." He closed his eyes, thinking. "Okay, go look through the files, her files. Anything you can get into. Employee records, car registration. Anything. It's a matter of life and death. It's okay to break the rules. I'll hold."

She was back in less than two minutes, sounding breathless. "Okay, I think I found something. She has a car registered to an address out there. I guess it's cheap-"

"Tracy, just give me the address, please." He copied it down and headed out.

CHAPTER NINETY-SEVEN

Evelyn | Eden

Sheriff Savoy turned onto a narrow, unpaved road and switched on the car's brights. Evelyn squinted to see into the forest ahead, but darkness had fallen, and visibility was near zero.

"Man weakness," she said. "Picard, Sonnier... even Lambert. All so weak. But that's history, right?" She made a little clucking sound and smiled to herself. "Time flies, right?" She picked up a water bottle, took a drink, and tilted it towards Evelyn. She noticed Evelyn's right hand on the inside passenger door. "Don't bother," she said.

"Uh... I...," Evelyn spluttered.

"No handle. Child locks too. The whole car. So," she said and shot Evelyn a look of mock resignation, as if she, Savoy, were the one trapped. "Don't bother. You can't get out."

They drove in silence for a few minutes. Evelyn's chest ached from the beat of her heart. Her mouth was dry despite the water, and she was having difficulty controlling the panic, which she knew from experience would make rational thought impossible.

Savoy started again. She looked at Evelyn, who only stared back. Mute. *This nightmare wasn't happening,* Evelyn told herself. "Lambert, poor bastard. Never really knew how hot the fire was, right?"

"Fire?" Evelyn was unsure whether Savoy's speech had confused her or if panic was clouding her thinking, but she was feeling disoriented.

"Yeah, you know, like the toad in the frying pan. Turn up the heat all at once, he jumps out. Turn it up slow, real slow, and he'll just cook himself to death." Savoy cocked her head at Evelyn and smiled and then narrowed her eyes. "Evelyn, do you have any idea how much people will pay to hide the things they've done in their past? All I did was make them pay. All of them. John Picard, Mary Sonnier, Finney, Judge Fulsome, and all those men that spent the seventies fucking children they'd bought from Tom Sonnier. Some paid with their lives, some with money. And you know what else?" She glanced over, but Evelyn thought the Sheriff was so intoxicated by re-telling of her own story she wasn't addressing anyone outside her own head. "No matter how much I took from them, they kept right on paying because they didn't have a choice. That's the best part. I trapped them like they'd been doing to others for so long."

Jesus, Evelyn thought, *she doesn't hate men. She hates everyone.* She blurted without thinking, "You killed all those people. You-"

Savoy didn't hesitate. "Yeah, and I'll tell you what, if it were up to me, I'd kill every single one of those bastards again. Very slowly. I think maybe I'd rip out their balls, then let the nutria eat them alive by the side of the road." She smiled, and the expression was terrifying. "But you can't have everything, right? So, I took the money. Your mother learned it the hard way. She couldn't keep her nose out of business that had nothing to do with her." Savoy looked at Evelyn. "Like you."

"You-" Evelyn couldn't finish the thought. Nausea threatened to overwhelm her. She tasted vomit.

"Yes, me. It wasn't hard. Such a trusting woman for someone who'd been through so much. She had to share it with me. Her secret. No matter the danger." Savoy shook her head. "A shame."

"She told you?" said Evelyn, the words coming out cracked and dry.

"She did. She trusted me. Called me up."

"And you—you poisoned—"

Savoy grimaced. "Nasty word. Poisoned. I prefer euthanized." She wrinkled her nose. "Gwen wasn't well, you know? It was hardly a surprise." She'd let go of the steering wheel and was driving with her one arm casually draped over the wheel. "I just stopped by for a chat." She smiled. A pleasant memory. "A little magic medicine in her lemonade." Savoy held up her right hand, thumb and first two fingers held apart as if gripping a saltshaker. She pantomimed dumping out the contents. "Boom, she was out. The hard part was killing her. Your mother was tougher than she looked." Savoy glanced over again. "But I guess you probably knew that." *Marks around her mother's neck. Bands of purple encircling the milk-white skin.*

"I don't understand," said Evelyn, although she supposed she did.

"I think you do. I'll do what I have to do, Evelyn. Always have. If that means collateral damage along the way," she said, pointing at Evelyn. "So be it." She rolled the car to a stop and cut the engine. "Here we are." When they stepped out of the car, it was into the deepest, darkest forest Evelyn had ever seen. There would be no escape from this, no miracle survival, and no homecoming. *Collateral damage*, she thought, *like Broussard, like Junior Sonnier, like Gwen.*

∙　　∙　　∙　　∙　　∙

Evelyn, who was now handcuffed to a chair, which was in turn bolted to the floor, had seen enough movies to know that a victim was supposed to keep the abductor talking. *Make her see you as a person.* She couldn't think of anything to say.

Sweat dropped off Evelyn's forehead. Stung her eyes. Her head ached where it had been, gashed in the accident. Her hands were moist, and she worked them back and forth in the cuffs. She could feel the metal cutting into her wrists. Blood dripped into her palms. She didn't care. "My sister... what did you do?"

Savoy looked at her, almost pitying, with a narrow smile. "Evelyn, the real question you should ask yourself is, what did *you* do?"

She stared at Savoy. A memory opened up in her mind, like a slide coming gradually into focus. No, no, no. What had Libby said in her message? The diary. Evelyn, ten-year-old Evelyn, had written about it. *I did something bad, and now Carolyn is gone.* She squeezed her eyes shut, willing herself to remember. *Something bad.* She was floating again, away from her body, out of the room, into the wilderness and up into the inky black sky overhead.

A girl in her room. A girl searching for something. A girl running across a field into the dark. Fleeing. Carolyn running away from the house.

In the morning. People in the front room. Her father is angry. Yelling. Scaring her. It's time for Carolyn to go. We need to find her, Evelyn. Do you know where she is? Where is she, Evelyn? You need to tell us. Mr. Mike asking her, repeatedly. Where is she? Where is your sister? Sugar Smacks falling down the front of her T-shirt. Plastic bowl toppling to the floor. She backs up against the television. Where is she? Mr. Mike in her face. Leaning in. Asking. Demanding. Tell me. Tell me where your sister is hiding.

Carolyn's arms and legs flailing as Mr. Mike carries her across the yard, past the laundry swinging on the line. Mr. Mike moving across the yard with a bundle. Shoes, jeans... things Daddy wanted to send to the hospital for Carolyn. His broad back, the stack of clothing... the sticky-soled shoes... across the yard... into the car... away. But suddenly, Mr. Mike's silhouette against the sunlit backdrop is fuzzy, the outline breaking down, melting, disappearing.

"Oh my God," Evelyn whispered the words. "It wasn't Mr. Mike." Evelyn sucked at her breath. She was suffocating. Dying. Collateral damage, that's what she'd said. "He was there, but he left. He left before... and he didn't..." Her throat felt swollen and thick, rubbery. "He wasn't holding her." The truth, the obvious truth she'd seen back at the doctor's house, was opening up, wider, taller. As if she'd drawn back invisible curtains to reveal previously unseen, unimagined vistas beyond. "Oh my God," she repeated. She closed her eyes, trying to conjure the image she'd seen in her mind so many times over the years. It wouldn't come. In its place was... nothing. "He didn't take her, did he?" Silence, eyes glittering in the darkness. Evelyn's mouth had gone desert dry.

Savoy was staring at her, still grinning. "You remember, don't you?" She made a sarcastic tsk sound. "Poor girl."

Suddenly, she could see it. Daddy standing in the sunlight at the bottom of the steps. *Tell me,* he says, *tell me where your sister is hiding. Evelyn.* And then, his face tight up against hers. The smell of tobacco heavy on his breath, his voice gravely, eyes gone squinty and mean in the light. *Tell Deputy Savoy where your sister is hiding.*

Evelyn's spine went icy. She shuddered. Forced her hands apart, allowing the metal handcuffs to bite further into the skin of her wrists, forcing herself to think. "It was never Mr. Mike," Evelyn whispered. Blood throbbing at her temples. "It was *you.*"

CHAPTER NINETY-EIGHT

Evelyn | 1986 | Eden

They'd argued, she and Carolyn. About the photograph. "I don't have it," Evelyn had lied. "Leave me alone. Go away."

Carolyn had gone crazy and ripped apart their bedroom, looking for it. Hissing at Evelyn. It made Evelyn hate her more and made her even happier that she'd stolen it. Then she'd said it. "You're crazy, Carolyn. You're totally crazy, and everyone knows it, and they are sending you away. Did you know that? They're sending you away to a place for crazy kids. To the crazy house." Evelyn had lost control. Pain, fear, grief, and loneliness pummeled her young heart in a hailstorm of emotions she couldn't understand. "I hate you, and I hope you go away and never come back."

But she didn't hate Carolyn. She loved her and depended on her. Needed her. Carolyn was all she had left after Gwen died, and she'd destroyed her. Out of anger, grief, and spite, she'd killed her own sister.

Carolyn had stared at her, disbelieving. "No, you're lying. Nobody is sending me away."

"They are," said Evelyn, full of a ten-year-old's defiant self-righteousness. "I heard them talking about it. Mr. Mike and Daddy. I heard them in the kitchen. Daddy said he can't handle you. That's what he said."

Carolyn shook her head. "That's not true," she said, but her words sounded weak. She was trying to convince herself.

"It is," said Evelyn. "And I'm glad. I want you to go away and never come back."

• • • • •

Carolyn had run. Later that night. Carolyn's words whispered across the darkness. "Shh, go back to sleep," she'd said. "It's ok. Just go to sleep." She'd left the sweater, her favorite sweater, tucked inside Evelyn's bed covers. A last act of love. Of loyalty. "It's ok," she said. "I'll be back." Then she'd run. Hidden. Evelyn sat in her bed, watching Carolyn take off across the meadow in the moonlight. Watching her head straight for the barn. Evelyn had known where she was going right away. She'd known exactly where Carolyn would try to hide.

• • • • •

The next day. Her father was angry, yelling, searching. Sugar smacks falling down and milk soaking into her T-shirt. Wetting her skin. The TV. The bowl on the floor.

"Where is she?" Deputy Savoy is in the doorway. "Evelyn," says her father. "Tell the deputy where she is. Tell Deputy Savoy where your sister is hiding."

Out to the meadow, into the barn, to the hole in the slats. "In there," Evelyn says, thin fingers reaching, pointing. "In there. She'll be in there." Terrified and excited at the same time. Carolyn is in trouble and she deserves to be in trouble. She's been so mean.

"What's that you're holding, Evelyn? What's in your hand?" Deputy Savoy asks.

"I found this," she says. The first of so many lies roll off her tongue like butter. "I found it in Carolyn's stuff. She... she had it. I don't know why."

Alice Savoy's face in hers, smiling, kind. She reaches a hand down, taking the paper from Evelyn. "Hmm, good girl, for letting me have this." She leans closer. Evelyn smells the spearmint gum on her breath. "Tell me something," Savoy says, quietly. "Do you know who this is? This man in the picture?"

CHAPTER NINETY-NINE

Evelyn | Eden

Evelyn squeezed her eyes shut, trying to remember then opened them. "The photograph, I gave it to you."

Savoy stopped whatever she was doing at the sink and turned around. "I should thank you. Your father called me to help find your sister. She was, uh," she hesitated. "Misplaced, I guess. They had plans for her, sending her away, but you know that."

"But you killed her."

"Well, that's the thing, isn't it? I hadn't planned on it. I was only there to help... uh... retrieve her. But then," she grinned. "You handed me that photo, and what choice did I have?"

Spearmint gum. Tell me something, do you know who this is? This man in the picture?

At first, Evelyn says nothing. She's frozen there. Her feet in flip-flops, sinking into the mud. Her heart beating so hard she could hear it like thunder in her ears. Finally, she shakes her head.

No, she tells Savoy. She doesn't know the man, but, she says, Carolyn does. Yes, she's sure. Carolyn can tell you who that man is.

Oh, God. She remembered. Letters and numbers. Dates? "Notes? There were notes on the back."

"There were," agreed Savoy. "CB 1975, DD 1976, TW 1978, WR 1981... your mother was a smart woman."

"The dead girls," said Evelyn. "Initials of those girls who died."

"And the dates they died. Or thereabouts. Your mother figured it out. Like I said, collateral damage," said Savoy, and lifted the water bottle to her lips.

CHAPTER ONE HUNDRED

Carolyn | 1986 | Eden

The day Carolyn discovers the truth is the fourth straight day of summer rain, and the Louisiana bottomland is threatening to swallow Eden whole like a communion wafer.

She's been reading the little red diaries a little at a time ever since Mama died, but she has to sneak into Daddy's room to steal them when he's asleep. She always puts it back when she's done, and she's extra careful to take only one at a time-there are four of them-and to leave them in the same spot so that he won't know. He'd be mad if he knew. He is almost always mad anyway, but she doesn't want to make things worse than they already are. On this day, she is sure the rains will never stop, and she does not want the books to be lost when the lightning starts and the floods come. Daddy doesn't know she's been reading them, so she cannot ask him to move them to some place safe. She's not sure he remembers he put one of them under his bed the last time he got angry and took them away from her. The other three he left in Mama's bottom drawer.

That's not yours, he'd said. *Those are private words,* he'd said.

It is mine, she'd screamed; *she was my Mama, not yours.*

But he hadn't listened. Only grabbed it away from her and went to hide it in his room.

•　　　•　　　•　　　•　　　•

She waits until he passes out in his chair and then goes into his room and reaches for it under the bed and slides it out, and puts it into her backpack, where it sits all day. Every hour she takes it out and reads a little more. She wonders how she'll protect it while she sleeps. She waits for him to say something, but he never does, and she thinks maybe he's forgotten about it, and she'll just keep it with her all the time. That makes her happy. She is rarely happy. At bedtime, she is reading it under the covers with a flashlight, so her little sister won't see what she is doing. Her sister, who is only ten, would want to know what it says, and Carolyn doesn't think ten is old enough to understand. For a minute, Evelyn sees, and Carolyn tells her it's private. Not for babies. She knows Evelyn is angry. She'll have to make it up to her later.

It's terribly hot and stuffy, reading underneath the sheet, but her sister is refusing to go to sleep, so Carolyn has no choice. She is turning pages slowly so that it doesn't go too fast, and something falls out of the middle and lands on the comforter. Picking it up, she can see it's a newspaper picture of someone she does not know. She holds the flashlight directly over the photograph and changes her mind. Yes, she thinks, she definitely knows this man. He's dead now. Maybe three- or four years dead, but she recognizes the marks on his forearms. His smile is creepy, and she doesn't like his eyes. She turns the photo over and reads the writing on the back, her mother's writing: CB 1975 DD 1976 TW 1978 WR 1981. She flips back through the diary. Crystal Bergeron. Debbie Dugas, Tracy Wilkerson. Wanda Rabalais. The dead girls. Her mother has printed their names in her journals. Carolyn looks at the newspaper photo again. This man, this man in this picture, killed those girls. Her mother had been keeping track.

She decides to tell someone, but not her father. He's already so burdened, losing Gwen. Besides, he never believes Carolyn anyway. She has to think about it. Who to trust? Who to tell? Someone who will believe that her Mama was a wonderful mother and would never have left her all alone.

•   •   •   •   •

It's Evelyn who tells her about the plan. Evelyn says they're sending Carolyn away. To the crazy house. That's what Evelyn calls it. They can't handle her anymore, or Daddy can't. She panics. It's too soon. She hasn't figured out what to do about the picture in Mama's diary. She hasn't figured out who to trust There's no time. She has to get away; she'll hide somewhere until she can figure things out.

•   •   •   •   •

She hears them first. She's been hiding up in the Back Field all night. Trying to sort out what to do next. She can't let them send her away. Her father. The social workers. She wishes she'd brought some food. Her stomach grumbles and aches. No, she thinks, they won't send her away, not now. She needs to tell someone the truth about her mother. But Evelyn stole the photograph. She knows Evelyn has it. The little brat is lying. She'd asked her about it, and Evelyn had lied. Anger surged within her, nearly overshadowing the fear. Nearly.

It's still early when she hears them. She sits behind the juniper bushes, peering out as they come through the barn. They had to widen the hole in the slats. It was too small for grown-ups.

As they step through, she is up and running through the field; the mud oozing in over her sandals is cool, although the morning is already dank and hot. The people call her name. They've seen her. They are close. She runs fast to the edge of the forest. Her breath, coming in, spits and coughs. Soon she'll be unable to continue. Terror drives her forward another few seconds, but then she's bent over, gasping and heaving, unable to move.

She hears the ground crack behind her. Once, twice. She lifts her head. Something catches her and has her by the hair. She screams as she feels it rip one handful out of her scalp. Then a gloved hand grabs her arm and shoves her to the ground, where she curls into a ball, covering her head with her arms. She squeezes her eyes shut and wills herself to disappear. For a moment, she thinks it might have worked. The thing lets go of her, and silence falls like a blanket over the forest. She can no longer hear the birds, and the chaos of a moment ago seems stilled, frozen.

Then, with a great yank, the thing has her again. It's her arm this time. She hears a terrible crack, and pain, like none she's ever experienced, explodes from her wrist and careens around inside her body. A second later, she hears a whirring sound as something massive swings past her right ear.

She's on the ground again. Only this time, she cannot move. Something hot is pooling under the backside of her head and dripping into her ears. She thinks of the warm washcloths Mama used to bathe her when she was sick. She thinks maybe she's sick. Maybe her Mama has come back to make her feel better. Something leans in to look at her. Examining. It is a woman, but it is not her Mama. The face is close, down next to hers; so close she can see the eyes glisten, even in the forest darkness.

She knows this woman. Relief spreads over her. Warm and sweet like honey. She'll be saved. She whispers, "Deputy Savoy?"

Now she is cold, so cold, and she wishes her Mama would bring back the warm washcloth. *Mama*, she says, but only inside her head because her mouth is not moving the way it should. Then, before she can say anything else, her body is sinking into the earth, and she knows that the bottomland has come to swallow up Eden after all.

CHAPTER ONE HUNDRED-ONE

Evelyn | Eden

They sat in the dark and waited. Evelyn in a kitchen chair and Savoy on a stool beside her, side by side facing the living room's large picture window. They might have been friends, sisters even, waiting for a show to start. *Except for the handcuffs. Except for the gun.*

Minutes ticked by, the thick silence muffled the clock's sounds over the mantel. Fear spreads like cancer into all her vulnerable places, and the pain in Evelyn's wrists burns in her brain. She glanced for the hundredth time at the gun and wondered what it might take for Savoy to shoot her now. Anything was better than waiting to be executed. Escape or death. She'd been backhanded across the face for asking why they were waiting. After a bit, she tried asking again. This time, she got no response at all. The slap would have been better. Maybe death would arrive quickly. She didn't deserve to live. She'd killed Carolyn. It was her fault.

Even at age ten, she'd known what she'd done. She'd spent the next thirty-plus years trying to forget it. Or bury it. Or something. What was that saying: The Truth Will Out? Suddenly she remembered. The bracelet Gwen gave Carolyn. It hadn't read: *To Thine Own Self Be True.* What it said was: *Truth Will Out.* As a child, Evelyn had not understood its meaning. Thought it strange. Now it made perfect sense. Gwen carried secrets her whole life. She must have wanted so badly for her daughters not to be burdened the same way.

Evelyn tipped her chair slightly to the right. A fraction of an inch. Then she tipped a bit more and a bit more and even a little more. *Just maybe, if she could grab the gun.* The chances were slight, but Evelyn figured her chances of survival otherwise were zero.

Ba. Boom. Ba. Boom. Her heartbeat was so loud, Evelyn was certain Savoy would look over just to see what the pounding was all about. She imagined the sound of a bullet ripping through the fleshy part of her torso, the smell, the smoke. *Focus.* Another fraction of an inch... A bit more... *Look at the gun, look at the gun.* Her heart kept on - *Ba... boom... ba... boom. Ba* - Savoy is still staring straight out the window. She'd look up any second and...

Light flooded the cabin's interior, illuminating it like a circus tent. *Headlights, please let it be headlights,* Evelyn silently begged. She squinted and straightened her chair. Savoy stood and held the gun to Evelyn's head, the hard steel outline of the barrel jamming itself into her temple.

"Sheriff," Nick's voice from outside. "Come on out now. I know you're in there, and I know you have Evelyn."

"I do, Nick. I have Evelyn, and you need to come and see us." Savoy sounded manic. Nick stepped away from the car lights, and Evelyn could see him peer into the window. She was sure he had a clear view of Savoy holding the gun to her head.

"Don't hurt her, Alice. Let her go. Just let her go. Hurting Evelyn will not help you, and you know it."

"I won't hurt her, Nick. Not if you come on in and talk to us. Come on now."

"Let me see her, Alice. Let me see, she's all right."

"Well, she's busy right now, Nick. If you want to see her, I'm afraid you'll have to come inside."

"Let me talk to her, then. Let her talk. I need to hear she's okay, at least."

Alice nodded at Evelyn but never moved the gun barrel away from her temple. "Tell him you're fine," she said.

"I'm okay, Nick; I'm fine. She hasn't hurt me. But don't-"

"Shut up now." hissed Savoy as she slammed a piece of electrical tape across Evelyn's mouth.

Nick was moving around toward the steps up to the front door. "Evelyn, you still there? Are you okay?" He called out. The cabin was only two rooms. One functioned as a living room and kitchen, and the other as a small bedroom. As soon as he opened the front door, he'd be face-to-face with Savoy and Evelyn. The door swung open, and Nick stood in the light. He pointed a gun out before him, but Savoy had disappeared. Evelyn's arms were bound behind her, with her mouth now gagged. She could neither point nor speak. She rolled her head wildly in the direction from which he had come, but, in the fraction of a second it took him to understand what she was trying to say, Alice Savoy stepped out from behind the open door and slammed Nick across the back of the head with her nightstick. He crumpled to the wood floor. Then, Evelyn felt a sharp pain in the back of her arm, and seconds later, the room slipped away.

CHAPTER ONE HUNDRED-TWO

Nick | Eden

Nick opened his eyes to the tremendous pain in his head and the overwhelming smell of gasoline. The fumes were thick enough to make his eyes water and his stomach sick. He looked around. He was lying flat on his back on the wood floor of the cabin, and Evelyn was lying unconscious next to him, her hands still cuffed together but no longer hooked over the chair. Blood streamed from her wrists in rivers across her palms. From this angle, he saw gasoline pooling on the floor, encircling them both, pink where some of Evelyn's blood had dribbled. Savoy had doused everything with gasoline, most of the furniture, and their clothes.

At first, he did not see Sheriff Savoy. Then he did. First, only her boots from under a table across the room. Then she moved a few steps, and he saw her upper body, her gun strapped securely to her belt. She was an excellent shot. No way he'd get that away from her before she'd kill at least one of them. Probably both. She was readying herself to leave. Collecting items, packing up. Muttering something. Nick reached out and poked at Evelyn. She opened her eyes, heavy-lidded, then wide with fear. He quickly covered her mouth with one hand and put a finger to his lips with the other, warning her to keep quiet. He pointed to his gun, which lay on the floor about five feet out of reach. She nodded.

Slowly, he began inching his way across the floor, one eye on Savoy. When she stopped murmuring and moving, he froze. When she started up again, he moved a little more. After a full minute, he'd advanced about six inches. He could see now that Savoy had a box of wooden matches on the table. Her intent was clear. She'd torch the cabin and take off. He hoped Evelyn had not seen the matches. He kept moving. Twelve inches. Eighteen. Two feet. Still, Savoy hadn't noticed. A minute later, he'd made it to within a foot of the gun. Nick pressed his face, now drenched with sweat, into the gasoline-soaked floorboards and reached forward, stretching his muscles so out of joint he thought he might dislocate his shoulder. His fingertips just brushed the cool metal of the gun, then came a gruesome crunch. A white-hot bolt of pain shot up his arm and wrapped itself around his brain. He gagged and willed himself not to scream. Looked up. Savoy was standing on his hand. She'd broken at least a few bones.

"Looking for this?" She held the gun in the air, eyebrows raised in a question, head cocked to one side. "Guess not." She tucked the weapon into her gun belt and looked down at Nick. Frowning. "This is too bad, Nick. Really. I didn't want you involved, but you had to go and call Tracy. What did you think? That she wouldn't let me know you were coming?" She shook her head. "I mean, come on, Nick. What were you thinking?"

"T" for Tracy, of course. If he weren't flat out on the ground with Savoy's enormous boot on his hand, he would have hit himself in the head for being so stupid. He'd wondered what that initial around the Sheriff's neck meant. How long had they been lovers? How many seconds had it taken that bitch Tracy to call Savoy and rat him out after he'd collected the information on the cabin location? Not that it mattered now.

Abruptly her expression changed to one of cheerful resignation. "Oh well, can't be helped, I guess. Sorry about that." She smiled at each of them and rolled her foot off Nick's fingers, causing another wave of pain that blurred his vision and made him groan. She picked up her bags, heaved them over her shoulder, and turned towards the door. Abruptly, she turned back. Picked up the box of matches, sliding one out. Nick lay on the floor, his hand in agony, still outstretched, and struggled to turn towards Evelyn.

Savoy held the match aloft and had barely touched its orange tip to the strike plate when suddenly Nick saw her neck kick back at an unnatural angle, and a fist-wide trench open vertically in her face. A massive spray of blood and brain matter hit the kitchen appliances and cabinets behind her, then her body crumpled vertically to the floor, a heap of blood and tissue, her gun belt buckled and weapon securely strapped to her hip.

· · · · ·

"Detective MacCallum?" A voice from over his shoulder. Nick turned. One of the CSIs was approaching. Carrying something in a plastic evidence bag. "So, there's a whole lot of stuff in the trunk of her car, Detective. Two suitcases. Cash, jewelry. Looks like she was planning a trip. A long trip. I've got guys bagging and tagging. But I thought you'd want to see this. She had it in a special compartment. Looks like it was important." He handed over the baggie.

Nick held it up so that the crime scene floodlights illuminated its contents. He peered into the baggie. A newspaper clipping. On one side, writing, in a sloping, elegant hand. Four sets of initials. Four dates. He flipped it around. A photograph. Small. Black and white. An obituary photo. Immediately recognizable. Tom Sonnier's sinister face smiled back.

· · · · ·

The combined psychological and physical effects of their experience, culminating in witnessing Sheriff Savoy's head explode like a watermelon shot at close range, were so profound that both Nick and Evelyn suffered short-term memory impairment from the events surrounding the Sheriff's death. When questioned later about it, Evelyn could not recall she had seen Judge Fulsome preparing to follow the car in which she had been abducted by the Sheriff earlier in the evening. Nick would not remember the image of an old man with a shotgun standing for just a moment in the vehicle's headlights on the other side of the shattered picture window before turning on his heel and disappearing into the night.

Nick knew only two men in town who could have made a shot like the one that killed Savoy. One was Lambert, dead by his own hand, and the other one, as far as Nick was concerned, would go unnamed. *If his daughter's life had been in danger,* Nick thought, *wouldn't he have done the same?*

CHAPTER ONE HUNDRED-THREE

Evelyn | Eden

Tuesday, June 13
Present Day

The morning arrived sunny and promising. But by nine am, the day outside had darkened as if on a dimmer switch, and storm clouds were rushing west with purpose. Evelyn was increasingly worried about Libby, who hadn't returned her messages this morning. "She'll call," Nick had tried to reassure her. "Don't worry. It's early there. She'll call when she wakes up." Evelyn hoped so.

Looking out the window, Evelyn smiled a little, thinking about the torrential rains she and Carolyn had loved to splash around in when they were small. Louisiana rain wasn't rain at all. It was a sky waterfall, and a warm sky waterfall was a glorious experience. Except for the lightning; they should have been more careful about the lightning.

The water came down in sheets as she watched.

Then she was crying. A tissue box sat on the small table next to the window, but Evelyn didn't take one. Instead, she just sat watching lightning slash the sky and the clouds thicken and break. She thought about John Yates. Who had he been? A drunk, a lover, a father, a husband, a hero, and a failure? Or was he just a fool who sat back while his wife spent a lifetime loving another man? Perhaps, Evelyn thought, he had been a man like other men, trying to survive this life, doing the best he could. He'd clung to a delusion; unable or unwilling to see the rot as it bloomed around him, as he was forced to bury one child to protect another. In the end, he was just a man whose life was so gutted by loss and regret he stopped existing at all. Evelyn had spent her whole life hating John Yates for his neglect, hating her mother for leaving her; telling lies to avoid the truth about Carolyn and hating herself for all of it. And now, she thought, who was there to hate? Tom Sonnier? Mary Sonnier? Finney? All those unknown old men in the cemetery mausoleum? Lambert? Confused, crazy, damaged Alice Savoy? Herself? When she looked down inside herself for the rage she expected to find, she found only sadness and a grief so deep it seemed infinite.

After a long while, her tears stopped, and for the first time since coming to Eden, she felt like she could breathe.

●   ●   ●   ●   ●

At noon, the phone rang.

"Mom?"

"Lib," Evelyn stood, heart-pounding; Libby's voice sounded miniature, far away. "Oh god, I've been trying to reach you. Where are you? How are you?"

"I'm not sure."

"Honey, tell me what's happened. Tell me where you are." Evelyn tried to make her voice sound calm.

"I'm... I'm here. I mean, here in Eden."

CHAPTER ONE HUNDRED-FOUR

Libby | Eden

Libby sat on a bench at the bus station and waited. She knew she looked awful. Thin, wet from rain, disheveled, depressed. She probably looked as if she'd been through a war. She couldn't remember when she'd last eaten. The food on the plane sucked. She hadn't touched it, and then, figuring out how to get to Eden with little sleep, had taken all her focus. She'd taken Uber, realizing that she did not know where to go from there after she arrived in town. She had no address. The driver suggested the bus station for reasons unclear to Libby, except that he probably didn't want to drop her in the middle of the road.

Evelyn arrived within ten minutes. Libby stood as she approached. Apprehensive. You never knew. Her mother was unpredictable. Would she be angry?

But Evelyn only clutched her, stared into her face, and said, "Baby girl, baby girl, I love you so much." She stroked Libby's hair and held her, and Libby let her do it. Before she could say anything, her mother's arms were around her. They sat like that on a wooden bench in the bus station for fifteen minutes. Listening to the storm rumble and watching clouds roll further west, carrying the rain away.

Finally, Libby looked up at her mother and said, "You're not mad?" Evelyn shook her head and smiled and held Libby closer.

"Mad? No, sweetie, I'm not mad. I'm so happy you're here. So happy you're safe."

In the car, Libby said little. Only that she'd been on her way to the rave when she'd heard Evelyn's message, she knew something was wrong by the sound of her mother's voice, and when she tried to call back, it went straight to voicemail. *A million times,* she said. *I called a million times, and you didn't answer. I was so scared.*

I'm sorry, baby. I'm so sorry. Her mother kept repeating.

Then she was silent, staring out the window. She felt suddenly exhausted.

"Are you hungry?" Evelyn asked after a bit.

"Not really. I guess. I don't know," she answered.

"Tired?"

"Yeah."

"Do you want to sleep?"

"Mommy?" She hadn't called Evelyn Mommy in years.

"Yes?"

"Will you be mad if I tell you something?"

"No, I won't. Sweetie," she turned to Libby, "tell me what happened. Tell me anything. I won't be mad. I love you and listen to me; I have some things to tell you as well."

Libby took a breath, which caught as a sob escaped. Evelyn pulled the car over, took Libby in her arms, and let her cry as long as needed. When she was done, Libby sat back and started again. This time she told her mother about Conner and the party and Mitch and what she could remember of the events that followed.

CHAPTER ONE HUNDRED-FIVE

Evelyn | Eden

They'd requested time alone with Libby, standard procedure after an assault like this, the doctor explained. The social worker would talk with Libby first and then with Evelyn if that was alright. Of course, Evelyn said, anything, everything Libby needed. The hospital was bright, white, and open. It smelled of antiseptic and illness, like every other hospital and Evelyn, who despised hospitals, should've hated it, but she didn't. Right then, the comfort offered by the doctors and nurses and social workers overwhelmed her. There was honesty here, and safety. It was ok. She would trust them. As she waited in the pediatric lobby, thoughts tumbled around in her brain. Eden had always seemed like the problem. Like a source, a reservoir, from which sprang all her internal pain. But now Evelyn wondered if that was true. Could she have been wrong? About everything?

She stopped pacing and looked out the windows over the expanse of Bonfante Parish. The day was bright. She could see all the way to Eden. From this vantage point, it was beautiful. The land was soft and moss-green, like carpet. Water ran through it in deep bayous and small rivulets, like a watercolor painting. The pale, blue sky touched down in the distance and lay a silky blanket over the landscape.

Evelyn thought about the little bookshop next to Marnie's. How sweet the light inside had looked one evening she'd passed by. What if she could get a job at a bookshop like that? She needed little money. What would starting over be like, Evelyn wondered? She and Libby. She felt herself smile just a little and looked around to see if anyone noticed. Embarrassed.

•   •   •   •   •

Nick arrived at the hospital a half-hour later. He was breathless, and she imagined he'd raced in from the parking lot. Evelyn explained what had happened, what Libby had told her.

"Oh Evelyn, I'm so sorry. What do the doctors say?"

"She's with the doctor now and a social worker. They need to see her alone for a bit. They have to run tests but she wasn't-" Evelyn's voice broke. Nick wrapped his arms around her. "The bastard didn't... oh god Nick she got away." He held her for a long time, saying nothing. "You know, I called Stuart. He didn't know she was gone. The son of a bitch did not know she was gone. He said she was sleeping at a friend's house. This is my fault. I should have done something."

"Hey, hey." Nick put his hands on her shoulders and bent down so she had to look at him. "Evelyn, this is not your fault."

They sat side by side in the stiff plastic chairs in the family lounge for a time. They spoke little. Nick waited with her until a doctor appeared. They both shot up from the chairs, Evelyn moving quickly across the linoleum tiles. Libby was stable, the doctor said. She'd be just fine. She could go home as soon as the last blood test came back. Evelyn felt the tension leave her body with a violent whoosh. She nearly lost her balance. Nick steadied her, wrapping an arm around her shoulder and drawing her close.

"Oh, thank you," she said to the doctor. "Thank you so much."

"I'll let you go see her," Nick said. "You let me know if you need anything, ok? Call me?"

She looked at him; thumbs hooked into his pockets like a schoolboy- his tired, angular face, neat hair grown to just a little longer than he probably liked it. The scar. Eyes haunted and shadowy but still lovely. *Such a strange man.* Such a peculiar, good man. "I will," she said. Unsure if she would. She touched his arm and drew closer. "Thank you, Nick. For everything."

•   •   •   •   •

The afternoon was brilliant. The storm had left the sky as clear blue as a gemstone, and the rain-washed world was wet, sparkling in its newness. Even the parking lot blacktop looked diamond-studded, and the heavy olive-green foliage beyond was oddly exotic in juxtaposition. The hospital, built in the time before politicians and insurance companies invented terms like *third-party payor* and *corporate medicine*, was a lovely building. The original architects had incorporated a series of walking paths and tranquility gardens leading down behind the main building to a small natural waterway called The Hodges. Libby wanted to take a walk before going home. She had questions, she said. They took the sandstone path to the right of the entry doors and started down to the river. Strolling, they stopped now and then to rest and admire the Birds of Paradise and coleus planted along the way.

"It's so pretty," said Libby.

"Yeah, it's lovely; I used to wander back here when my daddy came to the hospital."

"Your daddy?"

"Oh, yeah," she said and bent to press her face close to a cluster of English Roses the color of cotton candy. "He was a drunk, Lib. A bad drunk, but he wasn't a bad man. Just a sick man."

"That's what it is, isn't it?"

"What?"

"Drinking? It's sick." Evelyn nodded. They walked a while in silence before Libby said, "Mom?"

"Yeah?"

"Can you tell me about it? I mean, about your family. Really?"

Evelyn looked at her, studying her expression. The age in her eyes was too much for such a young girl. Truth, Libby deserved the truth. Yes, Evelyn thought, she would tell her daughter, and she did. About John Yates and Mama. About the time in her life after Carolyn and life with her father when he was drinking.

They reached the river and followed the gravel path for a bit.

"What about Carolyn, Mom? What happened?"

Evelyn took a breath. She hadn't had a drink or a pill in over twenty-four hours. The world was taking on another dimension. Colors brighter sounds clearer, or it had always been that way; she'd just missed it. She looked at Libby, her eyes hopeful. "Yeah," Evelyn said. "Ok, I'll tell you. Let's sit."

They sat on a bank, looking at the river for a bit, its green-brown water moving in lazy circles, full of secrets they would never know. Evelyn talked. Told her daughter the things she didn't think she could ever tell anyone. When she stopped talking, a warm silence hung between them. Connecting them. Invisibly.

After a bit, Libby said, "It wasn't your fault, Mom. You were only little."

"I should have known," murmured Evelyn. "I should have known she was in danger. I was the only one who knew where she'd hide, and I-" Her voice broke. "I led her killer directly there." She shook her head and wiped the tears. "I handed over that photo. Sealed her fate."

"No," said Libby, her voice taking on a maturity Evelyn had not heard before. Serious. Intense. "No, Mom. It wasn't your fault. You were ten. What if I were ten? What if I did something with consequences like that? Would you blame me? Blame a child."

That was easy. Of course not. Ten is a baby. She touched her daughter's cheek. "Never," she said. "I'd never blame you."

"See?" said Libby. "Please, Mom. Forgive yourself. I need you to forgive yourself."

Evelyn paused and smiled. "When did you get so smart? So, grown-up?"

Libby shrugged, smiled, and leaned toward her mother.

When they'd said all that needed saying, they found a small grove of trees, live oak and magnolia, grown and twisted together so intimately it was no longer possible to tell one tree from another. They lay down on their backs in a patch of soft grass beneath a set of enormous branches projected out parallel to the earth. Secreted away, behind the Spanish moss which hung from the branches like curtains, they closed their eyes, inhaled the thick perfume of the magnolia and the earthy smell of the river, and rested. When it was time to go, Evelyn slipped her hand into Libby's, and they walked all the way back to the car in silence.

CHAPTER ONE HUNDRED-SIX

Evelyn | The Gulf

One Week Later
It was Libby who requested a memorial for Carolyn. She pointed out that Carolyn had missed so many birthdays, holidays, and dances, it wasn't fair. It struck Evelyn that Libby was so like Carolyn. Her sister would have said the same thing. *It wasn't fair.* They both shared Gwen's sweet soul as well. Prone to moods and fancies but also capable of great love and even greater kindness. So, they'd waited. For the conclusion of the investigation, the release of Carolyn's remains. The cremation.

Grand Isle, south of New Orleans. By the time they arrived, the sun was well up. The ocean's expanse shimmered under a cloudless summer sky, and the bone-white sand was warm and soft as baby powder under their bare feet. Patches of ice plant and seagrass dotted the landscape, and an occasional pelican swooped down, splashing headfirst into the calm sea, but otherwise, they had the entire beach to themselves. They spread a blanket and sat side by side, each with elbows propped on knees and face toward the water, for a long time, just watching the gentle waves in silence.

After a bit, they took the urn holding Carolyn's ashes, together with a daisy chain Libby had made, down to the water's edge. They stood silent for a few minutes, letting the soft water lick at their toes. Finally, Evelyn glanced at Libby, who nodded, then Evelyn opened the urn and let the ashes fall into the waves. Some sank, some bobbed and floated feathery atop the surf for a while. Libby lay the daisy chain on the water's surface, and they both watched as the ashes and white flowers sparkled in the sun, gradually carried by the current, far out to sea. Libby reached over and wrapped her arms around her mother, and, like that, they watched the waves for a long time.

Afterward, they wrapped up their belongings and shook the sand from the blanket and walked slowly back to the car. They passed back through the swamp and into the bayous as the sky turned indigo. Around them, the cypress trees were dark shadows, silhouetted against a luminous sky. Twilight gradually faded to a bruised blue and, all that stood between them and Eden was the sweet night and the song of the cicada. Evelyn reached over and touched her daughter's hand. Libby curled her fingers into Evelyn's palm, and together they drove on.

THE END

ABOUT THE AUTHOR

W. A. Schwartz writes short stories and novels of literary fiction focused on psychological suspense and interpersonal relationships. Her work has been given special mention by the literary journal *Glimmer Train* (2018) and has been long-listed for the Alexander Chee Short Fiction Prize (2020). Born in Berkeley and raised in both the US and the UK, Ms. Schwartz was educated at the University of California and LSU in New Orleans. She and her husband, a native of Baton Rouge, spent many years living and working in Louisiana. She holds a BS in biochemistry and an MD from the University of California. She studied literature at UC Davis and novel writing at Stanford. These days, she lives in Northern California with her husband and children.

NOTE FROM THE AUTHOR

Word-of-mouth is crucial for any author to succeed. If you enjoyed *Eden*, please leave a review online—anywhere you are able. Even if it's just a sentence or two. It would make all the difference and would be very much appreciated.

Thanks!
W. A. Schwartz

We hope you enjoyed reading this title from:

BLACK ROSE
writing™

www.blackrosewriting.com

Subscribe to our mailing list – *The Rosevine* – and receive **FREE** books, daily deals, and stay current with news about upcoming releases and our hottest authors. Scan the QR code below to sign up.

Already a subscriber? Please accept a sincere thank you for being a fan of Black Rose Writing authors.

View other Black Rose Writing titles at www.blackrosewriting.com/books and use promo code **PRINT** to receive a **20% discount** when purchasing.

Made in the USA
Las Vegas, NV
03 July 2023

74187547R00249